BLUE FIRE
and
BLACK AMBER
[TWO NOVELS]

BLUE FIRE

AND

BLACK AMBER

~~~~~~~~~

TWO ROMANTIC SUSPENSE NOVELS BY

Phyllis A. Whitney

HAWTHORN BOOKS, INC.   Publishers/NEW YORK

BLUE FIRE
Copyright © 1961 by Phyllis A. Whitney

BLACK AMBER
Copyright © 1964 by Phyllis A. Whitney

Manufactured in the United States of America

Blue
Fire

For Morea

1

HE SAW HER almost at once. In spite of the confusion spilled across the South Side tracks, where there had been a minor collision, she was easy to spot. A chap at the Chicago *Bulletin* had said she was out on a job and had mentioned the accident. If the need was urgent, she could be found there. "Look for a half pint of girl with a full quart of camera," he had directed. The urgency was not that extreme, but Dirk had come nevertheless, with a curious wish to see her unguarded at work in her own environment.

The August afternoon had turned drizzling dark and this was not a section of Chicago that set its best foot forward. Gray was the predominant key for mist-blurred trains and tracks and milling people, for the sky and the lake and nearby buildings. Despite the soupy murk, he found her easily, hopping around through the crowd like a lively sparrow, pausing for a camera shot here, ducking out of the way of an ambulance attendant there, her orange scarf a tongue of flame that made its wearer easy to follow. Her hair was tucked under a shapeless brown beret, a trench coat engulfed her slight person, and flat-heeled loafers carried her in agile leaps as she searched for suitable camera angles.

Dirk lighted a cigarette in the shelter of a tilted boxcar and watched with a mingling of amusement and interest. The accident was apparently not serious, so she should be through with her duties soon. No need to get on with it immediately—he would bide his time.

Strange that he should remember so clearly the last time he had seen her. She had been seven and he sixteen. That morning she had been clambering about on an arm of rocks that thrust out across the sand of Camp's Bay at the other end of the world. She

1

had held a camera in her hands that day too—a child's box camera. And she had insisted on taking his picture. Perhaps he remembered that long-ago morning at the Cape Peninsula so well because no one since that time had ever regarded him with the same warm adoration that little Susan van Pelt had shown toward a somewhat uncertain young man of sixteen.

He continued to watch the girl with the camera, wondering what his best approach might be. Perhaps he'd better not tell her at once who had sent him here, or why.

Having taken her fill of pictures, the grown-up Susan swung her equipment over her shoulder and started toward him across the tracks. She still moved with the news photographer's watchful eye for an unexpected picture, so that she did not look too carefully at the rails and crossties under her feet. The toe of one small brown loafer caught in stepping over a rail and she went sprawling before Dirk could spring forward to catch her. It was an ugly fall, but she was up before he reached her, looking first to the safety of her camera.

To Dirk her anxiety, her look of near fright as she turned the camera about, examining it for injury, seemed a bit extreme. Probably it was borrowed from her paper and expensive to replace in case of serious damage. Only when she had made sure that the bulky camera had received no hurt did she pull up her plaid skirt to examine the bloody smear across one knee, where cinders had torn stocking and flesh.

"Ouch!" she said. And then more gently as if in afterthought, "Damn!"

Dirk hid his amusement at such hesitant profanity and stepped to her side. "That was a nasty spill. May I help? Let me take that camera and get you out of here."

The odd, trembling fear was fading and the look she gave him was straight and clear, her brown eyes enormous in her small, pointed face. A faint sense of shock went unexpectedly through him. She had been a homely little thing, with freckles on her nose and eyes too big for her size when he had first known her. She was not pretty now, but here was a face to arrest a man and make him look again. There was still a shadow of freckles and the mouth was generous and mobile. In the bulky trench coat her figure was invisible, but her ankles were good and small boned, her wrists fragile for the load of that heavy camera. Her mother had been a small

2

woman too, he remembered—an American, and something of a scatterbrain.

She resisted when he tried to take her camera, but accepted the help of his arm, limping for a few steps until she forced herself to walk steadily.

"I'm all right," she said. "I've got to get these plates back to the paper right away." Her accent was wholly American. There was no trace of English or Afrikaans left in it.

"Let me take you there," he said. "We can find a cab on the next street. Think you can walk that far?"

"I can walk," she assured him, and her gaze came wonderingly back to his face. The brown eyes, hazel flecked, searched puzzled for an answer. "I know you, don't I? I've met you somewhere?"

They had reached the sidewalk and he raised a finger to a cruising taxi, postponing a reply. The girl hesitated only a moment and then got in when he opened the door. As the cab headed north, she dabbed gingerly at her raw knee with a handkerchief. Then she pulled off the ugly beret and ran a hand through her cropped hair. He started at the sight. Strange that he had remembered her eyes and forgotten her hair. It was a bright color, just short of a true auburn, but with fire in the chestnut. She wore it shorter than he liked. She must be persuaded to let it grow, he thought, as if it were ordained that he should influence her life.

"Tell me where we've met," she persisted, studying him again.

The cab was following Michigan Avenue now, and luxury shops rimmed the boulevard like shining beads on a gray thread. In the tall buildings ahead lights gleamed in a thousand windows, brightening the mist with their glow.

"I'll give you a hint," he told her. "Can you picture a wide beach with very white sand and a piling up of big flat rocks cutting out toward the sea? Can you remember a line of peaks leaning all one way and repeating themselves against the sky?"

She gasped and one hand flew to her lips. "The Twelve Apostles! South Africa, of course. And you're Dirk—Dirk Hohenfield!"

"So you do remember," he said, a little surprised at his own pleasure.

Her eyes danced into eager life. "Remember? Of course I remember! How could I not? I was madly in love with you then. You were a smattering of all my heroes rolled into one, including Paul Kruger and Cecil Rhodes."

3

A faint smile curled her lips and he had an odd wish to see her smile with gaiety, to laugh aloud. Her face was not a gay one in repose.

He took her hand, the left one, and pulled off the worn pigskin glove. At least there was no ring on the third finger. That should make the old man's wishes a bit easier to gratify.

"You slapped me with this hand once," he reminded her. "I can remember how surprised I was that such a little girl could slap so hard. Your right hand was holding a doll, I believe."

"I remember too," she said. "You hurt my feelings. You made fun of my dear Marietjie and I had to make you think I hated you."

"But you didn't." He spoke with confidence. She, at least, had never sensed his uncertainties, or the resentments of a brooding, sensitive boy. "What a funny little scamp you were. I liked playing hero for you, even if I didn't deserve to have you feel that way."

She withdrew her fingers and unwound the orange scarf from about her neck as if she sought some occupation for her hands. The elusive smile had vanished.

"Did my father send you for me?" she asked directly, and the gentleness was gone from her voice and manner.

"I'm on a combination business trip and holiday," he told her, but she would have none of that.

"If he sent you for me, the answer is still no. I'm twenty-three now. I hadn't heard from him for sixteen years until he wrote recently, following my mother's death. I don't know him. I don't want to know him."

"We must talk about that," he said. "Will you let me come to see you? For my own pleasure," he added hastily as he saw refusal coming. "This evening, perhaps? Will you have dinner with me?"

The hint of resistance melted and she relaxed in the seat beside him. "I should have known who you were the moment I heard you speak. I haven't heard the accent of South Africa in years, yet every word comes back to me."

"I'm no South African by birth," he reminded her quickly.

She nodded. "Yes, I know. Your father was German, wasn't he?" In spite of himself he stiffened, and she must have sensed his withdrawal.

"Why don't you come to my place tonight?" she asked. "I'll fix supper for you, if you like. It will be easier to talk than in a restaurant. Have you been in Cape Town lately?"

4

"I live there now," he said. "I work for your father, Niklaas van Pelt."

The cab had stopped for a red light that halted the wide stream of Michigan Avenue traffic. The bridge was just ahead, with the Near North Side beyond. They were almost there.

"He must be terribly old—my father," she said. "In his seventies? He was close to fifty when he married my mother. She was young—too young for him." The girl turned her direct look upon Dirk. "How did he learn that Mother had died? He's never shown any interest in us before. How would he hear?"

"Your father has friends in America," Dirk told her casually. He must be careful now, make no slip about the letter which had alerted the old man to his wife's approaching death. It was clear that the girl knew nothing of her mother's letter.

Susan seemed to consider his words, neither completely accepting nor denying.

"He hurt her so much," she went on, her tone youthfully bitter. "My mother was sweet and gay and fun-loving. I can still remember the cold way he treated her when he didn't approve of her frivolity. He broke her heart—and her spirit too. That's why she ran away from South Africa and took me with her."

Dirk watched the cars slipping past, not looking at the girl beside him.

"My father did something wicked and went to prison for it, didn't he?" she said, sounding prim and disapproving, like a child who has been taught to parrot grown-up words.

The cab pulled up to the curb and Dirk opened the door and stepped out, relieved to bring a halt to her words.

"We'll return to this tonight," he said, and helped her to the sidewalk, camera and all.

She gave him her address, and he walked with her to the door and into the echoing cavern of a vaulted lobby. For just a moment he held her hand lightly and looked into brown eyes that had a shading of grief in them.

"Until this evening then," he said. "*Tot siens*—till we meet again."

At the homely Afrikaans farewell, tears came into her eyes and she blinked them back furiously. "Perhaps I shouldn't see you after all. I don't want to remember too much. Remembering hurts."

There was, he found, a somewhat surprising tenderness in him

5

toward her, and he smiled, knowing that she would not withdraw her invitation. She turned abruptly and walked toward the elevators and he stood looking after her. The jaunty set of her shoulders seemed touchingly deliberate. She swung the shapeless beret from one hand, guarding her camera with the other, and the bright fire of her hair shone in the lighted lobby. He watched her until she disappeared through an elevator door.

Then he left the building and strode along Michigan in the direction of his hotel. He was ready now to question the tremulous letter her mother had written—all that sticky sentiment about her innocent and helpless chick with no nest egg to save her from harm. This girl was far from helpless, and yet there was about her an air of innocence that was as unexpected as it was appealing. He could see a streak of her father too, which gave her a stubborn resistance. She might be harder to convince than he had expected, but he would give it his best try, for more reasons than one.

A subtle excitement had begun to stir in him and he whistled as he walked along the avenue. Had there been any about to recognize the tune, they would have known it for an old riding song of the Boers. All about a young man who was willing to ride his ten-pound horse to death on a night-long journey in order to be with his love in the morning.

> I'll think of my darling as the sun goes down,
> The sun goes down, the sun goes down,
> I'll think of my darling as the sun goes down,
> Down, down below the mountain.
> I'll ride, I'll ride, I'll ride, I'll ride,
> I'll ride all night,
> When the moon is bright . . .*

———————————

The girl felt the excitement too. Through the rest of the day she thought a great deal about Dirk Hohenfield—and about what little she knew of the past.

Her mother had been born in Chicago and had lived there after her parents' death. Her one excursion out of the country had been with a world-circling musical troupe for which she had played the

* From "As the Sun Goes Down." New words and new music by Josef Marais. Copyright 1956 by Fideree Music Corp., New York, N.Y.

piano. When the tour had ended in financial disaster, Claire had stayed on in South Africa. There she had married and remained until something she would never talk about had terminated her life with Niklaas van Pelt. This was at the close of the war and she had been able to return to the States and the city she knew best—Chicago. At home, with a small daughter and herself to support, she had held various positions as receptionist and hostess—a type of work that required good looks and a charm of manner that Claire was happily able to supply.

Her mother's illness and untimely death only a few months before had left Susan with a devastating sense of loss. She had always been a rather lonely person, but that had not mattered so much when there was someone to whom she could devote herself. Now there were reminders on every hand of the companion she had lost, and there was no one who needed her.

During the past year or so she had made friends in her newspaper work, it was true, but that rather sophisticated world was still new to her. She wanted very much to belong to the fourth estate, but she suspected that her coworkers did not yet take her seriously. There was no one to whom she was truly close.

Dirk Hohenfield's sudden appearance was like having a rocket shoot across a bleak horizon. Like a rocket he would soon be gone, but for a little while she would delight in his presence and even in his link with a place she had never been able to forget.

It was understandable that the day dragged and that she was preoccupied with her own thoughts until the moment when she could get away. Then she stopped at a grocery store to shop and went home to the little apartment on the Near North Side that she had shared with her mother. In the tiny kitchen she went to work, feeling happier than she had for a long time.

Now she could think without interruption of the man who was coming here tonight. She did not know all the circumstances, but she knew her father had taken him as a ward when Dirk's parents had died. Apparently he had continued in a close relationship to her father after he had grown up.

When a casserole of scalloped potatoes was browning in the oven and the salad greens were ready in the refrigerator, the steaks prepared for broiling, she wandered into the living room to look about with a sense of dissatisfaction.

She would have liked Dirk to see her as she really was, and she

7

was not a pastel-pretty person like this room that had so well suited her mother. But there was nothing to be done about the matter at this late date. She wrinkled her nose ruefully at the rose-pink cloth she had spread over a gate-legged table by the window, and at pink candles in rosebud-painted china holders. Without disloyalty she knew that these things were Claire and not Susan, and she could only hope that Dirk would understand.

How well she remembered the boy he had been—the very way he had looked the last time she'd seen him, his bright fair hair shining under the South African sun, his eyes as vivid a blue as the Cape Town sky. They had clambered out upon a great stretch of rocks that reached into the Atlantic and he had been watchful of her, lest she slip and tumble into the water. She had wanted to take a picture of him with her small camera, but somehow it had never come out. He had teased her as he posed, and laughed at her, though never unkindly. With the single-mindedness of a lonely child she had looked up to him and there had been an aching in her beyond her years, sensing as she had that she was about to lose him out of her life forever. Such a loss seemed especially poignant for a child, moving at the bidding of adults and helpless to save what she loved.

By comparison, of course, Dirk had been grown-up—yet not wholly so. He was always willing to romp with her, and sometimes even to talk to her about his own adventurous dreams that still had about them an immaturity which she had been too young to recognize. Sometimes he told her of how he would be a great lion hunter when he was older, or perhaps he would find gold and become enormously rich. He had been the only person she knew with the spirit of adventure burning high in him—and thus akin to the heroes of the stories she loved to read.

Now he was here and real, they were both grown-up, and her feeling of excitement persisted and heightened.

A gilt-rimmed mirror over what had once been a real fireplace gave back her reflection and she studied it critically. Her beige dress with the green belt was right for so warm an evening, but she was uncertain of the green velvet band she had wound through her hair. Was that ribbon Claire or Susan? Sometimes it was very hard to tell.

She had just raised a hand to remove it when the sound of the buzzer startled her. Too late now—the ribbon would have to stay.

8

She flew to push the button that would release the door catch three floors down.

"All the way up!" she called over the hall rail and heard the breathless sound of her own voice.

He came up bareheaded and the memory of the way he had looked in the sunlight that last day in South Africa was upon her again. Of course he was older now, but in so many ways the same. Still breathless, she retreated to her doorway, trying to hide this betrayal of her own eagerness. She must not let him think her too absurdly young and expectant.

He climbed easily and reached her with no loss of breath. His eyes were as intensely blue as she remembered them—no less so in the man than in the boy. There was an eagerness in him too and her heart thumped foolishly at the knowledge. This meeting could mean nothing, she reminded herself. A rocket could not stay its flight, and Susan van Pelt would never return to South Africa.

In his arms Dirk held an extravagance of yellow roses and she took them from him, letting her pleasure shine in her eyes. He followed her into the apartment, looking only at her.

"There were no proteas to be had," he told her.

The word, so long forgotten, brought a bright recollection of South Africa's flower—the fabulously beautiful and exotic protea that grew there in endless variety.

"Please sit down," she said, shyly formal. "I'll be only a moment. I want a vase for these roses."

In the kitchen she filled a pale-green vase with water and arranged the flowers tenderly, her fingers a little clumsy with excitement, fearful as always lest she break something. That moment with the camera today had frightened her badly. Her neurosis! she thought wryly, and hoped Dirk had not noticed.

When she carried the vase back to the living room to set it on the coffee table, she found him standing before a row of photographs on the wall. It pleased her to see that he had singled them out for his attention, since these pictures were Susan and not Claire.

There was one dramatic shot she had taken of a fire which had damaged a West Side tenement some months ago, another of an excursion boat loading children at a Chicago River landing. And one of a snowy night on Michigan Avenue with shop windows magically ablur through the storm. The one she liked best, however, was a study of an elderly newspaper dealer at his sidewalk stand. The play of light and shadow was exactly right, the composition perfect. She had been proud of the result and pleased to sell it to a national magazine.

Dirk studied the pictures and she was glad of the opportunity to study him. The charm he had held for her as a child was still there, but magnified as the boy had matured into a man. How very attractive he was, not only because of his fair good looks but in the kindness he showed her, in the quick intelligence that was so evident in him—all adding up to an appeal so strong that it dismayed her a little.

"Do you enjoy this sort of work?" he asked, still considering the pictures. "I should think it might be hazardous and a bit rigorous for a woman."

"I love it," she said fervently, but she liked the fact that he was thinking of the girl behind the photos. "Before I went to the newspaper I sold photographic supplies in a store in the Loop, and I never really liked that. I always wanted to be out taking pictures."

"These are good," he said, and she warmed to his approval.

He turned to look directly at her and there was an appraisal in his eyes that made her a little self-conscious. She chose a chair in a shadowy corner and let him take the sofa facing the light. She did not want to be looked at and measured too closely, but only to look, to fill her eyes with the bright dazzle of him. This moment was one she would treasure and remember when he was gone.

"There's a great deal to photograph in Cape Town," he reminded her, a faint amusement underlying his tone as if he sensed something of the effect he had upon her and rather enjoyed it.

But that was a road she would not follow. "It's no use," she said firmly. "I'm not going back, if that's what you mean."

"Have I asked you to?" The timbre of his voice had changed with the years. It was no longer a boy's voice, but that of a man, deep and vibrant. "I told you I wanted to see you for my own pleasure first of all. The rest can wait a bit."

She brought him a drink and as they sipped companionably, she asked him about his work for her father in Cape Town.

"You were always going to be a famous hunter someday," she reminded him. "Or discover a fabulous vein of gold."

He laughed aloud, pleased that she remembered. "I'm afraid my present hunting is on the prosaic side, though it has its moments of interest. After—what happened—your father sold his home in Johannesburg and moved to the Cape Town house, where he has lived ever since. He has become an exporter of native craft work and has two shops as well. His store in Johannesburg is particularly fine, and there's a smaller one in Cape Town. My hunting these days consists of going out to places he can no longer reach—in the Transkei, Zululand, Northern Rhodesia. Your father's standards are high—we don't look for cheap things, but for real native art work. It's remarkable how keen he has remained, how alive he is."

She did not want to hear about her father. "I can barely remember the house in Jo'burg," she said. "It was always the Cape Town house I loved best. Protea Hill! Such a lovely name for it. When we went there for the December holidays in summer I had a room with a wonderful view."

Dirk set down his glass, his eyes holding hers. "A view that's still waiting for you, Susan. I doubt that it's changed in the slightest."

"I know," she said. "The mountain wouldn't change."

She excused herself, went off to the retreat of the kitchen to put the steaks under the broiling flame and toss the salad. But he would not remain a guest in the parlor. He joined her and carried in plates and glasses as though he enjoyed helping her, though he must be accustomed to servants.

When they had settled down to the meal, she asked him more about his own life so that he would open no further dangerous doors.

"What did you do before you went to work for my father?"

His smile was rueful. "When I finished school I got the diamond fever so you see it was diamonds by then, instead of gold. I did a little prospecting on my own, though not very successfully. Your father still owned land around the Kimberley area at that time and he told me I could have anything I discovered there. He was mainly interested in quenching my fever, I suppose."

He reached into a pocket and drew out a leather wallet. From an inner fold he took a small packet of paper.

"I still have one of the stones I found at that time. I've kept it for a lucky pocket piece and to prove I've been a digger."

She bent her head to watch as he unfolded the square of paper, and was aware of his own fair head so close to hers that his breath touched her cheek.

"There," he said. "I'll wager that's like no diamond you've ever seen."

The tiny stone shone orchid pink and translucent against the white paper and was irregular in form. The rough natural shape of the diamond was revealed, but it lacked the brighter sparkle of a cut diamond.

"This is what they call a fancy stone," Dirk told her. "Fancies are odd, off-color diamonds. Perhaps pink or green or yellow. Sometimes even black. This one isn't large enough or perfect enough to be of any great value, but I have a certain sentiment about it. Of course it's uncut, or I would have been breaking the law by bringing it into this country. Only uncut stones come in duty-free."

Susan picked up the little stone and nested it on her palm, seeing not the diamond but a very young man with a hunger for adventure in his heart, working for a dream that had never materialized.

"I thought De Beers owned all the diamonds in South Africa," she said. "How is it you were permitted to do any prospecting on your own?"

"The syndicate owns the important holdings," he explained. "But there are still diggers who work their own claims and sell what little they find to De Beers. As a matter of fact, it's against the law to possess an uncut diamond in South Africa unless you are an authorized person. As a licensed digger who found this stone myself I'm able to keep it." He returned the pink diamond to the paper and folded it away in his wallet. "Have you ever heard of the Kimberley Royal?" he added.

She shook her head, fascinated by this talk of diamonds and of a South Africa she had long ago put away from her and reconciled to painful memory.

"The Kimberley Royal was one of the great finds," Dirk said. "A remarkably beautiful and valuable stone. Bigger than the Hope diamond and nearly flawless. I saw it once as a boy. The very machinery that sorts diamonds these days may crush or damage the unusually large stone, but that's a chance that has to be taken.

The present system is geared to a realistic commercial output. It takes, on an average, four tons of rock to give one carat of diamonds. But now I'm getting a bit technical."

She did not mind. She loved to listen to him and she gave him her absorbed attention all through the meal. Later, when he had gone, she would think about everything he had said.

When dessert was finished and she had cleared away the dishes, they sat among the pale pinks and baby blues and drank large cups of American brewed coffee. But now Dirk seemed restless, as if he felt time was slipping away and the subject for which he had really come had still not been opened between them.

In this mood his appeal for her was more disturbing. There were contrasts in this man, vibrant changes that would ask much of any woman who cared for him. But the thought of caring for him seriously was ridiculous and she dismissed the notion impatiently. She must be on guard against herself if her thoughts followed such a course.

He set down his cup and moved about the room again, glancing once more at the photographs, picking up a small carved antelope figure from the bookcase and holding it out to her with a smile.

"So you still keep a bit of Africa around?"

"It's an impala," Susan said, the remembered name coming back to her unbidden.

He studied the stripe-grained golden wood of the carving, turning it about with experienced fingers. Tall lyrate horns rose from the slender, gracefully turned head. The ears were pricked, the muzzle delicate, the eyes long and luminous, even in a wood carving. The figure was at rest, its forelegs curled beneath the body, the haunches smoothly rounded, with the strong hindquarters of a leaping animal. The curving grain suggested the haunch stripe of the impala and about the whole was an air of life and sensitive alertness, as though the creature might at any moment leap from its oval stand and go flying out of Dirk's fingers.

"A good piece," he said in approval. "The artist has caught the feeling of a wild thing, even at rest."

Susan stared at the figure. Until Dirk held it up the carving had meant nothing in particular to her and she had not thought of its name in years. Her mother had never connected the carving with South Africa. Yet suddenly knowledge was there, rising without warning from the forgotten past.

He set the figure down, moving closer to her, and this time he picked up a book from a table at her elbow and turned it over with a low whistle of astonishment.

"You want nothing to do with South Africa, yet you read the books of John Cornish?"

"Someone on the paper recommended it," Susan told him, a little startled by his tone. "The jacket flap says that his mother was an American, like mine, and I believe he lives in America now. Except when he's off to get material for a new book. That one is about Algeria."

Dirk turned the book over and studied the face pictured on the back of the jacket with an air of displeasure.

"Cornish used to write about South Africa," he said. "That's where he grew up. In fact, it was an article of his that helped to send your father to prison. Did you know that?"

She had not known it and she sat staring at him in silence.

"Cornish is back in the Union now," he went on. "The Johannesburg papers were running pieces about him when I left. I even ran into him one day there in the Carlton Hotel. It was not a fortunate meeting. I hope he'll stay away from Cape Town."

She wanted to ask more about John Cornish and her father, but remembered in time that these were matters in which she had no interest.

Dirk put down the book and came toward her, stood over her, so that she had to look up into his face. "Why are you so afraid of returning?" His gaze commanded her, yet there was a gentleness in him that kept her from turning away.

"My mother told me a few things about my father," she said. "He really cared very little for us. There's no reason to go back just because he's lately changed his mind about seeing me."

"But it was your mother who ran away at a time when he needed her most," Dirk said.

Indignation flared in her. "That's not true! He didn't need her, didn't want her. She was thinking of me, of getting me away from what might happen to us because of him."

He countered calmly with a question and she saw pity in his eyes. "Didn't she ever tell you why your father went to prison?"

"She said it was best that we both forget. For years it's never been mentioned between us. Anyhow, all that has nothing to do with me now."

The truth behind her willing ignorance was something she could explain to no one. There was about it a faintly nightmare quality she knew better than to rouse.

"I know enough," she hurried on. "My father must have been an important man in his day. Mother told me he was well-known in the diamond world—one of the most valued men with De Beers. He ran for the South African Parliament at one time too, didn't he? He was a leader, a respected person. Yet he threw it all away. Threw his family away—everything!"

"Listen to me," Dirk said, and the gentleness had gone from his manner. "It's time you knew the story. It's true that he broke the law, and no one knows why. But he's paid for that mistake a good many times over. So it would be a fine thing if his daughter—"

Susan jumped to her feet, familiar panic rising in her. "I don't want to hear!" she cried. "If you go on, I won't listen."

He looked clearly astonished at her show of emotion. Quietly he sat down on the sofa, and drew her to the place beside him, put a quieting arm about her shoulders. She shivered at his touch, all too conscious of his warmth and nearness. It was dangerous to get too close to a rocket. The tears she had been holding back since her mother's death welled up in her eyes. Softly, helplessly, she began to cry. He turned her head so that her cheek was against his shoulder and his fingers smoothed the bright hair back from her warm, damp brow.

"I'm sorry," he said. "I'd forgotten that you've had a bad time lately. I'm not sure what it is you fear and I suspect that it's unreal. But I won't trouble you about it now."

She suffered herself to rest against his shoulder for a few blissful moments and then raised her head and gave him a wavering smile.

"There—I'm all right now. And terribly ashamed. I didn't invite you here to be cried on." She blew a nose that she knew was pink, dried her eyes, and silently despised herself.

Dirk glanced at his watch and stood up. "I mustn't forget that you're a working girl and probably have to be up early in the morning. I appreciate your good dinner. It's been wonderful to see you again, Susan."

He was impersonal now and almost brusque. She knew she had sent him away with her tears, her nonsense. "Wh-when are you

15

returning to Cape Town?" she asked, her voice fainter than she intended.

"At the moment I'm not sure," he told her. "This assignment may take me longer than I'd expected. To be perfectly truthful, I'm going home just as soon as you're ready to go with me."

He waited for no answer to that, but kissed her lightly on the cheek and took his departure before she could summon words to answer him. She stood frozen in the doorway, and listened to the sound of his steps as he ran lightly down the turning stairs. Before he reached the bottom he began to whistle and the tune touched some chord of memory in her mind. When the street door opened and closed, she went back into the apartment and stared about her vaguely. Somehow the place had a different look to her now. The valentine touches no longer mattered. Dirk had known they had nothing to do with her.

On the table lay the book by John Cornish. She picked it up and, as Dirk had done, turned it over to study the face portrayed on the book jacket. The picture was a candid shot and she had not thought it professionally good. It showed the rather brooding face of a man in his early forties or late thirties—a face with a strong bone structure beneath the flesh, the eyes deeply set beneath heavy brows. The mouth was straight and unsmiling, with a relentless quality about it, yet there was a mark of sensitivity to the lips. It was a face worth photographing skillfully, and this had been a haphazard shot.

What role had this man played in her father's life? She knew of him only as a highly respected writer on African affairs. Today America regarded him as an American. She put the book aside abruptly. She did not want to read John Cornish after what Dirk had told her about him.

She reached for the carved impala and sat on the sofa holding it tightly in her hands as if for comfort. She knew very well what it was she tried to postpone, to fend off. In spite of the fear that had its roots in her half-forgotten childhood, there was a faint edge of eagerness encroaching upon her resistance. Was it possible that she might in the end give in and go back to South Africa with Dirk Hohenfield?

She shook her head stubbornly, fighting off the thought. No, certainly she would never go back. Not if it meant any contact with Niklaas van Pelt, who was her father.

The tune Dirk had been whistling still haunted her memory, running through her mind over and over again. The words came back to her suddenly.

I'll think of my darling as the sun goes down,
. . . Down, down below the mountain.

2

AFTERWARDS SUSAN WOULD always think of the days that followed as the time of the pink diamond.

In the beginning she tried to steel herself against Dirk and his confident, persuasive ways. But she could not refuse to see him, did not want to, and with each new meeting her defenses crumbled a little more. He behaved as if all the time in the world were at his disposal and he could afford to wait. The late August days were hot in Chicago and some evenings, when she was free from her work on the paper, they would walk down Michigan Avenue together or perhaps find their way to the lake front along Grant Park. During these walks he would often speak of South Africa, of Cape Town, and a long-forgotten homesickness began to stir in her. With it there came, in spite of herself, a softness and a yearning that warned her of what was happening.

She had fallen in love two or three times before, rather foolishly. There seemed in her a perversity that drew her to someone who, for one reason or another, could not possibly consider her seriously at the time. It was almost as if she had protected herself by the very impossibility of the person on whom her attention focused. As if she bided her time, playing at love, waiting. She did not want to go through this again. Dirk would soon be off to Cape Town and she must stay on here. With such reminders she tried to fight the softness in herself.

It was during this period that headlines began to shout of new violence in South Africa. Trouble had erupted fiercely in one of the squalid locations near Durban, and Susan showed Dirk the paper as further buttress against her returning to Cape Town.

"I don't think I'd want to live in South Africa now," she said. "There are so many terrible things happening there."

"This is in Cato Manor, where there's always been trouble," Dirk said. "It's a thousand miles from Cape Town."

"But there's been trouble in Cape Town too," she reminded him. "You can't shrug Langa aside."

"No one's shrugging it aside. Listen to me, Susan. You're talking to a South African now. The press here is never fair to us. Living in a place isn't like reading headlines. You'll find it's business as usual in Cape Town. The coloreds are on our side and you'll see very little agitation. It's an explosive and complex problem. Don't try to judge it sitting here in Chicago."

He was right, of course, and she let the matter go.

The time came, however, when Dirk dropped his pretense that the passing days were of no consequence.

"Susan, Susan, you must hurry!" he said. "If we wait too long we'll miss springtime in Cape Town. September and October are the most beautiful months in South Africa—we mustn't let them go."

One evening at her apartment, when she had given him dinner again, he spoke to her more brusquely than ever before.

"I must get back to Cape Town," he told her. "Your father needs me and I have my work to think about. This afternoon I booked my flight home. I'm leaving for New York at the end of the week."

A darkness of despair welled up in her and she found herself remembering that other departure when it had been Susan van Pelt leaving South Africa. But then she had been a child, helpless to stop what was happening. It was far worse to be grown and equally helpless. Yet because she was grown she must hide her feelings somehow. By an effort she kept her voice steady as she answered him.

"I'll miss you," she said and was proud of the fact that she spoke lightly when there was so much hidden pain beneath the words. "But of course you must go. There's nothing but wasted time for you here."

He had taken a restless turn around the room and now came back to her with an unexpected light in his eyes, alive with all the dynamic energy that was so vital a part of him. He stood over her as he had done that first time he had visited her here and held her attention by the very force that seemed to move him.

"Believe me, Susan, I didn't ask for this to happen," he said. "It's going to complicate my life quite frightfully. I'm not sure I'm pleased about it. Yet I think I knew it was going to happen that first day when I stood on the tracks and watched you hopping about with a camera that was almost as big as you were."

She stared at him in dismay, not knowing what he meant, and he took something from his pocket and dropped it almost casually into her lap. It was a small blue and gold jeweler's box and she looked at it without touching it.

"Open it," he commanded.

She put a finger to the metal catch and raised the lid. A ring lay against the white satin—a thin gold ring with a polished pink stone in the raised setting.

"The jeweler said it was unheard of to mount an uncut stone," Dirk said, "but I thought you might like it that way. A bit of polishing has given it more of the look of a diamond. It means something to me this way—uncut. Does it fit, I wonder? I had it made for a very slim finger."

She looked up at him, unable to believe what was happening, and was startled to see the anxiety so clearly evident behind his quick impersonal manner. He was tense and a little fearful, not at all in proud control of his own emotions as she had believed. She found what she saw in his face more endearing than anything else might have been, and she held out her hand.

"Put it on my finger, please," she said.

All the angry impatience drained out of him and with it the uncertainty, leaving the engaging younger Dirk she remembered. He sat beside her and took the ring from the box, slipped it onto the third finger of her left hand. There was only tenderness in his manner, and a pleading.

"Now my luck is in your hands, darling," he said. "Treat it gently."

Not until she was in his arms did she truly believe in what was happening.

"I booked places for two on that flight to South Africa," he told her. "And space for two on the plane to New York. Though I've been terribly afraid I was going too far. Now there's the matter of your passport and inoculations, a marriage license, and all the rest.

Let's go to New York and get on with it. Let's not waste another moment."

Get on with it they did. She would never have believed that she could break all the threads of her accustomed life with such dispatch and so joyously. Fortunately she had already packed or given away most of her mother's things. The apartment was sublet to a friend on the paper. Dirk drove her across the state line for a quicker marriage than could be arranged in the city, and Susan found herself on the plane for New York with a man who was now her husband.

In spite of the breathless quality of all that was happening, there was time for the happiness that lay between them. This, Susan knew, was what she had been waiting for all these lonely years. This was the answer to her nostalgia, to her sense of something left unfinished. She knew why no one else would ever do. In her was some guiding force wiser than conscious thought which had waited only for Dirk. Whatever South Africa held for her, she would now be able to face it because Dirk was part of her life, she of his. This was the most satisfying thing of all—his need of her, so tenderly clear.

Only now and then did she remember Niklaas van Pelt and try to bargain a little.

"If you're marrying me just to take me home to my father, you're making a mistake," she told him, teasing a little. "I still haven't promised to see him, you know."

Dirk was offhand. "We'll talk about that when the time comes. I've written Uncle Niklaas airmail about our change in plans. Though if I thought you were serious about the accusation you've just made—"

She kissed him warmly to prove that she had not been serious. His reassurance was hardly necessary. It was clear in his eyes, in his touch, that he was a man in love.

Their days in New York shone through a haze as pink as the diamond on her finger. She glowed with happiness and contentment and Dirk said she grew prettier every day.

The only part of her old life that she had brought with her was her own small 35mm. camera and Dirk humored her in her picture taking.

"So I've married a career woman, have I?" he laughed when she insisted that camera and light meter accompany her on their day-

21

time jaunts. She explained gently, but with a certain firmness, that there was no reason why she should not continue to sell pictures to American and British magazines and papers. The eyes of the world were turned toward Africa these days.

She particularly enjoyed taking pictures of Dirk—shots that showed his bright, laughing quality and ignored the captious side that occasionally showed itself in an unexpected moment. At times she suspected that something was worrying him, something he kept from her, and that some problem awaited him in South Africa. She suspected that it might well concern her father. Perhaps he would disapprove of this sudden marriage of his ward to a daughter he did not know—the daughter of a woman who had left him. She hoped she was wrong if this meant hurt and a difficult situation for Dirk. But for the moment she could only try with all her heart to adjust to these moods of Dirk's and keep from questioning him. She did not, however, want to record such shadows with her camera. These were the sunny days, and must be captured as such.

It was still September, still spring in South Africa, when they boarded the big American plane at New York's International Airport. Even by jet it was a long and wearying trip, and Dirk had allowed for stopovers in Accra and Brazzaville. They left French Equatorial Africa in the early morning and set down in Johannesburg in midafternoon. Jo'burg was the port of entry—the City of Gold, "Goli," as the dark people called it—a relatively young and booming metropolis of great wealth and great poverty.

When they had gone through immigration and passports and baggage had been checked, they sat in the busy waiting room before huge bay windows of glass and watched planes taking off for every part of Africa and the world. They were truly in South Africa now, and Susan saw the Slegs vir Blankes signs for the first time. Signs that were translated as "Europeans Only," "European" meaning "white." She winced at the signs just as she would have winced at similar signs in the American South.

All signs were given in the two languages of the country, and so were the announcements over loudspeakers. Susan had forgotten her Afrikaans, but as she listened, the sound of it began to return and it seemed not unfamiliar.

Once, to her surprise, Dirk's name was paged over the loudspeaker and he hurried away to pick up the message. When he returned he looked a little angry.

"Was it word from my father?" she asked.

"No." He shook his head. "It was merely a warning."

The word startled her. "A warning?"

"Oh, it's not as bad as all that," he said, managing a smile. "Someone thought I ought to know that John Cornish is going to Cape Town. He'll be aboard our plane."

He said nothing more and seemed to lose himself in his own remote thoughts, so that she was left wondering. Why had it seemed necessary to let Dirk know that Cornish would be aboard their plane? If the harm John Cornish had done lay in the past, how could his presence in South Africa affect her father now? And why had Dirk used the word "warning"?

When their flight to Cape Town was called, they started across the tarmac to a plane with a springbok symbol marking the nose. Suitably enough, since the South African gazelle with the curving horns had the habit of springing high into the air.

"I feel as though I were going too fast," Susan whispered, clinging to Dirk's arm. "Some of me is still back home. I haven't caught up with me yet."

Dirk did not hear her. He was watching a man up ahead mounting the steps to the plane.

"Look quickly," he said. "The tall chap up there wearing a gray topcoat—that's John Cornish. He'll be aboard, all right."

She looked in time to see the tall man vanish through the door. The glimpse of a straight back told her little and he was out of sight by the time a stewardess showed them to their seats.

"Do you know him well?" she asked, letting Dirk help her with her seat belt.

"I knew him as a boy," Dirk said.

"How well did he know my father?"

"Actually, he knew him very well. Cornish grew up on a veld farm near Kimberley and your half brother Paul was his closest friend. They were in the war together—as commandos."

"Tell me about my family," Susan said. "I know so little. It doesn't seem real that I've had half brothers and a half sister. I know the eldest boy died as a child, but I'm not sure about the others."

"Your sister married and went out to Australia to live," Dirk said. "Paul died in Italy during the war. Cornish was wounded at the same time and was shipped home to recover. He had a bad time with his leg and that put him out of the fighting. He still limps a bit. When he came home he went into the field that always interested him, journalism. Your father eased his way more than once. Which made it all the harder for Uncle Niklaas to take when Cornish turned on him a year or so later."

The plane was taxiing into place for the take-off, and Susan forgot John Cornish and all that concerned him. In the days when she had lived in South Africa, the Blue Train had still been the main luxury accommodation, taking a good many hours to cover the thousand miles to Cape Town. Now the airplane was the popular and luxurious means of transportation.

The sign of the springbok was everywhere in the plane, woven into the green aisle carpet and into the seat covers. But this was a springbok turned Pegasus and Susan had yet to catch her breath. She was experiencing not only the normal difficulty of today's air passenger in keeping up with the speed of her flight but also the feeling in her own case of rushing too rapidly back into the past.

They flew over the crowded huddle of Johannesburg, where the white man had space and the black man did not. The strange yellow-white mounds of gold mine dumps loomed below, square with slanted sides, and then the plane was away, and Susan looked down upon open country. The green faded quickly and the veld spread below, a bare and tawny land, not yet wakened, as it would be briefly, by the touch of spring.

Africa had surprised her because, except for the equatorial belt, there had been so little jungle green. So much of the land was tan and dull gold and sometimes reddish. In the past it had been wholly lion country, of course, and that was still its color—the tawny yellow of the lion.

Dirk read a magazine, hardly glancing out the window at a view long familiar, but Susan, in the window seat, could not take her eyes from the scene that swept below the plane. Nothing as yet had brought a sense of recognition, but she knew that would come eventually. Ahead in Cape Town the mountain awaited her. She had never forgotten the mountain. Sometimes it came into her dreams, pressing vastly above her as if it would crush her by its very mass of high-thrust granite.

Before they reached Kimberley, dusk hid the land and in the

great spreading darkness below there were few lights to be seen. The distances of Africa were immense and so often empty of human life.

"Talk to me," she pleaded, slipping a hand beneath Dirk's on the arm of the seat between them. "Africa frightens me a little. It's rushing toward me over the years. Right now there's nothing but space and emptiness around me, but when I come down Africa will be waiting. And I'm not ready for it." She tried to laugh, but there was a catch in her throat.

He put aside his magazine and covered her fingers with his own. She leaned back in her seat and let the new delight of sensation that his touch could arouse sweep away obscure fears. For now, this was enough. Love was her protection for whatever awaited her in South Africa.

"What do you remember best about Cape Town?" he asked quietly, as if by the very softness of his tone he would avoid rousing her sleeping fears. "What do you remember of your father?"

She closed her eyes in order to invite the pictures. The mountain was there so easily, whenever she summoned it. And glimpses of the house in Cape Town—Protea Hill. She could remember Dirk too, flashing in and out of the pictures with his bright fair hair and blue eyes. But when she tried to think of her father, to recall his face or even to summon back the look of her mother as she had been sixteen years ago, the vision blurred as if she had dropped pebbles into a pool, causing the surface to waver into distortion. With every throb of its engines the plane was hurling her toward her father and, though she had made no promise to see him, the inevitability of their meeting was there like a wall against which she was sure to fling herself. She dreaded the probable crash, and dared not think about it.

"Don't ask me to remember now," she said. "Let all that take care of itself when the time comes. Tell me about you instead. How did my father happen to take you as his ward?"

Dirk's fingers released her own and he stared unseeingly at the magazine in his lap. "My father, as you know, was a German," he said at length. "He was interned and I never saw him again because he died before the war was over. He had worked on the farm for your father. Afterwards my mother died. Of grief, I've always believed. Niklaas van Pelt took me into his home. It was a simple enough thing."

He spoke without emotion, yet Susan sensed a depth of feeling that denied the simplicity he claimed. There were dregs of painful memory in Dirk. She must learn to know these things a little at a time. The very learning meant a loving exploration. Only in the closeness of marriage could the delight of knowing another person be fully plumbed. But such a plumbing could not be managed quickly. Falling in love was one thing. *Loving* was another. There must be growth and time for growth.

"Perhaps we should both leave the things that hurt alone until we really want to talk about them," she said. "I won't ask you again. I'll make a pact with you on that. There's plenty of time."

Dirk looked past her out the big oval of the window. "We're over Kimberley," he said, "and coming in for a landing."

The distraction served and she hardly noticed that he had agreed to no such pact on his part.

A stewardess announced that they would have approximately forty minutes on the ground and then the plane was taxiing along a runway of the small airport.

Dirk flung Susan's coat about her shoulders as they left the plane and she was grateful for its warmth. The spring night was cold, the air sharply invigorating.

MIND YOUR HEAD—PASOP U KOP. She saw the sign between two small buildings as they walked from the plane to the fenced enclosure where passengers might wait. After a look about inside the small restaurant, they returned to the brisk clear air and stood beneath the stars, content enough to be close to the earth for a little while.

Others from their flight stood about talking, or merely waiting, and Susan noted the smartness of South African women. They wore the furs and expensive suits and spiked heels of New York or London or Paris. Looking at them one felt merely a sense of recognition. Common fashions had a way of pulling the world together. One might trade hemispheres and seasons these days with scarcely a sense of the scene having changed. Only something inside her rushed and rushed, trying to catch up.

She had forgotten their fellow passenger until she saw John Cornish standing by the enclosure fence not far away. She recognized him at once from the photograph she had seen. Dirk saw him too and quickly turned his back toward the other man.

"He may try to speak if he sees me," Dirk said. "I'd rather

avoid him. If he should come over and I have to introduce you, I shan't mention that you're Niklaas's daughter. Let's not get his journalist's nose pointed in our direction any more than it is."

Susan nodded her agreement, but she still felt puzzled. She saw Cornish leave the fence for a turn about the enclosure, saw him start past them, then glimpse at Dirk's averted head and stop.

"He's seen you," she murmured to Dirk and sensed the stiffening that went through him.

As the writer approached, she looked at him with frank curiosity and saw that he was to a great extent like his picture. There was a touch of gray in his dark hair and a craggy look to his brows and nose and well-defined chin. There was the same somber, relentless cast to his face that the picture had revealed, and even though he smiled as he held out his hand to Dirk, his expression did not light to true friendliness.

"What luck," he said. "I've been hoping to run into you again."

Dirk's hesitation was momentary before he took the other man's hand, but Susan suspected that Cornish was quite aware of his reluctance. He turned a look of surprise upon her as Dirk introduced her as his wife.

"You've married an American girl," he said. "My congratulations, Hohenfield."

He held out his hand to Susan and she was aware of the substance of his fingers as he took her own. They were lean and hard and there was a hint of wiry strength in their pressure. She remembered that this man had been a commando in the war and the knowledge was not reassuring.

"What luck to run into you," he said again to Dirk. "I've been hoping to see you. The letters I've written Niklaas van Pelt haven't been answered. I've done all I can with my book in Pretoria and Johannesburg. I'm going to Cape Town now and see if I can persuade van Pelt to see me. Will you intercede for me, Hohenfield?"

Dirk's shrug was casual as if he were close to the edge of being rude. "As you know, Uncle Niklaas makes his own rules. If he has determined not to see you, then I expect that is the end of it."

"It's not the end of it as far as I'm concerned," the other man said coolly. "If you're unwilling to give me your help, then I must do without it."

"Exactly," Dirk said.

The moment was sharp with antagonism on Dirk's part, though this fact seemed to slide off John Cornish as if he were totally indifferent to discouragement. Susan had the dismayed feeling that Dirk was quite capable of causing a scene if he lost his temper, and she spoke hurriedly to stave off a possible explosion.

"What sort of book are you writing this time, Mr. Cornish?" she asked with a little rush of false enthusiasm she did not intend.

His attention was clearly focused upon Dirk and there was the alertness in him of a man who could think and move quickly if he had to.

He answered without looking at her, almost absently. "It's a book about diamonds and South Africa."

"Another one?" Dirk's blond brows rose derisively. "Isn't there a surplus of books about diamonds already? Books on everything from the history of De Beers to diamond smuggling!"

John Cornish answered impassively, and there was something a little frightening about his refusal to take offense or yield his stand. This was a man who would make an implacable and dangerous enemy, Susan thought.

"It's possible that I have a different approach," he said. There was a pause, as if some crackling significance hung in the air between them. Then he turned to Susan with an air of having answered Dirk and dismissed him. "Kimberley is the right place for this talk of diamonds. You must come back another time and see something of the mines."

"I'd hate to go down into a mine," Susan said quickly, wanting to oppose this man because Dirk opposed him.

"Mines are only the beginning of the story," Cornish said. "The real excitement lies well aboveground. I suppose it's a truism to point out that diamonds are harmless enough in themselves. It's what men do with them that breeds the trouble. And that's what my book will be about."

A loudspeaker called them back to the plane, and Dirk took Susan's elbow, turning her away from John Cornish. But the other man came with them, walking along toward the plane as if he sensed no lack of welcome. Susan was aware of his slight limp, though he kept pace with them easily.

"I shall hope to see you in Cape Town," he said in the tone of a man who expected to be asked to tea.

Dirk made no answer and Susan walked uneasily between the

two. This interchange had seemed to threaten her father in some way and she sensed that Dirk was resisting the other man's fixed purpose with an inward anger and stubbornness of his own. But none of this made sense to her and in any event it was not her affair. As long as possible she meant to avoid seeing Niklaas van Pelt. And in all likelihood she would never meet John Cornish again. It was ironic that she who so longed to avoid Niklaas should be confronted by a man whose only purpose seemed to be to force a meeting with her father.

When they were once more airborne, Susan gave herself over to the wifely duty of soothing Dirk's irritation.

"I don't blame you for disliking that man," she said. "The very fact that he would choose to be a commando makes me feel uncomfortable about him."

Dirk did not take to such soothing. "Why should you feel uncomfortable? It requires courage to make a commando. Some of the first commandos were ancestors of mine—on my Afrikaner mother's side."

When she glanced at him blankly, he went on.

"That's where the word comes from. The men who went along with the voortrekkers as fighting men, as guards, were called commandos. It was a designation of bravery and honor."

"You sound as though you were defending John Cornish," Susan said in bewilderment.

"I'm defending him only on the score of an unreasonable feminine attack," Dirk said. "I have no use for him and I mean to keep him away from your father. But not, my darling—" he gave her a quick, exasperated look "—not because he was briefly a commando in the war."

Susan lapsed into hurt silence, convinced for a moment that men were given to being unreasonable, ungrateful and unfair. But when the numerous dinner courses began to be served she recovered in spite of herself, and Dirk seemed to regret his sharpness.

"We're both tired after a long trip," he said penitently. "John Cornish isn't worth quarreling over."

One of the likable things about Dirk was his regret when he had hurt her and the eagerness with which he made up for any momentary loss of temper. She knew that he was volatile and high-strung; indeed these very qualities were part of the attraction he held for her, part of a personality that would never be stodgy and dull. She must learn to wait for the gentler mood, the contrition that would always come if she gave him time.

She quickly regained a happier state as Dirk began to describe the dark invisible land over which they were flying. They were above the tawny veld that bloomed so briefly in spring with a vast carpet of wildflowers. The veld with those unexpected hills that from the plane looked like no more than small bubbles thrust up from the landscape. He complimented her on remembering that "veld" was pronounced "felt" in the proper Afrikaans way.

He told her of the mountains that rose where the land descended from the high central plateau of Africa to a lower plateau—like giant steps descending to the sea. And at last of the jagged peaks that guarded the Cape Peninsula and the final downward drop to the level of the Atlantic.

Now there were lights to be seen below—the clustered lights of towns—and all through the plane passengers began to stir and take down their parcels, put on their coats.

"Someone may meet us," Dirk said. "I wired your father the plane we would take."

Susan glanced at him in surprise. They were coming down now, descending in a gentle slant.

"Do you mean that my father might come to the airport?" she asked, disturbed at the thought. "You should have warned me. I—I'm not ready—"

"I doubt that Niklaas himself will come," Dirk said, and there seemed a sudden tension in him that she did not understand. He reached for her hand where it lay on the seat arm between them. "Susan dear—" he began and then broke off.

"Is something wrong?" she asked in dismay. "I mean about my father? Something you haven't told me?"

His fingers tightened upon her hand. "Darling, will you trust me? Just trust me, that's all. As long as you're with me, we'll work things out, I promise you."

Lights were rushing toward them and in a moment the runway markers were flying past and the plane's wheels had touched the concrete with a faint jar.

Susan could feel the thudding of her heart as the plane rolled to a stop and she got into line in the aisle to move with Dirk toward the exit. This was not really Cape Town yet, she reminded herself. Malan Airport was at a distance from the city and not even the mountain could be seen through the darkness. The moment of recognition could not come until morning and she would be better prepared for it then.

They did not see John Cornish among the passengers as they went through the barrier gates and into the broad main hall of the handsome building. Dirk moved toward the luggage pickup without so much as a glance about to see if anyone had come to meet them. Susan went with him, keeping close to his side, feeling that she was truly in a strange land now. The tension she had noted in the plane was still upon Dirk, and an impatience too, as if he were braced for something which might prove to be an ordeal and which he resented having to face.

As he pointed out their bags and was handing over the checks, Susan saw a man and a woman approaching the luggage counter. The woman had seen Dirk and she walked with a purposeful step that carried her directly toward him. She was young, less than thirty perhaps, and strikingly attractive, with a complexion that was clear and glowing. Bareheaded, she wore her heavy fair hair coiled in a loose knot at the nape of her neck. A smartly styled tan coat hung carelessly from her shoulders and her slender feet were encased in high-heeled brown pumps. Susan's eye for pictorial detail registered her as remarkably photogenic.

Just behind followed a light-skinned colored man in a chauffeur's uniform. A man who was possibly about Dirk's age. Again her quick eye noted detail—the fact that he was fine looking and carried himself well. Yet she had seldom seen a face so carefully devoid of feeling, so guarded in expression.

Susan touched Dirk's arm and he turned and saw the two as they reached him. The air of defensive waiting was still upon him, but he made an effort to appear friendly.

"Mara!" he exclaimed. "I wondered if you would come. This is my wife, Susan. Miss Bellman. Good evening, Thomas. Will you help us with the bags?"

The colored man answered his greeting with a touch of finger to cap and stepped up to the counter to reach for the bags Dirk indicated. Mara Bellman smiled brightly at Dirk.

"Congratulations and all that sort of thing," she said, and turned her violet gaze upon Susan. "Welcome to Cape Town.

I'm your father's secretary and general assistant. I'll have to confess that Dirk's marriage has taken us a bit by—surprise."

Susan tried to return her smile, but her lips felt stiff. "I suppose it has taken us by surprise too," she admitted.

She wanted to ask about her father's reaction to their marriage, but a restraint lay upon them all, something unspoken but real, and she said nothing.

"Let's get along to the car," Dirk said. "We're both fagged and this is no place to talk."

Thomas picked up the bags and started toward the doors. They followed him into the cool night air, walking briskly toward the car. But now, having dismissed her father in her own mind, Susan slipped a hand through the crook of Dirk's elbow, drawing him back.

"Tell me," she whispered, "which way is Cape Town?"

He understood and his impatience faded. "It's that way. To our right. You can see the lights. By daylight you could see the mountain from here. But that will have to wait until morning. At least there's the Southern Cross. Do you remember it?"

He pointed and she looked up at the dark, star-tossed sky, her eyes searching eagerly until she found the constellation—like a small kite in the heavens. Not particularly impressive, yet capable of rousing in her a choked sense of emotion. She could recall a dark night away from the lights of the city, and someone showing a little girl the Southern Cross for the first time. Had it been her father?

The old, unappeased longing, the nostalgia, was upon her again —for what she could not tell. Dirk felt her shiver and slipped an arm about her.

"Come along, darling," he whispered.

She went with him toward the car. The sense of space rushing dizzily away had ceased. She was here and Cape Town was waiting for her.

It has to go well, she told herself. We must make it go well. But the uneasiness would not leave her.

3

During the drive Mara made an attempt at light conversation, though Dirk helped very little, lost again in his own thoughts. Her accent was wholly South African, Susan noted, with much of the English in it, yet with a slurring of syllables that she remembered from the past.

Dirk broke into the middle of Mara's words as if he had not noticed that she was speaking.

"What did Uncle Niklaas have to say about our news?" he asked.

Mara was quiet for a moment. Then she began again, as if summoning up her bright, animated tones. "He hasn't talked about it, actually. But at least he has been making preparations and giving orders madly. For tonight you are to be taken directly to the hotel. You're to come to see him late tomorrow morning, Dirk. That will give you time to move out of the hotel and into the Aerie before you come to his place."

"The Aerie?" Dirk sounded surprised.

The movement of Mara's blond head in assent was graceful, but there was a hint of spite in her voice. "He thought you would want to be by yourselves. And the Aerie is vacant. Not too far away either. It should be convenient."

"At seventy-odd," Dirk said to Susan, "your father has lost none of his tendency to highhanded action. But at least this will spare us the need to do any house hunting immediately."

"What is the Aerie?" Susan asked.

"It's a smaller house your father owns," Dirk said, "and not as pretentious as it sounds. Sometimes he houses visiting buyers there. One of the things you'll have to get used to in Cape Town

33

is the way we name our houses, instead of giving them numbers. If a stranger wants to find a house, all he can do is ring bells along the street until he locates it. This house is furnished and in good repair—I had a look at it myself not long ago."

"We've added a few touches to make you more comfortable," Mara told him, still brightly vivacious. "We moved down some extra furniture from Protea Hill and we've fixed up a little office with your desk in it, Dirk. And your clothes have been sent down, of course. The servants won't be there till tomorrow, which is why you can't move in tonight."

"You have been busy," Dirk said, his tone dry. He turned to Susan. "We're following Rhodes Drive. The road curves around Devil's Peak just above us on our left. The mists have started down, so you can't see the peak tonight."

She knew her directions now. The unseen mountains curved like a broken amphitheater, she remembered, with Devil's Peak and the Lion's Head making the two opposite wings and reaching down toward Table Bay. Though the sky was still starry, clouds blanked out the peaks and to her disappointment she could not see Table Mountain itself—the mountain of her memory. Nevertheless, she knew it stretched hugely between the two wings, forming backdrop and stage. Cape Town itself filled the spectators' seats and spread around the Lion's Head to the suburbs on the sea. Cape Town tonight was a panorama of brilliance fanned out below the drive, extending to the far rim of lights that edged the bay.

It was beautiful, but it did not speak to her. She must still wait until tomorrow for a glimpse of the mountain. Only then could she know she had come home.

The car, a right-hand drive, had been following the left side of the road in the British manner. Now it turned left through tall Grecian columns that marked the impressive entrance to the hotel. It climbed the curving drive past centered palm trees and came to a halt before the front door. They were close beneath the mountain now, but the mist had thickened, reaching down the lower slopes, and there was nothing to be seen except the bright pink hotel façade looming among the palm trees.

Mara came into the lobby with them and stepped efficiently to the desk to make sure that all was in order with their reservation. When Dirk was signing the register, Susan walked a little way into the lounge to look about.

This was the after-dinner hour and men and women of varied ages, the women well cloaked against the chill in mink stoles, were enjoying coffee at small tables scattered through the long, high-ceilinged room. The well-bred atmosphere of an English novel prevailed, except that these people seemed more sensitive to the cold than any true Englishman would have been.

Once assured that all was well, Mara bade Dirk and Susan a somewhat hurried good night and returned to the car. A boy took them upstairs in the small lift. Their room had a surprisingly cozy air about it, and less of the impersonal quality of most hotel rooms. After the chilly halls, the warm glow of an electric heater made them welcome.

There was still a strangeness about Dirk. Susan wanted to cry, "We're here!" and go straight into his arms the moment the boy had gone. But now he kept his distance and made an effort at casual conversation that held her away.

"I'm fond of this hotel," he said. "They go in for old-fashioned British comfort of the sort that used to be demanded by officers who served in India and spent their holidays in Cape Town. There was no nonsense about those old boys when they wanted something."

He was still much too keyed up and clearly as afraid of silence as Mara had seemed to be in the car. But Susan could hold herself away from him no longer, and slipped her arms about his neck.

"What is it?" she asked, her cheek against his. "Ever since the plane started down you've been waiting—as if you expected something unpleasant to happen."

"It has happened," he told her. He held her to him briefly and kissed her cheek, but the evidence of being wound up did not leave him. He had withdrawn from her in some strange way and instinct warned her not to push him when such a mood was upon him. Whatever was wrong, he would not talk to her now. And for the moment, in spite of her disappointment in this entire homecoming, she was almost too weary to care.

It was wonderful to get out of her clothes and into the white-tiled bathroom. She turned on the oversized taps in the enormous English tub, dropped in the big chained plug, and gave herself up to the luxury of steaming hot water. Afterwards she crept between sheets warmed by a hot-water bottle, and pulled the blankets and slippery satin puff over her. She was sound asleep by the time Dirk came to bed, and she slept longer than he did the next morning.

She awakened lazily to the waiter's knock and watched him bring in a breakfast tray with covered silver dishes and a coffee pot. He set up a table in discreet silence and bowed himself away. Dirk was up and already shaved, his fair hair sleek and darkened from the water, his skin glowing above the towel wrapped around the neck of his terry-cloth robe. Susan lay watching him through half-closed eyes, savoring the novelty of wifehood, wishing he would forget about breakfast and come to tell her how much he loved her. His manner, however, was brisk and impersonal.

When the waiter had gone, he poured a cup of coffee, weakened it with the usual English touch of hot milk, sugared it too generously, and brought it to her.

"This will wake you up," he said, plumping her pillow so that she could sit up in bed. "I ordered breakfast up here so we could make an early start. How are you feeling this morning?"

She wasn't sure as yet, but she tried to answer cheerfully that she was fine. The diluted coffee was a little sickening to her taste, but she did not want to offend him by pouring it out and starting over with a strong black cup that would shock her awake. Somehow he could never believe that she liked her coffee black or that she preferred to get up and wash and dress before she had anything at all.

He turned to the window to fling draperies open to the daylight, and she watched hopefully. If the day was bright and sunny, perhaps her spirits would rise correspondingly. But from the bed she could see now that the sky was white with solid clouds, the early morning gray and drab.

When she slipped from under the covers and went to the window, she found that their room faced the bay, with the mountain out of sight behind. To her left the Lion's Head was hidden by clouds—an omen of continued bad weather, she remembered—and mist curled along the flank that stretched toward the bay and was known as Signal Hill. The red roofs and white houses of Cape Town lay spread beneath the window, with the big buildings of the downtown section making an island in themselves near the shore of Table Bay. But there was no bright color in the scene today, no sunshine to cheer her, no lifting of her spirits. And no sense at all of recognition, of coming home. Shivering, she turned back to the electric heater.

Dirk was serving a portion of omelet onto her plate, offering toast in the silver rack that assured its arriving cold.

"Let's hurry a bit," he said, the touch of impatience in his manner no longer hidden. "I'd like enough time to get you over to the house and settled before I go to see your father."

She sat down obediently and tried to eat. But the sense of things going wrong made a lump of discouragement in her throat and it was hard to swallow.

At least Dirk had made no suggestion that she go with him to see Niklaas van Pelt, and she was grateful for that.

While she was dressing in a gray-wool suit against the chill that the electric heater did not entirely dispel, the telephone rang and Dirk answered it. Miss Bellman was waiting for them downstairs with the car and the news gave no lift to Susan's spirits.

As they went down and out to the car, she felt increasingly depressed. Nothing seemed auspicious for the beginning of their married life together in Cape Town. Nothing was going right or turning out as she had hoped it would.

This morning Mara was alone and at the wheel of the long gray Mercedes. Susan and Dirk joined her in the front seat and once more Susan was aware of the girl's vital beauty, her assurance and air of efficiency. She seemed enormously alive, and by contrast Susan felt drained of vitality.

"Your car's ready for you whenever you want to come to Protea Hill to drive it away," Mara told Dirk. "I suppose you'll pick it up this morning when you come to see Mr. van Pelt?"

Dirk nodded. "I'll be glad to have it back. Susan, unfortunately, doesn't drive. Her education has been neglected."

Susan smiled weakly and gave her attention to this old section of Cape Town through which they were driving. The streets were narrow and took unexpected turns up and down steep hills. White cottages, built in the old Dutch style with gabled fronts, were visible on every hand, and there were glimpses of lacy wrought-iron balconies and fences that suggested Spain more than Holland. Rain drizzled across the windshield and mist still shrouded the mountain. Everywhere people were hurrying to work and there were many dark faces among the light. In their dress the people on the sidewalks and in the double-decker buses looked like those one saw in New York or Chicago. This might have been a rainy day anywhere, except for an occasional native blanket or Moslem veil. Whatever lay behind headlines which had been shouted across the world was not visible on the surface this morning in Cape Town.

The car was taking a general uphill course in the direction of the Lion's Head and at length it pulled up before a two-story stucco house with Spanish arched windows and a red-tiled roof.

"I've found a cookie for you," Mara said as they got out of the car, and Susan remembered the familiar name used for cooks. "And a Bantu boy for the yard. By tomorrow I'll have your house-maid and I'll bring her up myself. Hope you can make do till then."

They would barely be able to endure, Susan thought wryly, and reminded herself at once that these were different ways and she must be grateful for all that Mara was doing to make them comfortable.

"You've been efficient, as always," Dirk said pleasantly, covering Susan's silence.

Mara got out of the car in her brisk way, slamming the door after her. She seemed displeased as she went ahead of them through a gate of iron grillwork set in a white stone wall. Following her, while Dirk watched the Bantu boy unloading the bags, Susan noted a small bricked courtyard with a delphinium border. The steps to the arched door were shallow and at the top she walked directly into a wide hall with a darkly polished floor, its gleam unhidden by rugs. At the rear a staircase railed in iron grillwork turned at right angles and disappeared toward the floor above.

Mara ran ahead up the stairs to fling open doors in the upper hall. Moving after her more slowly, Susan had the increasing sense that this was wrong as a homecoming. Dirk was not even at her side. Another woman showed the way, another woman had made all the preparations of welcome, had arranged both flowers and furnishings. She tried to brush such unreasonable resentment aside. Later there would be time to acquaint herself with the house and make it her own and Dirk's.

Upstairs Mara had chosen a room for them and furnished it

with linens and freshly hung curtains and draperies. Her high heels clicked across the polished wood of the floors as she explained this and that, and called orders to the Bantu boy to bring up the bags.

"You may have a little trouble getting him to understand," Mara said, speaking to the boy in Afrikaans. "But Cookie is one of our coloreds and she knows English, so you can get her to translate. If you'll excuse me, I'll run down and show Dirk his office."

Susan thanked the native boy as he set the bags down in obedience to her gesture, and he went away, moving quietly on bare black feet.

The bedroom was pleasantly spacious, but undistinctive, with twin beds, dressing table and bureau, a wardrobe closet. Like fashions in clothes, furniture also pulled the hemispheres together, making it easier to forget other differences. Only the wardrobe closet—a wide armoire—set this room apart. Yet there was, Susan felt, a wrong note about the whole. The over-flowered draperies did not quite harmonize with the spreads. The furniture seemed placed without thought for balance. It was as though an unfriendly hand had arranged everything on a purposely jarring key.

There were windows on two sides, so at least there should be a fine view on a clear day. Now they overlooked a world of mist. Leaning on the sill of a window on the garden side, Susan found that the house was perched high on the lip of what appeared to be a dry, woodsy ravine. Beneath her window stretched lawn and garden, with a retaining wall at the back. Beyond, the hill dropped steeply away to the deep recesses of the ravine. There mist wreathed the flat, parasol tops of a thick stand of Mediterranean pines. Some distance below were other houses on the far side where the hill climbed up from the slit of the ravine. "Aerie" might not be a very original name, but Susan could see that for this house it was appropriate.

She pulled off the small soft hat she had traveled in and ran a comb through her russet hair. Then she went out of the bedroom and down the stairs.

Mara and Dirk stood near the front door, engaged in earnest conversation, speaking softly as if what they discussed was private. Some instinct of warning halted her on the stairs. She remembered Mara's forced volubility in the car yesterday and Dirk's rising uneasiness as the plane came in to land. Then too there was Mara's almost officious manner of taking over the preparations in this house, and the jarring touches Susan had sensed in the bedroom. The work perhaps of a woman whose intent was not wholly amiable? Disturbed and alert now to anything that might lie beneath the surface, Susan went down the stairs.

Mara heard her step and looked up, her lovely face blank of any emotion. Whatever her words had been with Dirk, their import was not visible in her expression.

"Mr. van Pelt expects to see you tomorrow, Mrs. Hohenfield," she said matter-of-factly. "Suppose I call for you in the car right after lunch?"

The tide of warning did not subside in Susan. This was too sudden, too soon. She would not be managed like this against her will and she did not believe a visit to her father had been the entire subject of this whispered conversation.

Before she could object, however, Dirk spoke quickly. "That will be fine, Mara. My wife will be ready."

The other woman gave Susan a bright, slightly vacant smile and went to the door. "I'll leave you then. You won't need the car to get over this morning, Dirk?"

"I know the way on foot," Dirk said, his voice dry.

Mara ran down the flagged walk and got into the car. With a careless wave of her hand she pulled away from the curb.

"I will *not* be ready," Susan told Dirk in a low, indignant voice. "You had no right to arrange this without consulting me. I'm not ready to see my father."

Dirk closed the door upon the damp mists. He put a hand beneath her small stubborn chin and tilted it upward.

"I'm sorry, darling. This has been a bleak homecoming for you, hasn't it? I know you didn't mean to see your father so quickly. But it's better to get it over with and put it behind you. He expects you."

She refused to be appeased. "I don't like that woman! I don't like it a bit that she has arranged everything in this house to please herself. And now she's trying to manage me!"

To Susan's surprise Dirk put his head back and laughed. "I do believe you're jealous," he said.

She stared at him angrily, realizing that she was off on the wrong foot but not knowing how to make a graceful recovery.

He put an arm about her and drew her to him as they started upstairs. "You have my permission to put her down all you like," he said. "She's a bossy piece, and if you don't care for her arrangements in this house you have only to change them. Otherwise, don't give her a thought."

The relief that flowed through her washed away her anger. If he felt like this, then Mara didn't matter at all.

Upstairs in the bedroom Dirk returned to the subject of her father. "Don't forget that this meeting will be as much of an ordeal for your father as for you. Especially since he won't be able to see you."

Susan turned from arranging her toilet articles on the dressing table. "Not see me? What do you mean?"

"You know that he's blind," Dirk said.

"Blind? Of course I didn't know!" Susan stared at him in dismay. "You never mentioned it. You never told me—"

"How could I, when you always stopped me from talking about your father? Besides, I'd supposed—"

She walked away from him and stood at the window that overlooked the ravine and the parasol tops of the pine trees. But she saw nothing of the view before her. As though a curtain had been rolled up, her father's face had flashed back into her mind more clearly than at any time since Dirk had found her in Chicago and wakened long-suppressed thoughts of Niklaas van Pelt. Her father's eyes had been gray, with a direct, penetrating look about them. They were eyes that could see through you quite clearly— or so she had believed as a child. It had always been difficult to keep a secret from him or to deceive him in any way. Her mother saw only what she chose to see, but Niklaas van Pelt saw the truth. And with every child that was sometimes a thing to be hidden. It seemed unbelievable that so clear and vigorous a look was now quenched forever. She would need to fear his eyes no longer. She had been fearing them, she realized. Yet the thought brought her no relief, only a sad stabbing of pain.

"I'm sorry if I've shocked you," Dirk said gently. "I had no idea that you didn't know. After all, he's quite an old man now, and he has been accustomed to being blind for many years. It hasn't changed him, except that sometimes he must be more dependent than he likes to be. But that is what I am for—and Mara too."

As he spoke he moved in and out of the adjoining bathroom,

putting his shaving things in the cupboard over the washbasin, setting a bottle of shaving lotion on a shelf. Susan followed him into the room that was so much larger than most American bathrooms, and reached for a glass. Shock had left her a little sick, though she was not sure why. Long ago her father had been dismissed from her life, from her affection and her fears. Why should it matter now to learn suddenly that an old man whom she no longer knew, who was nothing to her in a personal way, had long been without his sight? Why should the knowledge give her this feeling of faintness?

She reached for the cold-water faucet to fill the glass, but somehow her grip was insecure and the glass flew out of her hand, struck a corner of the wash basin, shattering on the floor. She stared at the debris with a sense of horror that was out of proportion to the damage done.

"No harm," Dirk said. "The glass doesn't matter. But perhaps you'd better sweep it up so we won't step on it later."

Awkwardly she obeyed. There was a hand brush in a cabinet and she knelt on the floor, sweeping the bits of glass into a pile. Her fingers were shaking ridiculously, though she tried to hide their trembling from Dirk. Her tendency to drop things and then be upset out of all proportion to the damage was a senseless weakness of which she was ashamed, and she was glad that Dirk was preoccupied and did not seem to notice.

When he was ready to leave for her father's, she went with him to the door and he kissed her, tweaked her ear affectionately, and went off down the street. She watched him out of sight, not altogether reassured. In more ways than one she had behaved badly this morning and the knowledge depressed her.

The cook, a small, brown-skinned woman with a *doek* about her head—the white kerchief draped in the special manner of South Africa—came in to ask about lunch. Susan tried to be friendly, but the woman seemed uncertain of a strange American, and ill at ease. She must fix whatever she liked, Susan told her. Whatever was available. Such vagueness in an employer was clearly unfamiliar to the woman and again Susan felt inadequate. How could she manage to cope with the duties this house would demand when she was at a loss when it came to so small a task as giving directions to the cook?

When the woman had gone doubtfully back to her kitchen,

Susan began to look about the downstairs portion of the house. The dining room seemed dark on this gray day and she spent no time there, but went on to the living room. This promised to be cheerful and attractive. A big bay window with a cushioned seat beneath it overlooked Cape Town. There was a higher, wider view to be had here than she had seen this morning from her hotel window. The room possessed a small fireplace too and, while the furnishings were undistinctive and lacking in color, a good deal could be done with personal touches.

Pictures always helped bare and characterless walls. This, at least, was a start she might make in the right direction. There were a few of her mounted photographs in her bag upstairs. Dirk had objected to their weight but she had wanted them with her. They would help to make her feel at home. Glad of a purpose to occupy her, she ran up to the bedroom and got the photographs from her bag.

Four of them, well arranged against the end wall, would lighten the room with their white mats and lend a spot of interest that would not be wholly impersonal. She carried the stack of photographs—some eight or ten in all—down to the living room and spread them out on the floor. There she knelt before them to make her choice.

A little pang of homesickness went through her at sight of these Chicago scenes and she braced herself against it. She was where she wanted to be—with Dirk. Wherever he was, there she would make her home.

News pictures seldom came out best for her. She liked to try for good ones, but she knew she was still very much an amateur. Sometimes such a picture was inherently dramatic because of the circumstances involved. But when she was photographing a person it was possible to take more care and obtain a more striking graphic effect. She picked up her favorite picture of the aged news-dealer at his stand and studied it with pleasure.

A sudden ringing of the doorbell made her jump. She dropped the picture and stood up as if she were a child discovered playing with forbidden toys. Unaccustomed to servants, and not sure of her own role, she wondered if she was supposed to let one of them answer the bell. But nothing happened and there was another ring. Probably neither the yard boy nor the cook was expected to answer the front door, and she would not have a housemaid until tomorrow, Mara had said. She went to the door herself and opened it.

Silhouetted against the gray morning stood John Cornish, tall and angular and grave. He said nothing for a moment, his deepset eyes observing her as though he might expect some show of displeasure.

"G-good morning," Susan faltered, taken aback. After the antagonism that Dirk had shown toward this man in the Kimberley airport, Cornish was the last person she had expected to see, and so quickly, on her own doorstep.

"Good morning," he said. "May I come in?" His mouth was straight and unsmiling, his look knowing as if he fully understood the predicament he placed her in.

She did not move from the doorway. "Dirk isn't at home. If you've come to see him—"

"I haven't," he said calmly. "I've come to see you, Mrs. Hohenfield."

She knew very well that Dirk would not want this man in his house, but there seemed no way to refuse him entry without being ruder than she was able to be. Had he found out that she was Niklaas van Pelt's daughter and come on that account to further his aims?

Wordlessly she gestured him into the hall and took his damp coat to hang on the hall rack. Then she led the way reluctantly into the living room where her pictures lay spread across the floor. When Dirk found out about this visit, she would be in for his displeasure, she was very sure. She hated to try his patience further. Why did John Cornish have to add to her problems on this gray, uneasy day?

4

"I won't keep you guessing," Cornish said as he followed her into the living room sidestepping the pictures. "I don't suppose you've had an opportunity to meet Mr. van Pelt yet, but of course you will be meeting him shortly."

So he didn't know her identity as yet. She invited him to a chair, sat down on the window seat, and waited in silence for him to go on.

"Your husband seems to have prejudiced himself against me without a hearing," Cornish continued, watching her keenly from beneath craggy brows. "But you are an unprejudiced newcomer on the scene, and an American besides. Is it possible that you might hear me out on this?"

"What has my being an American to do with it?" she asked.

He permitted himself a frosty smile. "I live in America now, you know. And I've found American wives often given to independent thoughts and decisions of their own."

She did not want to be an American wife, she wanted only to be loyal to Dirk, and this man's presence in the house already involved her in something close to disloyalty. She must be rid of him quickly.

"All this is my husband's affair, not mine," she told him. "If you are here to ask me to intervene and try to arrange a meeting for you with—with Mr. van Pelt, you're asking the impossible."

"I see." The look of appraisal was still in his eyes and she had the sudden instinct that he was here not merely for the obvious purpose which he had stated but for some further reason that he did not mean to tell her. She suspected that he had never

45

believed she would really go against Dirk's wishes. The uneasiness she felt in his presence increased.

He glanced at the photographs which lay spread in a row near his feet. "Interesting," he said. "Do you mind if I look?"

She shook her head helplessly. It was clear that telling him she minded would do little good.

He picked up the picture she had taken of a fire on Chicago's West Side, and held it up to the light, studying it. "What a good shot. Fortune certainly played into your hands."

She prickled to her own defense. "Even shots of dramatic circumstances don't always come out well. A news photographer has to be quick to see a picture, and he has to have the patience to wait."

"Granted." He set the photograph down and picked up another—the one of the newsdealer that she liked best. "A good friend of mine in New York does news stories on assignment for a big magazine. I've gone the rounds with him a few times and he has helped me with occasional photos for my books. I find there's a similarity in some ways between the journalist's approach and a photographer's."

Casually he carried the picture over to her. "Take this shot, for instance." He held it out for her to see, though she knew it by heart. "Here you didn't quite wait for the story, I think."

She could understand very well why Dirk did not like this man. He was a person who did not hesitate to speak his mind, no matter what toes might be stepped on.

"What do *you* think the real picture should have been?" she asked stiffly.

He tapped the photograph with one long finger. "This is good composition and interesting in itself, but not particularly revealing. You've caught a well-balanced shot of an old man with a tired face working behind a stack of newspapers, but you haven't told us much about him. You didn't wait for the moment when his expression would light up and come to life—either over a sale, or in disgust at a customer, or some other way that might show what he's like as a person."

"Doesn't his face show that?" Susan demanded. "After all, he has lived his face."

Cornish shrugged. "You're annoyed with me, aren't you? Not that I blame you. I had no business popping off like that."

46

"I sold the picture," Susan said more quietly.

"You should have, of course. It's worth printing." He leaned toward the row of pictures and replaced the one he held. "You're very good, you know. Don't take the words of an amateur critic too seriously. If you keep on you'll be able to laugh at the critics."

She wanted to resent his words, to consider him rude and officious, but he gave her a slow, grave smile that lessened the somber quality of his face, and she felt herself unexpectedly disarmed. It was true that he spoke from a position of greater maturity and experience. However, her very softening toward him put her on guard again. It was his purpose, of course, to disarm her.

"How did you know where to find us?" she asked. "How did you know I would be alone?"

His sardonic left eyebrow quirked. "A good reporter never reveals his private sources. It wasn't particularly difficult to manage. Do you mind if we talk a bit about Niklaas van Pelt?"

She saw that she was neatly caught and must either be as rude as she should have been in the first place or hear him out. At least she would not tell him that Niklaas was her father. His private sources had not revealed everything and she wanted no place as Niklaas's daughter in this book John Cornish was writing.

"I'd like to finish my work here as quickly as I can," he went on. "That's why I've let no grass grow under my feet. I want to get out of South Africa and back to the States."

"You were born here, weren't you? Isn't South Africa your home, even more than the States?"

Cornish frowned. "It was Mr. van Pelt we were going to talk about."

"You were going to talk about him, not I," Susan said.

"Exactly. As I mentioned in Kimberley, I'm writing a book about diamonds and what they can do to men. It's the men I am interested in more than the diamonds. One of the men who had an influence on the diamond business, and was affected by it in turn, is Niklaas van Pelt. He belongs in the book. His name will run through it and he will have a chapter given over to him, whether he likes it or not."

"As I understand it," Susan said quietly, "you had a hand in injuring him rather seriously some sixteen years ago. Haven't you done enough?"

He was silent for a moment and she sensed again the relentless determination in this man, though exactly where it led she was not sure.

"If what happened can stand unchallenged, then that is what I shall write," he said. "But there were certain aspects of the affair that I have never understood. Perhaps van Pelt can be persuaded to talk about them now."

He would have gone on, but Susan heard the sound of a key in the front door and knew that Dirk had come home.

"Here is my husband," she said. "You had better talk to him."

Cornish stood up. "I doubt that he'll listen to me, but I will see you again."

Before she could say that she had no intention of seeing him again, Dirk was in the room. At the sight of John Cornish he threw Susan a questioning look and faced the other man, antagonism bristling as it had before.

"What do you want here?" he demanded.

Cornish answered without hesitation. "I want an appointment with Niklaas van Pelt."

"You'd better realize," Dirk said, his voice tight with anger, "that I will arrange no such appointment. Mr. van Pelt does not wish to see you under any circumstances."

"He has answered none of my letters, and I quite understand how he may feel," Cornish said calmly. He went into the hall, took his coat from the rack and bowed gravely to Susan. As Dirk opened the door for him, he paused for a moment longer. "Nevertheless," he added, "I will manage to see him."

Susan returned to the living room and stood staring absently at the row of pictures on the floor. She felt not a little frightened by the anger in Dirk's face. Anger that might now be directed at her. She braced herself against whatever was to come. In some long-ago time she had learned to retreat from angry words, to shut herself away in a world of her own making where violence could not reach her. But Dirk's anger was cold and nonexplosive—the outburst did not come. Perhaps the deepest anger was always deadly cold, and all the more alarming for that very fact.

"Susan—" his very tone was chill—"I will not have that man in my house. He's not to be trusted. Whether you care about your father or not doesn't matter. I am deeply concerned about protecting him from the harm this man may do. Cornish spells disaster for all of us. Do you understand me?"

She looked at him distantly, unable to return at once from the inward retreat to which she had withdrawn. For a long moment he faced the remoteness in her eyes, then he went abruptly from the room and she heard the sharp closing of the door as he left the house.

She pressed her fingers to her temples and felt the pain of sensation flooding back. What was happening? What had gone so wrong between herself and Dirk that suddenly they did not understand each other? Why had she not gone to him quickly and promised whatever he wished, since that was all that really mattered?

Something nebulous and threatening seemed to crowd about her, gathering like mists on the mountain, menacing all her new-found happiness in some dreadful way. If Dirk stopped loving her, there would be nothing left—only empty loneliness again, and all her hopes ended. Yet at the core of her there was a small, hard spot of anger—not cold like his, but hot and bitter. She could not be wholly meek in her loving. If she had the scene with John Cornish to relive, she would be forced to do again as she had done and ask him into the house. There had been no harm in her action, no complete justification for Dirk's attitude toward this man.

Unless? "Disaster for all of us," Dirk had said, and the sharp chill of his voice seemed to linger in the room.

With a sweeping gesture she gathered up the photographs and carried them upstairs. She did not want to hang any just now. There was no comfort for her in looking at them.

When Cookie came to tell her that lunch was served, she went downstairs and sat at the dining table alone. It was hard to swallow, and sugar beans, cooked with meat and served over rice, tasted as flat as her spirits. Which was not Cookie's fault. She tried to pretend an appetite she did not feel, and lectured herself firmly as she ate.

John Cornish had spoken of her as an American wife. The fact that she had married a South African husband must also be considered. The English husband and the Afrikaner and Dutch and German husbands were not, as she must never forget, entirely like the American husband. The Old World still held the man to be master, and perhaps in the long run that was a better and more satisfying thing for any woman. She knew that Dirk liked in her the very youthful qualities she was inclined to regret, and that he did not enjoy any tendency to oppose him and go off on some headlong tangent of her own. It was up to her to learn how to be a South African wife and suppress her occasional headlong American impulses.

Dirk remained away all that day and into the evening. Susan went early to bed between chilly sheets, not yet being hot-water-bottle minded.

It must have been after midnight when he came in. He undressed quietly and she pretended to be asleep. In spite of her good resolutions, her wounded spirit resisted him, turning from him, yet longing perversely to have him break down her resistance.

He did not come near her, however, and she heard his even breathing in the next bed while she lay awake for a long while. At some time during the late-night hours she fell into an uneasy slumber, but she was awake again at dawn, to find a cold clear light seeping into the room.

She knew she would not sleep again, so she slipped out of bed in her thin nightgown and went to a window, heedless of the cold. There she parted the draperies so that she could look out. The window faced at an angle across the irregular amphitheater of mountains and town, so that the Lion's Head, the right wing, was out of sight, just behind the house. The broken pyramids of Devil's Peak rose straight ahead on the far side of town. She had to turn to her right a little to view what all Cape Town affectionately called "the mountain," and with her turning the full impact of it struck boldly across her vision.

The mists had blown away and the dawn sky was clear, with a rosy tinge beyond Devil's Peak. No cloud "tablecloth" lay over the mountain's top this morning. It stood clear in awesome power, its great mass stretched behind Cape Town, its head a long straight line ruled against the sky. The light of dawn struck across the rocky face of sheer precipice and set it glistening. Thirty-five hundred feet it rose, so massive and close that every cleft and ravine and steep fall of rock was visible in detail. Here the black gods of old Africa had lived in times long past before the white man had come to the continent. And here they would live when the white man's power was gone.

Upon Susan the impact was tremendous. She had no thought for the chilly room behind her or the cold pane of glass beneath her fingertips. She had half expected to find the mountain dwarfed when set against her childhood recollection, but the reality was more impressive than her memory of it.

She had come home. This was the Cape Town she had loved, with Table Mountain ruling the sky and Devil's Peak raising its jagged head across the valley. She liked best an older name for the peak—the Wyndberg. What a home for storms it was, when great winds beat across Cape Town winter and summer. Today the white houses and red roofs no longer looked dim and gray. There was a clean, well-washed gleam to them, untouched by industrial grime.

She did not hear Dirk when he left his bed, did not know he was near until he put his arms about her and drew her slim body against his own. For an instant she stiffened, and then warm love flowed through her and she was alive again.

"I'm sorry, darling," he said softly and kissed the place where her short hair curled above her ear.

She forgot the mountain and turned her face to him. Relief was a wave engulfing her, carrying her free of darkness. She put her arms about his neck and pressed her cheek against his own.

"Dirk, it's been dreadful! You went so far away and I didn't know how to reach you."

"I know," he said. "There's a devil of perversity that gets into me at times. And you closed yourself away from me behind those wide eyes of yours. We mustn't let this happen, sweet. You know I love you. Never forget it."

And he knew how much she loved him, she thought. He did not need to hear her say it. It was something she told him with her hands framing his face, with her lips upon his own. The embrace was all the sweeter because she had been for a little while so frighteningly far away from him.

Before they went back to the warmth of blankets, she turned once more to the mountain. "I remember what they call it—the Old Gray Father. Oh, Dirk, it's good to be home again! Yesterday I couldn't find myself. I couldn't find you and I was afraid."

His hands pressed her shoulders gently. "Do you see the ravine that cuts down the hill below us? The house you lived in as a child is just across. Your father's house. Can you find it there, lower than we are, on the opposite hill?"

Her gaze swept the width of the ravine and moved along the hill beyond to a white house with red-tiled roof and the intricate lacework of wrought iron around its porches and balconies. From this angle it did not look altogether familiar, but she knew it was the house she had visited with so much joy as a little girl and dreamed about with longing through the Johannesburg winter.

"Your father expects you today," Dirk said. "Mara will come for you this afternoon and you mustn't be afraid."

"Will you be there?" she asked.

"Probably not. There's work for me away from the house. But you mustn't disappoint him. He's counting on this."

The picture of an elderly blind man, grown pitifully helpless, had taken hold of her imagination and she had been able to put aside the disturbing memory of a piercing look that saw everything and a judgment that could be merciless.

"I'll go," she promised. "But remember that I'm doing it for you, more than I am for him."

He laughed and there was something exciting in the sound. He tousled her short hair almost roughly and tangled his fingers in it as he kissed her again.

"You're to let your hair grow," he ordered. "I want to see it down to your shoulders. I don't like being married to a crop-haired boy." He picked her up and she clung to him as he carried her back to her bed.

Afterwards she lay awake for a time, a dreamy contentment upon her from which all fearfulness had fled. She loved him so very much. She wanted only to please him, to serve him, to be what he wished her to be. The ancient longing of Eve, of Woman, possessed her and she wanted—for the moment—nothing else.

Even after she rose for the second time, even after Dirk had gone to work, the sense of having at last come home remained with her. When she was alone she went lightheartedly to every window in the house and looked out upon the clear bright day, savoring each remembered view. Behind the house the Lion's Head was free of clouds, raising its nubby rock top from the hill that separated Table Bay and the ocean beyond.

She even got out her camera and checked her film supply, tried a shot or two from upstairs windows, just to get her hand in again and because every view filled her with delight. Once more she felt alive and eager to plan.

Dirk had said there was a downstairs bathroom she might fix

up for a darkroom, if she liked. She must purchase supplies, set herself up in business, as it were. This morning she could even remember without resentment that John Cornish had said she had talent. Perhaps she might take a few pictures around Cape Town that he would approve of. If she ever saw him again—which was unlikely. Knowing now how Dirk felt, she must take no more chances. If he came to this house again, she would not be at home to Mr. Cornish. The spell of the repentant Eve was still upon her.

5

IN THE AFTERNOON Mara came over, bringing the new maid—a dark-skinned girl named Willimina Kock. "Willi" for short, Mara said. The girl had a gentle manner that was appealing, and she spoke English naturally as a language she had grown up with. Mara gave orders briskly about Willi's duties as if she hardly expected Susan to know what they would be. The girl said, "Yes, Miss Bellman," quietly and went to change into her working clothes.

"She'll manage quite well for you," Mara said casually. "She's had a bit more education than is necessary, but she needs the work. If you're ready now, we'll get along over to the house. Your father is waiting for you."

Susan felt like saying, "Yes, Miss Bellman," to all this brisk efficiency, but she suppressed the urge. Undoubtedly this handsome, blond young woman was hired for her ability to handle such matters with authority.

When Susan had put on her coat, she slung her camera over her shoulder, hoping to find an occasion to use it later. As they got into the car and drove along the short, narrow street to a sharp turn, Susan glanced at her companion speculatively.

Today Mara seemed less brightly vivacious than she had been before, and while she was courteous enough, there was a chill behind her manner, and perhaps disapproval. Did this, Susan wondered, reflect Niklaas van Pelt's feeling about a marriage between his long-ignored daughter and his ward? At any rate, remembering Dirk's laughter at Mara's expense, she would not be troubled by her today.

Though the van Pelt house was not far across the ravine, it was necessary to follow the road uphill to the place where it bridged the cut and go the long way around down the other side. From this approach the house looked more familiar to Susan. It was built in a fat L, with lacy iron railings along the upstairs and downstairs verandas. The short part of the L extended toward the front and was capped by a peaked roof, red tiled. Under the eaves were old-fashioned gingerbread curlicues. A low stone wall, painted white and topped with more of the fanciful iron grill-work, was further fortified with a high box hedge, behind which towered a huge rhododendron bush.

Mara turned the car into the driveway and ran it around to the garage in the rear.

"I'll take you in," she said shortly, and Susan let herself out of the car and walked beside the brisk-moving Mara toward the front of the house.

There were a few flowering shrubs, Susan noted as they walked through the yard, but the rare proteas her father had once raised and which gave the house its name were no longer in evidence.

As they neared the steps wings of nervousness began to flutter inside Susan. This sudden attack of anxiety was nonsense, she told herself. It was ridiculous to be seized by a groundless fear that bordered on panic just because she was to meet this old man whom she really did not know.

Mara seemed unaware of Susan's uneasiness. She went up the front steps and across the wide veranda, with Susan following after. The front door had narrow panes of glass running down a strip on either side. The sight brought recognition. Susan could remember a child peering out at the street through one of those panes on a rainy day when she could not go outside to play.

A maid, wearing the usual white kerchief, opened the door at Mara's ring and they entered a wide hall, with a stairway running up at one side. A small Oriental rug lay against the dark floor, and a chest of drawers made of some dark, handsomely grained wood stood against the wall, a ladder-backed chair beside it. On top of the chest brass candlesticks flanked a tall Chinese vase filled with glowing pink flowers.

"If you'll wait here a moment," Mara said, "I'll tell him you've arrived."

Susan was glad enough to wait in the dim light of the old-fash-ioned hallway and try to get her own bewildering emotions in hand. Something in her accepted the house in warm recognition, remembering the hallway, the very stairs, the glimpse of a dining room beyond, with more flowers on a long sideboard. Yet when it came to facing the man who was her father she could feel nothing except a tendency to panic and she did not know why.

The colored maid took her coat, but Susan kept her camera over her shoulder as if its very presence helped to identify her with a world she knew and belonged to. When the maid had gone she turned to the vase of flowers with a further sense of recognition. So spring proteas were blooming in Cape Town. The waxy petals of this variety were thick-fleshed and stiff, the centers a solid, prickly mass. Woody stems supported the blossoms and the green leaves were waxy like the blooms. She touched a tentative finger to a leaf, knowing that the surface would be faintly sticky.

Behind her, at the far end of the hallway, the assured click of Mara's spiked heels sounded and she turned about.

"Come this way, please," Mara said. She had taken off her coat and wore a blue knitted suit that revealed her figure effectively.

At the rear the hall turned at right angles, ending with an open door. As they approached the door, Thomas Scott came out, carrying a sheaf of envelopes. Susan said, "Good morning," and he bowed his head, murmuring a scarcely audible response. For an instant she was aware of dark eyes that held a hint of anger in them. Mara paid no attention to him as they went through the door of Niklaas van Pelt's study.

Now the sense of engulfing recognition brought with it a dread that was nearly overpowering. There was something disturbing about this room, some association it held for her. Yet it was a pleasant room, with French doors opening upon a terrace, the walls done in soft grays and grayish greens. It was not the colors of the room she remembered, however, or even the pictures on the walls. These things had been changed since her childhood. The great desk of native stinkwood stood in the same place. The heavy dark bookcases were the same, and the slippery chairs that were difficult for a child to sit upon without sliding. All these she saw at a glance as a background for the man who occupied a great red leather armchair behind the desk. Toward him she had no feeling of recognition at all, and the very fact helped to quiet the fluttering of anxiety as she faced him.

"Here is your daughter, Mr. van Pelt," Mara said.

The old man behind the desk barely lifted his fingers in a gesture of dismissal and Mara went softly away, silencing her clicking heels, closing the door without a sound behind her.

"Susan?" he said. There was a resonance in the deep voice that was not unmusical, but there was no warmth in the sound, no eager greeting. It was merely a question addressed to a yet-unsensed presence.

"Yes," she said, equally cool. "I am here, Father."

He reached toward a chair beside the desk and removed a heavy silver-headed cane that leaned against it.

"Sit down, please," he said.

She obeyed, her eyes never leaving his face. It was a thin face with deep grooves in the cheeks. The beaked nose was the same, strong and aggressive. But the keen eyes she might have remembered were hidden behind dark glasses. His hair had grown grayer than she recalled, but it was not yet white, and it still grew thickly back from a fine brow. She knew him and she did not know him. Around her the room watched and bided its time.

"I am glad you have returned to South Africa," Niklaas said, his tone formal. "Though it is a surprise that you return as the wife of Dirk Hohenfield. That is something I neither planned nor expected."

"I'm sorry if you're not pleased," she told him. "I know you like to plan all matters close to you yourself."

She had not meant to say that. The words had presented themselves unbidden and they sounded rude in her ears. But there was no way to take them back.

A flicker of some expression that was not a smile crossed his face and was gone. "I see you are still outspoken. You were a gentle child, yet you had a surprising way of speaking your mind at times."

"I had no business saying that," she apologized. "Dirk has been like a son to you for years, and you don't know me. There's no reason why you should be pleased to see him marry me."

"Your voice is a woman's voice," he said, as though he had listened only to the tone and not the words. "But the image in my mind is of a straight-haired little girl with bright reddish plaits, brown eyes, and a stubborn chin. I must change that picture."

For the first time she sensed what he might be experiencing and was moved. She at least could see the change in him, she could comprehend the fact that they were strangers. He could see nothing of the far greater change in her.

He put out a hand and touched her shoulder, felt the strap of the camera, followed it down to the case, and she knew he was seeking to replace his eyesight by means of his fingers.

"What is this?" he asked.

"A camera, Father," she told him.

"Yes, of course. Dirk has said you were working at picture taking on a newspaper in Chicago, and that you wanted to keep it up."

He touched her shoulder again, reached upward lightly to her short hair and then withdrew his hand as if the feel of it distressed him. Tears stung her eyelids. Tears of pity for a once vigorous man who was no longer whole.

He made no further exploration through his fingers, but sat back in the deep chair, his hidden eyes turned in her direction, his expression impassive, remote. She had the feeling that he had put her aside as someone he did not know. A silence grew between them, as if he withdrew into his own darkness and forgot she was there.

Waiting for him to speak, she looked about the room and saw the touches of Africa that were new since she had been here as a child. On the wall behind her father hung a mask carved in some dark-brown wood: a face with the thickened lips and flattened nostrils that made it almost a caricature, yet a face that possessed dignity. The earlobes were elongated, with tubes of ivory thrust through them, and the eyes were lost in hollows. Yet there was a vitality here that made one know a man like this had lived in proud authority and been respected by his fellows. In a corner of the room stood a native assegai, and against one wall a tall, cylindrical drum waited for fingers to beat old rhythms upon the tightly drawn skin.

But the silence grew too long and Susan stirred uneasily, finding herself at a disadvantage. After all, he had summoned her here; she had not asked to come. He had no business treating her as if he had gone away and left her here alone.

"Why did you want me to come to South Africa?" she asked him boldly. "Why should you want to see me when so many years have passed?"

He seemed to return from a distance as he touched a paper on the desk before him. "Your mother did not tell you she had written to me? She did not tell you what she asked of me before her death?"

Susan was startled. Her mother had written to Niklaas van Pelt? And without letting her know! She felt shocked and a little betrayed.

"I didn't know she had written," she said. "What did she write to you about?"

Raised blue veins marked the hand with which he pushed a letter toward her across the desk.

"Here it is. Read it for yourself."

She picked up the sheet of airmail paper almost reluctantly. The sight of her mother's rather childish handwriting opened a wound that was far from healed. The letter began on a slightly frantic note, and she sensed the despair with which it had been written. The doctor had felt it wiser to keep the truth from Claire, and Susan had agreed. But now it seemed that her mother had not been fooled after all. The letter began with the statement that she had not much longer to live, that she had never asked anything of Niklaas for the child before, but that she must ask it now. When she was gone Susan would have no one. Claire's own family was long dead. There would be no one to advise the girl, protect her, care for her.

Susan looked up from the letter at her father. He had withdrawn again. The blank, smoky surface of the glasses told her nothing. From a humidor on his desk he took a cigar and snipped the ends, then lighted it with the ease of a man long used to managing all small actions by touch. Susan watched in uneasy fascination, as she considered the words she had just read. Her mother's concern in the letter was touching, but not very realistic.

"You needn't have sent for me because of this," she said. "I'm not so helpless as she represents."

He puffed his cigar and said nothing. She read on. Now her mother was speaking of some personal matter that lay between herself and her husband. Susan did not understand and read the words through a second time:

I know you always thought it my fault that the Kimberley disappeared. You believed I tricked you. You believed

59

I was a thief. How could I bear that, Niklaas, when I truly did not know what happened to the stone? How could I stay on in South Africa as your wife when you thought I had betrayed you in such a terrible way? I told you the truth—though you never believed me.

Susan looked up from the letter. "What is she talking about?"

"Have you read it through?" her father asked.

Her eyes returned to Claire's words sloping along the page:

At the time I had a feeling that the child knew something about the diamond. That perhaps she had witnessed something, or was unwittingly in possession of some knowledge about it. But she was in a wildly distraught state during the period before we left the country. When I tried to question her she would only sob hysterically. The only thing to do was get her away from South Africa where she would not have to grow up under a shadow.

I encouraged her to forget. I taught her never to look back. Just as I had to forget and never look back. It was the only way. Though many a time I've wondered what might be locked away in her childhood memories—something she might know without knowing that she knows it. Perhaps you can draw it out of her, if ever you see her again.

There was nothing of further consequence to the letter. It closed stiffly, formally, and then the writer hurled herself into an emotional plea for Susan's welfare in a postscript that was typical of Claire.

Susan put the letter back on the desk within reach of his hand. "I don't know what she meant by all this. I've never so much as heard of a lost diamond."

"She was referring to the Kimberley Royal," Niklaas said. "One of the famous diamonds of South Africa. It disappeared many years ago and that was the end of it."

His tone was even, without emotion. He felt for Claire's letter and returned it to a folder while Susan pondered the words she had read. A glimmer of the reason for them was beginning to form in her mind and she spoke the thought aloud.

"I believe I know what my mother meant to do. She couldn't be sure that you would interest yourself in me after all these years. So she tried to offer you a clever bribe. At least she must have thought it clever. She could weave the most fantastic notions at times."

"I don't understand," her father said.

"I know it sounds a little silly," Susan said apologetically, "but I knew her so well. It's exactly the sort of thing she would dream up. If she could convince you that I knew something about this lost diamond, then perhaps you would interest yourself in me. You might go out of your way to take me under your protection. Isn't it possible that is what she intended?"

Once more the silence between them lengthened. He did not answer her suggestion. He neither admitted nor denied. Yet the more she thought about it the more logical such reasoning seemed. It would never have occurred to Claire that Susan might hate to be brought to South Africa by means of such a ruse. Or that it might be a tiresome and disturbing thing if her father and others began prodding her into trying to remember something she could not possibly remember, never having had any knowledge of it in the first place.

Apparently the ruse had worked. Niklaas van Pelt had sent for his daughter promptly. Even Dirk—who had undoubtedly read this letter—had asked her back in Chicago if she had ever heard of the Kimberley Royal. But Dirk had not been truly interested, she remembered thankfully. He had not pushed the matter and never returned to it.

If this was why her father had called her home, she wanted only to escape his presence and end this disillusioning interview.

"Apparently you don't agree with this reasoning," she said. "And if that's the case there's nothing more I can say. I had better be going."

He heard her rise and reached for the silver-headed cane beside his chair as he stood up. He made no effort to keep her, but held out his hand. She put her own into it, aware of the sensitive touch of his fingers, as though he were again using them to see, learning the fragile structure of her bones, the span and length of her hand. But he did not ask her to come to see him again, nor did she suggest another visit. Because of Dirk she would undoubtedly be forced to visit this house from time to time, but there was nothing left between them of a father-daughter relationship.

Mara came to meet her as she left the study, and Susan glanced a bit wistfully up the stairs. There was in her a greater sense of recognition of the house than of her father. She would have liked to wander upstairs, to return to the past through its rooms and corridors. But this was not something she would ask of Mara Bellman.

"Thomas can drive you home if you like," Mara offered.

Susan shook her head and patted the camera slung at her side. "Thanks, but I want to walk. Perhaps I'll find some good shots along the road."

Mara saw her to the door and Susan was glad to be out on the steeply slanting street again, climbing toward the high place where the road rounded its horseshoe curve and turned toward home on the higher level of the opposite hill.

More than anything else she wanted to be alone. An unexpected sense of pain and disappointment filled her. In spite of her efforts to convince herself that her father meant nothing to her and that she could expect little from this meeting, there must have been an unaccepted hopefulness in her based on the memory of a child's deep affection for her father. The fact that her mother's ruse had succeeded and he had sent for her, not out of a like, remembered affection but only because of her value to him in the possible recovery of great wealth, left her with an aching sense of disappointment.

Where the street began to curve Susan once more had a clear view of the mountain and she paused to gaze sadly up at it. The climbing houses ended well below the highway that cut horizontally along the mountainside, leaving a visible gash. Above the road the slopes were grassy, steepening as they extended upward to the level where rocky buttresses began. How blue and clear the sky was above the mountain this morning. In other parts of Africa the sky had seemed surprisingly white and thin. But the skies of South Africa could blaze with a deep-blue light.

To distract herself in this moment of painful disappointment she snapped a picture of the mountain. As she did so something moving at one end of the great fall of rock caught her eye. A tiny cable car was swinging up the face of the cliff, its support invisible, as if nothing suspended it between mountaintop and earth. She watched it travel clear to the small white block that was the building at the top where the cable ended. She must go up in that car one of these days. She would get Dirk to take her. For some reason no one had ever taken her up there as a child.

As she moved on toward the Aerie, she thought of how clean the streets of Cape Town seemed, and how pleasantly old-fashioned in this section. The white gabled houses still echoed the Dutch architecture, and the white stone walls, or picket fences with gardens beyond, seemed extraordinarily neat and well-kept in the true English manner. In one yard a poinsettia bloomed, and in another mountain mimosa, sweet-scented and pale yellow, sprinkled petals over the wall and upon the sidewalk.

But her surroundings could not hold her attention for long because the thought of her mother's letter was still upon her. There had always been a gentle fiction she had kept up to please her mother: the fiction that it was Susan who was dependent and helpless and Claire who cleverly solved all their problems. This had cost Susan little and it had helped Claire to build up the picture of herself that she found it necessary to harbor.

In reality, Claire had never had any notion of the physical difficulties of Susan's work or of the predicaments in which her daughter sometimes found herself in an effort to serve her paper. To Claire, being respectable had always been of the greatest importance. Underneath she might sometimes be as eager as a child for the gratification of her own wishes and pleasure. Yet all must be conducted with an air of gentility and decorum. She would never have been one, Susan recognized, to stand beside a husband who had disgraced himself, and thus disgraced her as well. Yet in the end Claire had been truly concerned about her daughter, had tried to ensure her future. And in a sense she had succeeded. At least the bait of the diamond had succeeded, Susan thought bitterly. It had caused Niklaas to act.

She wished now that she had asked her father more questions about the Kimberley Royal. In itself the story seemed unbelievable. Had there really been some suspicion on her father's part that her mother might have taken the stone, or was that still another of Claire's fancies? Had her father's imprisonment had anything to do with the disappearance of the diamond?

She had no answer for any of these questions.

The road climbed beneath the Lion's Head and she looked up at it, looming against the sky. The Lion overhung all this part of town, claiming ownership, as Devil's Peak on the far side of the amphitheater was ruler there. Yet both must pay homage to the more massive mountain bridging the space between them.

Tonight she would tell Dirk about this meeting with her father, ask him the questions that troubled her. The thought of Dirk brought something of her courage surging back. After all, what did Niklaas or his motives matter? She must forget, suppress, the child in her who had once so loved her father. She had Dirk now. With him she could be complete.

Her steps quickened. He would be in for dinner before too long and the warm memory of their reconciliation this morning hurried her toward home.

6

DIRK CAME HOME late and hurried to shower and change before dinner. Again Susan had left the meal in the cook's hands, but tonight the food tasted wonderful. *Bobotie*, meat balls with egg and curry, baked in a square English pie dish, was a favorite of Dirk's, he told her, and she found the well-spiced flavor delectable.

The table looked attractive with the white candles the new maid, Willi, had set in silver holders that had been a gift from Niklaas van Pelt. Blue cornflowers had been massed in a small bowl in the center to give an accent of color.

It was pleasant to have Dirk telling her about his work tonight. He had persuaded Niklaas to put in a stock of handsome silver jewelry, he said. Not work from the reservations this time, but fine silver craft done here in the Cape, some of it set with semiprecious stones mined nearby. He had brought home one of the pins for her and she unwrapped it from the tissue in delight. Cut into a raised silver oblong were tiny figures copied from ancient cave paintings: a naked running figure with a bow and arrow, another leaping with a spear upraised, and between the two human figures a doomed impala in graceful flight. She pinned the brooch to her blouse, touched by his gift.

John Cornish was not mentioned, and the meal went off without variance.

Willi served at the table so quietly that they were hardly aware of her. When she was out of the room Susan told Dirk that her father had shown her the surprising letter Claire had written him before her death.

"You knew about the letter, didn't you?" she asked. "You must have known about it when you met me in Chicago."

65

"Yes, I knew," Dirk agreed. "Your father showed it to me before he sent me to fetch you home."

"But then why didn't you tell me about it? Wouldn't it have been fairer to me if I had known?"

"Fairer, perhaps. But not so useful in furthering my purpose." There was both amusement and affection in his smile. "You were being a bit obstinate and I didn't want to add to my own handicap. If you'd suspected that your father had an ulterior motive in wanting you here you might never have come."

"But of course my mother's ruse about the diamond was nonsense," she assured him. "That was something she thought up to make certain my father would interest himself in me. And it seems to have worked." She couldn't help a tinge of bitterness in her tone. Dirk was undoubtedly right. If she had known about the letter she would have been much more set against coming.

Dirk reached across the table for her hand. "Think of it this way—it might be of real service to your father if you could recall anything that would give him a clue about the Kimberley."

Clearly he had not understood her point. "But, Dirk, that was only a made-up story! I don't know anything about a diamond. My mother was full of well-meant little feminine tricks like that. It's exactly what she would have done—and thought herself very clever and helpful."

Dirk's smile lighted his face with the bright look she loved to see, but at the moment it irritated her a little because it meant that he did not really accept her theory about the letter.

"How could my remembering anything about a diamond benefit my father?" she demanded.

"That's a question I can't answer," he said. "But I have a strong feeling that it might."

She was on dangerous ground now, she knew. Always before, she had avoided probing too far because that way fear lurked like a shadow at the back of her mind, ready to engulf her if she looked too closely. But she could not go on being a child about this forever. She had to know. She moistened her dry lips with the tip of her tongue.

"Was it because of this lost diamond that he went to prison?"

Dirk shook his head. "No, oddly enough, the diamond had nothing to do with what happened. Even though the Kimberley was presumed to be in his possession at the time. It had been entrusted

66

to him by its owner—a close friend of Niklaas's—to bring to Cape Town for a special exhibit. When it disappeared, his friend said nothing to the press or to the police, merely withdrawing his consent to have it exhibited. He was devoted to Niklaas and he did not let anyone know what had happened. So there was no prosecution, no public search, no fanfare. Not until years later when all the trails had grown cold did word of the diamond's disappearance emerge."

"But then why did my father go to prison? What was the offense that sent him there?"

"You should have asked me that in Chicago," Dirk said gently. "When I wanted to tell you, you wouldn't let me. Now your father has asked me not to go into all that past history, since you don't know about it. He feels it has no bearing on the present. If he decides differently he'll tell you himself. So that's the way it has to be, darling. I can't go against his wishes in this."

Willi brought in the dessert—an English dish called a "trifle"—made of sponge cake, jam and rich custard. It put an effective end to their discussion as she struggled to get it down.

Under the circumstances she could hardly insist that Dirk tell her what she wanted to know. He had not accepted her reasoning about her mother's letter and there seemed to be no way to convince him. In any case, it could not matter now that she was here. It was wiser to let the whole thing go. Besides, she was looking forward to her first evening at home with her husband and she wanted no friction to mar it.

After dinner, however, Dirk seemed restless, as if the idea of settling down to a quiet domestic evening were foreign to his bachelor nature. Willi lighted a coal fire in the small grate, and Susan set out some books and magazines invitingly, drew two chairs before the hearth. But Dirk did not notice her little byplay and she watched him, troubled, as he moved about the room, pausing at the bay window to look out at the lights of Cape Town, lost in thoughts he did not speak aloud. When the telephone in the hallway rang and he jumped like a cat, hurrying to answer it, she knew he had been expecting the call.

From the hallway his voice reached her, controlled and low. She rearranged books on a nearby table, making small sounds so that she would not hear his words. Dirk had enjoyed a life of his own for years before she had come into it. She mustn't expect his transition to be as complete and wholehearted as her own.

When he returned to the living room he looked both exasperated and angrily alive.

"I'll have to go out," he said. "There's no help for it. Do you think you can put up with a husband whose daytime work spreads into the evening hours?"

She was careful to smile, to hide her disappointment, but she would have been more reassured if he had offered some explanation about work so urgent that it demanded his presence after hours.

She went with him to the door, striving for an appearance of cheerful good humor, and he kissed her warmly before he hurried away.

When he had gone the house seemed still and somehow lifeless. Darkness created a seclusion of its own, a withdrawing from the life of the city all about, so that each home became a unit existing of itself, without relation to the whole. The Aerie's high perch made this seem doubly so.

At least she was not yet entirely alone in the house. Small sounds issued from the dining room and Susan crossed the wide hall and went into the room where Willi was tidying up.

Once more Susan had an impression of a consideration and courtesy that was natural to this pretty, dark-skinned girl. Willi must be about her own age and Susan wondered about her as a person in the uneasy life of today's South Africa. It was clear that she was not typical as a servant, and Susan had wondered at Mara's choice of her for this work.

"Have you always lived in Cape Town, Willimina?" she asked.

"Not always, Mrs. Hohenfield," Willi said, setting the coffee service in place on the sideboard. "My parents were originally from the Cape, but they moved to Johannesburg when I was quite small. We returned here a few years ago." She glanced at Susan and then away, offering nothing more.

In Chicago Susan had known colored girls in school and had made friends with one who had worked on the paper. She liked what she had seen of Willi. She wanted to know her. And Willi would not take the initiative, so Susan spoke frankly.

"I've heard that the color bar is easier here in the Cape Province than it is in the Transvaal. Do you find that true?"

A spark of something quickly suppressed showed in Willi's eyes. "It is better here," she agreed and went on with her work.

"Are positions difficult to find?" Susan persisted.

The girl shrugged slender shoulders expressively. "So many come here hoping things will be better. There are dozens applying for every job. Especially in certain types of work."

Susan remembered her friend on the paper—a colored girl who was a graduate of Northwestern University. It had been hard for her too, even though opportunities were increasing. She and Susan had enjoyed several talks on the subject. But Willimina did not know her yet, and friendship could never be forced.

"At least you've been able to get in some schooling, haven't you?" Susan asked.

The look of spirit was there again in Willi's eyes. "A little. I wanted more, but it was necessary to help at home. Otherwise I wouldn't be—" She broke off, but the inference was clear. With the schooling she had wanted she would not have had to work as a domestic.

She took the bowl of cornflowers from the center of the table and placed it between candlesticks on the sideboard, then removed the tablecloth and folded it up.

"Is there anything else you would like me to do this evening, Mrs. Hohenfield?" she asked.

Susan shook her head. "I don't think so. Do you have very far to travel to get home?"

A flicker of surprise crossed Willi's face. "Miss Bellman said I was to have a room here. In fact, I've already moved my things into it."

Susan laughed. "I'm sorry, I didn't know. Perhaps you'd better tell me about the arrangements. Do the cook and yard boy stay here too?"

"No, they both go home to their families. Our house is a little crowded just now, so I was glad to have a room here. That is, if it is all right with you, Mrs. Hohenfield."

"I'll be glad to have you in the house," Susan admitted. "I've been thinking that it seems a bit empty when my husband is out. Where is your room, Willi?"

"I'll show you," the girl said.

She led the way through the kitchen, where the cook was giving things a last wipe-up, and went out through the back door. The night air was cold after the sun-warmed day, and Susan shivered as she hurried across the yard behind her. The girl stopped before a door that appeared to lead back into the house and pushed it open. It gave directly upon a small square room, meagerly but neatly furnished with bare essentials.

"I haven't had time to fix it up yet," Willi said. "I've brought some of my own things, but they aren't unpacked."

There was no door from the room into the house. The closest approach would be across the yard and through the back door.

"I should think this would be difficult in bad weather," Susan said. "Why didn't they have a door open directly into the house?"

"This is the way it is done here, Mrs. Hohenfield," Willi said, and looked away.

Susan understood. For years white people in South Africa had been living in a state of acknowledged jitters. And with some reason. All Africa was pushing at a door which was being held shut by a comparatively few white men in power—the descendants of the Boer settlers—the Afrikaners of the Nationalist party. It was these men who were calling the tune and making the laws. One of these laws, Susan remembered reading, was to the effect that servants were not to sleep inside the house of a white employer at night. It was necessary, everyone said, to take no chances. In Johannesburg many people slept with a gun on the bedside table. After the last demonstrations in Cape Town, Dirk said, there had been a run on the stores that sold firearms.

Not wanting to intrude on Willi further, Susan told her good night and hurried back through the kitchen, where the cook was getting ready to leave. When Susan spoke to her the little woman darted a quick, birdlike glance her way, as if she were vastly curious about this stranger from America, and not entirely comfortable with her as a "missus."

When she had gone, Susan tried the door behind her and then laughed at herself. This sort of fearfulness could be contagious and it was a disease she did not want to catch. There was no reason why anyone should mean her harm. This was a lovely night with the stars bright and clear and she decided not to wander about inside the house in a lonely, tiresome fashion. Instead she would go outside and enjoy the evening.

She slipped into her coat, tied a scarf about her head, and let herself out the front door. Following a paved walk around to the side of the house beneath the bedroom windows, she found that a street light spread its radiance through the garden. Along one side ran a low stone wall and when she looked over she saw that the hill dropped away beneath, disappearing into the shadowy ravine, where pine trees clustered. Beyond she could see lights burning on the opposite hill, and was able to pick out her father's house.

She sat on the wall and watched the panorama of Cape Town lights spreading densely up from the shores of the bay, to thin out and lose themselves on the lower slopes of Table Mountain. Tonight the mountain rose in massive darkness against the star-flecked sky. Her eyes sought the Southern Cross and she was enchanted as a child to find it again. How far away America seemed, and how vast and troubling was this tip of the continent. All up and down Africa freedom was on the move. Yet here beneath this lovely, peaceful sky quiet was held only by force and by those who believed against history that they could turn back the tide that moved, not only in Africa, but across the world.

She thought of Willimina, remembering very well from her childhood the gentle, friendly, highly intelligent people who were known as the "Cape coloreds." These people were a greatly mixed race that might include Portuguese, Indian, English, Dutch, Hottentot, Malay, and a good many other strains. They had come to be set apart from the black population and had fared better in the Cape Peninsula than the "blanket native," so recently from the reservation.

Somewhere close at hand a voice began to sing plaintively, sadly, of a soldier from the old Transvaal and his longing for "Sari Marais." She knew the tune for a song of the Boer War that she had heard as a child. The melody deepened the sense of loneliness all about her, and when it ended the silence seemed intense.

She returned to the house, wanting now to wake it up with sounds of her own making so that she might shut away the haunting loneliness. She was not truly alone. Dirk would soon be home and she must find ways to be busy and happy when he was absent.

There were so many things she must do, changes she wanted to make. All through the house there were touches of Mara Bellman that she felt impelled to erase and replace with her own. Now this was to be *her* house.

When Dirk came home he found her sitting on the floor in the bedroom, surveying her handiwork. The dressing table had been moved to a new place where the light was better, the beds pushed closer together, the throw rugs on the floor set in a new pattern. She sat with her hands clasped about her knees as she contemplated further changes, and he laughed aloud at the sight.

"I didn't expect you to be at this sort of thing so soon," he said. "Though I've been told all wives go in for rearranging the furniture periodically."

He did not mention his appointment and she was careful to ask no questions. Just having him home was enough.

Nevertheless, her sleep that night was dream-haunted. Once she wakened cold and trembling, with an impression in her mind so vivid that it stayed with her for a long while before she went to sleep again.

In the dream a door had opened and she was walking through it with a feeling of hope and confidence. The room she stepped into was alive with a great glitter and dazzle. For an instant the flashing blue light seemed more beautiful than anything she had ever beheld. Then the brilliant fire turned evil and somehow cold. And she knew what it was. A monstrous flashing of diamonds surrounded her. She was lost in a cavern of diamonds from which she could not escape. The door behind her had disappeared and there was no way out. She was enveloped in cold blue fire, drowning in it.

When she fought her way back to consciousness, the flashing still seemed so intense that she could see it all around her. She sat up in bed, fighting the memory of the dream, lest it return and engulf her in further terror. But the conviction of reality remained. The blue fire had been real—she had seen it with her own eyes.

"What is it, darling?" Dirk spoke from the next bed.

She slipped from the warmth of blankets and flung herself across the space and into his bed, to be held close and comforted.

"I dreamed about diamonds," she said. "Everything around me was burning in a dreadful blue fire. Just as though I had really seen a fire like that."

He held her close, stilling her trembling, his lips against her ear. "Perhaps you have. Isn't it possible—"

But she would not accept that. "No, Dirk, no! Hold me—don't let me think, don't let me remember!"

He held her, at first tenderly and then more warmly, but though

72

she went to sleep in his arms she could not free herself entirely of the subtle horror of the dream. Whenever she wakened it was there with only Dirk's arms between her and the fear that waited to possess her.

Not until morning did the nightmare begin to fade. Later she tried to explain it to herself. It had been caused by her mother's letter, of course, and Dirk's talk about the Kimberley Royal. These things had disturbed her and become a part of her dreaming. It was nothing more than that, she assured herself.

In the days that followed she was able to busy herself in a number of ways. Dirk took her downtown to visit her father's Cape Town store, where he had his office in the rear and kept an eye on things when he was not traveling to Johannesburg, or to some distant source of native art work in the far-flung reservations.

The shop enchanted her. There was no tourist clutter here. All was arranged with taste and an eye to subtly dramatic effect. Pieces of special worth were set apart against suitable backgrounds where they could be admired by the discerning. There was a corner for masks and fine wooden carvings, a current display of copperware from Northern Rhodesia, a glass case of delicate, carved ivory.

Dirk took her about, pointing out objects of interest—the painstaking beadwork, colorful blankets and woven mats—from the Transkei, Basutoland, Swaziland, Zululand. His knowledge was enormous, yet he displayed it in an offhand manner as if it were something that came naturally and which he did not particularly value.

"I can see where my father could hardly do without you," Susan told him proudly.

But Dirk disclaimed his own importance. "Hardly a day passes that Uncle Niklaas doesn't come down here," he assured her. "There's not much we handle that doesn't receive his attention before it goes on display. It's amazing the way he keeps a running plan of the store in his mind and knows just where everything is. Not a thing is changed unless he approves."

Susan could not share Dirk's feeling toward her father. Obviously there was much to admire about him, but remembering why he had brought her here, she had no desire to recapture old affection. She enjoyed the shop, but she did not look upon it as merely an expression of her father.

At the Aerie she went to work turning the house into a home for Dirk. He was willing to give her a free hand and she enjoyed being able to make her own plans. Her shopping list grew long and she began to learn about the stores of Cape Town.

Dirk had the rest of his own things brought up to the house and he and Susan had the fun of unpacking them together. One trunk still contained articles that had belonged to his father and mother, and this trunk he would not unpack. Susan had begun to sense that there were matters in his childhood that had left wounds he was reluctant to reopen. That his German father had been interned and that his mother had grieved herself into illness after his death—these things she knew. But he would not elaborate. There was a deep hurt in him that could be easily aroused and she learned not to tread upon quicksand.

One thing he sought for, however, in this family trunk, after he had it brought up to the bedroom. Though he would not unpack it, he reached along the sides and beneath the layers of clothing until he found what he had looked for. When he drew it out, Susan was startled.

The thing he held in his hands seemed to be a rounded, flexible black stick. It was over three feet long and perhaps an inch thick at one end, tapering to a point.

"It's a *sjambok*," he explained. "This one is made of rhino hide, cut wet, and then salted for preservation, rolled, and dried. It's the sort of whip the Boers used to drive oxen. Or it could be used for flogging, when necessary. In fact, the police still use *sjamboks* today. This one belonged to my father. See—he cut his initials into the thickened part that makes the handle."

He held the whip out to her, but she did not touch it. There was an ugly look about it that repelled her.

Dirk raised the *sjambok* and lashed it whistling through the air. Behind her Susan heard a soft sound of dismay. She turned to see Willi, her hands laden with fresh towels, standing in the doorway. Her eyes were upon the whip in something like horror.

Laughing at her expression, Dirk gave it another whack through the air, while Willi stood frozen, watching him.

"Don't do that again," Susan pleaded. "You've frightened Willi and you've frightened me. I don't like whips."

Dirk smiled at the colored girl. "This was just a practice session. I haven't had it in my hands since I was a boy."

74

Willi did not return his smile. Her gaze dropped and she went mutely away with her towels.

"You really did frighten her," Susan said. "It's a brutal-looking thing."

"She probably thought I was going to beat you with it," Dirk smiled.

"But why do you want it? Why did you get it out?"

He pulled the tough leather of the whip through his hands as if he enjoyed the feel of it. "Mainly because I thought it would make an interesting wall decoration. The voortrekkers used whips like this. They're part of our history."

She had no wish to oppose him, but she was not particularly happy when he fixed brackets on the living room wall and set the whip upon them. The pattern it made was far from decorative in Susan's eyes, and it lent a violent and disturbing note to their quiet living room.

7

SINCE DIRK PREFERRED to avoid any social fanfare over their marriage and Niklaas van Pelt shunned publicity, no announcements were given to the papers. The news was allowed to spread gradually among Dirk's friends.

Susan was happy enough to postpone the day when she would have to take up the social role that might be expected of her as Dirk's wife. A life of leisure, of belonging to a club, of going in for tennis and watching cricket matches, was not entirely to her taste. In her own mind she was still a working girl with a desire to earn a reputation by means of her pictures. Toward this attitude Dirk remained tolerant and encouraging, but she knew he did not take it seriously.

So far she had made no really constructive steps in the direction of furthering her work. Though she had a darkroom set up now, she had done no more than snap odd pictures like any sightseer. She must, she knew, determine upon some plan that would make her pictures marketable. Magazines were more interested in picture stories than in isolated shots. So she must work out such a story to photograph. There should be a good many possibilities in Cape Town.

One morning, ten days or so after her arrival, she awakened with a strong urge to get away from the house and wander on foot, tracking down a real story. She would set out, she decided, in the direction of the Public Gardens, which she still remembered affectionately from her childhood.

Learning her way about Cape Town had been an easy matter. The downtown streets crossed one another in the straight lines of a checkerboard, with Adderley Street running down to the bay as the main business thoroughfare, crossed near its foot by the Strand. Susan had already gone downtown on shopping trips and was learning to get about by bus and trolley.

But this morning she wanted to walk. When she set out soon after breakfast there was a brisk wind blowing and she was glad of the loose coat flung about her. Over one shoulder she carried by their straps both her camera and the big leather handbag in which she could put her light meter and extra rolls of film.

More than once she stopped for shots—of a sidewalk fruit stand, of a two-wheeled pony-drawn vegetable cart heaped high with bright orange carrots and green cabbages, of a house with the beautiful iron lacework that reminded her of New Orleans. She paused to watch boys on the way to school, dressed in the short pants and identical caps of the English schoolboy, and she caught a picture of them indulging in a bit of horseplay. Colored children were on their way to school as well, moving along with an air of independence, as though adult burdens had not yet descended upon them, and they too wore neat uniforms. It was notable, however, that the two groups of children ignored each other as if they did not exist.

The streets looked tranquil in the morning sunlight and, if this was South Africa, the screaming headlines seemed far away. Yet beneath the surface she knew the cancer of apartheid was at work. All was not as it seemed from this quiet viewpoint. The hint of a picture story began to stir in her mind and she walked on, watching all she saw with a renewed interest.

She came at length to the upper end of what everyone in Cape Town called "the Avenue." Government Avenue had its history in Cape Town's beginnings, when the first vegetable garden had been planted by Jan van Riebeeck on the site of the present gardens.

The wide path of reddish earth was closed to vehicles and all day long pedestrians used it as a pleasant thoroughfare that led directly into Adderley Street. On either side oak trees had been planted and the day would come when their branches would arch overhead, but now they were still young trees, unable to rival the giants over in the Public Gardens at her left. This morning scores of gentle ringnecked doves were out and their bubbling coo was everywhere. If any sound was truly typical of Cape Town in spring and summer, it was the ubiquitous cu-cu-cooing of the doves as they walked and fluttered about the gardens and avenue.

When she came abreast of the noisy aviary, Susan left the walk to wander among flower beds aglow with everything from the conventional blossoms of England and America to South Africa's brilliant and exotic blooms. Paths wound beneath great trees that had been brought here from distant parts of the world. A belombraboom with huge uncovered roots caught her eye, and a clump of papyrus. Everywhere doves and pigeons paraded watchfully, their bright eyes ready for tossed peanuts. Squirrels came tamely down from their trees to feed from the hands of small children, out early with their English nannies. All this Susan had loved as a child and she took pictures purposefully of the quiet, peaceful scene.

Farther on, past a fountain where a boy clasped a dolphin in his arms, she came upon a statue of John Cecil Rhodes. His upraised arm pointed across the bay and there were words on a plaque in the stone: YOUR HINTERLAND IS THERE.

This she found puzzling. The bay opened to the ocean and there was no hinterland for South Africa off there to the west. She had walked around the statue twice, considering the matter, when she became aware of a man observing her. She saw him out of the corner of her eye, and when he continued to watch her, she threw him a quick look. It was John Cornish.

Her first instinct was to walk quickly away. This man had caused her enough trouble and it would be wiser not to speak to him at all. But he came toward her and she was caught.

"Good morning, Mrs. Hohenfield," he said.

She answered his greeting and turned to walk on, but he did not appear to see her movement away from him.

"I hope I didn't cause you any difficulty the other day," he went on. "I'm afraid your husband was displeased at finding me there."

This was something she had no intention of discussing, yet in spite of the disapproval she knew she might expect from Dirk she was still curious about this man. A few moments of casual talk could do no great harm. She glanced up at Cecil Rhodes for help.

"Why is he pointing out to sea?" she asked. "There's no hinterland out there."

Cornish gave her the grave, slow smile that had so little warmth in it. "Like most *uitlanders*, you've turned yourself around. The newcomer forgets that Cape Town, and the mountain too, face north. The Atlantic is really off to your left beyond the Lion's Head. Across the bay to the north lies Africa."

She felt like telling him that she was no *uitlander*, but remembered in time that he had no knowledge of her identity. Her curiosity about this man's determined purpose still held her from walking away.

"Have you managed to see Niklaas van Pelt?" she asked frankly.

He shook his head. "Not yet. But I've not given up. The chance will come."

Having committed herself thus far, she plunged on. "But why is it so important to you? Why can't you write about him out of the material that must already be available? And out of your own past knowledge of him?"

"Perhaps the past is the very thing I want to know more about firsthand," he said.

It came to her that here lay an opportunity to find out the things her father had forbidden Dirk to tell her and that she felt an increasing desire to know.

"Will you tell me what happened?" she asked. "These are things Dirk doesn't want to discuss. Understandably, since he works for Mr. van Pelt. But I would truly like to know."

He studied her from beneath craggy brows as if measuring her in some way. She sensed in him a deep intensity held well in check. He gestured toward a nearby bench where sunlight speckled through leaves overhead.

"Will you sit down for a moment? I'd like to tell you. Perhaps if you know the story you won't think me quite such a blackguard as your husband believes."

She seated herself in a place of sunny warmth at one end of the bench. Doves cooed hopefully at her feet and a squirrel chattered his indignation when he found she had nothing for him. In the serenity of these gardens the rocky face of the mountain was hidden and she realized that sometimes its ever-present mass could be a little oppressive.

John Cornish clasped long, rather bony hands, interlacing the fingers loosely and staring off into the distance of Rhodes's hinterland. Susan waited for him to begin.

"Everything goes back to diamonds," he said at last. "Diamonds

79

and their effect upon men. Niklaas van Pelt went to prison because he was convicted of stealing diamonds."

This seemed to be in contradiction to what Dirk had told her and she frowned. "Do you mean the big diamond that disappeared? The one they call the Kimberley Royal?"

"The bad luck stone?" he said. "No, not the Kimberley. That's another story, though I have my own idea of what may have happened to that particular stone. The cache found in the van Pelt house in Johannesburg was of much smaller diamonds—though still gem stones."

"Found in the van Pelt house?" Susan repeated, not quite believing.

"That's right. I'd been invalided out of the war." He patted his right leg, outstretched before him. "And I was working for a Johannesburg paper. I was given an assignment to do a piece about diamond smuggling. Always a popular subject in South Africa. I took it seriously and I was keen on doing a good job. In the course of my nosing about I came hot on a trail that I followed long enough to turn over to the authorities. The details are unimportant, but the search ended with Niklaas van Pelt."

A muscle had tightened in the rugged line of his jaw and she sensed how merciless this man might be as an enemy. In dismayed silence she waited for him to continue.

"My own father had died a few years before. Perhaps you don't know that Niklaas van Pelt was my father's close friend. My mother was American and she wanted to get home as soon as the war was over. I went with her when the time came, and stayed on in the States. But at this time I was fairly close to Mr. van Pelt. His son Paul had been my good friend and I was still broken up over his death in action. So you can see that I would not have unlocked this Pandora's box intentionally, knowing the van Pelts would be involved. Before I realized what might happen I'd cracked it wide open and the matter was out of my hands."

"Did they actually prove that Mr. van Pelt had taken the stones?" Susan asked, increasingly disturbed by what she was hearing.

"That wasn't necessary," Cornish said. "When he knew the jig was up he confessed the whole thing. He had been on the receiving end, though he would not name any accomplices. So the other, or others, got away free. He was given a three-year sentence and I found myself covering the story for my paper."

"But doesn't Niklaas van Pelt know this was something you couldn't help?" she asked. "Why should he still be angry with you and refuse to see you after all this time?"

"I suppose I could have quit my job. But I chose not to. I can't blame him for being resentful."

"Yet you don't believe he also took the Kimberley diamond? Why not?"

"While I don't believe he took it, I think it was a jolly good thing the big stone's disappearance was kept quiet at the time and the friend who had trusted him with it kept the whole thing under cover. His trust seems to have been justified because when Niklaas van Pelt got out of prison he made himself a poor man by paying back every cent of the market value of that stone. He had to build up a new life for himself on borrowed money."

Susan listened in increasing bewilderment. "But how could the same man who paid off the debt of that big stone have been guilty of stealing the other diamonds? The two things don't fit together."

"That," said John Cornish, "is exactly what has haunted me for all these years. That's the thing that has brought me to the writing of this book, brought me back to South Africa. But I can't clear it up unless old Niklaas himself is now willing to tell the story."

She was beginning to understand, and something of the animosity she had felt toward John Cornish was fading. Surely Dirk did not know all these things. He was protecting her father mistakenly.

"It must have taken a great deal of courage for Mr. van Pelt to begin all over again," she said. "He must have lost the trust of a great many people."

"But not all," Cornish told her. "There's a curious thing about this matter of diamonds in South Africa. You have to remember that the country isn't very old. No older, really, than Manhattan, which the Dutch were settling at the same time they moved into the Cape. Even that three hundred years belongs more to Cape Town than to Johannesburg and Kimberley. Jo'burg was a sprawling mining town just seventy years ago, and Kimberley is only a few years older. In those early days there was a lot of smuggling going on and people got a bit casual about it. Even now there are some who regard it as a minor crime, not quite so reprehensible as stealing a man's ox. I suspect the color of romance hangs about the whole thing, a little like the romantic notions of America's lawless western days. The diamond people, naturally, take a dimmer view since too much leakage of diamonds out of the monopoly would send the world price down. Still, sentences are not so heavy as they once were, and a man may live them down. Niklaas van Pelt has done that to some extent. Though the stamp of disgrace is still there because of the high position he held, and never to be quite overlooked."

"But there's such a discrepancy between being honor-bound over the big stone, and holding a cache of smaller stones in his own home. Haven't you any idea of the answer?"

The man beside her leaned over and picked up a pebble from the path, tossing it lightly in his palm as if he weighed the decision of whether or not to speak his thoughts. Then he dropped the stone and turned to her.

"There was a woman in the case. A pretty, rather frivolous American woman."

Susan stiffened. She folded her hands about the leather straps of camera and handbag to keep them quiet. She must say nothing, do nothing to stop him at this point, though something uneasy and fearful was wakening in her.

"Go on," she said softly.

"This woman was a good deal younger than Niklaas—she was his second wife. I believe she was stranded here after some sort of concert tour failed, and she went to work for De Beers."

"De Beers!" Susan could not help the exclamation. Claire had said she'd worked for some time in South Africa but she had never mentioned that it was for De Beers.

"Yes; that's where Niklaas met her. He was still connected with the company at that point, but he retired a bit later to give all his time to government matters. He wanted to run for Parliament and he became active in the government after his marriage. The woman—her name was Claire—had found herself a wealthy and distinguished husband. From then on she proceeded to ruin him."

"What do you mean?" Susan asked more sharply than she meant to.

John Cornish gave her a slow, searching look. "Perhaps I'm saying too much? For all I know, your husband may have thought very highly of the American woman who married Niklaas."

"I want to hear it all," Susan insisted, holding tightly to the leather straps.

"There's not much more. I suspect that it was Claire who had managed to smuggle out that little cache of diamonds into her own possession. Perhaps there were even more that she had disposed of from time to time. She must have held onto the remainder after her marriage."

"If this is true, why wouldn't she admit it when Niklaas was arrested? Why wouldn't she tell the truth and save her husband from going to jail?"

"So that she might go to jail in his stead?" Cornish raised a dark eyebrow quizzically. "It appears that she wasn't that sort of woman. It would also seem that Niklaas was a gentleman and would not betray her."

Susan let go of camera and handbag and faced him angrily. "I don't believe a word of what you're saying! It's all the wildest speculation! I should think it would be a horrible thing to release such a story after all these years and disgrace someone who can't speak for herself."

Cornish remained relaxed in the face of her indignation, though it must have puzzled him a little. "Oh, I intend to let her speak for herself. When I get as much of the story as possible out of Niklaas, I'll go back to the States and find her. I believe she's still living in Chicago. Of course she would be safe enough from prosecution by this time, even if she is guilty."

Susan had stood all she could. "At least she's safe from such a visit!" she cried. "You can't hurt her now—she's out of your reach."

He merely stared at her, and she rushed on, her words tumbling out almost incoherently.

"You might as well know the truth! Claire van Pelt was my mother. She died only a little while ago. And I won't let you touch her memory with your miserable, made-up suspicions!"

She was so angry she was close to tears and it was all she could manage to blink them back. John Cornish regarded her in dismay for a moment. Then the guard he had lowered a little seemed to slip coldly into place again.

83

"I'm sorry if I've shocked you by telling you things you didn't know. But you asked for this. After all, it was hardly fair to hide your identity at the same time that you were questioning me."

She had no interest in what he regarded as fair. "I can see now why neither my father nor Dirk wanted me to know about all this. They didn't want me to be hurt by such lies. It was better for me not to know."

He answered her without emotion. "If your mother was innocent, then that would be enough to protect her. She needn't have run away. In any event, it's better for you to know the truth. This isn't something you could hide from, or be protected from, forever. Not here in Cape Town."

She thrust back her anger as best she could. It was necessary to convince him that he was wrong—wickedly wrong.

"My mother was never a thief. She liked to be happy, and perhaps she was a little bit spoiled because everyone loved her and gave her what she wanted. Besides—what could she have done with illegal diamonds in her possession? How could she have disposed of them?"

"Sometime you might ask your husband to tell you about I.D.B.," Cornish said.

She knew there was no way of convincing him. Not now. And she could bear no more. Abruptly she stood up, scattering a flock of doves, but before she could turn away, he rose and caught her elbow firmly but lightly in his clasp.

"Wait," he said and there was a note of command in his voice that halted her in spite of her longing to get away. "You were right about one thing. I don't know the truth of this matter yet. I am only speculating. But neither can you be sure of the truth. It may be a painful choice either way. But less painful to the dead than to the living."

She saw his face through swimming tears, stern and merciless. "I don't care about the living!" she cried, and hated the way her voice choked. "My father means nothing to me. But I still love my mother. I was closer to her than anyone else was, and I know what she was like."

"Nevertheless," he said relentlessly, "the truth is something to be respected for itself, without regard to one's own emotional involvement or whether one believes this thing or that. If I'm wrong, why not prove me wrong?"

She drew her elbow from his grasp as if she found his touch repugnant. "What do you mean?"

"I think you know very well what I mean," he said, and his eyes held hers, though now he did not touch her.

This was a man who would never give up. She understood that clearly now and she began to feel a little frightened.

"What do you want me to do?" she demanded. "What do you expect of me?"

A smile touched his mouth and there was unexpected kindness in it. "I will leave that to you. Good morning, Mrs. Hohenfield." He touched the brim of his hat and walked away through the gardens.

She watched him go, noting the slight limp with which he moved, the erect carriage of his shoulders. And she detested him with all her heart. His very walking away so abruptly was an affront. It should have been Susan Hohenfield who had walked away and left him, spurning his ridiculous story. Still shaken, she turned in the opposite direction and began to walk toward home.

8

Not even the long brisk climb back to the Aerie assuaged her anger. She continued to feel keyed up and distraught, yet impatient with her own unreliable emotions.

Cornish, she reminded herself, was merely a journalist after a good story. His suspicions were not to be considered. He had not known Claire as she had. He could not realize how incapable of harm her mother had been.

In an attempt to quiet her thoughts, she went into the darkroom as soon as she reached home and shut herself in to develop the strip of pictures she had taken. Working in the quiet little room by the faint light of one red bulb had a calming effect upon her nerves. Here she could be busy with her hands, give her attention to the handling of her materials, and hold all thought in abeyance. It was a treatment she had used more than once in Chicago when things had gone badly at the paper.

By the time the film had been attached to a clip and hung up to dry she felt a little better, and was even able to eat the lunch that Willi served her. In the afternoon she returned to the darkroom to print the pictures from her strip of film, trying to keep herself interested in the mechanical work before her. But now as her hands busied themselves she began to think of her father as she had seen him at the time of their interview. An old man who had never allowed himself to be swayed by emotion. An intelligent and thoughtful man, perhaps, but a cold one, who had lost all touch with the warmth and excitement of living.

Why had Claire run away? The question she was holding off flashed through her mind. Why had she not stayed to support her husband in his time of trouble?

Claire's story had always been that Niklaas had done some wicked thing for which he deserved imprisonment. She could never forgive him, she said, or ever again trust him. She had given all her efforts to getting her daughter away from South Africa so that she should not suffer for her father's sins. These, surely, were not the actions of a woman who was to blame for her husband's imprisonment.

Nevertheless, whether Susan liked it or not, John Cornish had set squarely in front of her a problem she must eventually face. The darkroom had given her a respite, only a postponement. When she finished with her prints, the problem was still there where he had placed it. Regardless of how Dirk might feel about this last encounter with Cornish, she would have to tell him about it, set the whole story before him, and ask his advice. She could not endure this turmoil and doubting alone.

Having come to a decision, she grew eager to talk to Dirk, and the afternoon passed slowly. She did not broach the subject immediately at dinner, however, but held to other topics through the meal. Dirk had spent the day in the store, where some difficulty had arisen, and he was tired and faintly absent-minded.

Not until they were in the living room after dinner, with a cheery coal fire in the grate, did she tell him of her meeting with John Cornish that morning. At her first words his attention was arrested but, though she saw his mouth tighten, she went on, straight through to the end, trying to make it as fair a story as possible, giving Cornish credit for the purpose he claimed—an attempt to learn the truth. But her voice broke a little when she came to the part about her mother.

Dirk's manner softened. "I'm sorry," he said. "You shouldn't have been told so cruelly. There were always rumors, of course. But I think you needn't worry about them. At least this should bring home to you the reasons why I've wanted nothing to do with Cornish. There's no reason for Uncle Niklaas to be tried twice. Cornish is a man bent on stirring up old troubles. Perhaps more trouble than you dream is possible."

"Trouble for whom?" she asked.

"Let me worry about that. Just let these sleeping dogs lie."

Puzzled though she was by his words, her thoughts turned back to Claire.

"You don't believe my mother was a thief, do you?" she asked directly.

Dirk came to sit beside her and took her left hand into his own, turning it so that light struck the pink diamond.

"Listen to me, Susan. Listen for once with your mind instead of your emotions. Perhaps the best thing for everyone concerned would be for you to recall whatever you can about the Kimberley Royal. If that mystery could be cleared up, it would help your father. It might even help to dispel any lingering suspicions against your mother. And, in part, it would answer John Cornish."

This persistent notion that she had something to remember was too much. Impatiently she pulled her hand from his grasp with a jerk that sent it backward against a heavy bronze bookend on the table beside her. The unintentional knock bruised her knuckles and the pink stone clinked against the bronze.

Dirk caught her hand and turned it so that he could examine the ring. "Take care," he warned, and ran his thumb over the diamond. "I'd hate to see you injure my lucky stone."

Her impatience, her bafflement increased. "Considering that diamonds are supposed to be the hardest of all stones, I'm not likely to hurt it with a tap like that," she said crossly.

He laughed at her indignation and let her hand go. "Don't be too sure. Diamonds are brittle stones. That's the way they shape them, you know—by tapping them along the lines of cleavage. Sometimes good stones are ruined in the process, though it's true it has to be a pretty sharp blow. Anyway, do remember that I've given my luck into your hands—so be careful with it."

There was an amused note in his voice as if he laughed at himself, but Susan's attention was still upon the issue that had irritated her.

"It's silly to expect me to remember something when there really isn't anything for me to remember."

"How can you be sure? What about the dream you had the other night?" he reminded her. "Have you ever thought there might be a reason behind it?"

"I know the reason," Susan told him. "There was talk about diamonds that day. It haunted me. So it was only natural that diamonds should get into my dreams."

"But why did you see a *blue* fire? Why was the flashing in your dream always a blue light?"

88

She stared at him. "What do you mean?"

"Has anyone ever described the Kimberley to you? It was a blue-white stone with a trick of flashing an intense blue light."

No, she thought, startled, no one had told her that, and his words frightened her a little.

"There's no accounting for dreams," she said quickly and turned from the subject. "Tell me what John Cornish meant when he said to ask about I.D.B.?"

"Anyone in the Union could tell you that," Dirk said. "The letters stand for Illicit Diamond Buying, the plague of the country. In other words, smuggling diamonds and selling them illicitly."

"But he surely couldn't have meant that my mother might have engaged in smuggling," Susan said.

Dirk's patience had clearly been exhausted. "Who knows what Cornish meant?" he said, and glanced at the watch on his wrist. "In any case, I've work to do at my desk tonight and I'd better be at it. You'll excuse me, darling?"

She sensed his disappointment in her and perhaps his exasperation. But at least he had not scolded her this time for speaking with John Cornish. He had been genuinely sorry that she had learned the truth of the situation in a sudden, shocking way. But still he had wanted more of her than she knew how to give.

When he had gone into the small room Mara had set up for him as an office, she sat staring at the whip that hung like a black exclamation mark against the wall. The *sjambok* stood for something more than voortrekker history, she felt sure, and she wished she could know exactly why Dirk had placed it there. In a way it was a symbol of the impenetrable side of his nature which she did not understand, yet longed to understand because it was a part of him and must be accepted.

The firelight no longer seemed cheery, and away from its immediate warmth the room was chill. She had no desire to sit here alone, so she went into the hall for her coat. Then she let herself quietly out the front door and walked about the quiet garden. The low sustaining wall again invited her, and she sat down on the stone.

An aching loneliness was once more upon her, and the familiar soreness of missing her mother that the talk about Claire had revived. Perhaps she was even a little homesick for the life she had led for the past few years in Chicago. Though there had been loneliness there too, and a sense of waiting for something important to happen that would give her days some depth of meaning. Until Dirk's coming she had felt shapeless and unformed. When he had put the pink diamond on her finger everything had begun to take shape, to make sense, and she had believed that she would never be lonely again.

Her own long sigh was the only sound in the evening hush that lay over Cape Town. The bubbling of the doves had quieted, the lowered murmur of traffic was distant. On the air was a scent that spoke of pines and the sea. Nearby a tall blue gum rustled its leaves and fell silent, as if it too had sighed. A bright full moon was rising, touching the great mass of the mountain, brightening the hillside below the wall. Leaning so she might look down, Susan could see that a narrow pathway wound through the grass, dropping away toward the black shadows of the ravine where the thick stand of pines stood guard. Just this side of the pines several tall objects shone with a dark gleam in the moonlight and she wondered what they were. If they were rocks, they were huge ones standing upright in monolithic fashion.

Outside the wall on which she sat the path ran uphill, appearing to end at the next street above. Sometime soon she must explore the downward plunge of the path and find out where it went.

The quiet of the night began to possess her, and to ease and still her unquiet spirit. The soreness and confusion were easing, leaving her relaxed, yet with her mind clear and free for once of stubborn resistance. Now she could begin to think quietly as she had not done before. Now she could face the question she had been thrusting so persistently from her mind.

Was it possible that some knowledge did lie hidden deep in her memory? A knowledge of something that had happened in her childhood and which she had long since forgotten? What if, instead of trying to resist Dirk's suggestion, which after all was a reasonable one, she tried to open her mind, tried to go backward through the years?

But *how* was she to do this? It would be necessary to retrace her steps, to recall incidents she had forgotten, to remember the days she had spent here in Cape Town. And this was not so easy. Happy memories came to mind readily but they were spotted here and there, without surrounding incident to give them continuity and complete a picture. All that was hurtful and unpleasant had been banished to some hiding place to which she had lost the key. That door would not open at will. Yet there must be a way to open it.

The cool, bracing night air seemed to shake away her cobwebby confusion and bring her to a state of clarity. She pulled her coat collar about her ears and swung her feet onto the wall, drawing her knees up so that she could rest her head against them and close her eyes.

Go back! she told herself intently. Try to remember what happened!

She could see the house again clearly—her father's house that she had visited a few days ago. But now for the first time since she had come here she could see it with a child's eyes, looking bigger than it really was, and with her father's study the focal point, the heart of the entire house. That was the room she had most liked—and most dreaded. It was connected in her mind with punishment and with lectures from her father, but such matters had not made her seriously unhappy for long. There was something more that brought the room into focus. Yet even as she struggled to remember a sense of dread began to possess her. It was subtly chilling and fearful, so that her impulse was to slam the door upon it and bring herself quickly back to the present. She managed to resist the impulse and let her memories come as they would in a bewildering rush.

There were angry voices now, clattering through her mind. A flashing glimpse of her mother weeping hysterically, of her father's face stern and cold as death. In the midst of all this crouched a child who sensed that something dreadful was happening, something no one would explain to her, something she could not understand. The adult Susan shrank as the child had done and the door closed swiftly upon all that was fearful, shutting it away from present consciousness.

She did not give up at once. Though she was shivering from more than the evening wind, she attempted once more to force the picture to come clear. But the voices had faded and all that was frightening had vanished. Instead, she could remember the sound of waves against a ship's side and long walks with Claire around and around a deck. Her mother's voice came to her clearly: "Forget what happened, dearest. We're going away from South Africa and we're never coming back. We're going to the place where I grew up and you'll never have to be frightened again."

She could hear her own voice questioning. "Will Father be there too?" And her mother's answer: "No, dear. We must forget about everything connected with South Africa. We must—" But then her mother had burst into tears and would say no more. Soon the small Susan had found that Claire would cry whenever Niklaas was mentioned, so she learned not to bring up his name.

Even as they began to return, the pictures began to slip from her grasp. The power to go back faded like a mist as she reached out to hold it.

Somewhere on the hillside the voice she had heard before was singing in Afrikaans. She knew the words: "My heart is so sore, my heart is so sore . . ."

Swinging herself down from the wall, she turned back toward the house. She had met with defeat for the moment, but she had moved in the right direction. What better way was there both to please Dirk and prove to him that she had nothing important to remember than to recall all the details of that distant time?

The mournful words of the song followed her upstairs and possessed her spirit with their sense of time slipping too quickly away.

9

In THE DAYS that followed, Susan was unable to push remembrance any further or to solve the problem she had accepted that evening in the garden. Most of the time the door remained firmly shut and when she tried to think herself back into her father's house she could remember it only through adult eyes as she saw it now.

There were, too, new distractions in her life. Susan van Pelt's marriage to Dirk Hohenfield ceased to concern only themselves. The word had spread along the Cape Peninsula's grapevine and reporters from the *Cape Argus* and the *Cape Times* came up to the Aerie to interview her. The old story of Niklaas van Pelt was revived and reviewed and much was made of the fact that his daughter had returned to South Africa married to his ward. The stories were not unsympathetic, but Dirk said Niklaas was upset by them and had refused to see reporters. He had stated through Mara that his personal concerns were of no interest or concern to anyone in South Africa these days. He wished only to be left alone.

Once the word got about, a certain degree of social life reached out to include Dirk and Susan. People were socially minded here, though there was the clannishness too of old-established families. The Cape Peninsula boasted a genuine and gentle culture that was still unknown to that young and lusty upstart, Johannesburg.

One Sunday afternoon they drove with another couple in Dirk's car to the Kirstenbosch Gardens to see the breathtaking display of spring flowers that grew on the other side of Devil's Peak. On the way back they went through the grounds of Cape Town University, spread out handsomely below the jagged brow of the peak.

All this Susan enjoyed, yet she sensed that she and Dirk were somehow not a true part of Cape Town social life. They might be drawn to its perimeter, but they would never be deeply involved in its central activity. Perhaps because they did not wholly fit the pattern. Both, in their different ways, were outsiders—even Dirk. And there might be another reason. In spite of Cornish's claim that Niklaas van Pelt had pretty much lived down the blight of his disgrace, she wondered if the old scandal did not still linger in people's minds and reflect upon his ward and daughter.

Her own work with her camera offered a respite from uneasy thoughts, and her interest was growing as she developed the story picture she wanted to do. Sometimes it was necessary to take dozens of shots in order to get a few that would convey the impact of a story and so far the pictures she had taken were distinctly one-sided.

Her intention was to choose from many a few pictures that would show the peaceful everyday life of Cape Town, the easily visible surface life. Against these she would contrast a few penetrating shots of what lay beneath. But since the world of the dark people was not easily opened to her, this was hard to accomplish.

She had wanted to visit Langa, the native location where there had been so much trouble, but Dirk would not consider taking her there. Indeed, he warned her that under present circumstances she was liable to get herself arrested if she attempted to take pictures in certain localities.

Though blocked for the moment, she did not give up the idea. There would be a way. In the meantime she contented herself with shots of the SLEGS VIR BLANKES signs that managed to convey the indignity they represented. Segregation in Cape Town took odd turns, she discovered. Benches in the parks were for anyone. In the libraries men and women of different races sat elbow to elbow. Yet the greater liberality of the English community was not permitted to extend to theaters or sports stadia. Bus lines run by the Union government were segregated. Those municipally owned by Cape Town were open to all. She also found that the colored citizen sometimes set himself above the black African and could be as prejudiced as anyone else.

It was Willi who told Susan about District Six. A half mile or so from the center of the business section, on a hill below Devil's Peak, was an area where many respectable colored people lived. But crowding in upon them, almost engulfing them, were the dregs of the colored group. The crime incident was high, young teen-age toughs known as skollies preyed upon the more respectable and fought with each other. The smoking and selling of dagga —a form of marijuana—was flagrant. Poverty and depravity were the lot of many. District Six belonged mainly to the coloreds and only a few black Africans lived or worked there as watchmen or caretakers in the schools.

This district, Susan decided, would be a place where she might get below the peaceful surface of white Cape Town. She had a strong suspicion that Dirk, if he knew, would forbid her to go there, so she kept her plans to herself. She had no reason to be afraid. After all, she had taken a good many pictures in Chicago's slums and tougher sections, and she had only sympathy for the underprivileged.

She chose a sunny early morning that would be good for picture taking, and before she left the house she told Willi where she was going. The girl looked both astonished and dismayed. Crimes were committed in District Six almost every day, Willi warned her with that flash of spirit that sometimes contradicted her usual gentleness of manner. Mr. Hohenfield would not approve of her going into that section alone.

"I won't tell him until after I have my pictures," Susan said cheerfully. "Don't worry. I'm not very reckless and I won't stay too long."

She set off dressed much as she had been that day when Dirk had found her taking pictures of the train accident in Chicago, in a beret, an engulfing trench coat, and low-heeled shoes.

A short distance from her goal she left the bus and set out on foot to penetrate the neighborhood she wanted to see. In many ways it was like the slums of Chicago's South Side, probably like those of any city. There was a teeming humanity on every hand, living in homes that had once been the elegant residences of prosperous white people, long since moved away. Now the houses were crumbling to ruin, undoubtedly rat-infested, vermin-ridden. Probably there were white slum landlords here, as elsewhere, who fattened on the misery of those who lacked the power to ensure better living conditions. Children swarmed on the stoops, in the streets, tumbling over the sidewalks, some screaming and shouting like children anywhere, others sitting in vacant-eyed apathy. For the most part their elders paid her little attention. She was aware of sidelong looks from a few, of resentful glances from others, but most of those she passed took the safest course by pretending she did not exist.

She was getting her pictures now, yet this sort of degradation existed in slums everywhere; it was not uniquely South African. It had probably existed before apartheid had come into being. Indeed, moving people out of such slums might give the government some justification for building new locations.

Then, as she was crossing an alleyway that opened off what seemed to be one of the main streets of the area, she saw something that made her stop to watch. An Afrikaner policeman was standing before a sort of shed. Its doors and windows had long since vanished and it stood open to the alley. A colored woman with a sleeping child in her arms sat on a tipped-up box, talking to a man who was clearly a black African. As Susan watched, the officer stepped up to the man, speaking curtly in Afrikaans, demanding what he was doing, why he was not at work.

Susan had recovered enough of the language she had known as a child so that she grasped most of the interchange. The policeman, not satisfied with the answer he was given, asked for the African's pass. The colored people, so far, were not required to carry passes, but without a pass none of the native population could move anywhere in South Africa, and passes must be presented on demand at any time. Not to have one was to invite arrest.

As she watched, Susan did not forget her camera. Unobtrusively, behind the policeman's back, she caught the picture. The African was gesturing toward a jacket, hung on a nail a few feet away. His pass was there, he said. But the officer would not give him a chance to get it. He had broken the law in not having it on his person, and that was that. Before Susan's eyes the unreasonable arrest was made, and her camera clicked through the entire incident, with pauses only for hurried film winding. What she had witnessed shocked her, and she was all the more eager to make a record that the outside world might see.

On the heels of her final picture, the policeman turned, prodding his captive ahead of him, and came toward her. There was no time for escape on her part. His first surprised reaction was due perhaps to her white skin. Then he saw the camera in her hands.

"Why are you in this place?" he asked in Afrikaans. "What are you doing with the camera?"

"I've been taking pictures around Cape Town," she told him in English. "There's no reason why I should not, is there?" Her attempted calm was a bluff. It was hard not to show her anger over what had happened, hard not to rush foolishly to the aid of the African, whose position she would only worsen.

The officer held his prisoner by one arm, ignoring the man's further effort to explain that his pass was in the jacket hanging not six feet away. He gave his attention coldly to Susan.

"You are English?" he asked, changing to that language.

Susan's position was not one she could quickly explain and he gave her no time. He looked as if he intended to arrest her too, and she had no idea what would have happened next if there had not been an interruption.

Behind her a car door slammed and feet came running. In a moment Mara Bellman was at her side, smiling at the policeman, speaking to him rapidly in fluent Afrikaans. She was saying in effect that the young lady from America did not know any better, that she was of course sorry if she had offended. She herself had been looking for the lady, fearing she might be lost. The officer would understand, of course.

What of the pictures the American had taken? The officer asked stolidly, not at all overwhelmed by Mara's charm.

The girl turned quickly to Susan. "Did you take any pictures? If you did, remove the film and give it to him."

Susan hesitated, not at all pleased by this rescue, even if it had saved her from temporary trouble. She was still indignant with the policeman. Indeed, with Mara here to help her out, she ought to speak her mind.

"You should have seen what just happened—" she began, but Mara stopped her at once.

"Give him the film or I won't answer for the consequences. These are not ordinary times in South Africa."

They were both against her and there was nothing else to do. She opened the camera and took the film out without rolling it up, making sure that light reached her last few shots. At least there would be no evidence against her.

The policeman took the film and Mara thanked him graciously, giving Susan a little push toward Niklaas's car. She clearly meant to stand on no ceremony, and indignant though she was, Susan went. Mara started the Mercedes and drove down the street. She said nothing until they were out of District Six, and Susan sat beside her equally silent. She was furious at the policeman, furious over the loss of her pictures and with Mara for her highhanded rescue.

"It's fortunate that Willi phoned me after you set out this morning," Mara said when they had driven a few blocks. "I had some trouble finding you, or I might have stopped you more quickly."

"I didn't want to be stopped," Susan said. "If you hadn't rushed in, I might have been able to deal with the officer myself and saved my pictures in the bargain."

"You don't know our police," Mara told her dryly. "If it hadn't been for me, you might be in real trouble by now. They aren't fooling, you know, and they don't like such pictures being sent outside. I suppose that's what you intended?"

Susan had no wish to tell Mara what she intended. All her first instinctive distrust of the blond girl had swept to the fore.

"I'm a news photographer," she said a bit curtly. "I've been in difficult spots before and I've managed to get out of them. It was kind of you to interest yourself, but I'm quite capable of—"

"I didn't do it for you!" Mara broke in. "I did it for Dirk. I couldn't stand by and see you involve him in unpleasant publicity."

It was perfectly true that Dirk would not like what she had done, but Mara had no business assuming that publicity would necessarily have resulted if she had been allowed to handle the matter in her own way.

The car had been headed toward the Aerie, but suddenly Mara turned into a quiet side street of small white houses, drew the car to the curb, and switched off the engine.

"We might as well have this out," she said.

Susan, still lost in her own indignant thoughts, could only stare at her blankly. The other girl's cool poise had deserted her and she was breathing quickly, as if some long-simmering rage had suddenly boiled up in her and was out of restraint.

"You can't go on being fooled forever!" she said in a low, tense voice. "If it hadn't been for you, Dirk and I would be married by now."

Susan was as much appalled by the look in Mara's eyes as by her words. She said nothing at all.

Mara pushed back her heavy mass of blond hair as if the movement rid her of pent-up energy.

"I'm neither mad nor a fool," she went on. "I'm in love with Dirk and in the end I mean to have him back. So you might as well be warned."

Susan's amazement was growing. Somehow she could not take this outburst seriously. Mara was suffering from some dreadful delusion.

The blond girl had quieted a little, as if her first wild expending of emotion was over and she was groping her way back to her normal, guarded poise. Her tone was calmer when she spoke again, but there was still venom in the words.

"Don't you know why he married you?"

"Of course I do," Susan said promptly.

Mara went on as if she had not spoken. "It was because of the diamond. Because he wanted that fortune in his hands and if you could lead him to it, then you were worth whatever temporary sacrifices he might have to make."

"That's ridiculous," Susan said. "I suppose you're referring to the letter my mother wrote before she died. In the first place, that letter was a trick to gain me consideration from my father. Nothing else. In the second place, you surely can't believe that a man like Dirk would go so far as to marry simply because there might be a remote chance that his wife knew something about a diamond that disappeared years ago. The whole idea is silly."

Mara did not answer. She started the car and put it in gear.

"What do you think Dirk is going to say when I tell him about this?" Susan asked curiously. "Won't he be angry with *you* then?"

"You won't tell him," Mara said, and turned the car from the curb. "You won't take that risk. Because then everything would be out in the open and you wouldn't be able to pretend any more. Though if you do tell him it won't matter to me."

She sounded so angrily confident that Susan felt shaken for the first time in her own strong conviction. The evil of doubt had crept subtly into her mind and now questions were there that had not existed before. She thought about them in silence as Mara drove her home. She remembered again Dirk's strangeness before their plane had landed in Cape Town, his stiffness at the airport, and the way she could not get through his guard that first day in the Aerie. That day when he had again been in touch with Mara Bellman. Yet later he had enveloped his wife with a love that she could not doubt and the uncertainties of their arrival had faded.

When the car drew up before the front gate, Susan quickly opened the door. She did not want to speak to Mara again, but the other woman reached across and caught her by the arm just as she would have stepped out.

"I pulled you out of trouble this time," she said. "And if you like we'll say nothing to Dirk about what you were up to. I jolly well don't want to talk to him about it. But next time I hope your troubles are a lot more serious. And if they are, I won't rescue you." Her eyes had narrowed and all the beauty was gone from her face. "In fact, I'd take great pleasure in helping them along."

Susan went into the house feeling a little sick. It was rather dreadful to see another woman rip away the guise of civilization and reveal what lay beneath. Could she be like that too? she wondered—and did not know the answer.

Willi met her in the hall, her manner one of quiet dignity, and Susan offered no reproach. Willi had acted upon the prompting of her own conscience and was not to be blamed for feeling that she must telephone Mara. Susan went upstairs and tried a little desperately to regain her composure before she had to face Dirk again. The cold look of the police officer's eyes, the limp jacket hanging on its hook, the helpless plight of the man arrested, mingled in her mind with the things Mara had said. The painful doubts she had planted began to take root.

Yet when Dirk came home that evening his mood was cheerful and her concealment successful. All went smoothly between them and a little of her fear subsided. No matter what had happened in the past, she told herself firmly, Dirk loved her now. Mara was simply a jealous woman who wanted to strike out and hurt the person who had hurt her. Seen in that light, she was more to be pitied than feared.

Yet it was necessary, Susan found, to tell herself this over and over.

10

THE EXPERIENCE IN District Six stopped Susan's picture taking for a time. If she could not catch the ugly side of Cape Town life as well as the pleasant, then there was no point in her trying the story she had in mind.

Her first sickness and shock over Mara's words faded and she made an effort to bolster her own confidence. She could not bring herself to broach the matter with Dirk, however, and evidently Mara had kept her word and said nothing herself.

As the days passed, she thought increasingly of the obligation John Cornish had placed upon her. More than ever she wanted to answer him, and to reassure Dirk. Once full remembrance had returned, there would be no more nonsense about a lost diamond. No more suspicions of Claire, and no more possibility that Mara's attack might have any truth in it. John Cornish would be stopped in his purpose and her marriage with Dirk would continue serenely with no threat of quicksand to betray her. It was a happy prospect and she decided to further it without more delay.

She had not seen her father since her first visit to his house. No further summons had come from him. Nor had Dirk asked her to see him. But the conviction began to grow in her that the only way into the past was to seek him out again. Seek him out and ask that she be allowed to see the house she'd lived in as a child.

The morning she returned to Protea Hill was also the morning when she decided to explore the path that led downhill into the ravine. She told Willi she would be out for a while. Then she put on walking shoes and a sweater and went into the garden. The drop from wall to path was not great and she swung herself over the stone parapet and down into the grass on the far side. In bright sunlight the scent of pines was warm and spicy, and she took deep drafts of Cape Town's sparkling spring air.

The path dipped sharply beneath her feet as she followed it, and she saw that the upright objects she had glimpsed by moonlight the other night were indeed several rocks that stood upright like great monolithic shafts. They formed an irregular half circle away from the path and she looked behind them cautiously, a little fearful of snakes. There was something almost awesome about these rocks. Had some primeval force toppled them end over end to stand them at last in this position through all the ages since? The mountain above would remember that upheaval, she thought, gazing up at it. What she saw at the mountaintop brought her to a halt, watching in wonder as the phenomenon peculiar to Table Mountain happened before her eyes.

In an otherwise clear sky a fluffy cloud floated high above the mountain. Even as she looked, the mountain exerted its attraction and the cloud dropped swiftly to its top. There it spread out in a layer of white over the entire table, drifting a little way down the sides so that it looked as if a tablecloth had been spread evenly over the flat top of the mountain. Above, the sky was still brightly blue.

Susan had seen this happen as a child, but she had forgotten until now what an astonishing sight it could be. Up there on the mountain, where all had been clear a moment before, the rocky top was now hidden by thick cloud.

Happy to have seen the mountain's performance, she followed the path down into the shadowy coolness of the grove where flat-topped pines clustered and then out into the open beyond. Here an amazing variety of tiny wildflowers spread over the fields. She stooped to pick a small flower with six widespread white petals, edged with black, its navy-blue heart touched with black and yellow stamens.

The path continued its downhill plunge to a place where a side path branched upward toward the houses on this opposite side of the ravine. Susan looked up to see her father's house a stone's throw away. The side path seemed to wind its way between houses to the street, with no wall to climb at this point. She followed it quickly and found herself outside the stone and iron fence of Protea Hill.

The yard boy saw her and came to open the gate. She went purposefully up the steps and stood before the familiar door with its long glass panels on either side. A maid answered her ring and invited her in just as Mara Bellman came down the stairs. Though she had prepared herself for this inevitable meeting, Susan winced inwardly at the sight of the other girl.

Today Mara wore a green suit that set off her fair skin and pale-blond hair and there was an aura of sophisticated perfume about her. Her eyes rested coolly upon Susan and she greeted her politely enough, without any of the letting down of her guard that she had displayed at their last meeting.

"If you're looking for Dirk," she said casually, "he's not here this morning."

"I'd like to see my father, if it's possible," Susan said.

"He has gone out in the car with Thomas," Mara told her. "I don't know when he'll be back."

She made no attempt to invite her in, and Susan knew that she would have to take matters into her own hands.

"I believe I'll wait for a little while in case Father should come home soon."

Mara hesitated, but Susan was Niklaas's daughter and she could hardly turn her away.

"Come in, if you like," she said grudgingly. "Though I can't promise that you won't have a long wait."

All she wanted was to get into the house, Susan thought. To be left alone with it. It didn't matter whether she saw her father or not. To reacquaint herself with one room would be a start. She could not very well ask Mara to show her through the entire house without her father's permission.

Mara led the way into a big, comfortable living room that had been changed considerably since Susan had last seen it. The furniture was set well back from the center of the room, arranged close to the walls. It was a room that had been made safe for a blind man, with no unexpected stumbling blocks.

Apparently Niklaas van Pelt had brought furniture here from his house in Johannesburg, for Susan recognized some of the pieces. She remembered particularly a great cabinet of stinkwood—that beautiful, ill-named wood of South Africa, odorous only in its freshly cut state. The grain had dark-colored markings that made a handsome, wavelike pattern, and the drawers were set with Cape silver key plates and handles. Over the fireplace hung a long copper warming pan, clearly Dutch in character. These old things suited the room and somehow suited Niklaas van Pelt.

"There are magazines on the table." Mara was curt. "If you want anything, just ring the bell near the door."

"Thank you," Susan said and sat down on a long couch, wanting only to be left here alone.

But Mara stood in the doorway, reluctant to go. "Have you thought over what we talked about the other day?" she asked.

Her audacity was surprising. Susan hesitated for a moment, once more taken aback. Then she spoke quietly:

"What was there to think about? Whatever may have happened in the past has no bearing on the present. I haven't been brooding about it."

Open dislike was alive in Mara's eyes. "You're wise not to put the matter to a test. As long as you don't lead Dirk to the diamond, you're safe enough. For a time at least."

Susan said nothing, refusing to be drawn into an open quarrel. Mara shrugged and went out of the room.

Now all hope of regaining contact with the house was gone. The necessary mood had been destroyed and Susan knew it would not return. When the maid came in with the inevitable eleven o'clock morning tea, Susan drank a cupful, trying to still the quivering resentment that Mara had aroused in her. Did the woman mean to bait her every time they met? The prospect was unthinkable, but for the moment she knew of no way to stop her. She was not yet ready to turn to Dirk about the matter. Was it fear of the truth that held her back? she wondered. Surely what had happened before she married Dirk need not concern her now. If she told Dirk, he would reassure her, but he would also think her foolish. There was no need to speak.

The sound of a car in the driveway indicated that her father had come home. Mara did not appear again, but the maid came to tell her that Mr. van Pelt awaited her in his study.

Again her father sat behind the great desk upon which every object had been placed with meticulous care so that there might be a minimum of groping for what he wanted. The heavy, polished cane with the silver head leaned against his red-leather chair, ready when he wanted it. As he took Susan's hand and drew her into the chair beside him, she felt again the cool, dry clasp of his fingers. She did not wait for him to ask the reason for her visit, but plunged at once into what she had to say. At her first mention of John Cornish's name, she sensed a stiffening in him. But his dark glasses gave nothing away and his face was expressionless as he listened.

She told him of her meeting with Cornish in the Public Gardens and of the story he had unwittingly told her, before he knew she was Claire van Pelt's daughter. She went on to speak frankly of Cornish's suspicions concerning Claire, and her father heard her through without interruption.

"So you see," she ended a little breathlessly, "I want to remember. I want to find my way back. Perhaps you can help me."

He was still for a long moment and there was a tightness about his mouth. "I will not help you," he said at length. "Remembering is pointless. I know all that happened, and the only thing that is important to me now is to forget. I am sorry, indeed, that John Cornish has returned to Cape Town."

"But what if there really is something to that letter from my mother?" she persisted. "What if it's true that I may have known something as a child that I could bring back to mind if I really worked at it?"

"You mean concerning the diamond?" he asked. "Forget about that. I don't want to know what happened to it. The man who owned it is dead. And he was paid in full long before he died. The stone has caused nothing but misery in its history."

If he spoke the truth, then he had not been impressed by her mother's ruse, after all. He had not sent for her because of the diamond. In this realization might lie an assuaging of pain, but something else was more important now. She had no time to think of her own hurt.

"Do you think my mother took it?" she demanded. "Because that's what John Cornish believes and it's what he means to write about in his book."

"He will not do that," Niklaas said. "I will not permit it."

Remorselessly Susan went on. "He thinks she took the small diamonds too. He thinks she stole them when she worked for De Beers. He means to bring all this into the open in his book whether he has a chance to talk to you or not."

"Then I shall talk to him first." Her father's blue-veined hand slapped the desk before him and for an instant she saw him as she remembered him from her childhood—a physically powerful, forceful man, of whom many were afraid. Including, sometimes, herself and her mother.

Without intending to, she had favored Cornish's cause. She had changed her father's mind about seeing him. And perhaps this was for the best. There was no one in a better position than Niklaas van Pelt himself to stop Cornish and prevent these fabrications about her mother from being published.

"When will you see him?" Susan asked.

His fingers uncurled and rested limp upon the desk. The moment of force had drained from him. "There is no hurry. This will take some thinking about. I do not rush into things."

"But his book—" Susan began.

"This book will not be written overnight. There is time."

She knew there was no time. If John Cornish was to be stopped, then it must be done at once. The further he carried his plans the more determined he might be to complete them. And Niklaas was not the man he had once been.

"I think you ought to see him very soon," she urged.

He smiled at her unexpectedly. It was not a warm smile, but one that seemed coldly amused. It did not reassure her.

"You will have to leave this matter to me, my dear. But enough of Cornish for now. I wonder if you would care to come with me for a drive this afternoon? The day is comfortably warm and I'd like to get out into the sun. There's a spot in Cape Town that I often visit—the Rhodes Memorial. From it I can promise you an unsurpassed view of Cape Town. If you agree, I will pick you up this afternoon."

The sudden invitation surprised her. Perhaps he was merely offering her a distraction as adults sometimes did with a child. At any rate, she would go. Whatever small advantage she might have with him she meant to press.

"Thank you, Father. I'll be ready whenever you say," she told him and rose to leave.

The crack of the twelve-o'clock gun from Signal Hill reached her just as she started home. A plan was stirring in her mind and, even though she knew Dirk would not approve, she felt impelled

to follow her instinct. After all, it was because she wanted to answer Dirk and set his doubts at rest that she must do this very thing.

The moment she reached the Aerie she went to the phone and called John Cornish.

11

THE VAN PELT car, with Thomas at the wheel, followed the curving drive around the base of Devil's Peak. Here the table was no longer visible and there were only great crags like the back of a dragon, with steep rock sides, encroached upon to some degree by determined stands of pine. In the clear thin sunshine of spring the Hottentots Holland Mountains were visible, their sharply notched peaks showing beyond False Bay.

Susan remembered the story of their naming from her childhood. The Dutch settlers had known that the Hottentots looked upon their mountains with the same homesick longing with which the Dutch remembered Holland, so the name of Hottentots Holland had been given to the mountains. "Hottentot" itself meant "stammerer," and was what the Dutch had called the Bushmen because of their odd language.

There were tall blue gum trees along the drive, and carpeting the woodsy areas of the hillside were hundreds of arum lilies, growing wild. Once, when the trees opened and she could look upward, Susan caught a glimpse of white columns set splendidly apart on the crest of a small hill, with the dark peaks rising behind.

Thomas turned his head. "There is the monument now, madam," he said.

Her heart quickened, not because of the beauty but because of her own uneasiness over what she had done—the result of which must now be faced.

Niklaas van Pelt sat back in the seat beside Susan, his thin hands clasped upon the silver head of his cane. There was an air of alertness about him this afternoon as though all his senses ex-

cept that of sight were sentient and open to every impression that touched them.

This is my father, she thought—and felt nothing. Perhaps it was too late for any feeling between them, even though he claimed it was not her mother's words about the diamond that had caused him to send for her.

"Rhodes is not buried here, you know," Niklaas said. "He chose his own burial place in Southern Rhodesia—a wild mountainous spot near Bulawayo. Not a place where many go. I visited it once as a young man."

The car turned onto a side road that climbed upward, and now the monument was hidden until the road turned again and came upon it in profile. Susan could see the tall white columns at the top, the broad flight of stone steps mounting toward them between a guard of eight bronze lions. At the foot of the steps a bronze figure rode a prancing horse high on a pedestal of its own. On either side were green lawns and terraces and the parasol-topped pines. Close above, as always, were the craggy peaks.

Thomas parked the car and came around to open the door. Gently he helped Niklaas out and the old man stood leaning upon his cane until Susan stepped out to join him.

"Go along on your errand, Thomas," Niklaas said. "My daughter will give me her arm. And you'll find us here when you return."

The colored man touched his cap and went back to the car. Slowly father and daughter walked toward the parapet before the monument. Niklaas's left hand rested lightly on Susan's arm, the other used the cane as he moved easily and without hesitation.

"I'm troubled about Thomas," he said as they reached the cobbled expanse before a low semicircle of wall.

Susan was only half listening. Uneasily she glanced up and down the steps, searched the shadows of the colonnade above with a swift glance. John Cornish was nowhere in sight and she could not help feeling a certain relief. Perhaps he would not come after all. He had not been certain that this was the right approach.

Her father was still talking about Thomas when she began to listen again.

"He should be a teacher by now. It's in him to do splendid work along that line. But this chauffeuring and acting as a blind man's eyes is achieving little for him. His bitterness is our own doing, I'm afraid."

"He seems to be in the same position that Willimina is in—the girl who works for us as a maid," Susan said.

"Willimina Kock?" her father repeated, sounding surprised.

"Yes. Miss Bellman brought her to work for us on our second day here."

"That's strange," Niklaas said. "Mara never mentioned the fact to me. Willi is more or less engaged to Thomas, you know. Though marriage hasn't seemed possible for them. Mainly, I gather, because of a certain obstinacy on Willi's part. Or so Thomas says. Another reason for his state of resentment."

Susan recalled the flashes of spirit she had seen in Willimina. Gentle though she was, it was possible that she could be obstinate if she chose. Then, too, there was at times about the girl an evasiveness that Susan had been forced to recognize. Certainly she had not revealed the fact that she knew Thomas. But, then, there had been no reason for her to do so.

Her father drew his hand from Susan's arm and moved with certainty across the cobblestones until his cane touched the low parapet. In this open space the wind blew strongly upon them, and the great panorama of Cape Town and its suburbs lay fanned out below around the curve of the bay. Wind sighed in the pines, and somewhere there was the dripping sound of water. Niklaas turned toward the wind and it was as if he saw all that lay before him, as if he savored the grandeur of the view.

At length he moved away from the wall. "Let's climb to the top," he said. "I want you to meet Mr. Rhodes."

They climbed the flight of granite steps, past the figure of "Energy" on the prancing horse, and started up the several levels toward the colonnade at the top. On either side the reclining lions guarded the way. Two small boys had climbed upon the back of one beast and sat astride, their young voices breaking the silence of the secluded place. At the top of the wide steps, enclosed by roofed columns, was the heart of the memorial: a bust of the man who had so loved and served South Africa, and himself as well. The man who had dreamed an empire into being. Rhodes's head rested upon his hand and there was a distant brooding in his face.

Softly Niklaas van Pelt began to recite, as if he read the words engraved below:

THE IMMENSE AND
BROODING
SPIRIT STILL
SHALL QUICKEN
AND CONTROL
LIVING HE WAS THE
LAND AND DEAD
HIS SOUL SHALL BE
HER SOUL

With a vividness that startled Susan, the words came ringing back to her over the years. All this was remembered, familiar. She had heard these words before. That other time she had stood here as a small girl, with her hand in her father's. She had felt only love and trust and confidence in him that day. His eyes had been able to see the engraved words and his voice had been the voice of a younger man. Yet still the words rang as he spoke them and there was a love for this precious and beautiful land in his very forming of the words.

"You knew him, didn't you?" she asked softly.

"Only to see him from a distance. I was a very young man at the time of his death, and I had been fighting on the other side with the Boers. I knew Paul Kruger better—I had at least spoken to him. Both men were giants. Who is to say which was the greater of the two. This one loved the land almost too possessively."

"You are no longer in sympathy with the Boers—the Afrikaners—are you?"

"They are my people." The ringing note had faded from his voice. "Far more so than the Englishman is, when it comes to blood, though I married an English woman."

He paused, listening. He had caught the sound of footsteps on the cobbles below and he turned to her inquiringly.

"Someone is coming?"

"Yes," Susan said, "someone is coming."

John Cornish stood on the lower steps looking up at them. Susan made no move, caught up in her own sudden dread. Slowly he started up the great blocks of granite that made the steps. The two small boys climbed from their lion and ran downward past him, hurrying off to new explorations.

She must warn her father. She must tell him that it was John Cornish coming up the steps toward him. But before she could manage her voice, Cornish himself spoke. His words were in Afrikaans and Susan recognized the "Oom Niklaas" by which he addressed her father. The old man beside her tensed and she saw his hand tighten on his cane. He stood where he was without moving, the mask of his face betraying nothing, though he spoke to her in a low voice.

"You should have warned me," he murmured.

It was clear that he had not been deceived into thinking this a chance meeting.

He waited as the other man climbed the steps below him, and he did not hold out his hand in greeting.

"You were the friend of my son," he said in English. "You were the one he trusted."

For the first time Susan noted a difference in John Cornish, a gentleness of manner she had not seen before.

"Paul was my friend and I loved him," Cornish said. "I loved his father as well. I would like you to know how it was. May I tell you?"

Niklaas made a gesture of indifference and used his cane to guide himself along the level of a step until he reached the side of the monument. There he sat down on the high step above and waited, while Cornish came to stand just below him. Susan withdrew a little, gazing out across the wide vista of Cape Town.

Cornish told his story simply. He explained how he had been caught in spite of himself in a trap from which there was no escape. He had not, he said, ever believed in Niklaas's confession. It was his conviction that Niklaas van Pelt had been protecting someone. Now it was time for the truth to be known. There was no one left who could be hurt.

"There is the girl," Niklaas said.

For the first time Susan broke in upon their talk. "I'm not important in this. The truth is important. I want to see my mother's name cleared."

Her father nodded gravely. "There is no hurry. These are things I must think about. A book takes time to write—we cannot hasten this."

"I mean to hasten it," Cornish said. "Since you would not answer my letters or agree to see me, I've been pushing the writing ahead."

The old man broke in abruptly. "What letters, John? I have received no letters."

There was sudden anger in the younger man's eyes, but it was not directed at Niklaas. "I wrote you several. They were sent to you at Protea Hill. I have written you at least three times."

This was Dirk's doing, Susan thought unhappily. Dirk's orders to Mara, undoubtedly. But he had gone too far this time in protecting Niklaas. No matter how Dirk felt about John Cornish, it was for her father to decide whether or not to see him—not Dirk.

"Had I received your letters, I would have paid you the courtesy of an answer," Niklaas said. "I shall look into the matter. But tell me now why there is such need for haste."

"I want to leave South Africa as soon as I can," John said. "I've no wish to stay here and see my country destroy itself by this insane course it's taking. If you won't help me, then I must go ahead on my own."

"You sound like a man filled with bitterness," Niklaas said. "Yet you have known many Afrikaners in your lifetime. You know their worth."

John Cornish turned toward the colonnade above with a quick angry gesture. "This is one monument built by South Africa. But there is another. One that stands near Pretoria in the Transvaal—the Voortrekker Monument."

"I know it," Niklaas said.

Cornish went on, a ragged note in his voice as he described the great stone building crowning a hilltop in the rolling Pretoria country. So vivid and compelling were his words that Susan could almost see the vast structure standing foursquare and sturdy as the men who had built it. The huge square tower was surrounded by a circular outer wall of concrete set in the form of a *laager* of wagons guarding it as the voortrekkers had guarded themselves from attack behind real wagons. Inside on the walls of the ground floor were stone bas-reliefs, John said. All around the great circular room they ran, depicting the history of South Africa, showing graphically the sufferings of the settlers, the massacres, the battles, the triumphs.

"A great history," Niklaas said gravely. "A brave history."

Cornish went on relentlessly. "From a railing in the center of the floor you look down through a wide opening to a quiet, empty room below. Empty except for the marble tomb enshrined there engraved with the words 'ONS VIR JOU, SUIDE AFRIKA'—'We for you, South Africa.' Down there too in that quiet room there's a niche in the wall where an everlasting lamp burns—a torch that signifies the light of civilization that was carried forth by the voortrekker movement."

Again Niklaas nodded. "A worthy memorial to history."

"These were brave men, and if it were only that I wouldn't quarrel with it," Cornish said. "But the monument has been used to turn a knife in the wounds of memory. It says in effect, 'These cruelties were done to your fathers—never forget them. The black man is your enemy—never forgive him. The Englishman is your enemy—hate him.' These are the meanings being urged on descendants of the voortrekkers today. The lamp has been buried in that pile of concrete. For South Africa the light is going out."

Niklaas van Pelt sat with his hands clasped upon the head of his cane, his sightless eyes behind their glasses fixed as if on some inner vision and he made the younger man no answer.

With an exclamation of impatience, Cornish walked along the level of one step and back again. Then he bent toward Niklaas as if he wanted to reach past the guard of those dark glasses and make him see the truth.

"All Africa is on the move. Do you think a handful of white men can stop the tide?"

"This country belongs to white men," Niklaas said calmly. "White men settled it and built it into what it is now. It is our only homeland."

"I suppose that's true enough. Nevertheless, the only way the white man can continue to live here is to accept the fact that we're all, black and white alike, natives of South Africa. Not Afrikaner or English. Not white. Not colored, or Malay, or Indian, or black—but South Africans together. Don't you see that you no longer have any choice? It is this or chaos."

"You are almost an American now," Niklaas said. "You live in a glass house. How can you point a finger at others?"

Forgetting herself, Susan broke in. "Why shouldn't we point our fingers wherever we see prejudice? Lots of us point quickly enough at what exists in our own country—in the North as well as in the South. Racial discrimination ought to be condemned anywhere it exists, no matter by whom!"

Cornish smiled gravely. "I agree. America may move slowly, but at least it moves ahead. The national law is on the side of the angels. Here the movement is only backward."

Susan drew closer on the stone steps, absorbed by the argument. Her father seemed to be baiting the other man almost coldly as if he tried deliberately to anger him.

"There's the matter of education," Niklaas pointed out. "You can't expect the black man from the reservation to stand beside the educated white man or understand the white man's world."

"Whose fault is that?" Cornish demanded. "Lack of education is always the excuse given by those who've not made enough effort to educate. Time catches up with them. The education must come *now*. Don't think I'm unaware of the complexities of the situation, but I can't help remembering something I heard Rebecca West say not so long ago: that it would be to the glory and honor of South Africa for its people to work together and solve the problem, however difficult. But I see no evidence around me that South Africans mean to rise to the challenge."

"While it may be our own fault and the fault of a good deal of historic hostility," Niklaas said, "we nevertheless have a tiger by the tail. How do you propose that we let it go without being devoured?"

Cornish did not answer, but stood looking up at the bust of Rhodes above them.

Niklaas turned his blind face toward the other man and there was unexpected sadness in his voice. "You speak of a challenge, yet you, who are a young man, will run away from it."

John looked startled. "I've no wish to see the night close in when there's nothing I can do that will hold it off. I'm getting out. I came here to right a personal wrong that I helped to perpetrate years ago. So, whether you like it or not, I will get on with my book. There will be a chapter about Niklaas van Pelt. I know the story well enough. Those early days of yours in the diamond mines. The later days when you worked for your country in Parliament. The courage with which you met disgrace and took the blame for someone else's guilt. There are a good many friends of Niklaas van Pelt to be found in South Africa today. They'll give me the story. I'll write it and go away."

"You are a determined young man and a foolish one," Niklaas said. "What you plan is ridiculous, of course, and completely wrong." He sat for a little while in silence, lost in thought.

"There's nothing more to be said." Cornish looked about for Susan and his eyes thanked her without betraying her with words. His silence made no difference, she knew. Her father was clearly aware of how this meeting had come about. She would have to face him on this score when Cornish had gone.

"Wait a moment, John," Niklaas said. "Since you are both determined and stubborn, it will be necessary to change your mind. Will you come to stay in my house for a time? There are empty rooms—we can make you comfortable. Then you and I can speak at length of all these matters and cover them at our leisure. When you understand fully, you will change your course about this book."

For an instant John Cornish seemed astonished. Then he accepted with eager alacrity. "Thank you, Oom Niklaas. It would be good to visit with you again, even if there were no book to discuss. You won't change my mind, but I accept the invitation gratefully."

"Good," Niklaas said. "Pack up your things and come over at once. We'll expect you tonight for dinner. There's Thomas now—I know his step. May we give you a lift back to your hotel?"

Thomas had appeared and stood waiting at the foot of the monument.

"Thanks, no," Cornish said. "I've a cab coming to pick me up. But I'll be with you this evening, if you'll have me. *Tot siens*."

He gave Susan a smile that was less cool than usual and ran down the steps. At the bottom she saw him stop and speak to Thomas, as if he knew the colored man. A sudden recollection returned to her mind. On their first day in Cape Town someone had told Cornish where Dirk was making his home. Had it, she wondered, been Thomas? In which case, was he as wholly loyal to Niklaas van Pelt as her father believed?

"Mr. Cornish seems to know Thomas," she said in a low voice.

"Of course," her father said. "Thomas Scott's parents worked for my family on their farm. John knew him as a boy." The old man stood up and held out his hand to Susan. "Give me your arm, please. I'm not as sure on these steps as I used to be."

He leaned upon the arm she crooked for him and they went

down slowly. At the foot of the steps Thomas offered his own arm and they moved toward the grove of trees near which the car was parked. John's cab had apparently come and gone.

"Do you think you can convince John Cornish?" Susan asked, when she and her father were settled in the car.

Niklaas sighed as if the encounter had wearied him. "I shall try. There will surely be a way."

She was silent as the car turned toward home, expecting him to reproach her for precipitating this meeting, but he said nothing further, lost in his own thoughts.

She was not satisfied with his uncertainty. She had brought these two together for the purpose of preventing John Cornish from writing about her mother as he intended. But now it began to seem that it was Cornish who might convince her father. The thought was far from reassuring.

12

THE DAY HAD been a disturbing one and she waited uneasily for Dirk to come home to dinner. She knew she must tell him about the drive to the Rhodes Memorial and of the meeting there with John Cornish. She would have to confess her own part in what had happened and the probability of his displeasure, coming on the heels of Mara's hints and outrageous behavior, left her increasingly apprehensive. The calm counseling she had given herself during the past few days suddenly crumbled and left her without confidence or defense. Her mind could follow only one disturbing course.

Mara had been in love with Dirk. She had spoken of getting him back. She had said they would have married if Dirk had not left South Africa. If this was true, it would mean that Dirk had once been in love with Mara Bellman. And Mara would not be willing to allow whatever had been between them to remain in the past. Nor would she stop at anything to gain her ends. There was a promise of conflict in the days to come and Susan hated the thought. She wanted no game of combat with anyone, and least of all with Mara. More than anything else she longed for complete security in Dirk's love for her. All her life she had been waiting for him. If she lost him now there would be nothing left to hold to, to believe in. The thought was devastating and she knew that she could rid herself of it only in the reassurance of Dirk's arms, of Dirk's love. And so there was impatience in her for his coming that evening.

When the telephone rang, and Willi came to tell her that Dirk was on the line, she hurried to take the call, feeling that she could not bear it if he did not come home to dinner tonight. It was *now*

118

that she needed him. But he said merely that he would be delayed by a half hour or so and asked her to have Cookie hold the meal. She hung up the phone, both disappointed and relieved. At least the postponement would be a brief one.

After she had passed the word along to the kitchen she went outside. The sun was dipping behind the tawny head of the Lion and the softness of dusk lay over Cape Town. A walk before Dirk came home might quiet this feeling of urgency that would not allow her to sit down and wait.

Knowing the way now, she went easily over the wall and down the path. She would walk only as far as the pine grove and back. By that time Dirk would be at home and she could talk to him.

The sky was still partly light, with the night haze encroaching gradually from the east. Only the tall rocks and the pines in the ravine below were hidden in darkness. She walked briskly, meaning to turn back before she reached those black recesses. Not until she neared the half circle of monolithic rocks did she hear the sudden sound of voices from the direction of the grove beyond.

An uneasy awareness of the solitude of this spot came over her. There had been so much trouble of late in Cape Town that she had been warned not to go out alone in deserted places after dark. But it wasn't truly dark yet, and this was so close to home that she had given no thought to the matter of her safety. Now she paused to listen and heard the voices cease, heard the sound of footsteps coming toward her up the path.

Swiftly she stepped around the base of one tall stone, and let the shadows take her. It was wiser not to meet whoever was coming up the path. When he had gone she would leave her hiding place and hurry back to the house. Tensely now, she leaned forward against the base of the stone to blend herself into its shadow, and felt its rough cold texture beneath her hands, against her cheek. It was to be hoped that she would stir up no snakes' nest in this hidden place.

Footsteps went past her and she peered warily through a crevice of stone in time to see Dirk striding hurriedly uphill toward home. The fact in itself would not have surprised her. She knew there were times when he did not take the car and used the short cut of this path between the Aerie and Protea Hill. But tonight someone had been with him. She checked her first impulse to run after him, turning instead toward the grove. She had to know. She had to see for herself.

Careful to make no sound, she entered the darkness of the pines where the path turned and curved between the trees. Around the first turn Mara Bellman's light-green suit was visible, her figure silhouetted against the paler dusk beyond the trees. Her face was in her hands and she was weeping soundlessly.

Unheard, unseen, Susan stole away, running now as she hurried toward home. In spite of this meeting she had nearly been witness to, she felt more relieved than disturbed. For the moment she had no pity for Mara's tears. If the woman was crying, it was a good sign for Susan Hohenfield. One must be hurt for the other to be happy, and if it were Mara, then it would not be Susan. Her reasoning was primitive and direct.

Nevertheless, she did not want to meet Dirk before she was over the wall. She did not want him to know what she had seen. She slowed her steps a little, to give him time to go inside the house, meaning to steal into the garden before he knew of her absence.

But when the path turned upward to the wall, she saw that she was trapped. Dirk was in the garden, standing beside the wall, watching the path up which he had so recently come. Perhaps he was merely composing himself before he went into the house. In any event, he saw her before there was time for retreat and waited for her in silence as she came up to the low place in the stone. She felt a little frightened as she put her toe in a crevice and pulled herself up and over. He made no move to help her, but stood motionless and silent until she was beside him in the garden.

"You should know better than to go out alone after dark," he said. "There are always ruffians about ready for mischief."

Perhaps he was hoping that she had seen nothing, but such evasion she could not accept. Her own sense of caution had suddenly vanished.

"Mara had to go home alone in the dark," she said a little sharply.

Even as she spoke she knew the words were ill-chosen and impulsive. He stared at her for a long moment. Then he turned away without waiting for her further response. Following him slowly into the house, feeling shaken and sick, she heard him tell Willi that he would soon be ready for dinner.

The very thought of food was distasteful. She ran upstairs and into the bedroom. If she had not chosen her words so clumsily, he might have taken her into his arms and comforted her. Probably he would have made nothing of the meeting with Mara. He would have explained that whatever might have been between them was long in the past and that he loved only Susan. But she had antagonized him instead, and she could not blame him for turning away from her.

When Willi came to call her, she wanted no dinner. She had a headache, she said, and would lie down. Willi went softly away, and Susan slipped into a quilted robe and flung herself down on her bed. The tears came easily now and she did not try to stop them. The figure of Mara Bellman stood openly between herself and Dirk and she did not know how to fight a past that might imminently become the present.

She could see Mara now, not as a woman who had lost the man she loved, but as one who had never given him up. She could see her as Dirk must see her—beautiful and confident and poised. So many things that Susan was not. How important had Mara been to him? How important was she now? Over and over the same tormenting questions turned in her mind.

From the dining room downstairs she heard the sounds of a meal being served. In spite of herself, she followed them through each course to the end and then an aching hope began to rise in her. Perhaps he would come upstairs to her now that he had eaten. His anger would have abated. Surely he would recognize her hurt and come to comfort her.

But when the meal was done, she heard him go into the living room where they had their coffee after dinner. She heard Willi bring in the silver service and then return to the kitchen. Dirk was having his coffee alone, still remote, still angry.

She turned her cheek against the pillow and wept again, as miserably as a child. When someone tapped on the bedroom door, her heart gave a foolish, hopeful thump and she opened her eyes to see that it was only Willi. But the colored girl's appearance was something to draw her from her mood of self-pity and despair, and she recognized the need to brace herself and make an effort toward outward recovery at least.

Willi came in carrying a tray that she set down on the bedside table.

"I've brought you some good tomato *bredie*," she said. "Let me fix your pillow so that you can sit up and eat."

The savory South African stew gave off an appetizing steam and Susan considered the girl who had brought it to her, wanting now to keep her here as a distraction against her own misery.

"Stay and talk to me, Willi," she said.

"I'll stay if you wish, Mrs. Hohenfield," Willi agreed.

She plumped up Susan's pillow, set the tray upon her knees, then stood beside the bed, waiting.

"Do sit down," Susan said. "How can we talk if you stand up like that?"

A guarded look came into the girl's face and she made no move toward a chair. Susan took a spoonful of the *bredie* and found it delicious. An impatience with her own weakness was beginning to hearten her.

"Listen to me," she said, finding herself more impatient with South Africa than with Willi. "You're a woman and I'm a woman. Please sit down and talk to me."

Still a little wary, and with an instinctive distrust of someone who wore a white skin, Willi seated herself on the edge of a chair and waited.

"Why must you make a difference between us?" Susan asked.

"I am working for you in this house," Willi said gravely. "It isn't considered suitable—"

Susan broke in quickly. "I've never had anyone work for me before. I feel uncomfortable being a mistress. I've had no training at all in running a household."

Willi's dark lashes swept her cheeks and she said nothing.

Susan tried a new approach, tantalized by her inability to break down the girl's careful guard, her mistrust. "My father told me today that you're engaged to Thomas Scott." She ate another spoonful of stew, watching her the while. "Are you planning to be married before long?"

This time Willi answered with an air of quiet reserve. "I am not engaged to Thomas. I don't intend to marry him."

There was a spark of reproof in her words and Susan found herself flushing. "I'm sorry. I shouldn't have asked you. This is my day for being clumsy."

With an effort Willi attempted to overcome her own reserve. "I don't mind your asking. Marriage for people like Thomas and me isn't easy. We have to think of the future. What of our children? That frightens me. I don't want the responsibility of bringing children into the world we know today in South Africa."

Susan was silent, unable to offer any reassurance. She remembered John Cornish's words at the Rhodes Memorial that afternoon and of his own wish to get away from the ugly promise of violence in South Africa. But people like this girl could not leave the country even if they wanted to.

"There is another thing," Willi went on, as though something of Susan's sincerity had reached her and she had begun to relax a little. "Thomas has a university education. And he is lighter-skinned than I am. There are doors open to him that might be closed to me. Why should I handicap him with a dark-skinned wife? You don't know how hard it is to have a dark skin in South Africa."

She was beginning to know, Susan thought. She was beginning to feel this thing strongly within the safety of her own white skin. In the face of Willi's problem her own worries had receded a little. But at the sound of Dirk's voice speaking suddenly from the open doorway, everything swept back in a returning sea of misery.

"May I come in?" he asked.

Willi sprang to her feet and Dirk spoke to her curtly in Afrikaans, in reproof and dismissal.

"Thank you, Willi, for bringing me the stew," Susan said as the girl took the tray and went off.

"You mustn't encourage her like that," Dirk said. "You Americans spoil your servants. Part of the trouble we're having in South Africa these days grows out of just such people as Willi and Thomas. Too much education, too much ambition, and nothing to do with it. It's foolish to give it to them in the first place."

She did not want to oppose him in some new way, yet she could not live with herself if she let his words pass.

"You can't deny education to anyone who wants it," she said hotly. "Or the opportunity to use it either."

"No one wants to deny it to them." Dirk was clearly impatient. "Let them have it in their own schools and their own way. That's what apartheid is all about."

Aparthate, Susan thought. That was the way it was pronounced and it could hardly have been a more graphic word. It hurt her deeply to see this attitude in Dirk, yet she knew that it was something he had grown up with, just as certain Americans grew up taking racial prejudice for granted. Eventually they must talk about these things, but this was not the time.

He came to sit beside her on the bed. "Let's not quarrel about Willi. She's a good girl in her way. But I don't want to talk about her now."

Susan made no move toward him. She felt miserably torn between love and indignation and hurt. He put out a hand and pushed back the bright hair from her forehead. "I do believe it's beginning to grow a little," he said. "You're not snipping it off any more?"

She shook her head, sensing that he would come in his own way to the point if she gave him time.

"I wonder," he went on, "whether you can understand if I try to tell you something? Sometimes you're so capable and independent that you alarm me. And sometimes I wonder if I've married a child instead of a grown woman."

Still she waited, her heart thumping raggedly.

"You mustn't think I don't understand how you feel about Mara," he said. "I'd have preferred not to have you know. But since you've stumbled on something that you may build up out of its proper proportions, I think you must look at this realistically."

"Look at what?" Susan asked in a low voice.

"At the way it was before you came into the picture. Mara is an attractive girl. We were both unattached. Why shouldn't we console and amuse each other for the space of time that we were free? There was never any intention of marriage on my part. She knew I didn't consider myself the marrying kind. Perhaps she hoped to change that. I suppose women always do. Perhaps she isn't yet reconciled, though I didn't expect her to mind as much as she apparently has. I wrote her from the States as soon as I knew we were going to be married. But I haven't seen her alone more than once or twice since I've returned. When she asked me to meet her this evening I felt I owed her that—I couldn't refuse."

Susan leaned against her pillow and closed her eyes. The important thing was the fact that Dirk wanted to tell her all this, that he wanted everything in the open between them. She must accept the past realistically, as he wished. Nevertheless, there was a question she had to ask. She opened her eyes and looked at him.

124

"Why does Mara continue to work for my father? Will she leave now, do you suppose?"

"I doubt it," Dirk said frankly. "Uncle Niklaas would be hard put to train someone to his ways as thoroughly as Mara has been trained. She's necessary to him. Can't the three of us be adult enough to accept that?"

She was not sure she could ever accept such a situation and she was positive that Mara could not. But there was a softening toward her in Dirk's manner and that was all that mattered. She raised her head from the pillow and in a moment she was in his arms, her cheek in the comforting hollow of his shoulder. He held her to him, murmuring assurances of his love in her ear. This was what she had wanted and needed. Mara could not touch her here.

But long before she was ready to leave the safety of his arms, he took her by the shoulders and held her away so that he could look into her face.

"There's something else we must talk about, Susan. I've just learned that there was a meeting between Cornish and your father this afternoon. It's hard to believe it was an accident. Can you tell me how it came about?"

So he knew, and there was no help for it.

"I arranged it," she admitted. "I telephoned Mr. Cornish and let him know where Father would be this afternoon."

The moment of tenderness was past. Dirk let her go and rose, moving about the room as if to restrain himself. When he turned back to the bed, she watched him miserably.

"Cornish is actually moving into Protea Hill," Dirk said, "and what will come of it I don't know. He's a troublemaker, as I've warned you, and he can harm us all. Particularly your father. Now it will be harder than ever to save Uncle Niklaas from harm."

Here it was again—that threat of something hidden in their lives, and further evidence of a devotion to Niklaas that had grown from past gratitude into a near obsession.

"Father knows you kept the letters from him that John Cornish wrote," she said, trying to speak coolly herself. "Has he told you that?"

"Yes! And he wasn't pleased. Couldn't you see that I was acting out of concern for Uncle Niklaas? What am I to do about a wife who betrays me at every turn?"

The shock of his words was like ice water in her face. She put up her hands as if she might ward them off physically.

"I would never betray you!" she cried. "Never, never! That's not fair. You haven't tried to understand my feelings in this. How could I stand by and let John Cornish write lies about my mother? That must be stopped and Father is the only one who can stop it."

"Your father is an old man—he will stop nothing. But now you've offered him innocently into the lion's paws. How can you be sure that what Cornish might say about your mother is a lie? How do you know you haven't made everything worse by getting your father and John Cornish together in such headlong haste?"

"Claire was my mother," Susan protested. "I know how silly it is to think she might be guilty of what Cornish suggests."

"Is it silly?" Once more Dirk sat beside her on the bed. He took her hands into his own strong clasp. "I wonder how I can make you understand what your father has been through. Even what he's going through now, with your return to South Africa and the opening of old wounds. Even the publicity our marriage has been given in the papers lately has focused attention on him. Do you think he's a man to carry disgrace lightly? And what of our children, darling—growing up here? The grandchildren of an important and well-respected man who broke his country's laws and went to prison as a thief!"

She was silent, a little frightened by his vehemence. Somehow she had been divorcing her father and all that concerned him from her own life and Dirk's, as if the past could not touch them in any way. But it was true that she wanted children—Dirk's children. She had not considered this aspect of the future.

"I'm sorry," she said more humbly. "Perhaps I'm the one who hasn't tried to understand your viewpoint, or my father's. What do you want me to do to help?"

"Have you tried what I've suggested?" he asked. "Have you really tried to remember the things that happened to you just before you left South Africa?"

"I have tried," she told him in a low voice. "But nothing comes clear. I can remember a few things, and then everything disappears in a fog. Sometimes I think I'm afraid to remember."

"I've suspected that was true," Dirk said. "But if you understand the reasons behind what I'm asking of you—if you somehow force this thing through—"

126

"Through to what? I don't even know what it is that I'm trying to remember."

"Through to the Kimberley Royal," Dirk said.

There was a moment of silence in the room and Mara's words concerning her marriage swept sharply through Susan's mind. But that was the very thing Mara wanted. It was her purpose to rouse suspicion in Dirk's wife. And Susan would have none of that.

Dirk was speaking again and she listened. "Even your mother seemed to think you knew something," he reminded her, "that you might have witnessed something. If you don't remember, it will always look as though she took the diamond herself when she left South Africa. If she really did, then we ought to know because it may lead us to the truth about the other diamonds."

"It wasn't my mother," Susan whispered, the strength of her denial fading a little. "We never had much money and Mother worked hard all the time I was growing up. If we'd owned a fortune, don't you suppose things might have been different?"

"Perhaps she was afraid to sell it."

"If she had it, then I'd have found it in her possessions after she died. And surely she would have given me some warning about it."

"The warning she sent was to your father," Dirk said. "Now the rest is up to you."

Susan sat up on the bed and slid her feet to the floor. She had a feeling of being hopelessly cornered, so that whichever way she turned disaster faced her. But she no longer felt sick and sad. Dirk was right. The time for action was upon her.

"All right then—I'll try in every way I know to remember," she promised. "I'll do my best to find the truth, whatever it is."

He cupped her face with his two hands and kissed her warmly. "There's my girl. Between us, we'll clear old Niklaas yet."

She was not at all sure that would be the final result, but she knew now that she must move ahead in some positive way.

"First of all you'll have to get me into Father's house," she said. "I want to go upstairs. I want to see my old room. How else can I begin to remember?"

"That's easily arranged. Let's give your father a few days' time to get Cornish settled, and then I'll talk to him about your seeing the house. But we mustn't say it's because you want to recall something about the diamond. There are times when I think your

127

father doesn't want to know what became of it. He hasn't that much liking for diamonds. In fact, he's almost superstitious about the Kimberley."

"Perhaps he's right to be," Susan murmured.

Dirk laughed and drew her into his arms. "At least we've cleared up the doldrums. You're all right again, aren't you, darling? You won't worry any more about Mara?"

"Not if you say I needn't," she told him. The bliss of being safe again, of having his love close about her, was the only thing that mattered. She would do everything she could to please him.

13

A FEW MORNINGS later, with time on her hands once more, Susan went down to the library at the end of the Avenue, where Adderley Street began, to look up some books on photography. When she had what she wanted, she came out the door to discover Thomas Scott standing on the library steps with a book in his hands. He was leafing through the pages with such absorption that he did not see her, and she was struck by the change in him.

The usual guard he seemed to hold against everyone had lifted. He had lost himself completely in the book he held and it occurred to her that a shot of him here on the steps might fit into the series she was planning.

If he saw her, the picture would be spoiled, so she focused her camera quickly and set the stops. As the shutter clicked, Thomas looked up from his page and saw her. With a quick, almost secretive movement, he closed the book and thrust it under one arm.

"I hope you don't mind," Susan said, abashed a little too late by this invasion of his privacy. "You—you made such a good picture there on the steps and . . ." Her words died lamely away at his lack of response.

For an instant she saw hostility flare in his eyes. Then his guard was in place again as he came down the steps toward her.

"Good morning, madam," he said correctly and made no reference to the picture she had taken.

"How is my father?" she asked, wanting to hold him there a moment and perhaps find a way to soften her action, to apologize, if that would help.

Thomas gestured toward the gardens. "Mr. van Pelt is just over there, madam, if you wish to see him." He touched his cap and walked away, the book still under his arm. For all his courtesy, she felt that she had been reproved, and with justification. But the change she had seen so briefly in his face held her interest, and she wondered what book might have given him that different look.

She stood on the sidewalk for a moment longer, watching passers-by and the hurrying traffic. The usual assorted crowd thronged Adderley Street. There were Malay women with veils across their foreheads and under their chins, colored messenger boys wearing white pith helmets, now and then a "blanket native," barefoot and wearing wrapped about him the blanket that distinguished him from those who had left the reservation long behind. There were many white people, of course, and many of the colored people of the Cape.

When she turned toward the gardens she did not move quickly, not being entirely sure that she wanted to see her father. None of her meetings with him had been very happy ones, and perhaps he took no more joy in her company than she had found in his. However, since Thomas might report having seen her, it seemed only courteous to stop and speak to him.

She followed a path into this unexplored corner of the garden, past the marble statue of Sir George Grey, a gentleman in a long coat and tight trousers who had once been governor here. Then around an ancient and enormous holly oak where a colored man and woman sat together on a bench, speaking earnestly. There were no "Europeans Only" designations here.

The path led her toward a quiet and secluded corner and she saw the sign at once—this was a garden set apart for the blind. On a green bench in the sunlight sat her father, his hands resting in characteristic fashion on the head of his cane, and a look so dreaming and gentle upon his face that she hardly knew him.

"Good morning, Father," she said hesitantly. "I met Thomas just now on the library steps and he said you were here."

He accepted her presence without surprise, and motioned to the bench beside him. "Won't you join me? I've been sitting here thinking about your mother."

Always before when Claire's name had been mentioned there had been a coldness in his tone. But now there was a tenderness she had not heard before. She sat beside him in silence, not wanting to break this gentle spell that lay upon him.

"Do you remember how much your mother loved flowers?" he asked.

"I remember," she said. "That was the thing she liked best about South Africa—the flowers."

For a little while he was silent. When he spoke again his memories of Claire still claimed him.

"She used to love this little garden. She loved the small, scented flowers—the little English flowers that were so different from her South African favorites. Do you remember what she used to do when we came here?"

Susan did not remember. She could not recall ever having been in this place—except perhaps for Sir George Grey, who had looked vaguely familiar. Strange the things a child's memory retained or rejected.

Her father went on. "In those days we both had our vision. But Claire liked to play a game when we came here. She would cling to my arm and pretend she was blind. I would lead her about and she'd bend her pretty head toward the flowers to catch their fragrance. Then she would identify the scent, and nearly always she was right."

There was a tightness in Susan's throat, and she could not speak.

Her father went on, recalling a younger Claire than Susan could remember, and the note of affection in his voice was surprising. Always Susan had thought of Claire as running away from a man who had hurt her and did not love her.

"Why did she leave South Africa?" she asked. "What was she escaping from?"

He answered her indirectly. "We must remember that your mother was a fragile person. Her wings were easily bruised and she could never bear unhappiness. She would have crumpled under the strain of what happened to me."

"But you must have needed her then," Susan said impulsively. "How could she bear to leave you at a time like that?"

He turned the blank surface of his dark glasses toward her as if in inquiry, as if her words surprised him. But he said nothing and she knew he would give her no answer. With his cane he began to draw blind patterns in the earth at his feet and the silver knob shone in the sunlight, catching Susan's eye.

"I've noticed your cane," she said. "It's very beautiful."

He held the head of it toward her. "It was given me by friends some years ago. Do you see the enamel embossing on the silver?"

She took the cane from him and studied the raised symbols on the head and saw that they represented the three flags of South Africa. One the Union Jack of the British Commonwealth, one the flag of the Orange Free State, the third the *vierkleur*, the old flag of the Boer Republic. When she gave the cane back to him he traced the embossing with a forefinger.

"Three flags are not one flag," he said enigmatically, and she wondered which he favored.

He leaned upon the cane to rise from the bench and she stood up beside him.

"I mean to walk over to the flower market—would you care to come with me?" he asked.

"I'd like to," she said. "But before we go, may I take a picture of you here?"

He did not mind and she asked him to move about as he would if he were alone. For the first time she had seen in him something to which she could respond, and she sought for it in her picture. When it was taken, she went to walk beside him and drew his hand gently through the crook of her arm as they moved together toward the street.

"Would you have gone to the market alone, if I hadn't come by?" she asked.

He nodded. "I come here two or three times a week. First I visit the shop, and then Thomas leaves me for a while in the garden if the weather is fine. When I've sat in the sun long enough, I walk over to Adderley and there is always someone to help me through traffic. I prefer to get about by myself as much as possible."

When they reached the curb he felt for it with his cane and stepped down without hesitation. His sense of hearing had been intensified by his loss of sight and he seemed aware of the nearness of any person or moving object in an astonishingly sure way. As they crossed to the right side and followed the old-fashioned street with its elderly buildings and busy modern traffic, Susan asked him about the visitor in his house.

"Has Mr. Cornish moved in? Have you had any talks with him yet?"

"He has moved in," Niklaas said. "And I'm glad to have him under my roof and within easy reach. At the moment I'm afraid we're sparring and wary of each other. We've not been able to come together on the matter that interests us most. However, I've filled him in a bit on my early life—when my first wife and your half-brother Paul, who was his friend, were alive. On all this past history we are in accord."

It seemed strange to hear about these people whom she had never known—Paul, who was in school in England much of the time when she was small, and later in the war, never to come home. She listened with interest as they approached the arcade opening off Adderley Street, where the flower market occupied the center of an alley a block long.

Down the length of this arcade a double row of tubs and containers were set high on stands, revealing an almost solid bank of brilliant blooms. There were irises and poppies, tulips and jonquils. There were carnations and roses and cornflowers. And of course the exotic blooms of South Africa as well—flowers Susan had no name for. Along the outside aisles moved housewives and tourists, old gentlemen and young girls, all making purchases. Brown-skinned women stood amid the riotous color, urging their wares upon the customer, each calling attention to her own more superior blooms.

Niklaas van Pelt stood still for a moment at the entrance, breathing deeply of the fragrance. A nearby colored woman called him by name and began to speak to him in Afrikaans. He smiled and shook his head.

"We always play this game," he said to Susan. "They know very well that I will make a circuit of the entire market before I select what I want, but they always try to coax me to buy before I am ready. Come, let's see what they have for me today."

As he moved along the row with Susan at his side, a middle-aged woman, whose waistline bulged above her checked apron, spoke to him in greeting and reached out her hand for his cane. As she touched it, Niklaas gave it readily into her keeping. Apparently he wanted both hands free now and had no need for the cane in this restricted area. The woman placed it out of the way beneath her flower stand, and as they moved on down the row the flower buckets themselves seemed to guide her father along.

Once he put out his hand and held them above a great basin of marigolds, not quite touching them. It was as if he sensed the mass itself and would do the delicacy of a flower no harm by touching so much as a petal. Often he bent closer to breathe an individual fragrance and there was a quiet enjoyment in him that Susan found moving to see.

When they had circled the market, with the flower sellers greeting him and sometimes thrusting a bouquet beneath his nose, Niklaas began to make his selections. He seemed to remember exactly where the flowers were that he wanted, and he chose lavishly and with evident pleasure, often calling the market women by name.

Susan stepped back toward the street and took out her light meter. Only color film would truly do justice to this display, and she had none in her camera at the moment. Nevertheless, she was interested in the central figure of her father, the smiling flower sellers nearby, the expression on the face of the fat old woman who was returning his cane. She snapped the last two shots on the roll and began to turn the film on its spool. When she looked up again, she saw Thomas Scott waiting near the entrance to the market.

Niklaas raised a finger, as if he knew he would be there, and Thomas came to gather up the flowers the girls had wrapped into cornucopias with paper and string.

Susan bought a few roses and a bunch of green chinkerichees for herself. She had loved these South African "chinks" as a child, with their green buds that climbed a long stalk and would open later into long-lasting white flowers.

When she walked back to the car with her father, he offered her a lift home, but she thanked him and refused. The car drove away and she returned to the scented garden for the blind and sat on the bench which she and Niklaas had shared. There was much that she wanted to think about here in this quiet place.

One thing she had learned this morning and it was something she had never believed in before. Niklaas van Pelt had loved his wife deeply. He still retained for her a tenderness that he succeeded in hiding most of the time. Apparently he had reached a state of acceptance and understanding, so that he did not blame her for running away. Yet, in spite of this, Claire had raised her daughter with the belief that Niklaas had cared for neither of them, had not wanted them, had somehow betrayed them. For the first time a faint doubt about her mother began to rise in Susan's mind.

More than ever now she felt a reluctance about delving deliberately into the past. Whatever she found was sure to injure one or the other—her father or her mother. Yet she knew she must take the action she had promised Dirk. One way or another, she must have the answer.

14

When she reached home Susan was eager to see how her new pictures had turned out. She went directly to her little darkroom to develop the roll of film. Since her enlarger had not yet arrived, she could not complete her work as perfectly as she wished, but she could at least develop the film and make the first contact prints.

Just before lunch she finished her work and took the roll out to hold it up to the light. The shots of her father looked as if they had come out well. She hung the strip up to dry and was ready when Willi came to call her to lunch.

The thoughtful, shutaway time in the darkroom had increased her feeling that she must wait no longer to take the first step back into the past. She would not wait for Dirk to make the arrangement for her to visit her father's house. She would go there this afternoon on the very heels of Niklaas's kindness to her this morning and would hope that he might hear her request receptively.

After lunch she set off for Protea Hill. The colored maid admitted her and showed her into the living room, where French doors stood open. Afternoon sun shone into the room and she walked to the doors and looked out. On the terrace John Cornish sat before a table on which rested a portable typewriter. He looked up at once and saw her.

"Do come and talk to me," he said, as though he expected nothing but friendliness from her. "I'm getting nowhere today. Cape Town distracts me and so does the feeling of spring."

She crossed the flagstones to the low wall of the terrace. From here Devil's Peak was behind her, and she could see the full sweep of the Lion, from its tawny stone head to the flanks that reached toward the sky.

"I've had no chance to thank you for arranging a meeting with your father the other day," Cornish said. "Considering the rather brutal way I'd blurted out the story to you, it was kind of you to help me."

"I didn't do it for your sake," Susan told him frankly. "I wanted to see my father stop you from writing whatever you had planned. I had no idea that it would wind up with you here in his house."

John Cornish continued to study her with his oddly intent gaze until she began to feel uncomfortable beneath the scrutiny. There was never any knowing what he thought, or what plots this man might be hatching. There was still something in his purpose with her father that she did not understand and that made Dirk feel that he was dangerous. Was it, she wondered, because there was even more to what Niklaas van Pelt had done in the past than John Cornish had originally brought to light? Since her encounter with her father this morning, she disliked such a suspicion. But what else could Dirk mean?

Idly Cornish tapped the space bar on his typewriter. "How is your photography coming?" he asked.

This was a safe enough topic and she told him about the picture story she was planning and her efforts to get beneath the placid surface of Cape Town life. Before she was through, her father came to the door of his study and stepped out upon the terrace.

"Susan?" he said and waited for her response.

The softer mood of the morning was gone and he was distant again, even a little forbidding. She rose to greet him, but before she could state the reason for her visit, he drew a ring of keys from his pocket and began to detach one of them.

"Dirk tells me you want to explore the house," he said. "You're welcome to do so now if you like. You may go into any room you please—even Mara's and John's, with their permission. And of course my own. There's only one door you'll find locked. This is the key for it."

Her problem was solved more easily than she had expected. Relieved, she thanked him and returned to the house with the key in her hand. In the downstairs hallway she stood looking about for a moment. The great Chinese vase, filled now with African poppies her father had bought this morning, stood on the hall chest, a

137

glowing splash of color in gloom that sunlight did not penetrate. But now she had no desire to look through the downstairs rooms.

Quickly she mounted the stairs, following the right-angle turn to the floor above. Near the top was the open door to a room she remembered as her father's. She merely glanced in and went on. It was not her father whom she sought up here. Across the hall a second door stood open and she saw that this was the guest room John Cornish must be occupying. She glimpsed a desk with manuscript pages spread out upon it, and on a tall dresser the framed picture of a pretty, smiling woman.

Hastily she moved away, not wanting to pry. Somehow the picture surprised her. In her mind John Cornish had come to be more a symbol than a man. He was the well-known author, and more recently a rather sinister figure who had stepped threateningly into her own life. She had no idea who the woman in the picture could be—wife, fiancée, sister? No one had ever mentioned a woman in connection with him.

She crossed back to the room next to her father's. This had been her mother's room, as she knew very well. Was it here that she would need the key? But the knob turned under her hand and the door opened at her touch. It was strange to have her returning memory of the room erased in a flash. Everything had been changed. There remained not a stick of furniture that her mother had used, though this was clearly a feminine room. A pale-blue negligee lay across the bed and there were jars of cream and bottles of perfume upon the dressing table.

For an instant a queer vertigo possessed her. It was as if the world about her whirled and fell into angry sound and she felt with compelling conviction that something dreadful was about to happen. She steadied herself and closed the door upon the wave of fragrance that she recognized as Mara's French perfume. She had been half afraid that she might see a picture of Dirk upon the dressing table, but there was nothing save those bottles and jars and boxes. Yet it was not her sense of Mara's occupancy that had caused this sudden dizziness. For a moment it had been as though something had reached out of the past to smother her in nightmare fear. But as she stepped back from the threshold her head cleared and the oddly threatening impression was gone.

Shaken, she moved on toward the rear of this upstairs hall. It was her own room that she was now approaching. There was no fear in her now, no sadness. She had loved this room as a child, and had always looked forward to returning to it for the summer months that the family spent in Cape Town. There was no need to try the door. She knew it would be locked, knew the key she held would open it. The key slipped easily into place, but before she turned it she closed her eyes and rested her forehead for a moment against the darkly varnished wood. This time she did not want memory to be suddenly dispelled, and she called back a clear vision of the room in detail, impressed it upon her consciousness so that it might be recalled even if everything in the room was different. Then she pushed the door open and stepped across the sill.

Her first impression was of a place that was dark and dusty and long unused. There was a stuffy odor and the very opening of the door roused a stirring of dust. As her eyes grew accustomed to the gloom, she saw that all was the same as it had been when she was a child. There was a small bed and a low bookcase still filled with rows of books. A worn leather hassock stood before the bookshelves as if it had been used only yesterday by a little girl who loved to read. There was a small desk, and a chair too, and a full-sized chest along one wall.

Softly Susan crossed the room, hesitant to disturb whatever was left here of her childhood. She opened the casement window and unhooked green shutters to push them outward. In the frame of the open window the full sight of the mountain, gray and rocky and massive, caught away her breath. This was the view she best remembered, and it was the one she had both loved and feared. Sometimes the mountain had seemed her friend and guardian. Its strength and eternal presence had seen her through many a childhood problem. Yet at other times that mass of rock could seem relentless in its judgment of her. There had never been any way to hide from the mountain. It knew everything.

The block of the lower cable-car house made a spot of white at the place where the slope began to steepen. As she watched, a tiny car started upward, rising like a bead upon an invisible thread. Up, up, slowly—and there was its counterpart coming down. The cars passed like the figures in a formal dance and each disappeared into its own white cubicle at the foot and at the top. The mountain remained unmoved, untouched by this display of human engineering. In spite of the continuous assault made upon it, no human figures could be seen along that vast expanse of the table. The mountain would have dwarfed them, made them invisible. Only when one came close could an occasional climber be seen, finding his precarious way up that great face. The easier paths were hidden in ravines, or lay out of sight on the other side. Every year the mountain took its toll in human sacrifice. Its strength and immobility affected all Cape Town, set a stamp upon it, but sometimes its influence and import were less than benign. Yet every child who grew up in the Cape, both colored and white, loved to go climbing. Last Sunday, on her day off, Willi had gone up the mountain on a date with Thomas, and Susan knew that if she had stayed here as a child she would sooner or later have gone up the mountain herself.

She turned her back now on its stern face and looked at the room. She found it both touching and disturbing to realize that her father had kept her room exactly as it had been in the days of her childhood. Had he expected that she would someday return? Had he kept it waiting for her, even though he had wiped the memory of his wife's room from existence?

There was a tightness in Susan's throat as she went to the chest that stretched along one wall. It was a fine old *kist* made of beautifully grained stinkwood and it had been given to her by her father to keep her treasures in. She did not question now what she would find inside. If all else had not been changed, this, surely, would remain the same.

She pulled over the leather hassock and sat down before the chest, pushing the heavy lid back against the wall. Sure enough, an all-too-familiar jumble of toys lay within. Not all her toys, it was true, but only those she had brought to the Cape Town house the last time she had journeyed here from Johannesburg. She pulled out a stuffed toy rabbit with one pink glass eye and grayish fur. There was a small box camera with a broken lens, a china doll with a missing arm—how she had loved that vacant-eyed doll. And then—at the bottom of the chest among other odds and ends she discovered a treasure. It was the album of old snapshots she had taken before she had broken the camera.

This was a find. Perhaps these pictures would be something to jog her memory. She took the big book with its woven grass cover out of the chest and was about to close the lid when she heard a sound from the doorway. Looking up quickly she found Mara Bellman watching her.

"Your father sent me to see if you were all right," Mara said. "You've been quiet for quite a while and he began to worry."

"I'm fine," Susan said curtly and waited for her to leave.

Mara, however, came into the room with unconcealed interest.

"Bluebeard's closet!" she said. "I always expect to find a body hidden in here, or at least evidence of some crime."

Susan said nothing, merely waiting. This was an intrusion she heartily resented and she was not deceived by the other girl's suddenly affable manner. Mara remained insensitive to her wish to be alone. She strolled idly to the window and looked out at the mountain.

"We're allowed in here only once a year, for spring cleaning, you know. The rest of the time your father keeps it locked. I understand he had the room closed when he came down here to live after he was released from prison. Not that he ever saw it again himself. I suppose you know that his blindness came on while he was in prison."

"I didn't know," Susan said in a low tone. There was pain for her in the sudden revelation. It seemed doubly tragic that he should have gone into prison, never to see the bright free world again. It was as if the prison sentence still lay upon him and always would.

"How dusty everything is," Mara said. "I'll have to get the key away from him soon so the servants can clean up." Looking about, she noticed the chest beside which Susan knelt. "That, of course, is a treasure," she added. "A beautiful old piece. It's odd that it should have been given to a child to use for toys."

Restraining her irritation, Susan answered evenly, "When he gave it to me, Father said I was to take care of it. He always believed that children should learn very young to take good care of their possessions. He said this was to be my wedding chest when I grew up. I didn't dare let it get scratched or dented because he would have been angry."

Perhaps Mara did not care for the reference to a wedding chest. She moved on about the room, revealing her impatience now, opening a drawer here, touching a chair there. Ignoring her, Susan reached into the chest again. This time she drew out a faded pink candy box with a heavy content that rattled in her hands.

At once she remembered what it was and opened it delightedly, to reveal what had been her prized rock collection. She dumped the entire contents out upon the floor and began to identify bits of rock and shell that she had not thought of in years. This bit of shell with the mother-of-pearl colors had come from Camp's Bay, where her parents had friends and where she had often gone swimming. This piece of black porous rock had come from the top of Table Mountain. Dirk had brought it down after a climb, especially for her collection. Something with a bright gleam to it caught her eye and she held up a piece of quartz.

Mara had come to stand beside her, watching. "What's that?" she asked.

Susan's resentment at this continued intrusion brimmed over. "The one thing it is not," she told Mara, "is the Kimberley Royal," and she looked up at the other girl angrily.

For once Mara's poise failed her. A flash of dislike so intense flared in her eyes that Susan was startled. Without another word Mara went out of the room. Thoughtfully Susan began to put the bits of rock back into the box. She wondered if Dirk had any conception of how much Mara Bellman detested her.

When everything except the photograph album had been returned to the chest, Susan closed the lid and came out of the room, locking the door behind her. Then she took the key back to the terrace where Niklaas sat talking to John Cornish.

15

"KEEP THE KEY if you like," her father told Susan when she would have put it into his hand. "I have a duplicate. You're welcome to visit the room whenever you like. Everything in it is yours."

His manner had not softened and the offer was made almost indifferently. Yet so close was she at that moment to her childhood that the impulse to touch him in a remembered caress was hard to resist. She made no move toward him, however, and only thanked him softly.

He did not let her go at once. "I've been thinking about inviting a few people in for tea to meet you before long," he said surprisingly. "It's been a good many years since I've entertained in this house, but I believe there are some who would come. There are a few people I would like you to know. Would you have any objection? I've already mentioned it to Dirk."

"Why, no, of course not," she told him. "It would be very kind of you."

He nodded. "I'll set the wheels to turning then."

She said good-by and nodded to John Cornish, who had risen when she had come out on the terrace and stood watching them both with that look of his that was somehow different, Susan thought, from the way other people looked at you. Always there was an intensity in his gaze, a lively awareness of all that went on around him. Yet there was no knowing what his conclusions were or how he was summing you up.

"I believe I'll take a bit of a walk," John said. "I've sat at an unresponsive typewriter long enough for one day. Do you mind if I come a way with you?"

She did mind, but as always there seemed no way to escape him.

"If you like," she said carelessly and they left the house together, following the street and the longer way home.

"I've wanted a chance to talk to you," he said when they were away from the house. "Yesterday your father showed me the letter your mother sent him shortly before her death."

So now, Susan thought, John Cornish too meant to sound her out about that letter. She was silent, ready to resist whatever he might urge.

"It opens all sorts of strange possibilities, doesn't it?" he went on. "If your mother didn't take the diamond out of the country herself, it may long since be in other hands."

"Of course," she agreed a bit dryly. "I've thought so all along. Though I've wondered how such a famous stone could be disposed of. Wouldn't it be identified if it appeared on the market?"

"It would be, providing it reached a legitimate dealer's hands before anyone tampered with it. But an expert cutter can change any stone, disguise it, as it were, so that it wouldn't be recognized. Though if it went into black market channels, that might not be necessary. There are world powers eager for diamonds. And private collectors and dealers who are unscrupulous."

His words were taking an unexpected turn. He was not urging remembrance upon her, as others had done, but seemed to be deliberately opening another door, a door of escape from some of her worry.

"By a world power I suppose you mean Russia?" she asked. "But I thought Russia possessed treasures of cut stones herself."

"You're thinking of Czarist Russia. After the revolution diamonds poured out of the country in the hands of escaping nobility and were sold in a flood that dropped the price of diamonds everywhere until the outpouring ended and the price could be brought under De Beers control again. Now Russia occasionally sends out stones for sale, but for the most part she seems to be snapping them up in the illicit markets. Especially in the field of industrial diamonds."

Susan glanced at him hopefully. "If you think this is what may have happened to the Kimberley, then you won't have to write about my mother at all in your book."

"There are still the other diamonds," he said, not ungently.

"Those found in your father's house—the ones that sent him to prison."

She did not want to think about those stones at the moment and returned quickly to the safer subject of the big stone. If one side of the problem could be cleared up, then she would face the other side.

"One thing I've never understood about the Kimberley is why one man would give it so casually into the keeping of a friend to take from one city to another. You'd think something that valuable would be sent with an armed guard."

Cornish smiled. "You don't know South Africans. I've seen fortunes carried about wrapped in bits of paper. After all, that's the safest way to carry diamonds—unobtrusively. At any rate, your father had the big diamond in his possession. He brought it to Cape Town and after that what happened to it is anybody's guess. Though the letter from your mother opens a new possibility."

This was what he was leading up to, of course. Now he would do as the others had done. He would put the weight of remembering upon her shoulders and urge her to start thinking back into the past. Her resistance against him stiffened.

"You needn't ask me what I remember. I don't remember anything. And I hate to have everyone prodding me. Just now Mara Bellman came up to the room I had as a child and stood watching me as though she expected me to produce the Kimberley diamond at any minute."

"If I were you, I'd pay no attention," he said quietly.

"To Mara, you mean?"

"To anyone who tries to push you into remembering," he said. There was a sudden grave urgency in his voice that surprised her. "Don't try to remember, Susan. Don't let anyone force you back into the past."

His words astonished her. John Cornish had been the truth seeker, the one who had told her that she must face the truth, whatever it might be. She stole a look at him as he walked along beside her, and noted the craggy look of his head in profile, the stern set of his chin, the unsmiling mouth.

"That day in the Public Gardens you were the one who said that truth was to be respected for itself," she reminded him. "You said I ought to seek it out, no matter how involved I was emotionally."

"I've changed my mind," he said.

Somehow this unexpected reversal left her puzzled and disturbed. "But why? What has happened to make you change your course?"

They had reached a corner that brought the Aerie into sight a block or so away and John took her arm, drawing her to a halt on the sidewalk.

"Not my course—yours. This is difficult to put into words, and that's unlike me." He smiled ruefully. "There's a feeling about that house—Protea Hill—that I don't like and can't quite put my finger on."

"But what has that to do with me? What has it to do with whether or not I remember what might have happened years ago?"

"Perhaps nothing," he said. "But I have a strong feeling that it's wiser to let the matter rest. Perhaps, like a good many journalists, I play my hunches. Take care of yourself, Susan. Be very careful, won't you?"

Startled, she looked into his eyes, trying to read there the things he had not told her. "I—I don't know what you mean."

"I'm putting it badly. But will you promise me one thing. If you remember something, if you find the road back, will you make one move before any other?"

She could only stare at him blankly.

He spoke more gently, as if he wanted to soften the effect of his words, and there was a kindness of manner that she had seen in him before only in the presence of her father.

"If you remember anything that seems to be significant, go first of all to someone you can trust. And I mean someone you trust wholeheartedly. If there's no one near enough, then take what you know to the police." He touched her lightly on the shoulder, perhaps in admonishment. "I won't take you clear home and embarrass you with Dirk. I've done enough of that. Rather blindly, I'm afraid. Good-by, Susan. And think about what I've said."

This time he waited for no answer but went off, moving rapidly in spite of his limp. Both disturbed and astonished, she watched him out of sight before she turned toward home.

She did not understand any of this. Someone she could trust? Dirk? Her father? John Cornish himself? It was a chilling thing that she could give no confident assent to any of these.

Cornish she had trusted least of all. For the most part she had disliked and resented him, and yet as she walked the last block toward home the reluctant feeling of having found someone to depend on began to possess her. It was as if she had come up against a rock wall that was cold to the touch and would lacerate her flesh if she brushed against it, yet which stood there, unalterable, for her to lean against if she were at bay.

At bay? What a strange thought to cross her mind. Nothing threatened her—this was nonsense.

How strange too that he had urged her not to remember even if she could. This was no longer advice she could take. Dirk was her husband. It was he who must guide her. It was he who was trying to save her father from further pain. Besides, once the door of memory had started to open, it was unlikely that one could ever again keep it shut. This afternoon memories had begun to stir vaguely in the background of her mind. There had been that moment when she had stood, shaken, on the threshold of her mother's room, on the verge, it seemed, of some knowledge. The snapshot album that she had brought home with her might well open the door completely.

Nevertheless, when she reached the house she put the album down in the living room and left it there without turning so much as a page. John's words had made her hesitate.

She went next to the darkroom to see if the strip of film was dry. There was still time to make prints before dinner and she wanted to be busy. The film, however, was not where she usually hung it, and she looked around to see whether she could have put it absent-mindedly in some different place.

She even went into the dining room and the living room to see if she could have laid it down somewhere, having been called from what she was doing. But no amount of searching revealed the strip of film downstairs. She was about to go upstairs to look for it when she noticed a basket of sewing she had left on the coffee table. Her sewing scissors lay beside the work. As she picked up the scissors and basket to carry them upstairs something on the carpet caught her eye. She bent and picked up a stiff, transparent sliver with shadings of light and dark in it. When she held the sliver up to the light, it was easily recognized as a tiny strip that might have been snipped from a piece of film.

Increasingly puzzled, she put the sewing things down and looked into a wastebasket, finding nothing of any significance.

147

Then she went out to the kitchen and searched the garbage container, much to the cook's astonishment. No, missus, Cookie said, she had not seen any picture-taking materials.

There was a large outdoor container in the yard and Susan, possessed now by a hunch, hurried out to it. Hidden beneath a heap of damp potato peelings she found what she was looking for. Someone had deliberately cut her strip of film into tiny slivers and hidden them in this waste from the kitchen. More puzzled and shocked than angry, she fished out the mess of cut-up bits and wrapped them in a sheet of newspaper. Then she went into the house and rang for Willi.

The girl came from her room looking a little sleepy as though she had been taking a nap. In the living room Susan gestured toward the scraps of film on the paper.

"Do you know how this happened, Willi?" she asked.

The girl stared at the slivers with eyes that were expressionless. "What is it?" she asked.

Susan told her of looking for the length of film she had hung up to dry, of finding the clue of a bit of film not far from scissors that might have been used to cut it off, and of hunting down the rest.

Willi shook her head. She had seen nothing, heard nothing, knew nothing.

"Why would anyone do such a thing?" Susan cried. "I'd taken some really good pictures of my father and I was anxious for them to turn out well. Are you sure, Willi, that no one might have come into the house while you were in your room?"

"Not unless someone entered through a window, Mrs. Hohenfield," Willi said. "The front door is locked, and the cook has been out in the kitchen all the time. The only person who has entered the house is Mr. Hohenfield."

"You mean he came home early?" Susan asked in surprise.

Willi nodded. "He said he wasn't feeling well, and he went upstairs to lie down. I don't believe he has left."

She thanked the girl and let her go. Then she went upstairs to the bedroom door. Dirk must have heard her step for he called out to her.

"Come in, darling. I'm awake."

She opened the door to find him lying on his bed, wrapped in a maroon robe, his shoes off.

"Is anything the matter?" she asked quickly.

He shook his head. "Nothing to worry about. I had a rugged day and felt a bit seedy, so I chucked it and came home early. What's happened to you? You look as though you'd met a ghost."

Susan carried the newspaper over to his bedside and set it down. The paper curled open, revealing its soggy contents.

"What on earth?" Dirk said, and there seemed to be genuine surprise in his voice.

"I finished a roll of pictures this morning," she said, "and developed them before lunch. Then I went out for a while this afternoon. When I came home, my film was missing and I found it cut to bits and hidden under rubbish in the yard."

Dirk lay silent, his eyes closed for a moment as if he fought the return of a headache. "I suppose I'll have to give Willi and the cook a talking-to," he said.

"I've already questioned them. Neither one knows anything about it."

"Of course they'd lie if they did know," Dirk said. "These people always lie when they're trying to save their own skins."

Always before when Dirk had made derogatory remarks about the dark races she had either argued with him gently or tried to make allowances for his very different upbringing. There was always the hope that she could gradually get him to see these matters with a less prejudiced eye. But now outrage sprang up in her at his words and she made no effort to check it.

"That's a dreadful thing to say! There isn't any such thing as 'these people.' We're only considering Willi and the cook and I expect they are as honest as we are."

Dirk looked at her with an air of pained distaste and sat up on the edge of the bed. "Listen to me, Susan. This entire racial situation is dynamite. I've hoped you would stay out of it. You haven't lived in South Africa since you were a child and you don't know one thing about it. The romantic idea of equality between black and white, or even colored and white, is a dangerous one. If we give them too much, we are the ones who'll be thrown out. Look at the Congo. Leave Willi and the cook to me. What sort of picture did you take on that strip of film?"

She could see the futility of arguing with him further now, but the resentment his words had aroused did not die out. She was beginning to be sorry that she had told him what had happened.

But there was nothing to do except try to remember the pictures she had taken.

"Nothing of any consequence, I'm sure," she said limply. "A few shots around Cape Town. A picture of the van Riebeeck statue at the foot of Adderley Street. Several pictures of my father."

"You've seen him today?"

"I saw him this morning in that little garden for the blind, just off the Avenue. I took a picture of him there and then one or two more in the flower market."

He seemed to consider her words as he moved slowly toward the door, tying the cord of his robe around his waist. "And that was all?"

It didn't seem quite all. There were some scenes she couldn't recall, but nothing surely that was significant. Anyway, she no longer cared. She was too upset about Dirk to care.

"This sounds like malicious mischief," he said. "I'll have a talk with the servants now."

She did not go with him, but remained upstairs where she would not hear what he said. Restlessly she moved about the room, fighting the turmoil within herself. Dirk was set wholly in opposition to something she believed in with spirited conviction —and this diverging of viewpoints could hardly be ignored in South Africa. His own attitude hurt and grieved her and it promised continued friction between them unless some compromise could be reached. Yet this was a subject on which she could not compromise and still retain a sense of self-respect.

Idly she picked up the little carved impala she had brought from Chicago and smoothed the satiny wood, searching out the whorls of the carving. The diamond on her finger blinked as she moved her hand and she stared at it unhappily. The ring stood for happiness, marriage, the security of the love that she had believed existed between herself and Dirk. The impala seemed to stand in contrast to all this. It represented Africa and the dark strong heart-beat of its rising peoples. It stood for what was right—for the idea of freedom in which she believed so strongly.

She put the impala down and turned toward the window beside her. Must a choice between the two be necessary? Perhaps she could find a way. No man and woman were ever in agreement on every aspect of their lives in a marriage. Divergent viewpoints, even though fundamental, did not always destroy love and loyalty. Thinking of compromise, of giving somewhere in her own stand, she began to consider Willi.

The girl had been brought here by Mara Bellman. Not even Niklaas had known that she was coming here to work. Might that mean that Mara held her under some obligation which Willi could not escape? Was it possible that Willi would feel bound to let Mara into the house and would keep the secret of her entry? Mara was fully capable of malicious mischief, especially if it might disturb Dirk's wife.

This afternoon at Niklaas's house Mara had not appeared until that moment upstairs when the toy chest had been opened. Could she have come to the Aerie during that earlier interval? Or perhaps by the short cut while Susan and John Cornish were walking slowly the long way home?

Dirk's step sounded on the stair and she stiffened as he came into the room, offering him no inquiry, continuing to stare out the window.

He came up behind her and put his hands on her shoulders. "You can relax, darling. I gave them a very small talking-to and made no accusations at all. You'd have been pleased with me."

Relief flooded through her and she turned to him quickly. He was trying too; she didn't have to bridge this gulf alone after all. And if only he would try, she would make all the more effort to understand his viewpoint, even if she could not accept it for herself.

By nighttime the troublesome happenings of the day had receded to some extent. When she went to bed the load on her shoulders felt considerably lighter. Yet when her conscious mind slept, what lay beneath could roam as it pleased. During the early-morning hours she awakened once more with the sweat of terror upon her body and the flash of blue fire all about her. A cold fire that cut through her flesh with an icy thrust that seemed about to destroy her. She awoke struggling, fighting against something utterly fearful and shattering, to find Dirk holding her, gently shaking her awake, his voice coaxing her back to consciousness.

"You're all right, darling. It was that beastly nightmare again. It's over now. You're safe and I won't let anything come near to hurt you."

She clung to him, the terror still upon her, and it was a long time before she would let him go. The dream seemed a forewarning of the door that was slowly pushing open somewhere in her consciousness. A door with all the force of long-suppressed memories behind it. And there were no means by which she could prevent its opening. Nor did she really want to. Whatever was fearful and hidden must be faced, exorcised. Only then would she be free of it. Only then would the nightmare cease to recur.

16

Dirk stayed at home the next day. He was not ill, but there seemed in him a nervous dissatisfaction that worried Susan. How much was this mood a reaction to her own emotional vagaries of yesterday and last night?

When she told him of her father's plan for inviting a few people in for tea some afternoon, hoping the idea might please him, he grimaced.

"I know. Uncle Niklaas has mentioned it to me. If it gives him pleasure, let him go ahead. We can see it through, I suppose."

They were sitting together in the living room and Susan was waiting for Dirk to make some decision as to what they would do with this free day. Once she would have been full of suggestions, but now she hesitated, leaving it up to him.

"I thought it was kind of Father to suggest such a party," she said mildly.

Dirk shrugged and stretched, yawning. "I can warn you that the people he invites will be a bore. But he's unlikely to take our suggestions."

Idly he reached out and picked up a book from the coffee table. It was the snapshot album from her childhood.

"What's this?" he asked, and smiled as he opened the cover. The handwriting was her father's and Dirk read the words aloud: "'The picture life of Miss Susan van Pelt, aged six and a half.'" He glanced at her teasingly. "I remember you when you were the very young Miss van Pelt. Where on earth did you find this?"

"In my room at Protea Hill," she said. Was this the road back? Did the answer lie in these pages?

He turned the leaves and, drawn by her own uneasy fascination, she found herself looking at the pictures with him.

So young a photographer had been haphazard in her approach. Some of the pictures were blurred because the camera had moved. Some were crooked because it had been tipped. There was one of the Lion's Head that looked as though it was toppling away from the observer because the camera had been tilted directly up in snapping it. The better pictures had clearly been taken by adults.

"There I am," Dirk said, amused, tapping a picture with one finger. "There in my climbing outfit."

She looked at the page. How bright and shining a person he had seemed in those days; how wonderful to a little girl's eyes. In this picture he wore shorts and a jacket, cleated shoes, and a rope slung in a coil over one shoulder.

"You went up Table Mountain that day," she said. "You brought a black rock down for my collection."

He laughed. "So I did. I'd forgotten the existence of that collection. How important you felt about it."

He turned a page. "There you are with your collection. Isn't that what's spread out on that board in the garden?"

It was indeed. She could remember her pride in the labeling. Grownups had helped her to spell the words, though she had been able to make the letters herself. She had been seven by then and reading rather well. The pictures were too small to reveal the wording on the labels, but she could recall some of the details as she studied them. Invisible hands were pushing at the door again, widening the crack a little, and she shivered, suddenly afraid. This was too soon. She was not ready. She took the book out of his hands and closed it.

"What is it?" Dirk said. "What's the matter?"

But she could not tell him. "Let's not sit here looking at old pictures when a free day is waiting for us. Let's go outside and do something."

"What would you like to do?" he asked.

She suggested the first thing that came to mind, wanting only to get out of the house, to leave the album and all its crowding memories behind. Later she would face it, but not yet.

"Let's go up Table Mountain. It looks like a good bright day, with no wind." She knew the cable cars did not operate if the wind was high.

Dirk was willing. He seemed gayer now and more affectionate than he had been in a long while. When they were dressed in warm sweaters and Susan had put new film into her camera, they went out to the car and Dirk drove up the Kloof Nek Road, where a pass opened between the Lion's Head and Table Mountain.

On the way up Susan watched the little white cable house at the foot, but no cars seemed to be moving, in spite of the perfect weather. When they reached the Kloof and turned left to follow the road along the side of the mountain, they lost sight of the house for a time. But when at last the road curved beneath it and Dirk got out of the car to investigate they discovered that there were no cars running. A cable was being repaired and the cars would be out of service for a day or two.

"Let's get out anyway," Susan said.

Dirk drove the car off to the side of the road and they got out and climbed a little way up the rock-strewn lower slope of the mountain. The houses of Cape Town stopped well below this level and all about them great boulders jutted from the hillside with tiny wildflowers emerging from the stubby mountain growth. At their feet lay the town spread out between Devil's Peak and the Lion's Head, and behind rose the precipitous rock sides of the mountain, the table a straight black line against the sky. From the town below the ever-present cooing of the doves reached them.

Susan raised her face to the sun, clasping her arms about drawn-up knees. Dirk lounged lazily beside her, plucking at a scrubby clump of heather. A question she had been wanting to ask came to her mind and she put it into words.

"Yesterday when I visited my father's house and went through it upstairs, I looked into a room that must be the one John Cornish is occupying. I saw a picture on his dresser—of a woman. Does he have a wife?"

"Cornish again? The fellow's becoming an obsession with you." Dirk sounded annoyed. "He did have a wife. She was an English girl who died five years or more ago. He's been a lone wolf ever since, I gather. Anything more you want to know?"

She shook her head, wondering at herself for asking the question. The thought of John's odd warning had come back to her more than once, though she had been unable to puzzle out his meaning. But she had not expected to be curious about him personally.

155

It was pleasant here on the mountainside and she fell to dreaming a little as they sat in silence. A further remembrance of her visit to Protea Hill yesterday returned to mind: that moment when she had found her childhood rock collection. She stared up at the top of Table Mountain, from which Dirk had long ago brought her a piece of black stone. Above the mountain the sky was a bright warm blue—almost the blue of an alcohol flame. She closed her eyes to shut away the sight, but now the flash of blue fire seemed all around her, as it had been in her dream. Without warning, the thing was there in her mind—established in full detail. The door had blown open on a great gust of memory and she knew quite clearly what had happened.

Dirk must have seen the change in her face and sensed the tensing of her body. He left the rock on which he had been sitting and took her by the shoulders. He shook her gently so that her head fell back and her eyes looked widely up into his.

"Tell me what you've remembered," he said urgently.

She sensed by the grip of his fingers that he would shake her far less gently if she did not reply. Now that the thing had come through so clearly there was no way to keep it from him. In words that sometimes halted and sometimes rushed ahead, she told him exactly what had happened that long-ago day in Cape Town.

She had been playing with her rock collection out on the terrace behind Protea Hill one afternoon. The day was hot—the burning heat of their January summer. As a child she had always had an affinity for the heat of Africa, and she had set up her collection in the sparse shade of a blue gum, just as it had been arranged in those childhood snapshots.

That day she was admiring a new stone she had added to her collection. She could not remember when or how she had come upon it, but she had liked it better than any of the other stones. True, it was not as big as the shiny lump of quartz, but it had sparkled with a most amazing fire. A blue-white stone it had been, flashing blue fire when she turned it in the light. Her mother had come out of the house and seen her playing there. Even now Susan could remember her distraught and worried expression.

"Susan dear, I wonder if you've seen—" she began. And then her eyes fell upon the stone in her daughter's hands. She flew across the terrace and snatched it out of the child's fingers. It had been an alarming thing to Susan to see her mother, who was always gentle and loving, grow almost hysterically angry. She had slapped her daughter and scolded her thoroughly. What she said, Susan could not remember, but she could still recall how puzzled and wounded she had been by the outburst.

When Claire ran back inside and up the stairs, taking the stone with her, Susan, hurt and bewildered, crept after her. Not in order to spy, but wanting desperately to understand what she had done that was wrong, to understand why adult anger had struck out at her so unexpectedly, like lightning across a clear sky—when always before she had been praised and encouraged for her rock collection.

She went softly to the door of her mother's room. It had been closed, but the latch had not caught and she pushed it open without a sound. That was how she came to see exactly what happened. Her mother stood for a few seconds staring rather wildly about the room, her back to the door and the flashing stone in her hands. She looked as if the very touch of it burned her flesh. Then she went to her dressing table.

On its surface sat a glass powder bowl with a silver top that had always fascinated Susan. It was a Chinese piece with silver dragons entwined around the lid so that their raised heads made a knob in the center. Claire lifted the cover from the bowl, dropped the stone into the flesh-pink powder, and thrust it well out of sight with her fingers. Then she wiped off the powder with a handkerchief, wiped up a sifting of it from the dressing table, its delicate fragrance reaching the child who watched around the corner of the door. Claire's face was visible in the mirror, but she did not see the door ajar or Susan watching behind her. She looked only at her own pretty face and gradually the anxiety faded out of it. She began to look pleased as a kitten, as if she thought herself a very clever person.

The hidden Susan lingered a moment more, shaken as much by what she had seen as by her mother's anger. Her teeth had begun to chatter and she knew with frightening certainty that her mother would be even more angry if she discovered her here. Tiptoeing as if the very house watched her, she had returned to her rocks. But all her pleasure in the collection had vanished and the remaining rocks seemed dull and unmagical compared with the beautiful, shining stone it had been so wicked of her to possess.

"The Kimberley!" Dirk said tensely.

Susan came back from the sharply etched past to see his face. There was something almost avid in his expression. It was a face she did not recognize, had never seen before.

"So you did find it!" he went on. "You did know what happened to it. Go on with your story. Tell me the rest."

She stared at him blankly. So thoroughly had she been caught up in the illusion of the past that her feelings were those of the young Susan, and her eyes still watched her mother with a rising fear that was beyond her years. Why had she been so frightened? Why had so vivid an experience been thrust out of her mind, for so long buried and forgotten?

"Do go on," Dirk prompted impatiently.

She could only shake her head. "That's all I know. That's all I can remember."

Clearly he did not believe her. "That isn't possible. You must have been curious. You must have wanted to know why your mother hid the diamond in the powder and what became of it afterwards."

"I didn't even know it was a diamond," Susan said in a low voice.

"What does that matter? You thought the stone pretty, didn't you? You wanted it for your collection." Excitement had risen in him, and an urgency she hated to see.

Again she shook her head. "I don't know. Truly I don't know any more than I've told you."

The door had blown open on a wave of vivid memory. And as surely it had blown shut again. There was nothing left except a sickness at the pit of her stomach and a feeling that the threat of utter disaster hung over her head. New questions were crowding her thoughts. Was this something she had felt as a child or was it her reaction now—this foreboding and dread? What had really happened that day?

In any event, the moment had been spoiled. Dirk would not forgive her now. She stood up limply. "Let's go home," she said.

For a moment she thought he meant to urge her further. Then, without a word, he started down to the car, striding impatiently, and she went with him. But when they had driven to the Kloof, where the roads branched, he took the downhill highway that led through the gap and south along the Peninsula. He drove recklessly, wildly, and his speed on the turning road frightened her.

To their left lay the wine valleys and Groot Constancia, with all its history, but Dirk turned sharply onto the coast road and mountains shut away the calm, sunny valleys as the car sped toward the ocean level. Here they were beyond the flanks of the Lion and this was no longer Table Bay, but the cold South Atlantic.

Below the clustering houses, pink and yellow and creamy white, gay with red roofs, curved a crescent of white sand. The car plunged down a zigzagging road that led to Camp's Bay. Above them the sharp leaning peaks of the Twelve Apostles stood out against the sky.

Dirk braked to a jarring halt beside the palm-lined drive and came around to pull open the door on her side. He said nothing, but merely held out his hand. There was no gentleness in his fingers as he drew her from the car. Together they walked down a bank and out upon the warm sand. Susan stepped lightly, carefully, so that her shoes would not fill with fine white sand, but all her movements were automatic and she was shaken by a sickness of despair. Now she had truly angered him, and in a way she could not help. There was an ugliness in his anger that she had never seen before and she winced away from it as though he had lashed out at her physically.

A roaring of surf sounded where the rolling line of breakers pounded in. The water was still too cold for swimming and no one else walked the beach. They had the sand and the creaming surf, the breeze from the ocean, to themselves.

She did not move quickly enough for him and he caught her hand again to pull her along. Bits of broken shell strewed the rim of the high-water mark, and there were dry brown coils of seaweed like snakes upon the sand. Ahead a great mass of smooth, rounded rocks encroached upon the beach from shoreline to ocean, looking like huge animals with their wet brown heads in the sea. Dirk sprang ahead of her upon the nearest rock and held out his hand to pull her up. They moved from rock to rock and Susan saw the green marbling of the water where the surf roared in, saw it break high in the air over the farthermost point.

The calming effect of sea and sky, the physical effort, was quieting Dirk's anger and when he said, "Let's sit here for a bit," his tone was gentler than before. She took her place beside him on the warm smooth stone, but she could find no comfort in his change of tone. She sat staring mutely at the scene about her.

Toward the land golden lichen grew upon the rocks, and between them clung small purple flowers. On the water side seaweed hung like strands of long dark hair, drifting and lifting with the movement of the waves. Far out across the water was a small island where cormorants gathered on the beaches. And always, all about them, was the roar of the waves, rising and falling endlessly.

She knew why he had brought her here and there was only bitterness and sorrow in her at the thought.

"This is where we said good-by before I went away to America," she said, musing aloud. "I tried to take a picture of you that last day, but it never came out because I had broken my camera. Father never knew I'd broken it. It was a special gift from him and he was always angry when I broke anything. I was afraid to tell him. So I have no picture of you the way you looked that day. But I can still remember."

She did not know why she related these things, when obviously he did not care and they were not the memories he wanted. He was looking away from her toward the land, toward the familiar tipping peaks that numbered twelve and had been named for the Apostles. The strangeness had gone from his face, but there was no true relenting in him.

She brushed the warm surface of rock with her hands and saw the greenish shine of mica in the sun. Beneath her feet was a sandy crevice and she bent to peer into it—a flat cave large enough for a child to crawl through. On every hand was nostalgic memory. She leaned over to pick up a handful of sparkling sand from a crevice and let it sift through her fingers. Was this sifting away what was happening to her marriage? The boy she had said good-by to on these rocks was not the man she had married. Or was there perhaps less difference than she supposed? Had the promise of the man been there in the boy and she too young and adoring to sense in him the things she shrank from now?

Softly Dirk began to whistle and her heart caught in pain as she heard the tune, remembered the words. "I'll see my darling when the sun goes down . . . down, down below the mountain . . ." Sadly she turned the ring palmward on her finger so that the pink diamond would not glow so brightly in the sun.

He saw her gesture and it must have told him he would get

nothing more from her. This time it was he who said, "Let's go home," and there was a coolness in his eyes.

They clambered across the rocks and returned to the car. Dirk chose the lower road into Cape Town, below the flank of the Lion that made Signal Hill, and around Sea Point to the shores of Table Bay. Ahead the table was in view again and suddenly Susan felt oppressed and hemmed in by the mass of gray stone with its flanking, guardian hills. As she had always known, she could never escape the mountain. It knew everything.

17

THE TEA PARTY Niklaas van Pelt gave for Susan and Dirk proved a mixed success. The afternoon, to begin with, was gray, cold and drizzling. Mara, acting as hostess, looked beautiful but distant, so that her presence did little to warm the atmosphere.

It was clear to Susan that she detested the task that had been assigned her. When Mara's eyes met hers there was a fierce burning in them that was close to hatred. Susan, who had never found herself so intensely disliked before, recoiled inwardly and did her best to avoid the girl. Dirk seemed to notice nothing out of the ordinary and Susan could hardly appeal to him for protection against hostile glances.

In any event, it was impossible for her to give herself wholeheartedly to this affair when the aching soreness that had possessed her since that day on the mountain had never lessened for a moment. Dirk had not been unkind, but the breach between them had widened wordlessly. She knew he was blaming her for something she could not help. Memory would give her only so much and no more. There was no forcing it.

The matter of the destroyed film had gone unexplained. Dirk had not mentioned it again, nor had Susan. Indeed, it had begun to seem of little importance when set against the estrangement that had developed between herself and Dirk.

So Niklaas's tea came at an inopportune time, and Susan's heart was scarcely in it.

South Africans were a friendly people, and pleasant to know, but even the guests who came did not make it a complete success. It had been so long since Niklaas had entertained that there was a curiosity behind the polite façade of his visitors. And there was, as well, the usual undercurrent of uneasiness that so often presented itself in South Africa these days, so frequently possessed the conversation. Niklaas had many Afrikaner friends and their viewpoint was in political opposition to that of the English South Africans present.

One gray-haired English Capetonian spoke fervently to Susan on the subject. "I suppose you Americans are puzzled by what's going on down here. The majority vote is out of English hands—our own fault, too, since we practically gave away our birthright. And there's no way to save our necks down the beastly course we're being driven. Afrikanerdom wears blinders."

In opposition to this view, an old friend of her father's told Susan indignantly that the outside world did not understand the purpose of the great experiment of apartheid and should mind its own business.

"We want only to help the black man," he said with a fervor surpassing that of the Englishman. "When we separate the races completely, each can grow at his own pace and the black man will return to the tribal life that best suits him and govern himself as he wishes."

John Cornish had paused beside Susan to listen. "I know—I've been in the Transkei. But the white man still calls the tune there and makes the rules."

"We merely guide them wisely," the other man said and turned away.

John shook his head despairingly. "There's no ground on which we can get together. It's an Alice-in-Wonderland world when it comes to logic. The only thing that's sure is that everyone is badly scared and waiting for the next explosion. I hope I'll get my book done before it comes."

"How is it going?" Susan asked.

"Not very well. Your father manages to block me on all except obvious roads. We're still talking and at least I'm getting a clearer picture of the past."

Dirk joined them, nodding coolly to John, and after a few words the writer moved away, leaving Susan with her husband.

"How are you bearing up?" Dirk asked. "It's an odd lot Uncle Niklaas has invited here today. Oil and water. The trouble is that your father hasn't stirred himself to get out among people for so long that he doesn't know how fierce the issues are."

Someone spoke Dirk's name nearby and before he moved to answer he murmured a few words under his breath for Susan alone. "When we get home, darling, remind me to tell you how pretty you look."

His words surprised her and she tried to feel pleased and reassured, but everything had gone flat. She went over to where her father sat in an armchair, alone for a moment.

He spoke to her as she reached him. "Tell me about the gathering, Susan. Make me see it."

"I'll try," she said. "But, first, how did you know it was I?"

"Your scent, of course," he told her. "It's light and flowery, yet not too sweet. I could pick it out anywhere. I noticed it the first day you came to visit me."

"Appleblossom?" She must remember not to change, she thought to herself, touched that he had found this means of identifying her.

She took the liberty of painting the tea party in slightly more cheerful colors than were warranted as she told him about it. He listened attentively, but with a slightly disbelieving air.

"You describe everything with a photographer's thoroughness," he told her when she paused, "but I doubt if everything is going as smoothly as you say."

It was clear that he was not so ignorant of what was happening as Dirk thought.

A woman came up to speak to him and she could not answer. Later, after she had gone into the hall with someone who was leaving, she returned to the dining room to stand hesitantly near the door, looking about for Dirk, half concealed by a great jar of flowers on the sideboard. These days she was often at a loss when he was with her, yet when she was away from him she wanted unreasonably to be at his side again. As she stood there the voices of two women, hidden by the flowers, reached her.

"My husband says there's still a good bit of it going on, in spite of I.D.S.O., the security organization. There's always a leakage out of Cape Town."

The second woman's words were lightly mocking. "Perhaps Niklaas van Pelt is up to his old tricks?"

"That's unkind and unworthy of you," the first one said sharply.

The second woman laughed and they moved off together to have their teacups filled.

Susan went quickly away to find an empty corner of the living room where she could stand looking out at the gray day. The surge of angry emotion that swept through her was surprising. She had not known that anything could stir her to such anger in connection with her father. For just an instant she had needed to keep a restraint upon herself, lest she spring indignantly to his defense. It would do no good to involve herself and make a scene.

When the party at last drew to a close and guests began to leave, her one reaction was of relief because an ordeal was over. After the last visitor had gone, Dirk came to tell her that a question had arisen concerning the new stock of silver jewelry and he must remain for a little while with her father. He would be at home for dinner, and in the meantime Thomas could drive her home. But Susan said the drizzle seemed to have let up, and she would enjoy the walk.

Dirk joined her father in his study, and she went into the hall to put on the mackintosh she had worn against the rain. As she was buttoning it up, the doorbell rang and the maid appeared to accept a package from a man at the door.

"Mr. van Pelt's cigars," the maid said. She put the package on the hall table beside the Chinese vase and went back to her work of cleaning up after the party.

Susan considered the box of cigars for a moment. Why not take them to the study herself? Dirk had bustled her off rather hurriedly and she'd had no satisfactory opportunity to thank her father or to say more than a perfunctory good-by. The words of gossip she had overheard still left a bitter taste and she had the feeling that some small gesture toward him might help to erase them.

She reached out to pick up the package, but somehow the table runner of Indian brocade caught beneath it as she lifted the box. The big Chinese vase filled with proteas tilted forward at an alarming angle. Seized by her old horror of breaking anything, Susan dropped the cigars and reached for the vase, catching it just as it tipped toward her. Water splashed over her hands and the box she had dropped struck the corner of the table, bounced off to the floor with a crash and broke open, scattering its contents about. She had saved the vase at the cost of the cigars, but the latter mattered less.

With hands that were shaking she set the vase upright and searched her purse for a handkerchief to dry her hands. Then she knelt to put the cigars back in the box. She knew this trembling over nothing was ridiculous. Nevertheless, she fumbled clumsily as she picked them up. One had broken free from its cellophane wrapping, strewing tobacco on the floor. She snatched up the broken cigar, gathered up the shreds of tobacco and thrust the lot into the pocket of her mackintosh as guiltily as though she had been a child trying to hide some wrongdoing. Now she would have to tell her father what had happened, she thought in unreasonable dread. Perhaps he would let her buy him another box . . .

She was suddenly aware that someone was watching her and she looked up to see that Thomas had stepped into the hall. He came to help her and she was murmuring to him apologetically about what had happened when Mara came down the stairs.

Mara saw at once what had happened. "Don't trouble yourself," she said to Susan, sounding impatient over such clumsiness. "Do run along. We can take care of this. Thomas, fetch a brush, will you? That is, if you're sure, Mrs. Hohenfield, that you don't want him to drive you home." The spite in her eyes was barely veiled.

"No; it's not raining. I'll take the short cut," Susan said hastily. "But if you don't mind, I'll tell Father what happened first. It was entirely my fault."

"It's not necessary, but do as you like," Mara said curtly and began to rearrange the cigars in the box.

The moment Susan stepped into the study she knew she had interrupted some grave discussion her father was having with Dirk. Niklaas seemed a bit absent-minded as she explained about dropping the box of cigars, and Dirk looked distinctly displeased with her intrusion. She had half expected her father to reproach her for carelessness, as he used to do when she was a child, but he said merely that it did not matter, and dismissed her rather quickly.

When she returned to the hall Mara and Thomas were gone and so was the box of cigars. She let herself out the door and went through the dripping garden, feeling more disturbed and uneasy than ever. She had sensed some sort of cross-purpose between her father and Dirk and wondered what it was.

In the street she stood undecided for a moment. Overhead the sky looked threatening, as if it might pour at any minute. Should she go back and accept the offer of the car? But she did not want to return to the house. It would be better to chance the rain by way of the short cut and get home on foot.

The path was wet and muddy in spots, and she walked in the grass along the sides wherever possible. When she started the climb down into the ravine she moved more slowly than usual because of high heels, instead of walking shoes. The clouds overhead were scurrying before a wind that set the pine trees shivering and tugged the hood of her mackintosh back from her head. She had been letting her hair grow to please Dirk and she could feel the longer ends blow loose from their restraining pins.

On one hand the mountain stood black and wet, with silver falls of water down its face. The pine grove in the ravine was awhisper with raindrops falling from branches onto the brown, needle-strewn earth. Ahead, where the uphill climb toward home began, the tall rocks glistened like black marble, a little eerie in the gray light. The ravine was deserted, and it was foolish to be afraid of passing a mere huddle of rocks. Perhaps it was their shape that always vaguely disturbed her, as if they had been raised into position by some antique force that had left a malignant spell upon the place.

She thrust her hands deep into the pockets of the mackintosh, feeling the crumbled cigar beneath the fingers of her right hand. She had been foolish once today and once was enough. As she started up the hill toward the rocks she did not permit herself to hurry in the panic of her own imaginings.

There was no sound at all save the dripping of moisture from bushes and trees, and the movement of her own feet on the steepening path. The odor of wet pine was heavy on the moisture-laden air. She was safely past the rocks now and her fears had proved childish, as always. Soon she would be at the house and out of this cold wind. The crack of a twig on the path behind her sounded at the same instant that something struck her full in the back. She was flung forward to her knees, the breath knocked out of her, and something rough was thrust over her head and pulled down, smothering her cry, blinding her. A rude hand snatched the purse from her grasp and she heard the thud of someone running.

Kneeling on the wet stony path that bruised her knees, she

fought the coarse sack from her face and struggled free of its stifling odor of earth and potatoes. When she had pulled it from her
head she stumbled to her feet, the taste of earth in her mouth.
For an instant she glanced back at the black, silent rocks, the
dark cluster of pine trees and deepening shrubbery in the ravine.
There was no one in sight. Nothing moved, no footfall thudded.
Yet her assailant might be hiding there watching her. She turned
and ran toward home as quickly as her high heels would take her.

Willi met her at the door and saw her disheveled hair and the
mud on her mackintosh. Sensibly she asked no questions, but
picked up Susan's muddy shoes as she kicked them off.

"Someone was hiding in the ravine," Susan said. "Someone
snatched my purse. Willi, please call Mr. Hohenfield at my father's
and tell him what has happened. Ask him to come home right
away."

Willi went at once to telephone. Susan ran upstairs in her
stocking feet and began to walk nervously about the bedroom,
heedless of her wet mackintosh. She felt increasingly shaken by
what had happened, even though it might have been worse. At
least she had come out of the experience without serious physical
injury.

There was a sore place in the center of her back where the push
had come and her hands were scratched and bruised where she
had fallen on them. She wished they would stop their trembling
reaction and she thrust them into her pockets to steady them.
Again her fingers found the broken cigar and she drew it out,
aware of the not-unpleasant odor associated with her father, and
dropped it into a wastebasket.

Her mind was still going over what had happened to her—the
suddenness, the unexpectedness of the attack. Someone must have
been waiting in the shadow of those rocks, though that usually
empty path seemed an unlikely place to wait for a victim to rob.

She busied herself absently by taking off her coat and turning
the pocket inside out to rid it of tobacco shreds. Several bits of a
harder material fell out upon the carpet and she knelt to pick
them up. Four or five tiny hard pellets lay upon her palm. They
were dull in color—yellow, black, dark green. Bits of stone, they
seemed to be, smaller than a pea. Her attention caught, she retrieved the cigar from the wastebasket and crumbled the tobacco
over a piece of tissue. When the cigar had been reduced to powder,

she had collected a number of the tiny stones. They lay inert in her hand. Inert and possessed of terrifying implications.

Hearing Willi on the stairs, she wrapped the tissue quickly about her find and put it back in her mackintosh pocket. Willi reported that Mr. Hohenfield would be here at once, and remained in the doorway, her eyes questioning.

"I'll be all right," Susan assured her. "I was pushed down on the path with sacking over my head, but I wasn't really hurt."

When the girl had gone, Susan looked quickly about the room for a suitable hiding place. Then she tucked the packet of crumbled tobacco and tiny stones into the toe of a shoe in the armoire and set a shoe tree in against it. The cigars had been sent to her father and the knowledge left her alarmed. She did not want to tell Dirk or anyone else of her discovery until she had time to think about it.

Dirk came home a few moments later. He made her go over her story several times, explaining exactly what had happened. Then he phoned for the police. He was clearly concerned and did not remind her that he had advised against her use of the ravine path.

When the police came there was further questioning, though she could be of no help in identifying the person who had made the attack. The Afrikaner officer shook his head in grim disapproval over her walking about at dusk in the lonely ravine.

A search was made of the path she had followed and the potato bag was found, as well as her discarded purse, with the money missing. Sacking of the sort used might come from anywhere, and there were no other clues to be discovered. The path was used just enough so that there were footprints in muddy places of the few who had followed it. On the other hand, a man running in the grass along the side might leave hardly a trace of his passing. The officer concluded that it had been the act of some "Kaffir" who was interested only in the money she carried. She was fortunate not to have been seriously injured. Let this be a lesson to her.

Susan thought of the crumbled tobacco tucked away in the toe of a shoe in her wardrobe and said nothing. She could only hope there was no connection. No casual assailant could have known she had the cigar.

When the police had gone and the long-delayed dinner was served, she found it difficult to eat. The shock of what had happened had worn off a little, but she could not relax. The thought of those tiny significant pellets hidden away upstairs haunted her. She did not want to talk to Dirk about them. It was her father she must go to first. Tonight—immediately. But when she suggested seeing her father right after dinner, on the thin excuse of telling him what had happened to her, Dirk would not hear of her leaving the house.

He was gentler than he had been in a long while, but he was firm about the fact that she was to go up to bed right after dinner.

"There's a delayed reaction about this sort of thing," he warned. "I've already phoned the doctor to come in this evening and have a look at you."

Frustration made her all the more nervous but, though she fretted over Dirk's ministrations, there was nothing to do but give in.

When he had tucked the covers around her and gone downstairs, she lay awake with sleep the farthest thing from her mind. She could think only of the cigar and the tiny stones that had been hidden in it. Though she had never seen anything like them before, she could not doubt their importance. She knew very well what they must be. And her first hope that there had been no connection between what had happened to her on the path and her possession of that cigar was growing dimmer as she examined the possibilities.

Someone at Protea Hill was involved. Someone who knew she had dropped the box of cigars and broken it open, someone who suspected that she might have picked up a cigar from the contents and put it in her purse. There were just four people who knew what had happened, and there would have been time for one of them to cut ahead of her down the path and lie in waiting.

Thomas had found her in the hallway first, and then Mara. Leaving them, she had gone into the study and told Dirk and her father what had happened. A blind man could hardly have gone down the path to waylay her, even if he had been so inclined. But he might have sent someone else. She hated to believe that and turned her mind quickly to a readier suspicion. What of Mara? She knew perfectly well that Mara was capable of vindictive action against her. That rough thrust in her back might have carried the added strength of Mara's hatred.

Or had it been Thomas? She closed her eyes, shutting out the

170

light from a dressing-table lamp and thought about Thomas. Because he was a colored man she had a special reluctance to suspect him. That sort of thing was too easy, too much the obvious course to be taken by a person whose skin was white. Then, without warning, a vivid memory returned to her. She could see the man clearly as she had glimpsed him that day on the steps of the library, his rapt attention upon a book he had quickly hidden when he saw her. That day she had taken a picture of him. A picture that was on the strip of film that had been destroyed. A picture she had not remembered until now. She was beginning, all too reluctantly, to see where this might lead.

The doctor was long in arriving and Willi came upstairs with a cup of hot tea and an offer of encouraging sympathy. Susan watched as she moved quietly about the room, drawing the draperies across each window against the darkness.

"Willi," Susan said, her voice so low that it could be heard only in this room, "was it you who destroyed that strip of film?"

The girl was turning back the covers of Dirk's bed and her hands were suddenly still upon the satin coverlet.

"I don't want to hurt you, Willimina," Susan said, "but I need to know the truth."

The colored girl left her work and came to stand beside Susan's bed.

"Yes, Mrs. Hohenfield," she said. "I destroyed it."

"And it was Thomas who told you to get rid of it?"

For a moment longer the girl held to her outward calm. Then words began to spill out. They were spoken with spirit, revealing the often-hidden essence of independence in Willi. While she expressed regret, there was about her a dignity that was appealing. She had hated to do such a thing, she said, when she had been treated well in this house. Now she must leave, of course. She should have left before this. It was not right to stay on after what she had done.

"But why would Thomas tell you to destroy that strip of film? Was it because of the picture I took of him on the library steps? If he disliked my taking a picture of him, why couldn't he simply ask me not to print it or ask me to give him the negative? Why should the entire roll have been destroyed?"

Willi was quiet again. The moment of lost control was past. Her eyes met Susan's without fear but she stood silent, saying nothing. She might admit her own action, but it was clear that she would not further incriminate Thomas.

The bell rang downstairs and Willi turned toward the bedroom door. Suddenly Susan knew that she did not want to lose her, no matter what had happened.

"Wait a moment," Susan called, and the girl paused. "Don't leave us for good, Willi. Please stay."

There was surprise and sudden warmth in Willi's eyes. She nodded gravely, said, "Thank you," and went to answer the door.

Dirk came upstairs with the doctor and remained while he examined Susan's back and concluded that little damage had been done.

The sedative the doctor gave her did not take effect at once and when she was alone Susan lay thinking about what she must do. She must talk to someone, and very soon. John Cornish's words, so puzzling at the time, came back to her. He had warned her to be careful, though he had not told her of what. "Talk to someone you can trust," he'd said. Someone she could trust wholeheartedly. But who was there? She still shrank from going to Dirk though she did not want to examine the reasons for her reluctance too closely. And she was beginning to see that she could not go to her father either. She did not know how seriously he was involved. She did not want to judge him, but she could turn to him least of all.

No, it was John she must talk to. She could remember the odd sense of confidence that had come over her that day he had brought her home. There had been a feeling of strength about him, of a solidity which might serve her well if her need was great. Tomorrow she must find a way to see him without anyone else's knowledge. See him and show him those strange pellets she had found.

The sedative began to have its way and she dropped into a heavy sleep in which there were no dreams.

18

WHEN SHE WAKENED late the next morning, Susan felt a little groggy. Dirk's bed was empty, the covers thrown back. She had not heard him get up or heard him leave the house. Sleepily she touched the bell that would summon Willi and the morning cup of tea with which every proper South African began the day.

On the tray Willi brought to her was propped a note from Dirk. Susan sat up, sipping the hot, strong tea and reading Dirk's words as Willi flung open the draperies to a bright morning.

Regretfully, considering Susan's recent experience, Dirk was off to Johannesburg. Something had come up in her father's store there that needed his attention. Niklaas had told him yesterday, but he had not wanted to disturb her with the news after what had happened. He would be gone overnight and would fly home tomorrow on the afternoon plane.

"I hate to leave you at a time like this," he concluded. "But the doctor said there was nothing to worry about. Do be careful, darling. And miss me a little."

She folded the paper into its envelope with a sense of lassitude. Only a little while ago she would have been desolate at the thought of being parted from Dirk for a day. This was the first time he had been away from her overnight, and she did not care. Perhaps it was the drug the doctor had given her that had left this limp indifference. Except that it was laced with something like relief as well. She did not want to believe that she would not miss Dirk and yet, suddenly, that seemed to be the truth. It was a distinct relief to know that she need not see him today.

The telephone rang downstairs as Willi turned toward the door.

"Perhaps that is Mr. Cornish," she said. "He rang up earlier, Mrs. Hohenfield, and I said you were still sleeping."

She went down to answer the phone and Susan slipped out of bed and put on a dressing gown. She followed Willi downstairs and took the phone from her.

"Susan?" It was John's voice. "I've been concerned about what happened to you last night."

"I'm fine now," she told him, and the sense of relief she had felt over Dirk's absence increased. She was free now to talk to John. Willi had gone out to the kitchen and she lowered her voice. "I'd like to see you sometime today, if you can make it. Not here or at Protea Hill. There's something I want to consult you about. Dirk has gone to Jo'burg and won't be home till tomorrow, so I can get away at any time."

"Then what about dinner?" he said. "What time shall I pick you up?"

She glanced over her shoulder, but the hallway was empty, the door to the rear of the house closed.

"Let me meet you away from the house. And please don't say anything there about having dinner with me."

He named a small restaurant where she might meet him. She hung up with the certainty that John Cornish would know what everything meant. He would take the pieces out of her hands and tell her what to do. It did not even seem strange that she should be willing to place herself in his hands, when only a little while ago she had been bitterly set against him. Now she was only sorry that she must get through an entire day before she could be rid of her burden of worry and bewilderment.

When she had bathed and dressed and had breakfast alone in the dining room she tried to think of something to do with her day. Perhaps she would read awhile, sit in the garden with some sewing—anything to make the time pass. Twice she opened her wardrobe and checked the presence of the wrapped-up tissue thrust into the toe of a shoe.

It was nearly noon when the doorbell rang and Willi came to say that Mr. van Pelt was here to see her. Surprised, Susan hurried downstairs and found her father standing in the middle of the living room, one hand on his cane, the other upon the arm of Thomas Scott.

174

"Good morning, Father," she said, and gave the colored man a quick look. "Good morning, Thomas."

Thomas returned her greeting without meeting her eyes, and there was nothing to be read in his light-skinned, good-looking face.

"How are you feeling?" Niklaas asked, holding out his hand to Susan. "I want you to tell me exactly what happened."

"I'm perfectly all right," she said. "A little stiff, perhaps, nothing more. Thomas, will you bring a chair for my father, please."

Thomas drew forward an armchair, but he did not help Niklaas into it. The old man felt for it with his cane and sat down without undue groping.

"Don't go away, Thomas," he said. "We won't be long and I'll need you shortly."

Thomas said, "Yes, sir," and went to stand near the doorway to the hall. He faced the room, but he did not look at either of them.

"Now then," Niklaas said to Susan, "tell me what happened. From the beginning. When did you leave my house?"

She told him how she had hesitated over the weather and then started home by way of the short cut.

"And you saw no one along the way? Heard nothing?"

"Nothing at all," she said. "Nothing until I heard someone on the path just before I was knocked down. A rough bag that smelled of potatoes was pulled over my head and by the time I was able to struggle out of it and get to my feet whoever it was had snatched my purse and run away. I dashed for home and asked Willi to telephone Dirk. That's all that happened."

Again she glanced at Thomas and saw that he was staring at something on the opposite wall of the room with a fixed gaze that made her curious. When she turned her head she saw that the object which held his attention was the whip, the *sjambok* Dirk had fastened against the wall. But there was no telling from his face whether he really saw the whip or what his reaction was to her story.

Her father seemed lost in grave thought over what she had told him.

"Was there anything in your purse that someone might have wanted?" he asked at length.

She could answer that readily. "Only a little money, which was taken," she said. But her thoughts were upon those strange small stones hidden away in the bedroom upstairs. Did he know? Was that what he meant? Did he know perfectly well that what was sought had not been retrieved?

The dark glasses were like a guard upon his thoughts. Nothing was revealed behind them.

"You must avoid the short cut from now on," he said. "These are uneasy days in South Africa. Take care, my dear."

Was there a warning in his tone? She could not be sure.

He smiled at her suddenly, lightening the mood of the interview, changing the subject deliberately. "As soon as you feel yourself again, I'd like you to join me on a small trip. Every spring I take a morning's drive around the Cape. We'll make a little party of it this year. Perhaps a picnic at Cape Point. If Dirk agrees to drive the car, I'll give Thomas a day off. Eh, Thomas?"

"Thank you, sir," Thomas said and continued to stare at the wall.

"I must learn to get on without Thomas before long," Niklaas went on. "There's a school post coming up for him shortly in one of the new locations. I shall miss him, but I'll be glad to see him get what he wants. Perhaps you can talk Willimina into marrying you now, my boy."

Thomas said nothing, but for a moment the familiar bitterness showed in his eyes.

Susan saw it and spoke to him across the room. "Thomas, do you remember the time I photographed you on the steps of the library? What was the book you were reading that day?"

For the first time he looked at her directly. "It was a book by Mr. Cornish, madam."

"The one on Ghana?" Niklaas put in. "You read me several passages from it and I thought it very good."

Thomas offered no opinion and Susan felt increasingly puzzled. There would seem to be little reason why Thomas should be disturbed because she had seen him reading a book by John Cornish. Or why he should later have asked Willi to destroy the film.

"It is a book about freedom," her father mused. "About the difficulties and the price and responsibility freedom brings with it. Democracy has to be both learned and earned. Wouldn't you say so, Thomas?"

For once the colored man stepped out of his careful role. "At least, sir, they are stewing in their own juices in Ghana. Which is better than being stewed by someone else."

Niklaas nodded. "There's something to that, of course." He seemed oddly amused by his own words. Once more he changed the subject, turning to the personal as it concerned his daughter. "Tell me what you've done with this room, Susan. I knew the house years ago when a friend lived in it long before I became its owner. Tell me so that I can picture you in a setting."

She did her best to describe the room for him, explaining how the furniture was arranged, telling him of her own touches of small bright pillows that were not frilly and pink like Claire's. And of her framed photographs on the wall. When she had finished, she looked again at Thomas.

"Have I forgotten anything?"

"Yes, madam," he said and nodded toward the wall. "That." He did not name it, but left it for her to do so.

It was the whip he had indicated and Susan mentioned it reluctantly.

"Dirk has put a South African *sjambok* on the wall," she said. "A whip that once belonged to his father."

For an instant the room was as still as it sometimes was at night when Dirk was away from the house and the darkness seemed so quiet and ominous.

Abruptly Niklaas held out his hand. "Bring it to me, Thomas."

The colored man was tall. His long arms reached up to the brackets which held the black whip; he took it down and brought it to her father without a word.

The old man ran his fingers along the thickening of the handle. His sensitive, seeing fingers came to the initials that had been cut into the leather. He weighed the whip in his hand for a moment as though he were satisfied.

"It is the one," he said and gave it back to Thomas.

The colored man replaced it on the wall while Susan watched in bewilderment.

"What do you mean, Father?" she asked. "Have you seen that before?"

"I have. You might ask Dirk about it sometime." He stood up, tall and straight, and as cold as she had often seen him as a child. "If you please, Thomas," he said.

177

Thomas came at once to offer his arm. They crossed the unfamiliar room and Susan went with them to the door.

"Thank you for coming, Father," she said. "And you needn't be concerned—I'm quite all right."

He went down the steps on Thomas's arm and seemed to remember their number, so that he did not hesitate when he reached the walk, but followed it quite surely to the gate. Susan ran ahead to open it for them and her father paused before he went out to the car.

"On second thought, my dear, it might be wiser to say nothing at all to Dirk about that whip. Old angers are best left buried. Eh, Thomas?"

"Yes, sir," Thomas said, and there was no inflection of any kind in the words. He helped the old man into the car and they drove away.

When they had gone Susan returned to the living room and stared at the whip on the wall. What an ugly thing it was. And why, if there were angry memories bound up in it, had Dirk wanted to display it upon the wall of his living room?

She turned from it impatiently. How weary she was growing of secrets, of hidden threats, of knowledge withheld. What a relief it would be to talk to John Cornish tonight, to tell him everything and see what he could make of the odd pieces.

Once more she ran upstairs and checked the hiding place of the small stones. It was nonsense to worry about them, of course. No one was likely to steal them from under her watchful eyes. And this evening she would take them with her to show John.

Late in the afternoon, when she was dressing to meet him, she decided, half grimly, half in amusement at her own action, to set a few small traps. Here and there about the bedroom she made small preparations. Here a drawer left open an eighth of an inch, there a tracing of face powder upon a knob, a bedroom slipper set at an exact angle on the floor of the wardrobe, the hangers just so on the rod. And, as a last touch, the little carved impala put in an exact spot on the gold tooling of the jewel case on her dressing table. Then she took a last look at herself in the mirror and approved the simple black dress with its scoop neck and wide satin collar that set off to good effect her necklace and earrings of American Indian turquoise.

She put on a coat and a decorative veil over her hair. She had already told Willi and the cook that she would be out for dinner tonight and when the time came she phoned for a cab.

When they drew up before the small Swiss restaurant John had named, she recognized the van Pelt Mercedes at the curb. John Cornish was waiting for her inside.

"Your father generously offered me his car for the evening," John said as the hostess placed them at a corner table.

They were early for the regular dinner hour and for the moment had the small room to themselves. It was a bright, simple room, with scenes of Switzerland on the wall, a cuckoo clock in the form of a chalet, and yellow primroses set in small blue vases on all the tables.

He had dined here before, John told her, and the food was good. They ordered fondue and when the waitress had gone John poured wine for her from the bottle he had brought with him. One of the delectable wines of the Cape. Susan took the small packet of stones from her handbag and poured them into an ashtray on the table.

Four students came into the restaurant and took the next table —two girls and two young men. They too had brought their own wine, as was apparently the custom in an unlicensed place, and were laughing and talking, paying no attention to anyone else.

Susan pushed the ashtray toward John. "Are these what I think they are?"

He picked up a green stone and rolled it about on his palm, then dropped it back in the tray.

"Better put them out of sight before anyone sees them."

"Then I'm right?" She wrapped the stones in the tissue. "They're industrial diamonds, aren't they?"

"Bort," he said softly. "Diamond residue that won't make gem stones but is used for industrials and diamond dust. How on earth did you get the stuff?"

She told him about the cigars which had come to Protea Hill for her father, of her own carelessness in dropping the box, and of the way she had nervously picked up the broken cigar and put it into her pocket.

He heard her through, his expression grave. "Where do you think this leads to?" he asked, more as if he were curious about her conclusions than that he had any doubt about his own.

179

"Isn't it possible," she said, "that whoever snatched my purse yesterday was trying to retrieve the cigar with the stones hidden in it? If that's true, then someone in my father's house . . ." She paused, not willing to mention names.

John Cornish nodded a bit grimly. "It's not only possible. It is, I'm afraid, quite likely."

A waitress brought the steaming hot tureen of fondue and a green salad served at the table from a big wooden bowl. The students at the next table were lively and their voices filled the little room.

Susan speared a cube of bread on a fork and dipped it into the fragrant mixture of cheese, eggs and wine. Her attention, however, was scarcely on the food she was eating.

"I still don't understand. Why would anyone smuggle this—this residue from diamonds? If it is smuggling. How could it be worthwhile?"

"Illicit Diamond Buying—I.D.B., as they call it here—doesn't restrict itself to gem stones," John said. "The market for industrial diamonds is enormous. The demand is always greater than the supply allowed upon the market. In the past decade or so hundreds of new uses have been found for industrials and the United States, as well as Russia, has been stockpiling them. They're harder than gem stones and suited for the pressures of high-precision tools. Their value in the making of armaments is especially important. The West hasn't been willing to sell industrials to Russia, so she gets them on the black market and pays a good price."

"Then these are valuable?"

"Not when compared to gem stones. It takes a lot of carats of this stuff to add up to real money. But there are grades of value even here. What they call bort is really poor-grade stones. But up from that there are degrees of hardness, of quality, that raise the value. If I remember my figures—and I've done some research on this—industrials account for eighty per cent of the diamond business in bulk and perhaps twenty-five per cent in profit. Not to be sneezed at. Especially if a gem stone is smuggled into the lot occasionally, as is likely to be the case."

He was silent, dipping thoughtfully into the fondue. Frightening possibilities rose in Susan's mind. No wonder someone who knew she had picked up the cigar might be desperate to regain possession of it. Desperate enough, indeed, to make an attack upon her in order to search her purse. Who? Which one in Niklaas van Pelt's house?

She spoke the thought aloud. "John, who could it be?"

"I don't know," John said evenly. "There's not much use in speculating, is there? We can go in circles that way. Besides, there's something else that troubles me."

"What do you mean?"

"The cigars. Why would anyone try to smuggle diamonds by hiding them in a box of cigars?"

"Why not?" she asked. "I should think that would be a very good way to conceal them."

He quirked an eyebrow at her. "Exactly. And one of the oldest tricks there is. Cigars are always suspect when sent or carried across boundaries where inspection takes place. How did this package come to the house?"

"I think it was by special messenger," Susan said. "It must have been sent inside the country."

"Then a fairly obvious means of concealment wouldn't matter. Though I wonder why it should be used in the first place."

"They would have to go out of the country sometime," Susan said. "Perhaps they were intended to go from Protea Hill by means of another step."

"But why *cigars*? Why the most obvious means possible? There's something here I don't understand."

"I don't understand any of it," Susan said. And added forlornly, "Perhaps I'm afraid to understand."

The charm of the little restaurant and the excellent food were wasted that evening, and briefly Susan regretted the fact. Perhaps John Cornish would bring her back another time, on a happier occasion. Though that was unlikely. She would not be out with John again. As it was, this was one more thing she could never tell Dirk.

When they had finished the meal with fruit and coffee, Susan sat on at the table, reluctant to leave, feeling that the puzzle had deepened instead of being dispelled.

John sensed her concern. "We've a bit more talking to do, and since we have the car, why not go for a drive and discuss these matters further?"

She was relieved not to go home in her present unsettled state of mind. When they were in the car he turned toward the Kloof

Nek Road and followed its winding length up the hill. She wondered if he was going out along Table Mountain, but when he reached the place where the roads branched he made a sharp turn right onto the road that ran the length of the Lion.

A cool wind blew past the car and Susan turned up her coat collar, though she liked the feel of its freshness on her face through the open window. The road climbed in a straight line toward Signal Hill, and Cape Town lay below them, a bright carpet of light. When they had made a final circle around the hill and come out on top, the entire coast was visible, with the lights of sea towns beading the edge of the dark Atlantic.

They sat in the car for a few moments, held by the tremendous view. Then, pausing now and then, stumbling a little, Susan began to tell him of the way she had remembered having once held the Kimberley Royal in her hands as a child. And of her mother's taking it from her and hiding it in a silver-topped powder bowl. It no longer mattered that she had once regarded John Cornish with distrust or that his purpose had been to expose her mother to an accusation she could not defend.

"She had the diamond in her possession," Susan concluded. "Yet I still find it hard to believe that she actually meant to steal it. She was more like a little girl that day, playing a trick to amuse herself and fool someone. When she thought she had lost the stone she was frightened, but as soon as she had it again she seemed to be enjoying herself."

"What if I use what you've told me in my book?" John asked, studying her curiously in the dashboard light.

She returned his look, meeting his eyes without hesitation, liking what she saw. At the moment he reminded her of that badly lighted picture she had seen of him on a book jacket. His eyes were steady and deep-set, his mouth surprisingly sensitive in so strong a face. He no longer seemed a cold person to her, though he hid his feelings behind a reserve that broke down only when he was angry.

"If it's necessary to you, then you'll have to use it," she said. "Whatever you use will be the truth. I know that now."

"I don't want to hurt you, Susan," he said, "but sometimes the truth can be a shattering thing."

"I know," she agreed.

He looked away from her. "I'm sure now that there's something hidden going on in your father's house. My room's over the terrace and once or twice visitors have come at odd hours. I don't quite like it, but I don't know what to think."

Susan took the little wad of green and yellow stones from her purse. "To do with this, do you suppose?"

"What else am I to believe, now that I've seen these?" He took the tissue from her and opened it so that the dull stones were spread out upon the paper. "Some of these may be of good quality as industrials. And here's one that might even be a small gem stone. Some diamonds have a sort of greenish skin over them, you know, and there's no telling their worth till the skin is removed and the expert can look into the heart of the stone."

"Where do you think they come from?" Susan asked.

He shrugged. "There are many places. It's not too hard to smuggle diamonds in small quantity out of Sierra Leone these days. Or they might come from South-West Africa, or the Congo."

"But then they would have to be smuggled into South Africa, as well as out. Why would anyone go to that trouble?"

"Smuggling them in isn't nearly as big a problem as getting them out. Of course the more direct way would be through Beirut. In these days of planes Cape Town is a back door, yet it's still a good port for diamond smuggling. Ships stop here from every country. And there are deep-water coves along the coastline that can't be watched all the time. Of course it's even possible that this stuff is coming out of the Kimberley area or from around Pretoria."

"But aren't the big mines guarded?"

"No absolute way has ever been found to guard them. Trained dogs are used and high electric fences. Africans are let off the premises only at intervals and they are carefully searched. X ray has done away with some of the former indignities. But there are always white men who have to be trusted and who come and go without much interference. You can't X ray a man every time he leaves the mine—you'd kill him. So there are still leaks. This may be one of them." He folded the tissue carefully around the small stones. "Will you let me keep these for the time being?"

"I want you to keep them," she said. "I don't want them in my possession, now that I know what they are. Will you—" she hesitated—"will you go to the police about this?"

"I'd rather wait awhile," he said. "Once before I acted too hastily. I want to be sure this time. Have you told Dirk about these stones?"

"No!" she cried, and was astonished at the strength of her own denial.

John gave her a quick, sidelong glance as if her tone surprised him too. But he said nothing, and she was relieved when he switched on the engine and turned the car back along the road by which they had come. There were questions she had not asked, suspicions she had not put into words, a fear that she had not expressed. Now she did not want to. Any direction her thoughts might take seemed frightening and she could not choose their course safely.

John drove her downtown where the Cape Town streets were growing quiet, unlike Johannesburg after dark. At her request he put her into a taxi and she went home alone.

In the bedroom upstairs at the Aerie a lamp burned against her return and her night things were laid out upon the bed, her slippers on the floor. She had forgotten that of course Willi would be doing these things for her. So her little traps were foolish and no test at all. In the wardrobe her clothes had been slid a little way along the rod, her shoes moved on the floor when the slippers were taken out. The drawer that had been left a fraction of an inch open was neatly closed. And it all proved nothing.

Except—there was still one thing. There would be no reason why her small jewel box should be touched in any way, yet when she looked closely she saw that the little impala no longer sat upon the gold tooling where she had left it.

The discovery galvanized her into action. She ran downstairs and out the back door. The yard was hushed and still, with the nearness of the mountain somehow adding to the quiet. Light shone along the sill of Willi's door and Susan tapped upon the panel.

19

WILLI CAME AT once to open the door, a book in her hands. She stepped aside to admit her visitor and Susan saw other books on a table and scattered on the bed. They were schoolbooks, so Willi was apparently studying by herself.

Susan went directly to the point. "Willi, did anyone come to the house while I was out this evening?"

For an instant the girl's eyes wavered. "I've been out here reading, Mrs. Hohenfield," she said.

"Did you go upstairs and search the bedroom?" Susan asked.

"Oh, no!" Willi cried, and her distress was evident. "I put your things out for the night, Mrs. Hohenfield, and then I came straight out here to study."

"And after that? Who came to the house tonight, Willi?"

The girl clasped her hands tightly about the book she held and then released her grip with a helpless gesture and dropped it on a table. "Miss Bellman came," she said. "I let her in and waited downstairs while she went up to your room."

"Was she there very long?"

Willi sighed. "I didn't look at a clock. It seemed a long while. Perhaps half an hour."

Enough time for a rather careful search of a single room.

"What excuse did she give you?" Susan asked.

"She didn't give any." Willi threw further caution aside and spoke frankly. "When I came here, she warned me that it might be necessary to protect Mr. van Pelt in certain ways. She told me that because you were the daughter of the wife who left him, we could not wholly trust you, even if Mr. Hohenfield chose to shut his eyes to the danger. She said there might be times when we must watch what you did."

A nice little plot on Mara's part. With more reasons behind it than Willi knew. Mara, hating Dirk's wife, would be anxious to know all she could about her.

"Yet you're telling me all this now," Susan said.

Willi spoke without hesitation. "Because I don't believe you would ever try to harm your father, Mrs. Hohenfield. Because—" suddenly she discarded the maid's guise she wore in this house and became what she was, a young woman of courage and intelligence —"because I like you. And because I trust you more than I do Miss Bellman."

Impulsively Susan held out her hand. "I want to trust you, Willi. Thank you for telling me."

Willi took her hand in a firm clasp, but her dark eyes were troubled and Susan sensed torn loyalties in the girl. Not so much to Mara Bellman, but to Thomas, perhaps, and to Niklaas van Pelt.

"You can count on one thing," Susan assured her. "I would never willingly injure my father. We all know he has suffered enough."

"Thomas's parents worked on the farm the van Pelts used to have in the veld," Willi said. "So Thomas has known him all his life. He knew him at the time of his trouble, though he wasn't working for him then. Thomas would do *anything* for your father, Mrs. Hohenfield. I think there's no other white man he wholly trusts."

Her emphasis on the word "anything" was almost a warning, though Susan did not know what she was being warned against. She turned toward the door, then paused.

"I understand Thomas is to receive a teaching post," she said. "Will this make matters easier for you?"

"I'm not sure," Willi said. "I just don't know."

Susan then said good night and returned to the house. Twice now Willi had failed her, yet Susan's instinctive trust of the girl and liking for her remained. If Willi would only realize it, she and Susan were on the same side in their desire to protect Niklaas van Pelt from further harm. Might this be, in the long run, a difficult thing to do? An impossible thing—since John Cornish now held that little cache of stones?

Lately something of her old feeling for her father had risen in her again, and added to it were new respect and admiration for his courage in these trouble-inflicted years. She found it difficult to believe any wrong of him and she did not want to see him needlessly injured. There had been diamonds in the cigars sent to him, but that did not necessarily make him an accessory.

The emptiness, the quiet of the house was oppressive tonight. She could not endure the living room with that whip making an ugly black slash across the wall. The bedroom at least was brighter, but the loneliness here seemed even greater. It was almost a palpable thing that hung upon the air, something she drew in with every breath. She was shut away from everyone tonight—not only in her physical presence in this house but in her mind and spirit as well, through her own dread of looming calamity. Yet in her longing to stave off disaster she could turn to no one. Not to her father or Dirk, not even now to John Cornish, whom she trusted yet who might himself spell danger. Nor to Willi, who was coming to be her friend, but who had a prior loyalty.

She lay restless upon her bed, trying to think, trying to find an answer. Someone in her father's house was engaged in smuggling industrial diamonds. This much at least was clear. Mara Bellman had handled the cigars and knew that Susan must have picked up the missing cigar with its hidden stones. Mara had come to this house tonight and searched through Susan's things in this very bedroom. She had counted on Willi not to betray her.

But Mara might be no more than an instrument, just as Willi had been an instrument and perhaps Thomas as well. Whose was the brain and will behind all this? There were only two people from whom to choose. Her father and her husband. Perhaps both together?

She remembered the words John Cornish had spoken that time in the Public Gardens when he had made her so angry. Wasn't it better, he had said, to hurt the dead than the living? Her mother had held the Kimberley Royal in her hands. She had hidden it—whether playfully or cunningly, her daughter had no idea. The truth might reveal that Niklaas had been bitterly betrayed by a woman who had sought only to save herself. Painful though the choice between them might be, Susan no longer wanted to protect Claire's reputation blindly. Her father mattered more.

Yet now something else had come into the picture. There was a present-day connection with diamonds with which her mother had nothing to do. Had the gossip at the tea party been true? Could it be possible that her father, having the name, had decided that he would have the game as well? What was the meaning of those nighttime visits to the house John Cornish had mentioned? Who was coming to see him and why?

Then, as John had pointed out, there was the curious matter of the cigars. Why *cigars* if such a means was too shopworn to use?

She sat up in bed and wrapped her arms about her knees, rocking back and forth in bewilderment and worry. The house was so empty, so lonely. Yet this was nothing new. It was always lonely, she admitted in sudden honesty, even when Dirk was home. Falling in love had been an exciting thing, a rapturous, hasty, reckless thing, an unhoped-for gift of all she had ever longed for. Or so she had believed at the time. But growing in love was something else and a marriage that involved no growth was empty of meaning. Love had to be lived before it was truly real. And where was the living together in this marriage even when they were in the same house?

The pendulum swung once more through its confusing arc. What if it were not her father behind Mara? What if it had been Dirk? Dirk pushing her down on the path, thrusting that rough bag over her head, fleeing before he could be recognized. This was the thing she had been holding away, refusing to face. Had she the courage to face it now, to seek the answer deliberately, to know for sure? When she knew the answer—what then? What of life and marriage and love, if this thing were true?

The telephone bell downstairs shattered the silence. Let it ring, Susan thought. There was no one she wanted to talk to. But she knew she could not ignore it. The ringing might bring Willi inside to see why she had not answered. Besides, to call at this hour, the person who phoned must have good reason.

She went downstairs and took the receiver from the hook, spoke into it.

"I miss you, darling," Dirk's voice said over the miles from Johannesburg.

Something in her quivered and responded with heedless joy. She had loved him so long ago as a little girl. And she loved him now as a woman. The shimmering melancholy of loneliness that had seemed to hang in the air fell away and there was in her only a longing for Dirk's arms and his love securely around her.

"Are you coming home tomorrow?" she cried. "I hate it here without you!"

He was reassuring and affectionate and regretful. The business her father had sent him on would take longer than he had expected. He might go on to Durban tomorrow and perhaps to Basutoland. So he would be gone for several days more.

"Father is planning a trip around the Cape," she told him wistfully, though she knew this was a child's coaxing. "He wanted you to drive."

Dirk's laughter had a dry sound. "At least I'll be spared the trip this year. Go with him, darling, and keep him happy. Let him tell you about every landmark along the way and explain about the shipwrecks and the storms. But not for me. Not this year. If you like, we'll do the trip again by ourselves later."

"I'd love that," she said. "We don't do enough things together." It was easier to talk to him over the miles of mountain and veld than when he was in the room beside her and so quick to grow impatient.

"I know," he said more warmly. "And we must mend that. Let's make a date right now, darling. You've wanted to go up the mountain—so I'll take you up the very day I get home. That's a promise."

Whether it was the mountain or something else, she did not care, just so she would be with Dirk.

"I love you," she said. "I'll be waiting."

When he rang off she put the phone down and went upstairs, warm now and tingling. No, it was not Dirk! Whatever was happening it was not because of Dirk. She had been in a gloomy mood because she was lonely. Love, after all, was not a steady flame. It burned sometimes high, sometimes low, depending on those concerned. So long as it always leapt up high and warm again, there was nothing to fear.

There was no reason to believe that anyone was behind Mara Bellman. Or, if anyone was, then it must be someone who had no connection with Protea Hill.

She went to a window and flung open the draperies that Willi had closed. The mountain was there, waiting, and stars hung brightly above it. She had heard that the top was like some strange

189

landscape of the moon, bleak and awesome and vast. Had she lived here when she was older she would have climbed it, as all Cape Town children climbed it sooner or later, by way of the easy trails, if not up the precipices. For her first trip, however, she would gladly settle for the fun of the cable car with Dirk. And tea at the top.

"I'll be seeing you soon," she told the mountain and turned back to the room.

When Dirk came home she would tell him about Mara's coming here, searching this room. She would tell him about the stones she had found and entrusted to John Cornish's care. The pendulum had swung full arc again and, clinging to its high point, she could believe that this was where it would stay, improbably arrested at the peak of its flight and against all laws of gravity.

She slept well that night and there was no blue fire in her dreams.

During the next few days there was an interlude of calm while she waited for Dirk's return. An interlude during which she busied herself with small matters and thrust away whatever might disturb her or force her into thinking. It was not necessary to face these problems alone. When Dirk came home she would talk to him. He would help her. He would know what to do.

Toward the end of the week the spring weather turned cool and misty again and clouds lay over the table and hid the Lion's Head. A strong wind blew across Cape Town. At least it was not raining and Susan never minded misty weather. She put on her mackintosh and pulled its hood over her head. Then she set off for a walk downtown.

Today she chose Long Street because she liked its ironwork balconies and its two unexpected palm trees, around which traffic had to swerve. After a few blocks she cut across to Adderley, stopping along the way in a *boekwinkel* to see if they had John Cornish's book on Ghana. They had not, but took an order. Then she strolled beneath the arcades of Adderley and past van Riebeeck high on his pedestal surveying the town he had helped to create. Over in the Parade Ground hustlers picked up what change they could by making a great show of helping motorists to park.

Susan turned back on Adderley to her father's shop and stood looking into the always fascinating window. There was a display of beautifully carved animals: a rhinoceros with his great mouth gaping, a big-eared African elephant, a graceful springbok. She must ask Dirk to bring home some companions for the impala, she thought, walking on.

Little things were important, only little things. When the minor matters of the day became too inconsequential to dwell on, it meant that one's mind was troubled and depressed. Today she would not be depressed. She would remain in a state of pleasant suspension until Dirk came home.

Now she followed Adderley back toward the mountain till she reached the alley that housed the flower market. Here she would purchase more chinks to cheer up the house. She would bank it with flowers against Dirk's homecoming—which would be soon now, soon, though he had not yet told her when. But before she filled her arms with blooms she would take a few more pictures of the flower market to replace those on the film Willi had destroyed. Her mind flicked at the subject and winced quickly away. No, not today. This was the sort of thought she must guard against.

She gave herself over to reveling in color and scent and texture. She smiled at the colored women who offered her their wares, moved on to the far end of the market and turned about.

Niklaas van Pelt, leaning upon Thomas's arm, his cane in one hand, was entering from the Adderley Street end. This was perfect, Susan thought. Now she could retake the pictures of him in the midst of these flower stalls. She uncased her light meter to determine the exposure. Thomas did not see her down the length of the market. He left Niklaas at his usual place, touched his cap, and went away without glancing about.

Susan took a few steps down the long aisle of flowers, studying first the meter and then the subject. It was a gray day, lacking the shadows that gave a picture contrast and depth. But her film was fast and she would give it a try.

The same plump woman reached up to free Niklaas of his cane and he bent toward the nearest basin of flowers, absorbing their fragrance.

Susan stood stock still, suddenly arrested. The greeting which had risen to her lips was stilled. In a flash of searing clarity she understood how the second step of the smuggling was managed, and how cleverly and innocently it was done. No crude cigars were being used this time. This way was far better. She felt sick with the shock of knowledge, shaken to the point of nausea. And she could not bear to speak to her father.

Somehow she slipped past him, so close that she could have reached out and touched his arm. With the scent of the flowers all about, he would not catch her perfume today. No one noticed her except as a possible buyer of flowers, and in a moment she was on the street again, walking hurriedly toward the Avenue.

The mist was wet upon her cheeks—or was she crying? Crying because she had nearly found her father, only to lose him again. For good this time. Now she knew who had given the order to have that film destroyed. Thomas had seen her taking the pictures when he had come for Niklaas that day. He would have reported the fact, of course. The picture taken of Thomas on the library steps had nothing to do with the matter. The order had been relayed by way of Thomas to Willi. And again the order to stop her had been given when something had been missing from the cigar box. By whom, she knew now, and *to* whom did not matter. It was her father who had given both these orders. Perhaps to Mara, more likely to Thomas. Perhaps even to Dirk, if Dirk was aware of these matters. Though she would not yet believe that Dirk would accept such an assignment. She would see him soon and would ask him for the truth.

Along the red dirt path of the Avenue were little puddles and the young oak trees dripped moisture on either side. The handsome white towers of the Jewish temple rose against a misty backdrop of mountain, and all about her the doves burbled and cooed. Only a few moments before the peace of this place would have suited her mood. Now she scarcely noted where she walked as she climbed the hill toward home. When she turned through the gate at the Aerie, she found the light meter still in her hands.

Willi heard her step on the walk and left her work to open the door.

"Your father rang up about an hour ago, Mrs. Hohenfield," Willi said. "He was disappointed not to catch you."

Susan scarcely heard her. There was nothing she wanted to say to her father, or to hear from him, at the moment.

Willi took her coat and followed her into the living room. "Mr. van Pelt asked me to give you a message. He said the weather should clear tomorrow and be fine, so he is planning to motor around the Cape. Mr. Cornish has offered to drive. Mr. van Pelt will have a picnic lunch packed and if you are ready at nine in the morning he will pick you up. If this suits your convenience, he said you need not ring him back."

She could not go, Susan thought. She could not face her father until she had thought this thing through, decided upon some course of action. No action at all was now inconceivable.

Willi was watching her, puzzled and a little anxious. Susan tried to smile.

"Thank you," she said. "I may call my father later."

But she did not call him. By evening she still had not called. She had nothing to say to him. She could not even bring herself to tell him that she could not accept his invitation for the trip around the Cape. If he asked for a reason, what was she to say?

After Willi had retired to her room, Susan sat listening for a long while to the radio, trying to think against the quieting background of music. Someone was singing a program of songs in Afrikaans—old folk tunes of the sort that Dirk often loved to whistle.

"Marching to Pretoria . . ."

It occurred to her abruptly that there was something she could do if she went tomorrow. She could tell John Cornish what she had discovered. If she went on the trip, it was likely they might have a little time together while Niklaas rested. There was nothing else she could do, no one else to whom she could turn.

The weather report for the Union of South Africa came on and fine weather was promised. There was not even the hope that a storm would develop out of today's murk and enable her to do nothing, postpone all action, if that should be her wish.

By morning she knew that the weather report would hold true. She dressed in dark-green slacks with twin brown sweaters and a green kerchief tied in a band about her hair. Her every move was listless and the heaviness of her spirit could not have been greater.

When Willi came to say that Mr. Cornish was waiting downstairs for her, she picked up her camera, slung the heavy strap of her big leather bag indifferently over her shoulder, caught up a coat against the winds of the Cape, and went to face her father.

20

NIKLAAS VAN PELT sat in the back seat of the car, his head turned in the direction of the house, as if he listened for his daughter's step. When she said, "Good morning," and started into the car beside him, he stopped her.

"Why not sit up in front with John, my dear? I have the lunch back here. Mara was too busy to join us today, but she had something packed for us."

John had come to open the car door and Susan was aware of his look as she got in. She knew he had sensed that something was wrong, even more wrong than before. But he said nothing and turned the car toward the Kloof Nek where they could go through the pass and drop down the other side to run out along the Marine Drive. They drove in silence past Camp's Bay, and Susan remembered walking across the sands with Dirk only a little while ago.

How much did Dirk know of what occurred in the flower market? she wondered unhappily. Perhaps nothing. Surely he too had been fooled by the cleverness of Niklaas van Pelt. She must believe this, must hold to it until she saw him again and he could speak for himself.

As they followed the drive she watched the sea on one hand and the changing peaks on the other. Once she turned in her seat to look back at her father. He sat with his cane clasped between his hands, his head turning first toward the Atlantic, feeling the sea breeze against his face, then turning toward the mountains, as if he could sense their weight and presence. There was no gentleness in his face today, no betraying of thoughts behind the guard he had learned to wear.

How defenseless a blind person must feel, Susan thought. Those he could not see were free to study him as they pleased, intrude, perhaps, as a person with sight is never intruded upon. But Niklaas had learned to hide his secrets well behind the cold mask of his face, behind the dark glitter of his glasses. Only once had she surprised him without the mask—that time in the little garden for the blind. That day she had softened toward him as she could not soften now.

Niklaas spoke aloud, almost as if to himself. "Drake said it was the fairest of all capes, and Diaz called it the Cape of Storms."

"While we," John Cornish added, "call it, ironically, the Cape of Good Hope."

"Ironically?" Niklaas said.

"What good hope is there for South Africa?"

"That again? You must admit that our government has held down the disturbances," Niklaas said mildly.

"Toward what end result?" John was impatient. "You'd think we believed in the legend of the boy and the dike. If Hans stands long enough with his thumb in the crack the waters will recede. But any man of sense knows they won't. The pressure is building and the dike is going to be smashed flat, with chaos resulting. Nevertheless, Hans stands there stubbornly, shouting that others are interfering and he can hold back the waters alone in his own way."

Susan glanced at her father and saw that he was smiling.

"You think about these matters a great deal, don't you?" he asked John.

"How can I not?"

"Since you can do nothing, why not let events take their course and leave action to those who better understand the problem?"

"That's exactly what I mean to do," John said angrily. "Though I doubt that there's much understanding on the part of those in power."

Quietly Niklaas changed the subject, and Susan, whose sympathies were entirely with John's viewpoint, hardened a little further against her father.

"Where are we now?" Niklaas asked.

"Chapman's Peak is directly ahead," John told him. "Look your longest, Susan; this is the finest scenery of the Cape."

On their left the mountains rose in grandeur, jagged and steep, their stony slopes partly wooded. And where there were woods there were arum lilies—great white carpets of them—and everywhere wildflowers growing among the rocks. On the sea side the embankment dropped away in steep cliffs, gull haunted, with South Atlantic breakers rolling in at their base, roaring above the purr of the car.

"Here's a point where we can stop," John said and turned the car off the road beside a rocky lookout. He helped the old man from the car and led him gently to a place where he could stand with the sea wind in his face and the mountains massed behind him. Susan chose a spot a little away from the two. She did not want to be near her father or to touch him. The sickness of heart she had felt in the flower market yesterday had abated not at all.

John stood at the parapet, watching the frothing sea below, and his expression was grave and a little sad. "One has a curious feeling sometimes in returning to a familiar place. Earth and rocks and sea and mountains have such permanence. There's no change here, even though everything else in life may have changed."

Niklaas understood. "You came here last with Janet, didn't you?"

"Do you remember her?" John asked.

"Very well. A quiet, serene young woman. A good balance for you, I always thought. You were often too intense, too involved in the things you wrote about."

"Once it seemed a good thing to be involved," John said.

"But now," said Niklaas, "you are merely angry without being involved?"

John made a movement of impatience and spoke to Susan. "How is the picture series coming along?"

"It's not," she told him. "I'm still looking for scenes that will really tell the story."

"Perhaps I can help you," he said. "There are places I can show you around Cape Town. The *pondokkies* on the Cape Flats, for instance, where squatters live in the most utter destitution."

The old man seemed to have heard enough. He put his hand upon the sun-warmed rock of the lookout point with an air of authority. "Enough of this talk for now, or I'm afraid our trip will be spoiled. Susan, I've been in this place before too. More than once with your mother. She used to enjoy the drive around the Cape."

Susan said nothing, refusing to be softened by this reference to her mother. He must have sensed the resistance in her, for when he went on the chill had returned to his voice.

"John has told me that you remember seeing Claire with a stone that must have been the Kimberley. That you were playing with the stone and she took it away from you. Have you recalled anything more about that occasion?"

She answered him shortly. "Nothing more. I don't know what she did with it after she hid it in the powder bowl."

She expected him to urge her to recall the rest, as Dirk had urged her, but he did not.

"Perhaps it's better to let it stay forgotten," he advised. "Better not try to remember. Shall we go on now?"

Once such advice from him would have reassured her. It did not now. She could only remember how important all concealment must be to him. Perhaps of the past as well as the present.

They returned to the car and followed the intricate curves of the coastline down the Cape Peninsula. The scenes were varied: small beaches of white sand and little fishing villages; breaks in the mountain rampart through which green inland valleys cupped by hills were visible. Then the road took a center course as the land flattened toward the farthest tip of the Cape. But not, John said, the farthest tip of Africa. Oddly enough, Cape of Good Hope was not the end of Africa. Cape Agulhas across False Bay stretched farther south. Yet it was the Cape of Good Hope—the Cape of Storms—a sailor sought to round, and warmer currents were met when the point was passed, even though the Indian Ocean began technically around the farther cape.

They had entered the nature reserve now and Susan began to watch for animals. While none of the larger beasts were to be found here, many smaller varieties roamed free under protection. She remembered from her childhood the exciting watch for the wild creatures that blended so well with rocks and vegetation that one had to look long to see them. Once, close beside the road, they came upon an elderly baboon. He remained where he was, staring them haughtily out of countenance. Several of his female companions ran skittishly off to hide themselves in a pile of rocks, but the male posed with great self-possession while Susan took his picture.

As they moved on, the Cape narrowed and grew rockbound as

it pointed into the sea. On either side of the paved road wild-flowers grew in profusion. Cormorants perched on the sea rocks, and the *dassies*—those small-eared rock rabbits of South Africa—lay sunning themselves on landward outcroppings.

A rocky hill rising ahead was Cape Point itself. The car could to no farther.

John found a place to park and carried the basket lunch, while Niklaas took Susan's arm. They followed the lower road along the False Bay side, moving toward the new lighthouse. Above, on the peak of rock, was the older lighthouse, which had not been wholly successful, since ships had still wrecked themselves on the extending toe of rock below.

Here the sun was warm and pleasant and they were shielded from the Atlantic breeze. John found a big flat rock below the road and Susan helped him spread out blankets and cushions upon it. Soberly, with a distinct lack of picnic gaiety, she began to unpack the lunch.

Of the three, only Niklaas seemed contented and for the moment amiably disposed. He had remained unruffled by their earlier discussion, and while, as always, he seemed a little remote, he had clearly come on this trip to enjoy himself. They ate egg and sardine and watercress sandwiches, and nibbled sticky plum tarts.

In the distance the dim outline of Table Mountain was visible, and John nodded in its direction.

"From the top of the table you can see the entire Cape on a clear day," he told Susan. "Have you been up there yet?"

She shook her head. "Dirk has promised to take me up when he gets back from his trip."

"I'd planned to take you climbing up there by the time you were eight or nine," her father said. "Your mother disliked heights and would never go up the mountain. In the beginning when I was in prison I used to think about the time when I would be free again and you and your mother would return to South Africa. Then you and I would go up the mountain together."

Susan glanced at him uncomfortably. "But you never wanted us back. You never wrote."

He was quiet for a time. With one hand he reached out toward a scrubby bush beside the rock and plucked absently at its tough green spikes.

"I wrote," he said at length. "I wrote while I was in prison—to you as well as to your mother. And I wrote again when I was free."

Susan heard him in disbelief. "But there were no letters! Mother told me there were no letters."

He went on, paying no attention to her words. "When I sold the Johannesburg house and moved to Cape Town, I kept your room as it was in the hope that you would at least return for a visit. I suppose I kept it as a sort of hostage to fate. By that time I knew Claire would never return, but you still might if I kept it ready for you. I couldn't blame Claire. She was not one to be tied to a blind man."

"But she didn't know you were blind!" Susan cried. "Of course she never knew."

"She knew," Niklaas said quietly.

Susan stared at him, stricken. "But she never told me. She never said a word."

"Perhaps that was the kinder way, as far as you were concerned."

His tone was as cool and detached as though he spoke of some stranger whose wounds he could not feel, and Susan could not bear to hear him. She could not bear to be so torn herself. Torn between what she knew of him so recently and the anguish rising in her for what he had suffered in the past. How could she condemn him for what he was doing now when so much that was cruel had been done to him?

She had lost what appetite she had and now got up restlessly and sprang from the rock to the road. "If you don't mind, I think I'll climb to the old lighthouse. I'd like to take a few pictures."

"You were always snapping pictures as a little thing, too," Niklaas said. "I can remember how you treasured the small camera I gave you. And how devastated you were when you broke it."

Susan stood uncertain on the path, puzzled by his words. "But I never told you I had broken it," she said. "I can remember how frightened I was of letting you know. You always hated it when I broke anything and when you lost your temper I was terrified. So I never told you I'd broken it at all."

"Of course you told me," her father said. "You even brought it to me one day in my study to show me the damage."

She continued to watch him uneasily, though she did not know what it was she tried to read in his face. How could she have been so convinced all these years that she had never shown him the broken camera? Something stirred vaguely in the dim reaches of the past. Something frightening, something shattering. In memory angry voices sounded again in rising fury and there was the shrillness of a telephone that rang and rang. She covered her face with her hands, swaying a little.

"Are you all right, Susan?" John called to her. He jumped down to the path and took her arm, steadying her.

The mists receded. "It's nothing," she said. "A moment's dizziness. Will you walk with me to the top?"

"Go with her," Niklaas said. "I shall be content here." He had taken a cigar from his pocket to clip and light, and they left him smoking peacefully.

John and Susan walked back to the place where a steep concrete pavement led straight to the top of the rocky hill. The road was closed to general traffic, but open to pedestrians and the jeeps that served the houses clustered at the top. Far above two slim radio towers pointed toward the sky.

When they had climbed to the enclosure around the old lighthouse, John drew her to a place where she could lean on the wall and follow with her eyes the sweep of the Cape around the wide curve of False Bay. The Hottentots Holland range was misty blue in the distance. John's thoughts, however, were not on the view.

"Something has happened, hasn't it?" he asked. "I knew the moment I saw you this morning that something was wrong."

She had been waiting for an opportunity to tell him what she had seen in the flower market yesterday. Yet now she held back the words, reluctant to speak. What good would it do to involve the lost, saddened man who was her father? How could she lift a finger to injure him further, no matter what he might be doing now?

"I can't tell you," she said. "I must think first. I need more time to think."

"I won't press you," he said. "But, Susan—" the concern in his voice deepened—"don't put yourself in some dangerous position."

"Dangerous?" She glanced at him quickly. "What danger could there be?"

"Knowledge can be dangerous if it puts someone else in jeopardy. Are you sure this isn't something you ought to share for your own safety? Remember, there's been one attack upon you and there's someone still wondering whether you found those stones."

She shook her head, afraid to think of the stones, afraid to know the face of her assailant. John's eyes were kind and his mouth had lost its sober lines.

"Courage is something I admire," he said gently. "It's a quality I've sensed in you from the first. But don't let it carry you too far. Ask for help if you need it."

She looked into his face and saw more than kindness there, saw in him a hint of tenderness, as if she had been a very young person whom he wanted to protect. Did he mean the courage to hurt her father? she wondered. Or was there something else in his mind—something still more devastating?

"I don't know how much courage of any sort I have," she said. "All I know is that I'm confused. I'm not sure of my directions. I don't know yet which way I must turn."

Unexpectedly he put his hand beneath her chin and tilted her head so that his eyes held hers. What she saw in their depths made her a little afraid. More and more this man was coming to be a safe harbor—the one person to whom she could turn with confidence and trust. But this would not do. His face must not come between her and Dirk. She needed no such harbor. She turned abruptly from his touch, Dirk's image sharp and clear in her mind, and at once John drew back as if he too were aware of a barrier he must not pass.

She walked about the base of the lighthouse, peered down the rocky cliffs, made a great show of being interested in their surroundings, and John Cornish watched her in silence. When he spoke again his words startled her.

"Why do you have a *sjambok* on the wall of your living room?" he asked.

The suddenness of the question took her aback and she stammered a little in answering, not wanting him to know how much she hated the whip that Dirk had hung upon the wall.

"It—it belonged to Dirk's father, I believe. It was a—a whim of Dirk's to hang it on the wall. I'm not sure why."

"There are initials cut into the handle?" John asked. "The letters of his father's name?"

Susan's hands were still on the strap of her camera. "How did you know?"

"I've held the whip in my hands," John said. "I remember it

201

very well. This morning I saw it again on the wall of your living room."

There was something in his tone that caught her sensitive ear. "You know the story behind the whip? Will you tell me, please? Tell me what happened."

He made no attempt at evasion. "You and your mother were still in South Africa at the time, though you weren't at the farm in the veld when it happened. Janet and I had been recently married. We went there for a visit. One day your father used that whip in a flogging. I stopped him and took the whip away from him."

"But why would my father do such a thing?" Susan asked in dismay.

"He was capable of great anger when he was aroused. Life hadn't chastened him then. Once he was a strong and rather violent man. It's sad to see the fire burned out so that nothing rouses him now."

"Who was it he flogged?" Susan asked. "Someone who worked for him on the farm?"

John looked down toward the surf curling below the steep rocks of the point. He spoke without looking at her. "It was Dirk Hohenfield he whipped that day. Later your father thanked me for stopping him. For all his rage, he would never have injured Dirk when he was in his right senses."

Something turned painfully within Susan. "But what had Dirk done to cause my father to fly into a rage?"

John shook his head. "I never knew the reason. I didn't ask. I simply got the whip away from him and went into the house until everyone could cool off. I didn't see Dirk again before Janet and I left, and your father never mentioned the cause of what happened."

The surf far below had a chill sound as it broke about the rocks of the point. The South Atlantic held a steely glitter beneath the sun and the breeze had turned cold.

Susan could bear to hear no more. All feeling in her seemed drawn to a taut, thin strand that might snap at any minute.

"Remember that all this happened a very long time ago," John said. "Dirk was only a boy. Everyone has forgotten it by this time."

Dirk had not forgotten, she thought as they started down the steep roadway. Not with that whip upon the wall. But she did not want to think of that now. She wanted only to put the ugly memory of the whip from her mind.

Casually John caught her hand as they went down the walk and she found the pressure of his fingers comforting. Had he come here with Janet too? she wondered, and felt a sudden pity for his loss and his loneliness.

"I'm sorry about your wife," she said softly.

"This trip has brought her back," John admitted. "I've been thinking of her a good deal ever since we left Cape Town. But all that belongs to another lifetime. Not to the one I'm living now."

She understood what he meant. All lives seemed to break into segments. Her own too. The segment of her childhood in South Africa. The growing-up years in Chicago. The new world of the newspaper and all that pertained to it. Then the world of Dirk that she was living now. She pressed John's fingers gently and slipped her hand from his.

They found the old man as they had left him, his cigar smoked to a stub, his attitude one of listening, as if he waited for their coming, ready to start home.

The three of them had little to say on the drive up the opposite side of the Cape. Susan curled herself in the front seat, watching the clean little towns and villages slip past. But her thoughts were not upon them. She was remembering what her father had told her of the day she had brought her broken camera to him. A day she had buried carefully in the past—for what reason she did not know. This time she would not try to shut the door.

Let it open—let it open fully! She was ready for the answer now. A purpose began to come clear in her mind. She knew very well what must be done. A new impatience seized her to reach home and be off on her own private mission as soon as possible.

21

When Niklaas said he had some errands downtown and asked John to drive him there, Susan felt an enormous relief. She did not request them to drop her at her true destination, preferring to let her purpose remain secret for the moment. When they left her at the Aerie and drove away, she went into the house only long enough to rid herself of her camera equipment. Then, still wearing her coat and with her big leather handbag slung over her shoulder, she set off for Protea Hill. The key to her old room was in her bag and she was sure now of the one object that would bring memory flooding back.

Somewhere she had built up a block against what had happened, but there would be a way to level the barrier, to remember fully. She must finish this before Dirk came home. Then she would know whether or not she must tell him what she had discovered about her father.

The maid was long in answering her ring. Susan greeted her a little breathlessly. Asking no permission, she ran past her up the stairs and down the hall. She hoped Mara would not be about today. This was something she wanted to achieve quickly without her knowledge.

To her surprise, the door of her childhood room stood open and a breeze blew into the hall from the windows. She paused in dismay in the doorway to see that the promised spring cleaning was under way and that the housemaid was working here under the supervision of Mara Bellman. Mara herself knelt on a cushion beside the toy chest, with articles from the big *kist* heaped on the floor beside her. In her hands she held the small box camera and she opened the back to peer into it as Susan came indignantly into the room.

For a breathless moment the two stared at each other in open antagonism. All the pent-up resentment and distrust and jealousy Susan had felt toward this woman surged up in an angry wave of feeling.

"What are you doing here?" she cried. "I haven't given you permission to go through my things!"

A flush tinted Mara's fair skin, but she did not rise from her position on the floor.

"It's a job long overdue," she said, waving a scornful hand at the toys she had heaped on the floor. "All this seems to be trash and I was sure you'd be willing to let us get rid of it."

"I'm not willing!" Susan spoke sharply. "My father has left everything in this room in my hands and I want it left alone. Will you go, please?"

Mara made no move to comply. She still held the camera with its back open and again she looked into the small black box curiously. She shook it as if she half expected something to rattle or fall out. Susan watched her in an agony of impatience, wondering what she would do if Mara chose to oppose her. But the other woman shrugged in elaborate indifference, set the camera back in the chest, and got slowly to her feet.

"As you like," she said, and nodded to the maid to come with her out of the room.

The moment they had gone, Susan swung the door shut and ran to the chest. She picked up the camera and then stood looking uncertainly about the room. Was there anything else? Any other object that would speak to her as she had felt the camera would? There seemed to be nothing and she went to the closed door and stood very still, listening for any sound she might catch from the hall beyond. All seemed to be quiet.

She opened the door cautiously. No one was in sight. The door of Mara's room stood closed. Moving almost stealthily, Susan hurried along the hall and down the stairs to the landing. At the newel post in the entry hall below Mara stood waiting for her. The flush had vanished from her cheeks and she was very pale. Her eyes went at once to the camera.

For an uneasy instant Susan wondered if she might try to take it from her, but her entire purpose had been keyed to this moment. She would not be stopped or delayed. She went down the stairs with all the stubbornness and determination of her father and passed Mara without a word. The other woman did not try to stop her, and she went directly to her father's study and closed its door behind her.

The room seemed empty and strange without his familiar figure behind the great desk. But this was where she wanted to be, and she must be here when he was not present. There was no key by which she could lock Mara out and she could only hope that the woman would not follow her here. Quietly she seated herself on a small footstool in one corner, the camera in her hands. Even the choice of the footstool as a place to sit seemed right, and part of a pattern in which she now seemed to move without volition or choice.

Her father had been right in what he had said today about the camera. She had indeed told him of dropping it and breaking the lens. He had summoned her into his study to lecture her on the subject of being more careful with her possessions. He had told her to sit on this very stool—which had been just her size. She could remember the way she had stared at the pattern in the carpet while he talked to her about her increasing carelessness.

She had been upset, but had not then been filled with paralyzing alarm. Indeed, she had been more uncomfortable listening to his words than she had been frightened. Mainly she had been sorry about the camera, which she had treasured, and hopeful that he might mend it or buy her a new one.

It developed quickly that he intended nothing of the kind: "When I was a boy," he said, "and I broke something out of carelessness, I was told that I must either mend it myself or do without. I believe we've come to the place where this rule must be applied to you, Susan. I'm afraid you must now mend your camera yourself or go without."

His words were a blow, but still not terrifying. She sat hunched upon the footstool with tears in her eyes, wondering if she could move him to pity so that he would relent. But she knew this was not likely. When the telephone on his desk rang, he picked it up calmly enough. Neither of them had known that the call would change everything in life for them, that afterwards nothing would be the same again.

She remembered watching him a little resentfully, waiting for the call to end, so that his attention could return to her. But it had not. His face had blanched and his voice turned cold as he answered the person on the wire. She could recall the very words he had spoken, but who it was she never knew—a friend? a business acquaintance? the police?

"What you are saying is impossible. I have no uncut diamonds in my possession. Neither here nor in Johannesburg."

The man on the other end of the wire went on and Susan saw her father's expression grow strained and grim as he listened. When he hung up the phone he touched the bell that summoned the maid and sent her to find Claire. He looked so coldly formidable that Susan edged her stool into a corner and sat very still so that he would not notice her and vent his anger upon her.

How well she remembered her mother coming gaily into the room. She was wearing a flowered green dress, the color of ferns, and in her hair a white rose. Then she had seen her husband's face and the smile had left her own. This was when the time of terror had begun.

Coldly Niklaas told her that, thanks to a lead from some outside source, his house in Johannesburg had been searched and a cache of uncut diamonds had been found there. What, he demanded, could she tell him of this? Claire began to weep and deny, but Niklaas persisted in cold accusation. When she would not answer, he left his desk and took her by her soft plump shoulders, shaking her until she went limp in his hands. Limp and ready to admit everything. Yes, she had managed to take the stones when she was working for the company. She had not wanted to give them up. They had meant safety and security, no matter what happened. And diamonds were so pretty, so fascinating.

Neither had noticed the child in the corner, withered by the cruel anger, the accusations, and the rising voices. The telephone began to ring again, but Niklaas ignored it. He flung Claire from him roughly, so that she fell against the desk and bruised her arm. She had shown Susan the blue mark later as evidence of his cruelty. He had almost stepped on Susan, cowering in her corner, before he saw her. Then he had shouted at her to get out of this room and stay out. She had no business here. She was to leave at once!

Terrified, Susan fled from the room and upstairs, the camera still clutched in her hands. All her small world that was bounded so securely by her parents had been shivered into fearful splinters by those angry voices downstairs. Wounding splinters that pierced her spirit as glass might have pierced her flesh. Her father detested her, that was clear. He had looked at her with hatred in his eyes, and her mother had done nothing to come to her aid. Her mother, giving in to an excess of wild weeping, had forgotten she existed.

Her own room upstairs was lonely and the camera in her hands reproached her. The conviction was growing in her young mind that she had brought all these terrible things about when she had wickedly broken the camera her father had given her. For a while she sat on the bed in her room turning the small black box this way and that, wondering how she could fix the broken lens. If only she could mend it and make the camera work again, then surely her father would stop hating her and stop hating her mother. Her mother would stop crying and there would be no more angry words shouted between them.

Because of her enormous need, the answer came to her quite simply and clearly. It would take a very special sort of glass to make a lens, and it was possible that she knew where there was just such a piece she might use. Moving on tiptoe, without a sound, she ran into her mother's room and prodded with her fingers in the powder bowl. The stone was still there.

Now, so many years later, the grown-up Susan crouched on the footstool as the child had done, and her hands trembled as she opened the camera. Like Mara upstairs, she peered into the box. It was black inside and empty. There was nothing there. The film holder had long been lost and the camera was useless. She shook it hard as Mara had done and something shiny fell out in her lap. She picked it up and held it on the palm of her hand. It was only a piece of the broken lens.

Then she reached her fingers deep inside the box and felt behind the shutter. Nerves prickled at the back of her neck. Fumbling in her haste, she managed to pry up an end of sticky material that ripped loose when she pulled it. Stuck to her fingers was a strip of black mending tape that had been stuck crossways behind the shutter. Again her fingers searched and found the second criss-cross of tape. When she pulled it loose something came with it, adhering to the material. Held in place as it had been by the covering of almost invisible black tape, it had lain hidden all these years. Susan stared in fascination at the stone she held in her hand.

It was colorless and transparent, perhaps an inch or more in length and somewhat less in thickness, cut in an oblong shape.

In the shadowy room it lay lusterless upon her palm with none of the shimmer of a diamond. But diamonds, of course, once freed from the darkness of the inner earth where they were born in fire, could live only upon light.

She walked to the French doors and stepped through them. Bright daylight flooded the terrace. When she held out her hand the Kimberley Royal sprang magically to life. Light splintered into bright rainbows in its depths and glinted blue fire from the very heart of the stone. Yet it was a fire without warmth, and the stone was cold in her hand. It seemed to her a stone of evil omen and she was unable to suppress the quiver that touched her skin to gooseflesh.

Returning to the shadows, she sat in her father's chair with the camera before her on the desk. She could remember everything now. Men in uniform had come to the house and her father had gone away with them. There had been no time to show him the mended camera after all, so the bad fortune held, the evil she had done did not end. Her mother had cried endlessly, while the child, Susan, sat in her room and stared at the mountain until it seemed to lean menacingly toward her. Perhaps if she stared long enough, it would tip over and crush her—which was, no doubt, what she truly deserved.

So much she remembered!

How heavy the diamond seemed now in her hands, colder than any other stone, leaving her as chill as the stone itself.

There had been a further outburst from her mother when Claire had found the stone missing from her powder bowl. But she had not known whom to accuse or where to turn without betraying herself. She had questioned her daughter tearfully, but Susan by that time had been too frightened to confess what she had done. Besides, this was something for her father to see. Only he would understand about the camera.

She knew now why her mother had fled from Africa. Claire had been afraid that she would be the one to go to prison, and that was something she could not face. But Niklaas had taken her guilt upon his own shoulders and his "confession" had left her free to do as she pleased. The fact that the Kimberley was missing had not come to light until years later as far as the public was concerned. And in the meantime Claire had urged forgetfulness upon her daughter. "Forget, forget," her mother had said. "Don't try to remember what happened there." And Susan, confused, frightened, guilt-ridden almost to the point of illness, had drawn a merciful veil across her memory. Only now and then through the years had the veil fluttered, lifting away from the terror it had hidden. Whenever she dropped something or broke even the most trifling object, the gossamer shield would tremble, allowing incomprehensible fears to flow through her.

The sickness and hurt were back again in this moment, magnified many times over, though the guilt sense had faded. Her hurt was for her father now and all her love. She understood her mother's guilt and her father's innocence. Only that disturbing thing she had seen in the flower market stood unexplained in her mind, and because of what had happened in the past she would not now accept that without giving him a chance to answer for himself.

Distant voices sounded in another part of the house and she wondered if he had come home. She would wait for him here and when he came in she would give him the stone. He had paid for it with his own fortune. It belonged to him now. But more than that, she would tell him the things she had remembered and she would tell him what she had seen in the flower market.

Steps sounded in the hallway outside the door, but the footfall was firm and decisive, not the slightly shuffling sound of an elderly blind man's step. She had just time to slip the diamond into her handbag and click the camera shut before the door opened and Dirk came into the room.

There was an electric excitement in him, she saw at once. Something had happened to him that she did not understand and it made her wary. He swooped down upon her and pulled her out of the chair and into his arms.

"I *have* missed you!" he cried, his cheek against her bright hair.

When he kissed her she waited for the melting to run through her, and the familiar warm response of her blood. But nothing happened. Only the wariness remained and a resistance to his arms. He sensed her lack of response and dropped his arms from about her, but he offered no reproach.

"I went home first," he told her, "and then phoned here. Mara said you were in the house, so I came right over. I wanted to surprise you." His eyes searched her face keenly. "And I see that I have."

"You should have let me know, so I could be at the airport to meet you," she said, trying to cover whatever she might have betrayed. "I'm just home from the drive around the Cape with my father."

"And with John Cornish?" he said.

He reached past her across the desk and picked up the camera as she watched him uneasily. Her father must know before anyone else that she had found the stone. She had no intention of telling Dirk. He looked into the box almost idly and dropped it back on the desk. Had Mara told him of her sudden appearance in the room upstairs and of how she had taken the camera down to the study? But, though Mara had looked into the box, the black tape would have kept her from seeing anything. There was nothing she could have told Dirk except that his wife had carried away the camera.

"Are you ready to go up the mountain?" Dirk asked, still smiling in that oddly elated way.

"Up the mountain?" she echoed. "Now?"

"Why not? There's plenty of daylight left and the cars are running. I noticed on the way over. Remember—I promised to take you up there the very first thing when I got home."

"I've made one trip today," she objected feebly. "It's not as important as all that. Let's go tomorrow."

"It's important to me," he said, and she knew that the imperious mood when he would not be balked in his most trivial wish was once more upon him.

She shook her head helplessly, aware that opposition would only stiffen him in his purpose, yet not knowing what else to offer. She had no heart for the mountain now. She wanted only to sit at this desk and wait until her father and John Cornish came home.

"Of course we'll go now," he said. "You're dressed for it with low-heeled shoes, a warm coat, and slacks for climbing. Besides, we may not have time for this again."

There was an air of triumph in the puzzling words that made her stare at him.

"I've something to tell you," he said. "But let's get started first. We can talk about it at tea on the mountaintop. Come along, darling."

He held out his hand and took a step toward her. Then he paused, looking down at the carpet to see what he had stepped on.

Lifting one foot, he examined the sole of his shoe. Susan watched as he peeled a black strip of sticky tape from the leather. Instead of discarding it, he turned it about in his fingers, studying it as if it had something to tell him.

Quite suddenly Susan was frightened. She did not want him to suspect that she had found the diamond or that she carried it in her bag. She did not know how he would take the discovery of so much wealth that her father did not know existed. What if he tried to persuade her not to tell Niklaas? She forced her fascinated gaze from the bit of black stuff in his fingers and stood up, her handbag flung carelessly by its strap over her shoulder, as if it could not possibly hold a fortune.

"All right," she said. "Since you're in the mood, let's go up the mountain."

He dropped the strip of tape into an ashtray and linked his arm through hers. "Good girl! We'll be up on top in no time at all. I'll show you the greatest sight in the world, and I'll tell you my news."

What did it matter? she thought. It would be better to make the trip up the mountain and get it out of the way since he wanted to go. Safer, really, than to sit here behaving in a way that was clearly odd, waiting for her father to come home.

Dirk called upstairs to Mara to tell her where they were going and they went out together to his car.

22

Once they were on their way she felt a little better. Now that she had given in to what he wanted, he was in a gay mood—cheerful and amusing and affectionate. If she had not been carrying a fortune in her handbag, she might have felt more at ease with him.

They left the car in the parking place at the foot of the cable house and went up the long flight of stairs inside the building. A car was about to leave and when Dirk had bought tickets, they hurried to join the group going through the door. On the walls of the cable house were huge pictures of British royalty visiting the top of Table Mountain—pictures of the younger princesses Elizabeth and Margaret coming down the steps from the landing platform with their mother, the Queen.

In the tunnel-like room there was a steady clanking of cable machinery, and ahead people were packing themselves into the small car. The guard had a South African accent, dropping his h's and blurring his syllables as he performed an obviously routine task. The holiday visitors to the mountaintop were a gay lot, the girls ready to laugh, the men showing off just a little.

There were small end seats in the car, but no one wanted to sit down. Part of the fun was to look out the windows as the car went up the mountain. Dirk was the last one in behind Susan. The door closed and the car slid gently away from the platform and began its smooth climb up the cable to the top. No one seemed to mind the fact that passengers leaned dizzily out the open windows. When Susan looked down at the steepening rock cliffs below she was glad to have Dirk's arm firmly about her.

She inched her handbag more securely up the shoulder away

213

from the window and kept a hand upon its clasp. The thought of dropping the Kimberley Royal down a mountainside or of having her pocket picked made her feel quite hollow.

How small the car seemed against all this spread of nearby rock and distant hills and ocean. Even the tawny head of the Lion, with the sun dipping toward it, was left below as the car swept upward, its tiny shadow moving along the cliffs below. Murmurs from the passengers made Susan turn in time to see the sister car coming down, carrying its waving human freight. If only she could catch a little more of this holiday spirit and fill the queer hollow within, still the fearful shivering that had begun as the car moved up the mountain. It was not the height that frightened her, and the diamond was perfectly safe in her bag, so she was not sure why she trembled.

The trip took only a few minutes. As the car reached the final steep rampart of rock, Susan looked out dizzily to see a girl and boy in shorts and cleated boots, ropes tied about their waists, as they sought for toeholds in the sheer precipice. Again the quiver ran through her. Rock climbing, certainly, would never be for her. This ascent in a suspended car was quite enough.

Except for pointing out landmarks, Dirk had little to say on the way up and she was uncomfortably aware that he was watching her more than he watched the scenery. But, then, he had been up here many times and would naturally be interested in her reactions.

At the top the car slid into its cubicle in the tall white stone building that looked so small from below. A solid, squarish mass, the structure was, rooted in rock and undoubtedly able to withstand the gales that must belabor the mountain. They left the car to walk about the observation section behind guard rails, and Susan noted a warning sign: WHEN HEARING THE HOOTER PASSENGERS MUST PLEASE RETURN AT ONCE.

"Does anyone ever get left up here?" Susan asked.

"It's not uncommon," Dirk said. "Every year climbers get caught by sudden changes of the weather. Sometimes they spend a few cold, wet hours before they get down—if they're not close enough to reach the tearoom. Sometimes they get themselves stuck climbing up and have to be rescued. The Mountain Climbers Club is called upon for rescue duty every so often."

"I suppose there are falls too," Susan said, looking down over the dizzy cliffs of rock.

"The mountain still claims its sacrifices," Dirk said lightly.

She stood for a while studying the wide stretches of countryside spread out below. All of Cape Town could be seen, of course, and the far beaches beyond the Lion's Head. When they moved around to another vantage point, the entire Cape Peninsula stretched before them like a relief map. Susan could see clear to the distant point where she and John had stood earlier today. At the memory a queer regret touched her. How much more secure she would have felt if it had been John beside her now instead of Dirk, in whom she dared not confide.

The teahouse was built of stone and set in a hollow where tall boulders shielded it part way around and made it invisible from the ground below.

"This is a good day for the trip," Dirk said. "There's almost a dead calm up here. Let's have tea before we tackle the mountain itself," and he led her down a walk to the doorway.

They found a table in one of the stone-enclosed alcoves that occupied the corners of the dining room, and sat together on a cushioned bench curved about a round table. Windows circled the alcove, giving them a glimpse outside. However, what was going on inside was as interesting to Susan as the outdoors, and more reassuring.

A group of young people, barelegged, brown and rugged, had come in with their knapsacks and climbing shoes, to seat themselves at a table and compare climbing experiences over tea. There were small family groups as well, and older people who had come up by the cable car.

A waitress brought their order, and drinking hot English tea in the cheerful holiday atmosphere of the big room, Susan began to feel more relaxed. Soon they would go out to look at the mountaintop and see whatever views there were, and then they would be on the way down again. When she was back home she would manage to see her father as soon as possible.

"I want to tell you my news," Dirk said, lowering his voice so that those at the nearest table could not hear. "We're leaving South Africa very shortly."

She looked at him, startled, and he went on.

"This is no country to be living in now. Everyone knows there's a bad crackup coming. The government can hold things down for a while, but eventually—pfft! And it's not a country I want to live in if the blacks take over. So I've been making a few quiet arrangements outside."

"Wh-what are your plans?" she asked, feeling a little stunned. "You might have given me some warning."

He reached for her hand across the table and touched the pink diamond lightly. "Trust me a little, darling. You used to think everything I did was right and wonderful. Now you're puckering your nose and looking as though you might be obstinate. Give me a chance to show you what I can manage once we're out of South Africa."

Her fingers lay limp in his. This was too sudden and she could not respond. "Does my father know?"

"Certainly not," he said. "And you're not going to tell him. Or your friend John Cornish either."

"Do you think they would try to stop you?" she asked in bewilderment.

"Don't be melodramatic, darling. No one is going to stop me. Or even try. I mean to have it an accomplished fact before anyone knows I've taken the step permanently."

"But why must you do it that way? Why should you hurt Father with such secrecy? He trusts you and regards you as a son."

"You think he would be hurt?" Dirk made a derisive sound and let her hand go. "Niklaas has turned into a vegetable. There's no blood left in him. There's nothing left except cobweb dreams about saving the country."

Susan had never heard her father speak of such dreams. He had always seemed content enough to defend the status quo. None of what Dirk was saying made any real sense.

"No one will try to stop me," he repeated grimly. "Your father wouldn't dare. Do you think I don't know what's going on? I would have only to say a word to the proper authorities and he would be back in prison in a flash. No, I think he will not lift a finger when the time comes."

Susan made a helpless gesture with upturned palms. "I don't understand what you're telling me or what it is you're planning."

"That's as it should be. When we're out of the country, starting a new life, I'll tell you anything you want to know."

She could think only of the cruel blow to her father that seemed so senseless, so needless.

"Father took care of you when you were young and had no one to turn to. He—"

"He took me after he had destroyed my father by turning him over to the English, who interned him. And he killed my mother with grief. Whatever he gave me he owed me. Don't imagine that there has ever been any sentimental love between us. And don't imagine that I haven't been waiting for this moment."

Susan closed her eyes. The tea grew cold in her cup and the toast she had nibbled turned leathery. Nowhere was there solid ground upon which she could stand.

"Is that why you hung the whip on the wall?" she asked. "Was that to remind you?"

"So you know about the whip?" he said. "Who told you?"

"John Cornish. Today when we were down at Cape Point. He said he took the whip away from my father when he was flogging you with it. Yet you've always seemed to hate John."

"I don't like an interferer. That's what he has always been. He's at it again now. He's poking around and getting suspicious. Because of him I've had to push up my arrangements and get out of the country sooner than I wanted to."

Her mind was still upon the flogging. "What had you done that Father should take such fierce measures with you? You were only a boy—sixteen or less."

Dirk's laughter was unpleasant. "That's the ridiculous part of the whole thing. That he should have flogged *me* because I had taken my father's whip to punish disobedience. But let me tell you this—your father didn't stop me as quickly as John stopped him. Sometime you might ask Thomas Scott to show you the scars on his back."

Susan drew in her breath with a quick, shocked gasp. At every turn Dirk had seemed to place an enormous concentration upon her father, and she had always taken this for devotion. Now she knew better. Now she knew it to be something twisted and corrosive, building only toward destruction—something symbolized by the reminder of that whip.

"Now you will be able to help me with what I plan," he said.

It was strange, she thought, studying him almost remotely, that although she was sickened, she felt no real pain over this final destruction of the illusion she had been in love with. Something in her that she had not been willing to face had always known this day was coming.

"I will help you with nothing," she said evenly. "I am going home now and I am going directly to my father."

He laughed almost gayly. "And bring the whole house of cards crashing down about his head? Do you think his position isn't precarious on every score? Do you want to send him to prison again in his last years? I have only to tip off the police to finish him. And not only because of the odd lot of visitors he has at times."

She was beginning to understand now. An edge of cruel, clear light had begun to sweep across all that had bewildered her. She remembered the cigars with the diamonds hidden in them—sent to Niklaas van Pelt, so that he would be incriminated if they were discovered, but intercepted by Mara, as all packages were in that house. No, it had not been Thomas who had pushed her down on the path that night, even though it was he who had phoned Willi to destroy the picture she had taken of Niklaas in the market. Yet here was confusion again.

"Surely Thomas can't love you," she said. "How can you make him do what you want him to? And Willi through him?"

"Because he has been foolish enough to trust one white man—your father," Dirk said with biting scorn. "Thus he is involved—he's caught. His word would mean nothing in defense of your father, of course. He can only take whatever steps may keep Niklaas protected for the time being. So he does what I say. If I leave the country as quietly as I plan, no harm will come to your father. But if anyone tries to stop me—"

She did not believe him. She could not believe now that he would spare her father anything of the payment he had meant all these years to extract.

She spoke softly, her words hardly more than a whisper. "I saw—in the flower market. That is part of it too, isn't it? To weave the trap about my father, while you take the rewards?"

"You're far too clever, darling," he told her, his smile a little chill. "I'm afraid I've always underestimated you. I should have made you an ally from the first. Then we'd be in this together."

"As Mara is an ally?" she said.

"It's not exactly the same," he told her. "You, after all, are my wife."

"So it *is* you who have been smuggling diamonds?"

"Not alone, I assure you," he said mockingly. "Much as I have disliked the idea, I have had to accept certain—assistants, shall we say? But mine are the wits behind the operation. It would get nowhere without me. It's a tidy little sum I have being held for me when I get out of South Africa for good. We'll live moderately well, my dear. Not as well as I had hoped—industrials are not the most profitable commodity, but there have been a few gems to help out."

"What happens to them after the flower market?" Susan asked.

"You know enough for the moment, I think. Let's leave a little for you to puzzle out. I promise that you'll know everything once we've reached safety."

She wanted to repeat that she would not go with him, but now she dared not. The thought of the Kimberley in her handbag returned sharply to mind, and she barely held her hand from making an involuntary gesture. Whatever happened now, he mustn't dream that she had it in her possession. She had no illusion about how quickly he would take it from her and hold her to silence with threats against her father.

"Was it you on the path that day?" she asked him wearily.

For the first time he looked uncomfortable. "That was a necessary action. And I took care not to injure you, darling. After you came to the study and chattered naïvely about dropping the box of cigars, Mara called me out of the study to let me know something was missing. I dropped over the terrace wall and got out of sight on the path ahead of you."

She shivered, remembering rough hands pushing her down, the brutal thrusting of the bag over her head.

"By the way," he asked, "what did you do with the industrials you found that day? Where did you hide them?"

"I gave them to John Cornish," she said. "You aren't completely in the clear, you know. He does have some idea of what's going on."

"You have been a little fool," he said.

"Let's go home." She spoke dully. "It will be sunset soon and too dusky to see anything up here."

"There's still plenty to see," he assured her. "The lights at night

219

are miraculous from the table. However, I promise not to keep you up here after dark, if you'd rather go down. At least you must see the top of the mountain, now that you're here."

She did not want to go with him, but she felt too limp and beaten at the moment to struggle any further. For the moment there were only two things left for which she must fight. The knowledge of the diamond must remain hidden. It belonged to her father, and to no one else. And the fact that when Dirk left South Africa she would not go with him.

When he had paid for their tea, he took her arm in a mockery of affection and drew her up the rough rock ledges and out into the open at the top. The sky was still light and tinged with sunset colors over the ocean, but at the far end of this enormous bleak plain of tumbled boulders a hint of gray dusk had begun to settle.

She knew now what people meant when they said this was like a landscape of the moon. The great plain at the top of the mountain was longer and wider and far vaster in its spread than she had ever imagined. From where they stood at one end and near the center there was no view except the tops of nearby hills and in the very distance the Hottentots Holland was being swallowed in blue mist. The drop-off on every hand was too far away to be seen, and in a sense this was reassuring. She had no desire to go close to that dizzy edge.

"Come," Dirk said and took her hand. "Watch your step, my darling. Up here a fall might hurt you badly."

Near the teahouse concrete had been poured to make a sort of path, but as they ventured out upon the mountain there was only a vague way of dirty white sand strewn between rocks. After a few yards, the path was mainly guesswork and they had to pick their way. What looked from the gound to be an utterly flat slab of even rock across the table proved now to be anything but flat. On every side great black boulders, speckled with white and scabrous with age, rolled away over the great plain that had once been the bottom of an ocean. Scrubby green brush grew here and there, and once more there were the bright little wildflowers, finding sustenance in precarious crevices between the age-old rocks.

For all that there were a good many people up here, the table seemed to swallow everything human as soon as the teahouse was left behind. The place was huge enough for thousands, and the little parties scattered and were lost to each other at once. She noted with an odd relief that voices carried well up here, and that even those that seemed far away could be heard distinctly. At least she and Dirk were not really alone.

The air was clear and exhilarating and the dead calm had lifted. A slight, cold wind had begun to blow and Susan found herself wishing it would increase to a gale, so that everyone would be sent down from the mountain at once, summoned back by the hooter.

Dirk was pulling her along faster than she wanted to go, and she hung back, stumbling over rocks, stepping now and then into some pool of stagnant water held in a rocky basin. Once they ventured upon the edge of a slimy green bog and Dirk changed his course to circumvent it. Far away and out of sight someone was testing the echoes, shouting down toward the cliffs behind the mountain, then waiting while strange wild voices shouted back.

The boulders grew larger now, crouching like black animal shapes, eerie against the fading light in the sky. It became necessary to leap from one rock to another, instead of clambering laboriously up and down.

"Where are we going?" Susan pleaded. "I don't want to go any farther. It's all ugly and difficult. There's nothing to see."

"There will be soon," Dirk promised her. "But we must move along quickly or it will be getting dark and we'll have to go down."

She stood stubbornly where she was, refusing to budge another foot. He looked all around them and then capitulated suddenly.

"All right. This place will do as well as any. I don't want to tire you. Sit down and get your breath. You needn't worry. We'll go back in a moment. I know this tabletop like the palm of my hand."

She did not want to rest. She wanted only to turn back at once, to join the other groups that must by now be streaming back toward the cable house before the light should fade completely. But she was out of breath and when Dirk drew her down to sit beside him on a flat slab of rock she gave in. At least for the moment he was not hurrying her on.

"We're not far from the edge now," he said. "If you look over there you can see the lights beginning to come on in Cape Town."

She shivered at the sight and drew her coat more closely about her. The wind was growing bitter.

Dirk leaned forward to take hold of the strap of her handbag, tugging at it gently. "Will you tell me the truth now, darling? You found the diamond, didn't you? It was in the camera, of course.

Mara was suspicious about your interest in that little camera, though she couldn't see anything when she looked into it. We'd both been through that toy chest before, of course, but the camera seemed to offer nothing. I didn't guess until I picked up that bit of black tape on the floor of your father's study. Why don't you tell me the whole story now, Susan dear?"

She forced words between teeth that had a tendency to chatter. "I d-don't know what you're talking about."

"You know very well," he said. "Will you trust me with the diamond or must I take it away from you?"

"It's for—for my father," she said. "It doesn't belong to you!"

"It belongs to whoever holds it," he said softly. "Do be reasonable about this, darling. With the Kimberley in our hands we'll be in the strongest position possible. The world will give us anything we want. There's a rich, wonderful life ahead of us. For you and me, darling."

Susan steadied her trembling and forced the shiver from her voice. "Father knew my mother had taken the stone. Just as she took the others that were found in the Johannesburg house. Perhaps he still believes she took it out of the country. He impoverished himself to pay for it and save her reputation. He loved her deeply and I think she was incapable of loving him as much. The stone belongs to him. He has paid for it with a good deal of his life."

"You leave me very little choice," Dirk said, and the mockery of affection was gone from his voice. "I can get out of the country by ship tomorrow if necessary. The signals are ready to be given. I mean to take the diamond with me. You don't want to spend the night alone on the mountain, do you?"

Before she could speak, a sound pierced the air across the mountaintop. That was the hooter, the signal for everyone to go down. Susan stumbled to her feet, wrenching the strap of her handbag from Dirk's grasp. But before she had managed to get two boulders away, he was after her, whirling her about to face him, his hand across her mouth.

"Don't make a sound," he said. "If you scream, the edge is very close. They'll think you slipped and fell, and screamed in falling. I'll have tried hard to catch you—and only saved your handbag. A great tragedy, my dear. And especially sad for your father."

She saw his eyes, bright in the fading light from the west. The shining brightness she had loved was upon him—the brightness of a diamond and, like a diamond, hard. He would do as he said. Against his desire for the diamond her life was nothing.

When he saw that she would not move or scream, his grip relaxed a little.

"Don't be frightened," he said more gently, and she trusted gentleness in him less than she did cold force. "It will take a while for everyone to get in. There's plenty of time to join the last car. Or, if we have to stay, I know a fairly easy way down. There's even a hut we can take shelter in on the far side of the mountain if that should be necessary. But we can leave at once if you'll open your bag and give me the diamond. That's the sensible way to manage it, Susan. I'm fond of you, my dear. I'd never want to hurt you."

She looked at him with unconcealed loathing. With her eyes she told him the truth—that she despised him now as much as she had once loved him. That there would never be any life for them together anywhere. That she would betray him at the first opportunity and stop him, defeat him, if she could.

He read her look and reached grimly into his pocket. "My first plan won't do, after all. I can see I couldn't trust you, even with the diamond in my possession. So now we will have to arrange something else. It's your own fault, my dear. You leave me no choice."

He drew his hand from his pocket and she half expected to see a gun in it. But what he held was a looping of metal that looked vaguely familiar as he began to slap it back and forth across his hand in a speculative manner. A finger of fear traced itself up the back of her neck.

"Do you know what this is?" Dirk asked, once more at ease and even faintly amused.

He held the metal strand out for her to see and she recognized it as a looped bicycle chain.

"A favorite weapon of the Cape Town skollies," he said.

Skollies, she knew, were the young toughs who hung around District Six in gangs. Hypnotized, she stared at the links of chain being stroked across Dirk's palm.

"Do you see how cleverly this has been fitted for use?" he said and showed her how an end of the chain had been folded back and forth to make a handle, then bound with workman's tape so that it would not slip in the fingers. The remaining loop made a flexible lash.

"It can even be adjusted to the reach of an arm," Dirk said pleasantly, as if he were rather enjoying himself now. "A man with a long arm doesn't need as great a reach of chain. A shorter man can extend his reach by letting out the loop. It's pretty lethal as a weapon, and far quieter than a gun."

He took a step toward her and she saw death in his eyes.

"Open your bag," he said.

It was strange now that her hands did not tremble. She opened the clasp easily and reached into the copious depths for the stone. When she felt it in her fingers she drew it out and would have tossed it wide over the edge of the precipice, but he was too quick for her. His left hand closed about her wrist and he swung her about toward the rocky edge of the mountain. The hand with the chain in it was behind her now and she closed her eyes against the blow that was sure to come. She felt her fingers opening beneath pressure and the stone dropped into his grasp.

The moment her hand was free she whirled away from him, and saw in a terrified flash that she was on the brink of the mountain. The lights of Cape Town moved in a blur across her vision and she flung herself wildly back from the edge, flung her arms about Dirk, more terrified now of the precipice than she was of him. She was in his arms, closed in a deadly embrace, and she could not tell whether he was urging her toward the cliff or drawing her back from it. She felt her feet slipping over nothingness—and suddenly they were falling together, scraping against stone, rolling over the edge, sliding, falling, locked in each other's arms.

23

The blackness and the cold crushed down upon her. Behind her closed lids the world was made up of darkness, and there was pain everywhere. She seemed to hurt all over and it was hard to breathe. Someone was leaning over her, murmuring her name over and over, calling her back, though she did not want to come. She was being held in someone's arms, cradled there, rocked and grieved over—yet there was no comfort for her in the fact.

Painfully she opened her eyes and looked into Dirk's face bent close above her own in the last faint light before darkness came down. With the sight of him, memory swept back in frightening intensity and she tried to struggle away from him.

He held her still and there was a tenderness in his voice that startled her.

"Lie quiet, darling," he said.

But she pulled herself out of his arms and sat up. She was sore and scraped raw along one thigh, though her coat and slacks must have saved her to some extent. Her arms and legs seemed to move normally when she tried them, though she knew she would be black and blue tomorrow. If there was to be a tomorrow.

She saw now where they were. They had rolled together over the edge, it was true, but only to be caught several feet down on an earthen ledge cupped in rock extending below the upper table. A sloping buttress of rock down which they had slid had broken the full impact of the fall. The ledge which held them was fairly wide, but it sloped unevenly to the real drop-off of the farther pitch. Susan edged back against the rock buttress and stared at the spreading lights of Cape Town so very far below, yet so dreadfully close.

"You would have thrown me over!" Her voice was choked with horror. "You would have struck me with that chain. You tried to kill me!"

She had drawn as far from Dirk as she could on the ledge and he made no further move to touch her.

"No," he said, "I never meant to kill you. I knew there were ledges all along the edge of the mountain. I've climbed down to this very place before. I knew you wouldn't fall far." He watched her strangely. "At the last minute I couldn't let you go. I was afraid you might roll or hurt yourself seriously on the rock. I tried to pull you back—and we fell together."

There was no mockery in him now, but only a stark despair, and she knew he spoke the truth. But she no longer wished for his affection.

"What are we to do?" she asked dully.

"I can get back up," he said. "It would be harder for you alone. Impossible, perhaps."

"Then," she said, "if you still have the diamond, why don't you go?"

He had been kneeling on the ledge; now he stood up, and looked down at her.

"I have the diamond." He showed it to her in his hand and then put it away in a pocket of his jacket. "Susan, I want you to come with me."

She shook her head violently and pain throbbed at the back of her skull. "You know that's impossible. I can stay here. I have my coat. Tomorrow they'll find me and get me up. If you want to get away, go."

She could sense hesitation in him, an uncertainty that was unlike him. It was not part of his plans to be thinking first of someone else. And he was not able to do it for long.

"It's perfectly true that you'll be all right," he said. "I can get down alone, even in the dark, and tomorrow I'll be out of the country."

She expected him to turn and start up the sloping buttress of rock, but instead he knelt beside her again and suddenly his hands covered his face and his head was bent. A memory of the boy she had known so long ago seared through her and something in her twisted in pain. She reached out to touch his fair hair lightly, though she could not see its brightness now, and felt the ring on

226

her finger. With a quick gesture she pulled it off and held it out to him, nudged him with it.

"I'm giving you back your luck, Dirk. The pink stone belongs to you. I'll never wear it again."

The finality of her tone must have reached him. He raised his head and took the ring from her, dropped it into the pocket of his jacket with the other. As he moved his foot struck something on the ledge and he picked up the bicycle chain.

"I may need this," he said dryly and looped it into a neat and compact form before he thrust it into a pocket.

A steady repetition of sound had begun to penetrate Susan's daze and confusion. She recognized it for cars being started, driving away somewhere down the mountain. Unsteadily she stood up and looked directly over the edge. On the highway near the cable house far below and half the length of the mountain to her left, people who had ridden up were still getting into their cars, still leaving. If she screamed they might hear her, come to her help. Those in the cable house might hear her cries.

Dirk sensed what she intended. "Don't," he said wearily. "What good would it do you? It might take hours of hunting to find you. I couldn't let you scream more than once. Isn't it better for everyone if I get away from Cape Town? Better for your father. Better for you, Susan."

She felt too weak to struggle against him any further. And what he said was true. Whatever the cost to herself, this was the best way. He sensed her agreement and turned toward the rocky wall, began to pull himself up.

She waited fearfully, not sure whether she wanted most to see him go or to have him stay so that she would not be doomed to spend the dark hours alone in this dreadful place. Once she thought of pleading with him to help her get up from the ledge, to at least leave her on the mountaintop. But she knew without trying that such a plea would do her no good. Here she could make little trouble for him. On top he could not trust her.

He was good at rock climbing, he had done it all his life, and he found the toeholds, the crevices for his fingers. There was a man's strength in his arms and he went up and over the top.

She closed her eyes and sat very still and quiet against the buttress, listening for his departure. His voice came down to her.

"Good-by, my darling. I won't forget you."

He was whistling softly as he turned away, but the sound was melancholy and without cheer. Remembered words ran through her mind: "I'll ride all night . . . when the moon is bright . . ." and tears stung her eyelids. She heard his steps high above, heard a small stone roll as his foot struck it. Then all the mountain was quiet and she was alone. Even the sound of cars on the highway below had come to an end. Tears squeezed between her closed lids and a small sob shook her. Not for fear of her predicament or because of the long ordeal ahead of her, but for sorrow at the ending of love. So empty she was, so lost and lonely. Yet the man she had loved was someone who had never truly existed.

Her tears were brief, they dried quickly. She stood up with her back against the wall. Once more she stretched her legs and arms gingerly to try them out, and felt the sore place along her thigh. She was lucky, lucky. She might be dead by now. Her back could have been broken. She could have rolled on over the edge. She was safe and she was unhurt and she must remember only these things and hold to her courage for the night ahead. How cold and bright and deceptively close the lights of Cape Town seemed. So very close, so very far away. And how dark the bay beyond. It was strange to think of people down there, dining happily in hotels and restaurants and homes, never knowing that a girl crouched up here on a mountain ledge, cold and frightened and helpless in this darkly evil place. Out there on the Cape Flats were the *pondokkies* and a longer-lived misery than her own. Those people too had no thought for her shivering here, and perhaps would not have cared had they known.

All these years the mountain had waited for her. Even as a child she had sensed its malignant purpose, had known that it bided its time. Awesome and tremendous and enormously cruel it could be—cruel as the old dark gods who had ruled it long ago and who would be satisfied only when blood was spilled upon the black stones.

She crossed her arms about her body and held herself in a tight embrace, rocking back and forth. This was no place for such vivid imaginings to possess her. If she stayed quietly where she was no harm would come to her. Only her own mind could betray and injure her now. She had been shocked and shaken and held under a frightening strain. It was only natural that her thoughts should run wild in reaction, very nearly out of control. But not entirely. There was still something left in command. She laid her hands upon the reins of her galloping thoughts and pulled them in.

She must think only of physical things and her own immediate comfort and safety. She must be thankful that the full blast of sharp wind, sweeping away the warmer air of the day, blew over her head and did not strike her fully on this ledge. With the wind upon her, she would have been much worse off. She wished now that she had drunk all her tea, finished her toast. Wished for the remains of the lunch she had discarded today at Cape Point. Food would have helped to fortify her against this long night. Better not think of it.

Feeling for her watch, she found the crystal broken and one of the hands missing. It did not matter; she could not see the dial clearly anyway, and to watch the time would only make the night seem longer.

What was her father doing now? And John Cornish? The thought of John was steadying. He would surely come for her when he knew she had not returned and must be up here. This was a thought to hold to with all her might. In the morning he would come up the mountain—and he would find her. She had only to wait until then.

Her body was sore and achingly tired. Rest was the answer. If only she could sleep, dull her senses to discomfort, and sleep until it was morning and something could be done about her predicament. Carefully she began to feel about on the slanting ledge, groping with her hands for small stones that would hurt her body. At first she tossed them over the edge, but they made a sickening sound as they crashed on the stony slopes far below, and she took to piling them out of the way instead. At least there was a space of earth here, so her bed would not be wholly rock. Setting her big leather bag down for a pillow, she wrapped her coat about her, turning up her collar, and curled herself on the ledge. She was glad now for her two sweaters underneath. The night had turned very cold, and it would probably grow even colder.

For a time she lay quiet, her eyes open, watching the darkness, listening to the wind. The doves of Cape Town had quieted for the night and city traffic noises had lessened and were far away. Once she heard the sound of a car and raised her head to see headlights moving up the long slant of highway toward Signal Hill, where she and John had traveled together—so very long ago! The Lion's Head was a black knob against the sky. She stared at it until she began to feel drowsy.

She slept in rough snatches, waking, drowsing, dropping off into some wild dream, fighting out of it to a waking state, only to find that it was still night and nothing had changed.

Not much time had passed, she suspected, when she sensed a difference in the sky overhead. Below her the lights of Cape Town were still bright. They had not winked out into midnight thinness. But overhead there were no stars, no moon had risen. There was a damp smell on the air and as she stared upward something soft and white drifted like smoke along the lip of the rocky cliff. Clouds had come down upon the mountain and the knowledge shocked her fully awake.

The sight of that misty softness was terrifying. Darkness was one thing, but the cloth of cloud that could blanket the mountain was another. In mist there was no hope of escape, no hope of being found. Mist might cover the mountain for days and then no one could find her.

Frightened now, she stood up and began to call, remembering how sound had traveled earlier on the mountaintop. Dirk had said the people who ran the teahouse lived up here all the time. Perhaps they might hear her in their distant hollow at the end of the mountain. But the fog soaked up her voice like blotting paper, changed the sound of it in her own ears.

Yet now she knew she must not stay here. Perhaps the clouds had not thickened fully on top as yet. Here on her ledge the mist that crept down the mountain was still thin as a gossamer veil. There was no way down over this sheer precipice, so she must go up as Dirk had gone up. If he could do it, so could she, granted the will and the urgent need.

Her first assault on the buttress of rock was foolish and wild. She flung herself upon it and tried to claw her way up, succeeding only in scraping her sore hands further, yet finding nothing to cling to, no tiniest ledge for her fingers. It could not be managed that way, she realized, and drew back for a more careful examination of her position. Dirk had been given the advantage of at least a dim light. She had no light at all. Whatever was to be found she must discover by means of her hands, her fingers, her toes.

She leaned forward against the slanting buttress and reached upward as far as she could stretch, but she could not touch the edge of the mountain above her head. Yet if she could pull herself up even a little way, the edge could not be far out of reach. Its heavy rocks might give her a handhold and a leverage. Carefully, trying to be patient, she patted her hands over all the surface she could reach, and then moved around the buttress a little and repeated the process. Now, at the very height of her reach, she could feel a rough projection, a jutting of rock, and here, somewhat below, but too high for her foot was a tiny ledge that would surely give her a toehold if she could get to it. But she could not grasp the projection—it remained just out of reach and there was no way to use the promise it offered.

There must be a way up. There must be a way to do it. That was what her wits were for. Now was the time to use that wild imagination of hers and find some way of getting up. She turned about on the slanting buttress and leaned against it. In dismay she saw that the mists had thickened and Cape Town had vanished except for a faint glow. This was going to be even worse than she had feared.

Her foot had struck her handbag as she turned and she bent to pick it up, slung the strap over her shoulder. In an instant the possibility came to her. Eagerly now she stood on tiptoe, reaching toward the rough, just-out-of-reach projection overhead. When she had located it, she stood under it and looped the long strap of her handbag into a noose. Awkwardly she jumped and reached the noose up the wall above her. Twice she missed, and then the loop caught, hooked securely over the horny irregularity in the buttress.

With each hand she grasped one side of the strap and pulled herself up, praying that the leather would hold her weight. With almost ridiculous ease she walked up the buttress a few steps to the place where she could stand on the tiny ledge. Holding to the loop with one hand, she reached with the other and found the edge of the mountain only a little way above. She had no need for the strap now. She flung her handbag on top ahead of her and pulled herself up the remaining few feet, crawling breathlessly onto a flat slab of rock. She was once more on top of the mountain.

For a few moments she lay upon the cold stone, breathing hard with relief. Then she crawled away from the edge to safety and stood up in a pocket of rock to look about and plan a course of action. Now, surely, it would be possible to reach the teahouse and get help and a telephone. If she could find the way.

If.

She had never seen mist so thick. No lights were visible anywhere and there was an eerie stillness. Even the wind which had brought cold air into warm and created this heavy fog had stopped blowing and could not be counted on to clear the mountain of this quilting of cloud. The important thing was to keep her sense of direction. Behind her as she stood lay Cape Town, so she must move to her right. If she kept going in a more or less straight line she would reach the end of the mountain where safety lay.

But in the mists were no landmarks to enable her to hold to a straight line. Laboriously she felt her way, clambering over rocks, edging around them, stumbling now and then, moving ahead. But there were boulders too large to climb and the mists blotted out what lay behind her and in ten minutes she knew she had lost all sense of direction.

It was a dreadful feeling. The plain was so vast that she could wander on it for days if her directions were confused and she moved in circles. And there was always the danger of finding another precipice and this time falling to her death. Despairing and defeated, she sat down upon a low rock and leaned her head upon her knees, trying to think, praying for guidance. But now no inventive notion came to mind. There was nothing to do but sit where she was until the clouds thinned enough so that she could regain a sense of direction. Now there was no earthy ledge to lie upon, but only hard damp rock on every hand, rough and porous to her touch. Indeed, she was lost on the bottom of a prehistoric ocean bed and the world she knew had vanished from existence.

24

AT FIRST THE faint glow in the mist at her left meant nothing. She supposed the clouds had drifted a little thinner there. Then she sat up with a start, realizing that a light was indeed moving about, shedding a faint radiance far away in the fog. She jumped to her feet and cupped her hands around her mouth, calling, shouting, unnerving herself by the very urgency of her unexpected hope.

Had Dirk come back for her? But he would not have carried a light.

The fourth time she called the answer reached her faintly and she wondered if she heard only an echo. Then the sound of a voice came distinctly through the mist. Someone was calling her name.

"I'm over here!" she shouted. "Here, here!"

The voice reached her more clearly, and the intensity of light increased. She knew the voice now—it was John's. He had not waited till morning, he had come up through the dark and the mist. He had come for her!

When he loomed out of the fog close by, she saw that he was not alone. Another man had come with him. Thomas Scott leaped lightly down from a high boulder and stood beside him.

Susan waited on no ceremony. She flung herself into John's arms and felt them close about her securely. She wept in relief against his shoulder and he held her there, stroking her hair gently. She had seen tenderness in his eyes earlier today and had turned away from it. Now she wanted it safely around her.

"You're all right now," he said. "I couldn't have made it up here without Thomas, but he knew the way, and the mist isn't so bad down below."

She lifted her head to smile at Thomas. He held his own flashlight toward the ground, but his face was lighted indirectly by the torch John carried and there was a grim, unsmiling look in his eyes.

"Dirk left you up here deliberately, didn't he?" John said.

"Yes!" She did not want to stir from the security of his arms. "It's such a long story. I'll give it to you later. But he didn't try to hurt me. He only took the diamond away from me and went down the mountain."

"The diamond?" John said and looked at Thomas.

Reluctantly Susan drew herself out of his arms. There had been enough of weak relief and it was time to regain her self-possession.

"Yes. I found the diamond earlier down at Protea Hill. Dirk suspected that I had it and he made me give it to him. He's gone now—down the mountain. He means to get out of the country with it. I was caught on a ledge up here—"

"Don't try to tell us everything now," John said. "Do you feel a little better? Strong enough to try the way down?"

"The way down? Can't we go to the teahouse first? Why must we go down now?"

Again John and Thomas exchanged glances.

"The story isn't as long a one to tell as you think, Susan," John said gently. "We know some of it. Another batch of diamonds came to the house today. I'd warned Thomas to keep a lookout for any sort of package that Miss Bellman took charge of. Tell her, Thomas."

The colored man spoke in an expressionless monotone. "It was a package of drugs addressed to Mr. van Pelt. I watched and saw Miss Bellman take it up to her room before I went out today. When Mr. Cornish came home, I let him know."

"Mara had to talk," John said, sounding grim. "There was nothing else she could do. So we got a picture of the whole scheme. Almost any convenient means was used for smuggling the diamonds to Cape Town, but always in a way that would point to Niklaas if they were discovered. From what Mara said, I gather Dirk intended to involve him deliberately just before he got out of the country. She turned a bit hysterical then and told me about your going up the mountain with Dirk. She said you'd never come down. So Thomas and I drove to the cable house and watched the last cars empty. We checked every man and woman who came down those steps until the cars stopped running. Then we drove to the place where an easy trail starts up and left the car." He held out his hand to her. "Come along, Susan."

Someone else had said that to her tonight. "Come along, Susan." But now the words were different, comforting. She could go with confidence and trust. She did not understand why the climb down the mountain was necessary when she felt so sore and weary, but she would do as John said.

Thomas moved a little ahead to choose the way, holding his flashlight downward to light the rocks immediately at their feet. The mist did not defeat him as it had Susan.

"Dirk has the diamond now," she repeated dully as they started over the rocks. Somehow this was the only clear thought her mind clung to.

"Don't worry about it," John said. "Let's think of nothing except getting down the mountain. The police will have to come into this now and your father hasn't a notion of what's up. Before we call them in, he must know the whole story. That's why we're not going to the teahouse first."

Thomas seemed to have a sixth sense about direction or else there were landmarks he knew even on this desolate sea bottom. She kept thinking of it that way—as the bottom of the sea. It was only a mountaintop when you could see across it and know there was a world somewhere lower down.

The easy trail was not very easy in darkness and mist, but no fog was so thick that it could hide the immediate ground beneath her feet, and the flashlights made it possible to proceed a few steps at a time. John's hand was always firmly about her own and she did not slip or fall. As they descended the mists began to thin. The tablecloth lay only across the top of the mountain. Now and then, through trees growing in the cleft of ravine they followed, lights far below were visible.

Once, for Susan's sake, they stopped to rest. She sat upon a grassy slope and tried to catch her breath and gather her wits. Somehow she felt a little numb and capable of only one or two persistent thoughts.

"Will the police stop Dirk tomorrow?" she asked. "Perhaps it would be better if he could just get away." Better for everyone, she thought, remembering the threats he had made against her father. "He has the diamond now—what more can he want?"

235

Thomas moved impatiently. "Tell her. It's better to tell her."

John nodded. "Thomas is right. You'll have to know and it's better to tell you now. This is the trail by which Dirk chose to come down. We met him—not very far from the top."

Susan sat still and tense, listening as he made her see what had happened.

Thomas had been climbing ahead, finding the way. Dirk must have heard him coming up, and he stepped off the trail to let him go by.

"I doubt if he knew who it was," John said. "But I was throwing my light close to my feet and it reflected upward so he must have recognized me. We didn't realize he was there. He had only to wait till I went by and he could have had the trail to himself. But he didn't wait. He came at me swinging a bicycle chain before I had time to get out of his way."

Susan winced, remembering the chain.

John had ducked just in time. The chain had cut him across the face, but it had not knocked him out as Dirk intended. And John still knew his commando tricks. Dizzy though he was from the blow, he dived in for a hold and made Dirk drop the chain. After that a fair fight might have been possible, but Thomas, hearing the sounds, had run back down the trail. His flashlight caught the shine of metal on the ground and he picked up the bicycle chain.

"That was when Dirk saw him," John said. "He forgot me as though I didn't exist. My torch was on the ground and it showed Thomas standing there looking at Dirk with that chain in his hand."

John paused and glanced at Thomas, listening grimly to his words.

"This is the hard part to tell you, Susan," John said.

Susan spoke softly. "Dirk hated you. I think he would have killed you if he could. Tell me what happened."

"Thomas never touched him with the chain," John went on. "Or in any other way, for that matter. I didn't need help at that point. But Dirk saw him and I think his own conscience did the rest. I've seen frightened men before and Dirk was frightened. He knew the things he had done in the past and I think he expected no mercy from a man whose skin was dark. He thought Thomas meant to kill him with that chain and he was more afraid of him than he would have been of me or any white man. Because there was so much reason. That time with the *sjambok*, perhaps, and other times as well."

Susan could see the picture as John made it clear. Dirk had stood frozen in fear, staring at the chain in Thomas's hands. He said something like "Don't!" but the word choked in his throat. Thomas had known what was happening to him. Scornfully he threw the chain at Dirk's feet, knowing the white man could not use it.

"Dirk picked up the chain," John went on. "But his hands were shaking and his eyes never left Thomas. I said, 'Drop that!' but instead he stuffed it into his jacket pocket. Then he lost his head and turned to run. He fled without sense or reason—and we were still high upon the mountain and it was dark."

John took Susan's cold hands into his own warm ones and held them.

"He fell a long way," Thomas said quietly. "Down into a rock gully."

"We climbed down to where he was," John said. "But there was nothing we could do. He was dead when we got to him. We had to go on to the top after you. We emptied his pockets so he wouldn't be robbed in the event that anyone found him before the police could reach him in the morning. Then we covered him with his jacket and climbed to the top. Thomas has everything in his pocket. We can show you when we reach Protea Hill."

Susan was glad that John was holding her hands so tightly. Now she could think only of Dirk's fair head bent before her up there on the mountain ledge. And of Dirk as a boy down at Camp's Bay, laughing at a little girl who wanted to take his picture with a broken camera. All else was wiped away. There were no tears, only a thickness of old grief in her throat. She was aware that both John and Thomas were watching her.

"I'll be all right," she told them. They could not know that she had lost Dirk long before this and that her pity now was only for a man who might have been so much more than he was. A man who had been destroyed by what he had become. "Let's go down," she said. "Let's get back to my father."

Later she remembered few details of that climb down the trail in the dark. It was a relief when they came out at the bottom and found Niklaas's car where Thomas had left it at the foot of the path. It was Thomas who drove them home. Susan sat in the back seat with John's arm about her and they talked not at all.

Niklaas van Pelt was waiting in his study when they reached the house. They went in at once to see him.

"I've been waiting," Niklaas said. "Something has happened, hasn't it? Something is wrong. I think Mara has gone away."

"She can't get far," John said. "The police will pick her up tomorrow."

He told the story then as simply as he could and there was a deep sadness in her father's face as he learned of the smuggling of diamonds that had gone on in this very house, with himself as a shield. Now Susan could tell what she had seen in the flower market.

She picked up his heavy cane with the three flags embossed upon the silver head and ran her fingers down to the tip. The reinforced lower section was difficult to turn; no casual hand would have found the secret compartment. But when she unscrewed it the tube was revealed, where diamonds could be hidden. Under the shelter of the bench that held her tubs of flowers, the woman in the market had been able to remove the tiny industrial stones from their hiding place. This had been the next step on the way out of Cape Town—and again Dirk would have seemed free of any involvement and Niklaas van Pelt would have been incriminated if there had been a slip. No wonder Mara and Dirk, learning of the pictures Susan had taken, had been worried. Mara must have persuaded Thomas that the pictures could injure Niklaas in some way, and he had told Willi to destroy them.

But now it was over. Now the police could learn the truth without danger to her father.

While Susan told him about the cane, Niklaas took it into his hands and found the hiding place for himself. Sorrow lay heavy upon him and Susan knew that, no matter what Dirk might have thought, Niklaas had loved him and now grieved over what he had done.

"Diamonds have been destroying men ever since they were discovered," he said softly; "women too," and Susan knew he was thinking of Claire. "But there's something more important that concerns me now. John, have you made up your mind? Have the things I've told you this afternoon convinced you?"

"You have convinced me," John said gravely. "You and Thomas."

"Can we use him, Thomas?" Niklaas asked.

Listening in bewilderment, Susan looked from one to the other, and Dirk's puzzling words on the mountaintop about her father's notion of helping the country returned to her mind.

"We can use any who will work with us in good faith," Thomas said. There was an air of quiet invincibility about him.

"Men like you, John," Niklaas pointed out, "can't run away from South Africa in its time of greatest need just because you dislike some of the things that are happening here."

"I know that now," John answered gravely. "I mean to stay."

"But doing what?" Susan asked in bewilderment. "What is there anyone can do?"

"There's no such thing as a situation in which nothing can be done," her father said. "Not while there are men of courage. There are those in South Africa today, both black and white, who are in need of aid. A few of these have found a haven in this house. And it has been a quiet place for men to come and talk. And plan. There are more of us who believe in freedom than you might think —among Afrikaners as well as English-speaking South Africans. Many who believe that the only hope for the country is to act in whatever way we can against despotism and prejudice. And to make sure our numbers grow. There's work for you too, Susan. Perhaps through your pictures. The pressure of outside opinion matters more than it ever has before. Even Hans with his thumb in the dike must listen eventually. So, will you stay? Here in this house?"

"South Africa is my home now," Susan answered simply.

She was beginning to understand many things: her father's long and careful testing of John, his arguments that seemed to take the wrong course in order to challenge the younger man. Behind her eyes there was a stinging of tears, but they were tears of pride and love for her father. There was something tremendous about him and she could delight now in being his daughter.

"You brought Dirk's things?" John asked Thomas. "We might have a look at them before the police come."

Thomas reached into his pocket. One at a time he placed upon Niklaas's desk the articles that had been in Dirk's pocket. His billfold and loose change. His cigarette case and lighter. Then

239

something that clanked as he set it down on the polished surface —the coiled bicycle chain. And after that a small gold ring with an orchid-pink stone in its setting. Susan looked quickly away at the sight of it. It had not brought Dirk the luck he needed, after all.

The last article Thomas drew from his pocket was a folded handkerchief and Susan knew what it contained. All that had happened had driven the thought of the diamond from her mind. But now she wanted to be the one to put it into her father's hands.

"Please," she said, "let me."

Carefully she turned back the folds of the handkerchief. For just an instant the great diamond seemed to glitter in the lamplight in all its brilliance—yellow rather than blue because of the reflected light. Then Susan touched the handkerchief and, as they watched, the stone separated into a Y-shaped break before their eyes and lay upon the cloth in three pieces.

Susan gasped and could not speak.

"What is it?" Niklaas asked impatiently. "What has happened?"

John picked up the shattered diamond and put it into the old man's hands.

"It's the Kimberley," he said. "Or it *was* the Kimberley. It was in Dirk's pocket when he fell."

Nicklaas turned the pieces knowingly in his fingers. "Yes, this could happen. He fell upon rock, you say. The point of the diamond could have struck and if there was something hard in his pocket—"

"There was this," John said and pushed the chain toward the old man's hand.

Niklaas touched it and nodded. "Yes, it could have happened that way." He thrust the bits of stone aside and reached for the telephone. "It does not matter. It's time now to ring the police. We can wait no longer."

As casually as that he pushed the thought of a lost fortune from him and Susan, watching him, knew that it truly did not matter. There were other affairs to occupy her father.

While he was telephoning, she stood up and stretched her sore and weary body. There was still the ordeal of the police to endure before she could rest. She moved toward the French doors to look out at the night and Thomas came quietly to open them for her.

She smiled at him. "Will you phone Willi when you can? She'll be worried about us all."

He nodded and there was a moment of understanding and sympathy between them. Then Susan stepped through to the terrace and stood looking out over Cape Town.

It was past midnight and the lights were fewer and more scattered than they had been from the mountaintop. She heard John come to stand beside her and she turned to look up at the mist-hidden mountain.

"I was there," she said softly, unbelievingly. "I was up there tonight."

He did not touch her or speak. But he was close beside her and she knew he would wait until the time was right. They would work together through whatever dark times lay ahead. If only there were enough like John and her father and Thomas—enough who would stay, and who would listen and think and consult, persuading quietly, working for the good of all—then perhaps there would truly be a time of honor and glory in this lovely land of South Africa.

Black
Amber

1

BELOW HIGH BALCONIES that formed a veneer for the huge American hotel, the newer part of the city dropped steeply away to the shores of the Bosporus. A mosque at the water's edge, its whiteness diluted by gray March rain, pointed minarets into the sky —an indication of Istanbul. Otherwise the view was blandly modern and bore little resemblance to the Turkey of Tracy's lively imagination.

She stood on her private balcony, looking down through driving rain at the city she had been trying to reach. Now, all in one breath, she found herself both eager for the encounter and a little fearful over what it might hold for her. Where once her coming might have been a simple, joyful thing, now there were too many troubling questions in her mind. Whether she wished it or not, they removed her from the casual objectivity of the tourist, and brought with them an involvement she could not avoid.

An involvement, in fact, that she had deliberately chosen. She had moved quickly to seize the opportunity that had brought her here and she must not be turned back by the first obstacle.

With a quick, impatient gesture she pulled off the blue suede beret she had bought for this trip and let wind from the strait ruffle her shining fringe of brown bangs. That the wind carried with it a splash of rain, she did not mind. She raised her face to the cold drops as if they might quench her angry reaction to the letter she held in her hand. Clearly a cool head would be needed if she was to deal with the man who had written it. She was curious about him and not at all certain how many of the tales she had heard about him were true, but she did not mean to be summarily dismissed by his letter.

She had waited three months to get here. Waited because there was no way for her to come at once. Now that she was here—arrived at the airport this very afternoon—she was to be sent home ignominiously and without a hearing. The sheet of notepaper crackled sharply as she straightened it and read for the third time the strongly formed masculine handwriting.

DEAR MISS HUBBARD:

The arrangement I agreed to with Mr. Hornwright of *Views* was to the effect that Miss Janet Baker would be sent here to assist me in preparing the manuscript of my book for publication. Her years in the Middle East, her well-established background and knowledge of Turkish mosaics, have made her a suitable person for this work.

Now I have a cable informing me that she will not be free for another six months and that a temporary assistant is being sent in her place: "A young woman who has been doing excellent work for us during the past years."

I can only assure you that this substitution is not acceptable to me. I prefer to wait for Miss Baker. While there is nothing of personal criticism implied on my part, I can only suggest that you take the next plane back to New York.

Sincerely yours,
MILES RADBURN

Tracy folded the stiff sheet of paper. One part of her mind whispered that it would be easy enough to accept this edict. Surely no one in the home office could blame her for a defeat which was so clearly not of her own making. If she went straight home she could turn her back on all she might find disturbing about Istanbul—simply go home and forget the plea and the warning that had come to her, forget the persistent questions that presented themselves to her mind. Let the past keep its unhappy secrets, since she could not now affect the course of destiny.

Yet even as she considered the cajoling voice, she knew that if she turned and ran she would never forgive herself later. Again she folded the paper, creasing it emphatically. She would not permit the letter to anger her. She would keep an open mind about Miles Radburn. She could not know what was true about him and what was not until she had met him herself. His reaction to her coming was, of course, not unexpected. And in all fairness, it might even be justified.

Mr. Hornwright had been thoroughly upset when he came home from Turkey. Miles Radburn's book on the history of Turkish tiles and mosaics would be an expensive art number for the book publishing venture on which *Views* was recently embarked. The tremendous resources that had made the magazine one of the foremost in the country were behind the venture, and the name of Miles Radburn would bring prestige to the list. While it was true that Radburn, after a conspicuous rise to success in his younger years, had done little painting in his late thirties, nevertheless his portraits were in museums and art galleries around the country, and there was still a distinction to his name that spelled good publicity for *Views*. Unfortunately, artists were seldom skilled organizers. Mr. Hornwright, on his visit to Istanbul, had been appalled by the welter in which a possibly important book was buried.

Radburn had reluctantly agreed to accept assistance if he could have the help of Miss Baker, whose work he knew. Mr. Hornwright, procrastinating and treading water, had promised to see what could be managed. In her work as a researcher trainee, Tracy was in a position to hear the rumors going around. Mr. Hornwright had known very well that Miss Baker was otherwise occupied, and he knew as well that Miles Radburn was not ready for her at this point. What Radburn needed was not an expert on Turkish mosaics, but someone efficient enough to straighten out the general confusion in which he seemed to be working.

Once she knew what was in the wind, Tracy had not hesitated. She had gone to see Mr. Hornwright, plunging at once to the heart of the matter. She had pointed out that she was more expendable than almost anyone else in the department. Yet she felt herself equipped to do the job he wanted done. By good chance she had already completed two or three minor assignments for Mr. Hornwright, and he at least knew of her existence.

He smiled at her eagerness, not without sympathy. "How old are you, Miss Hubbard?"

"I'll be twenty-three this month," she told him with dignity.

"Hmm. Still young enough not to know the impossible when you see it. An advantage, perhaps. Though it's quite likely Radburn will decide to send you home the moment he lays eyes on you. What will you do then?"

"If I can get there, I'll stay," Tracy promised resolutely. Because nothing had ever come to her easily, there was an intensity about her that could be persuasive when she threw herself into something she really wanted.

Mr. Hornwright must have sensed this, for he considered her thoughtfully. "At least you're anxious to go. But if I send you, we'll have to move fast. We need to get you out there before he has time to oppose the plan. In fact, we won't let him know you're coming till you're on your way."

"I can leave as soon as you like," she said. "I already have an up-to-date passport." She did not add that it was unused and only a few months old.

There was still hesitation on Mr. Hornwright's part. "I don't know . . . Radburn won't like the switch. His mother was an American and he's lived here a good part of his life, but all the stubborn British half of him will rise up in protest. He has a remarkable trick of putting himself on the far side of a stone wall —with the other fellow out in the cold."

"If I can get there, I'll stay," Tracy repeated. She could be stubborn too. There were times when she thought that was the only reliable quality she possessed—a perverse stubbornness. She would reserve judgment about Miles Radburn and she would not let him frighten her. She would hook her thumbs into her belt, dig in her toes—and stay.

"Good," said Mr. Hornwright. "I like that kind of dogged spirit. But don't come crying to me if you run into that wall. If you go out there, you can't afford to fail. You might lose us the book altogether. A contract isn't enough to assure that he'll come up with the finished product. He's dragging his heels and you can ride herd on him, for one thing. You understand?"

"I understand," said Tracy.

"Then get started," Mr. Hornwright told her. She flew to the door, but he stopped her as she went through. "One more thing. If you know anything about Radburn's work, go easy on the painting angle. He's touchy about not working. He hasn't painted since a year or so before the death of his wife. You know, of course, about his recent tragedy?"

"I know," Tracy said. "I'll be careful," and she went down the corridor as if a stormy wind blew at her heels, whirling her along like a leaf.

The same wind whirled her breathlessly through two or three

crowded days of preparation and briefing. It had whirled her into quick shopping for necessities and the suffering of shots. It had, at length, hurled her at headlong rate over ocean and continent, and set her down on this high, windy balcony, where she stood with Miles Radburn's dismissal in her hands—his decree that she was to turn around at once and go straight home before she had so much as caught her breath upon arrival.

She left the balcony and retreated to her room. On the bed table the telephone sat silent, waiting. She went instead to the full-length mirror on the bathroom door and regarded herself critically. What would Miles Radburn see if she presented herself to him?

There were five feet, one inch of girl in the mirror. A girl with glossy, well-brushed brown hair worn in a smooth twist at the back of her head. Only the bang fringe went loose and unpinned. Her mouth was too big and her nose doubtful. Her eyes, beneath thick lashes, were warm-gray, not cold-gray, and their expression always betrayed any intensity of inner feeling, of eagerness and excitement, or sometimes indignation that she might be experiencing. The charcoal-gray wool dress she wore was severe of line and simple of cut, and Tracy cocked one dark eyebrow in mocking amusement as she considered it. She had made that dress herself, as she made most of her own clothes. She was good at this sort of thing—very good. Some of the smart women at *Views* had even asked where she shopped.

Someday, she thought, staring at her image rebelliously, she was going to break that plain neckline with loops of wildly colored beads. She was going to run amok with bright scarves and jewelry and furbelows to her heart's content and be as thoroughly fussy and feminine as she pleased. Today just two ornaments broke the overall severity—a stitched leather belt with a gold buckle, and a simple pin near the neckline. The pin curved gracefully in the shape of a golden feather and she touched it now for reassurance before she once more hooked her thumbs into her belt. The pin was an old friend.

At least she recognized her slightly defiant, toes-in stance and smiled because it went with the gesture of thumbs hooked into the leather belt. She knew what it meant. The stubbornness and determination she could count on were there. She had dug in her toes. She was staying.

Having accepted the fact, the next step was to get herself to where Miles Radburn was. She went to the telephone and lifted the receiver. The switchboard operator spoke English. Tracy gave her the name of Mrs. Sylvana Erim, and spelled out a town full of *y*'s and *k*'s that she could not pronounce. The Erim name seemed to mean something and before long a distant ringing began.

"A widow," Mr. Hornwright had told her. "A Frenchwoman in spite of her Italian first name, who married a Turk and still makes her home in Turkey. Quite wealthy and socially prominent. Radburn and his wife first met her on their honeymoon in Turkey some years ago. Apparently she has furnished a haven for him while he works on this book. He's staying at her villa in a suburb across the Bosporus. If anything goes wrong, talk to Mrs. Erim. She's a civilized woman in the European sense. Very charming. And she gets things done. Remarkably unexcitable for a French-woman."

A voice came on the wire, the words Turkish.

"I wish to speak to Mrs. Erim," Tracy said.

There was a silence that lasted so long Tracy began to think she had been cut off. Then a feminine voice spoke in her ear. A not unfriendly voice, pronouncing English with a French accent.

"This is Sylvana Erim."

Tracy identified herself.

"Ah, yes—you have been sent from the American publisher to assist with Mr. Radburn's book?"

"That's right," Tracy said. "I would like to see Mr. Radburn as soon as it can be arranged."

"But I have understood that a letter has been sent to your hotel," the cultured voice went on.

"I have the letter," Tracy admitted. "It tells me to go home. But I don't want to leave without at least speaking with Mr. Radburn."

There was a thoughtful pause and then a regretful, slightly amused sound. "But of course you wish to see him after coming such a distance. Sometimes he is like a bear—that one. Let us see what we can do. I will consider for a moment."

Again there was silence while Mrs. Erim considered and Tracy relaxed a little. She had a feeling that if this woman chose to help, her way would be smoothed.

The wait was not long. "As it happens, you have come at an

opportune moment," Mrs. Erim continued. "My sister-in-law, Nursel—Miss Erim—is in the city this afternoon. I know where to reach her. I will ask her to pick you up at your hotel in an hour and drive you here to the *yali*. Bring a suitcase—you must stay for the night."

Mrs. Erim waited for no thanks, waited hardly for agreement, before ringing off. One had the impression of calm force and authority at work. Mr. Hornwright had been correct.

Tracy put down the telephone and proceeded to tear Miles Radburn's letter into very small scraps and drop them into the wastebasket. The small violent movement did her good. He was *not* going to send her home. There was more at stake than Mr. Hornwright had any knowledge of. In fact, if he had guessed her own concern in this, he might not have let her come. She could only hope that no one else would guess it either. In an odd way she would be incognito here, while using her own name. It was better to have no one suspect her real secret. She could find out more this way, with no one on guard against her.

What a long way Turkey seemed from the Midwestern town where she had grown up. Though not as far as New York had been a few years ago when she had taken matters into her own hands, opposing the wishes of her parents. What warnings of disaster had rung in her ears! But she had found a job in New York. Then another job. There had been sadness over her mother's death, but not deep sorrow. She had lost all real touch with her mother long before. An estrangement with her father had continued and could not be helped.

Two years ago she had found this most fascinating of all places to work—*Views*. She had always wanted a finger in the creation of magazines and books. So far, it was a very small finger, but if she made good at this assignment with Miles Radburn, there was no end to the possibilities. Even more important, if she succeeded, she would be able to prove that Tracy Hubbard was someone in her own right, after all. Prove it to her father, to the world—and most of all to herself.

But she did not want to dredge up the past now. Not when she had just reached Istanbul. First she must see Mrs. Erim. One deliberate step at a time would keep her here.

She returned to the balcony and stood for a while looking down at the city that bore slight resemblance to the Istanbul she had read about. She had seen only a little more of it on the drive from the airport through the old city. Once within crumbling Roman walls, rain had obscured its outlines. She had been aware of the tight, cobbled streets of the old Stamboul section, slippery with mud; of erratic traffic in the narrow ways, and crowds of pedestrians, rainy-day-shabby, not unlike such crowds in any city anywhere. Of course Istanbul was not Turkey, any more than New York was America, she reminded herself. It was an entity in its own right, and not easily to be learned in all its complexities.

The hour was difficult to pass. She powdered her nose and repaired her lipstick. One step at a time was all she needed to manage.

Then the phone rang, announcing that Nursel Erim awaited her in the lobby. Tracy threw her gray coat about her shoulders, picked up her suitcase and handbag, and walked the miles of soft-carpeted corridor to the elevator bank.

Downstairs near the revolving doors of the entrance, the woman waited for her. She was young—perhaps only a year or two older than Tracy, and she had the great dark eyes, the beauty of feature that belonged to a Turkish background of wealth and family. She was dressed as faultlessly, as smartly as Paris or New York at their best, and while she wore no hat, her black hair was fashionably coiffed. A fur-trimmed coat hung open over her black dress. Around her throat several strands of pearls gleamed against the black, and one knew their luster was real. Standing beside all this elaborate elegance, Tracy felt herself painfully simple and unadorned.

The vision came toward her with one graceful hand outstretched. "You are Miss—Miss Tracy Hubbard?" She faltered slightly over the name. "I am Nursel Erim. If you will come with me, please. As usual I am parked against the law." Tracy gained the impression that small lawbreakings did not in the least disturb Miss Erim.

Outside they hurried through the rain to a small sleek car that was already blocking passage on the drive. The doorman shook his head despairingly, but he held an umbrella over them as Miss Erim opened the door. She laughed as she gestured Tracy into the front seat and went around to get in beside her.

"In his heart," she said as she turned the car out of the hotel driveway, "no Turkish man believes that a Turkish woman should

252

drive an automobile. Mustapha Kemal rid us of the veil, but human nature takes more than half a century to change."

They drove through rain-swept streets, downhill toward the waterfront, where they lined up for the car ferry. Nursel Erim, busy with a need for careful driving in late afternoon traffic, said little until they were on board the boat. Then they left the car and went upstairs to a dry, warm cabin for the short crossing from Europe to Asia. Here she became the courteous hostess, pointing out what little could be seen of the gray vista. Yet, for all her effort, there seemed a constraint upon her, as though she were not yet sure exactly how Tracy fitted into the scheme of things.

"This is the place where the Bosporus begins its course between the Sea of Marmara and the Black Sea." Miss Erim indicated roiling gray waters. "If you look closely in that direction, you can see Seraglio Point and the walls of the old palace showing through the mist. The site of ancient Byzantium was up there."

Tracy stood in the door of the cabin and gazed with interest upon the Marmara and the dividing protrusion of the famous point of land they were leaving behind as the boat moved toward the opposite shore. Crumbling stone walls ran down to the water, while in the mists far above rose palace roofs and windows.

"Of course visitors are always interested in the Seraglio and its stories," Miss Erim said. "It was just off that point that ladies of the harem who happened to be in disfavor were put into sacks and dropped into the Bosporus."

Tracy glanced at the girl beside her. Nursel Erim was regarding her with a somewhat sly amusement, as though she had told the story with deliberate intent to shock an American visitor and now awaited her reaction.

"At least it's a custom—you've discontinued," Tracy said dryly.

The Turkish girl shrugged. "The Bosporus has always invited tragedy."

"Do you live very far from Istanbul?" Tracy had no desire to think about Bosporus waters at this moment.

"Not too far. Our yali is in Anatolia, the area which makes up the Asian side of the strait. It is a very old house which has been in the family for more than a hundred years. You know the word *yali*? It means a villa on the water. There were many such villas on the Bosporus occupied by wealthy pashas in the old days."

"You live there with your sister-in-law?" Tracy wanted to bring the talk around to Miles Radburn, but she dared not plunge too hurriedly.

"My brother Murat and I live in the yali. Sylvana—Mrs. Erim, the wife of our older brother who is dead—has built a kiosk for herself, a land house, on the hill above. Thus we keep separate households, though my brother has his laboratory on the lower floor of the kiosk, where he can work in undisturbed quiet. He is a doctor but he does not practice medicine. He is well known for his contributions to medical research," she added proudly.

"Where does Miles Radburn stay?" Tracy ventured.

"Mr. Radburn's rooms are in the yali also," Nursel Erim said. There was the faintest change of tone in her voice as she spoke the name, but Tracy could not tell what it portended. The girl was on guard in some way and far from openly friendly.

By now the boat had slipped past Leander's Light—a squat white tower that rose near the entrance to the Bosporus. Oddly named, since Leander had drowned in the Hellespont, at the other end of the Sea of Marmara. As the boat swung wide with the swift current and nosed into shore at the town of Usküdar, several small mosques with their attendant minarets were visible through the rain and the aspect looked more like the Turkey of Tracy's imagining.

They left the boat and the car followed a road that ran north along low hills above the water. Small villages clustered along the way, with snatches of open country between, and now her companion drove faster as if she were impatient to end the journey. There was a half hour more of winding road before they stopped beside a grilled iron gate set into a stone wall. It was opened for them by a gateman who flashed white teeth in a smile beneath his thick black mustache. From the gate a private road dipped steeply toward the water, then straightened around a curve, ending before the door of a square, three-storied wooden house. The house had weathered to a soft silvery gray and its veranda rows were broken by a repetition of curved Turkish arches.

They left the car for a servant to put away, and Nursel Erim ushered Tracy into a long marble-floored passageway. A little maid bobbed into view, dressed surprisingly in a bright red skirt and darker red sweater, a red kerchief, flowered in white, covering her head.

Miss Erim spoke to her in Turkish and the girl answered, ducking her head shyly as she spoke.

"Halide says your room is ready," Miss Erim explained, turning toward the stairs. "Come, please—I will take you up. We do not live down here. The kitchens and storage rooms are here, and some quarters for the servants."

The stairs ran upward against the wall in a single graceful curve, a wrought-iron railing of fanciful design winding beside them as they climbed. Overhead, two stories above, an old-fashioned chandelier shed a pale glow upon dim stairs.

As they reached the second floor, a man suddenly confronted them. He wore a black, somewhat shabby European suit with a dark gray sweater and white collar showing beneath the jacket. His olive-skinned face was notable for its flourishing black mustache and eyes that were darkly vital and observant. No welcoming smile broke the somber quality of his expression, but Tracy felt that she was being weighed and assessed.

"This is Ahmet Effendi, our *kahya*—that is to say, our house-man, who is in charge of all the details of our lives. If you wish anything, Ahmet Effendi will procure it for you."

There was a note of fondness in her voice and she spoke to him respectfully in Turkish before they went on. To Tracy she explained further as they mounted the second flight of stairs.

"My brother and I have our apartments on the second floor. Mine is over the water, his at the back. I have suggested to Mrs. Erim that we give you our third-floor room, since it is a pleasant one—and empty at present."

Again Tracy caught the odd, sidelong glance, as though the Turkish girl awaited some reaction.

The stairs ended in a large bare salon, drafty and gloomy, serving perhaps more as a vast hall than as a room in itself. A tall blue porcelain stove which sent out a glow of warmth soon lost in the wide reaches stood against a wall. A few stiff chairs were drawn up about a round table covered with red velvet that dripped silken bobbles toward the floor. At either end of the salon were closed doors, and along the side opposite the stairs French doors opened upon an arched veranda.

"In the old days," Tracy's guide explained, "the haremlik, the women's quarters, was up here. The selamlik was in the more convenient rooms on the floor below—where the men stayed. Of course women had the run of the house, except when male visitors outside the family appeared. Then they retired to their rooms up here."

She turned toward the end of the house that overlooked the water, pausing before a vast wooden door with an ornamental brass doorknob. This knob was apparently a stationary handle. The latch was near the floor and Nursel Erim operated it with a quick flick of her toe.

She saw Tracy's interest and smiled. "We are very old-fashioned here, as you will soon find. Please enter. We hope you will be comfortable."

The room was huge, with a high, distant ceiling. A little to Tracy's surprise, its furnishings were of a light-grained modern wood. A thickly piled gold carpet occupied a good part of the floor and there was an exquisite dressing table equipped with folding mirrors and a stool padded in gold satin. Doors opened on three sides of the room—one to the salon, one apparently to an adjoining room, and double doors upon the arched veranda that seemed to run all about the house.

Miss Erim opened the door to the next room and gestured. "This was Mr. Radburn's study at one time. Now it is unused. He has now moved away from the water. It is rather cold on this side of the house in the winter months, though I do not mind. I never tire of the Bosporus. And soon spring will be here. In the meantime there is an electric heater, if you wish, and I see that Halide has already brought coals from one of the stoves to burn in the *mangal*."

She indicated a large brass brazier rather like an open lotus flower, in which glowing red coals sent out a surprising amount of warmth. When she had closed the door to the adjoining bedroom and locked it, she turned about.

"This was Anabel's room. His wife, you know."

Tracy stood very still in the middle of the gold carpet, waiting for a sudden chill to go away. The Turkish girl was watching her, waiting. For what, Tracy was not sure. Perhaps for some remark about the recent and tragic death of Anabel Radburn. She knew that this was a moment for caution. There was nothing the people in this house could know about Tracy Hubbard. She must speak naturally, pass over the moment quickly.

"You knew his wife well?" she asked, and hoped that she sounded casual.

Nursel Erim bowed her smartly coiffed black head in sorrowful

256

admission. "But of course. I knew her very well," she said, and was silent, suddenly remote.

She went next to the French doors that opened upon the veranda and set one of them ajar. There was still gray daylight outside, and the sound of rain falling on water. The Bosporus sped its winding course immediately below the jutting of balcony, but Tracy did not step outside to enjoy the view. She shivered slightly at the draft and clung to the relative warmth of the room. As Miss Erim closed the door, a white cat darted suddenly through it and jumped upon the bed. There it sat erect, watching them out of huge, unblinking green eyes. Tracy liked cats and she made a move toward this one, but Miss Erim stopped her.

"Please! It is not a friendly cat. It is what we call here an Ankara cat—or, as you might say, Angora. But this one does not like people."

"Tell me its name," Tracy said and moved quietly toward the bed.

"It is named Bunny," Nursel Erim said, smiling slightly. "A strange name for a cat, is it not? It is one Mrs. Radburn chose. She found the cat when she first visited here, and she made it her pet. Turkey is full of stray cats, and I think she wanted to adopt them all. But Miles—Mr. Radburn—would let her have only this one. Sylvana is not fond of cats."

Tracy fumbled with the buttons of her coat and did not look at either the cat or Nursel Erim. If she kept her hands busy, perhaps the cold sickness would go away. She had not dreamed how hard this was going to be, or what an assault there might be upon her emotions at every turn. *Bunny!* Of all things, Bunny!

Miss Erim looked at her with alert concern. "I will leave you now. You must be weary from your long flight. Please rest—and I will return in half an hour to bring you to Mrs. Erim."

"Yes," said Tracy in a small voice. "That will be fine. Thank you very much." She did, indeed, feel the need for rest.

She waited until her hostess had gone, then flung off her coat and lay cautiously down on one side of the great bed. The cat did not move. It neither scratched her nor leaped away in fright. It simply scrutinized her with that reserved and critical gaze. Nothing about it lived up to the frivolity of its name.

Bunny, Tracy thought, and felt suddenly helpless and alone. The coming meeting with Miles Radburn loomed as a frightening

257

prospect, and all her cool reserving of judgment seemed an exercise in futility. Why shouldn't she believe the worst she had heard about him? Why shouldn't she be afraid?

She lay staring at the distant ceiling where an all-over design of diamond shapes had been decoratively outlined in strips of dark wood. Only the ceiling and the arched windows of the veranda beyond spoke of old Turkey. This was a modern room, a feminine room, perhaps furnished to please the woman who had once occupied it.

She looked at the cat again. "Bunny?" she said tentatively.

The cat did not seem to recognize her name. At least not in Tracy's intonation, but she raised her pink nose slightly and twitched her whiskers as if she drew in some impression by means of these antennae. Coming to a decision, she sprang gracefully from the bed and removed herself to a cushioned chair across the room, rejecting untoward advances from a stranger.

The room seemed to draw about Tracy, weighing in upon her with a sense of ominous oppression. Slow warm tears gathered at the corners of her eyes and spilled back into hard Turkish pillows. At the realization that she was giving way to gloom and self-pity, she rose and went in search of the bathroom Nursel Erim had indicated earlier.

Here there was plentiful tile and a huge old-fashioned European tub with massive fixtures. Behind it stood an iron stove, with a pipe running out through the wall. Apparently one bathed in hot water only by appointment with the stove. Sure enough, when she turned the basin faucets the water ran icy cold.

Nevertheless, it refreshed her as she bathed her face, and she reminded herself that she was tired. Tomorrow she would feel more courageous and ready to face Miles Radburn. She could only hope that the ordeal of meeting him might be postponed until she had a night's rest behind her. She glanced at her watch, wondering what time it was in New York. But only Turkish time mattered from now on, and she returned to her room and shrugged the thought aside, surrendering still another link with home and all that was safely familiar.

When Nursel Erim came for her, Tracy was ready. Her eyes were dry, her emotions under control. She did not speak to the white cat in parting.

2

~~~~~~~~~~

"MRS. ERIM WILL see you now," Nursel said.

Again they traversed the big drafty salon. This time her guide went to one of the side doors and opened it to step out upon the veranda. Rain blew through the arches and the garden below was already dark and shadowy as daylight died. Hurrying, they rounded the house to the rear veranda where a passageway, covered with a roof and enclosed by glass windows, made its way over the private roadway that ended at the door of the yali, thus forming a bridge from the third floor of one house to the ground floor of the house higher on the hill. The kiosk, the land house, was very large, with trees growing all about.

"My brother's laboratory is down here," Nursel Erim explained, as they entered a marble corridor. "My sister-in-law's rooms are on the floors above. Our older brother built this house for her and gave it to her so that she holds it in her own name. Fortunately, he stipulated that Murat, his younger brother, be allowed this space for his laboratory."

A faintly resentful note was evident in the Turkish girl's voice. Apparently feelings were not completely amicable on the part of the younger Erims toward their sister-in-law. Tracy stored away the fact to be considered at another time, as all such facts about this household must be stored and considered.

Again curving Turkish stairs with wrought-iron railings took them upward. Again there was a central salon, apparently unused in the cold months. A sound of vehement voices speaking in Turkish came from a room at the rear of the house.

Tracy's companion knocked and then opened the door as a voice called to them to come in. The room had upon Tracy an

259

impact of light and perfumed air, bustle and sound that was overwhelming. As she stepped into its brilliantly lighted expanse she saw that there were a number of men in the room, all talking at once. And there was one silent woman.

It was a huge room, high-ceilinged, but brightly lighted against the dusk by means of a crystal chandelier and several imported table lamps. Turkish divans ran about the walls, heaped high with colorful silken cushions. All about were little tables, inlaid with mother-of-pearl, or set with mosaic designs in tile or fine wood. The carpets were richly Oriental and several had been piled one upon another to give layers of luxury and warmth. Upon these carpets knelt several shabbily dressed men, their garments patched and repatched, as nondescript and baggy as Ahmet's had seemed, displaying their wares as if before a throne. Sitting on a cushioned divan, slightly raised by a platform that enabled her to survey the room, sat Sylvana Erim.

She wore a dark red, embroidered robe of wool that flowed over the curves of her figure. Beneath its floor-length hem showed comfortable Turkish slippers with red pompons on the toes. It was her face, however, that drew and held the eyes of the observer once they had rested there. She was, Tracy suspected, the sort of woman who came to full bloom in her early forties and was now at the peak of her years. Her fair hair was golden in the brilliant light, without any hint of gray, and she wore it waved softly back from a smooth wide forehead. Her eyes were startlingly blue and very deep and lustrous beneath heavy lids. An aura of calm assurance seemed to lie upon her in the midst of confusion. She sat relaxed, without moving, while bedlam reigned at her feet. The kneeling men called her attention to scarves spread out here, a bevy of embroidered handbags there, brass trays beyond, all being energetically praised by their owners. Yet Sylvana Erim regarded all this in calm silence.

She saw Tracy and beckoned with a hand that moved without suddenness. "Ah—Miss Hubbard? Good afternoon. Please sit here beside me. I am sorry to receive you in the midst of my little bazaar. But it will soon be over. Ahmet Effendi—if you please—"

At once the mustachioed houseman stepped from behind the kneeling villagers and stood listening without servility as Mrs. Erim spoke to him in Turkish.

Since it seemed to be expected of her, Tracy seated herself on a lower divan next to the mistress of the house. Nursel Erim smiled with vague uncertainty at Tracy, and went away.

"If you will excuse me," Mrs. Erim said, "I will finish this small business."

Quietly Sylvana Erim singled out this article or that, rejected another, praising and blaming with equal calm. The men at her feet rolled up their goods, piled their brass and copper trays together, picked up their silver filigree jewelry, and took everything away that was not wanted.

When they had gone, Mrs. Erim reached for an elaborately shaped glass bottle from a nearby table and offered it to Tracy. "Cologne for your hands," she said. "Our pleasant Turkish custom."

The odor added further scent to the already perfumed air as Tracy sprinkled it upon her hands. It was fragrant and elusive.

"You like this?" Mrs. Erim asked. "It is attar of roses, but with an addition or two of my own. Myself I have distilled the essence from which it is made. A small amusement in which I take pleasure."

Tracy murmured her appreciation, finding herself somewhat in awe of this impressive woman. Mrs. Erim picked up a silken scarf that lay among the articles the men had left behind and shook out its bright yellow folds with a faint moue of distaste.

"A pretty thing, but the material and weave are of poor quality. I try very hard to restore our weaving of materials to the fine quality of the past. But we have lost some of our art and we have a long way to go. In articles of brass and copper we excel. For these I can always find a market abroad. But the weaving of silks has not yet reached a standard to be well received in America."

"Then you're not buying these things for yourself?" Tracy asked.

Mrs. Erim made a deprecating gesture. "No, no—these are made by people of the villages where I am trying to encourage more craft work for export. They know I wish to help them and that I can find buyers abroad for some of their work. This saves me the cost of sharing with an Istanbul dealer. It is not a business with me, but a small contribution to my adopted country. However, I have not invited you here to discuss inconsequential efforts. *Bien*—here is our tea. We may refresh ourselves as we talk."

Ahmet came in bearing a brass tray on which was set a small

samovar and two glasses resting on delicate china saucers. There was a dish of lemon slices and a plate of tiny cakes. Unsmiling, almost sullen in his manner, Ahmet took the small teapot from the rack atop the samovar and held it beneath the spigot. When the water, already heated by the tube of charcoal inside, had steamed onto the tea leaves in the pot, he set it back upon its rack to keep warm while it steeped. He brought a small plate and napkin for Tracy, and then Mrs. Erim waved him away. Though he obeyed her gesture, he glowered as if he had a wish to stay, and Mrs. Erim sighed as the door closed after him.

"Ahmet Effendi's disposition does not improve with age. But what is one to do? He was a servitor in my husband's family and is very loyal to us. He is difficult at times, but he knows our ways and is devoted to all who bear the Erim name. Now you must tell me about yourself, Miss Hubbard, and about why you are here."

Tracy explained as best she could, while Mrs. Erim poured the steeped tea into small glasses and passed the plate of cakes. As Tracy concluded, she nodded thoughtfully.

"It was not, I fear, a sensible plan on the part of your Mr. Hornwright. You will forgive me if I say that you are young and inexperienced for this work. Your use to Mr. Radburn can only be negligible. Is this not true?"

"I don't expect to be of much use to him in actual work on the book," Tracy admitted frankly. "Mr. Hornwright thought I might go through the material he has collected and find out exactly what remains to be done. Perhaps to sort and file will be the best service that can be offered Mr. Radburn at the moment."

Mrs. Erim's soft laugh had a ring of sympathy. "Files and order are, I fear, foreign to Mr. Radburn's nature. He will not welcome one who comes to tamper with his books and papers and sketches of mosaics."

"Perhaps tamper isn't the word I'd use, but I am here to sort through this material." Tracy's brows drew together in a frown of resistance. She must not permit herself to be swayed from her purpose.

The blond woman on the divan studied her frankly for a moment. "What you suggest is futile. The task would never end. But perhaps this is something you must see for yourself. It is possible that I can arrange for you to remain here for a week, at least."

"I'll need more than that for the job," Tracy said firmly.

Mrs. Erim's calm remained unruffled. "*Perhaps* I can arrange for you to remain a week," she repeated. "In that time the truth of the matter should be obvious to you. You will be able to report the hopelessness of this task to Mr. Hornwright. It will not be your failure, or the failure of anyone he might send, but simply the fact that Mr. Radburn does not wish to complete this book. When I invited him to come here to work, I had hoped that he would make this important contribution. But I am a realist, Miss Hubbard. I no longer have confidence that this is true."

Such a belief was not Mr. Hornwright's, Tracy knew, and she had no intention of accepting it herself.

"When may I see him?" she asked bluntly. "Does he know that I'm here?"

"Not yet. He is away and we do not expect him home until tomorrow. Perhaps then I can prepare the way a little. He has gone to the Istanbul side to visit a small mosque where the tilework is especially beautiful. Always he goes off on such trips. Always he collects more and more information, makes more and more sketches of mosaics. There is no end to this, though it is not necessary to represent the tilework of all Turkey in his book. A sampling from the various periods of history would seem sufficient. Your editor made this clear when he visited us. But tell me, my dear—why did Mr. Hornwright choose you in particular to come on this errand?"

Tracy answered carefully. "Mr. Hornwright thought I'd be useful at the moment. That is, if I can persuade Mr. Radburn to accept me."

"I like those who are open with me," Mrs. Erim went on. "It is possible that I may be able to smooth your way so that you may remain, as I say, for a week. I can promise no more. But that is something, is it not?"

Tracy could only nod. She did not know whether this woman was on her side or not, and she wondered about her claim that Miles Radburn did not want to finish his book.

"Tell me, Miss Hubbard," Mrs. Erim inquired, "do you know Mr. Radburn's paintings?"

"Yes, of course," Tracy said. "I've seen them many times in exhibits at home." She must be open, yes. But not too open. She was on uneasy ground here and she did not wholly trust this woman's calm and candid air. "Mr. Hornwright says he doesn't paint any more," she added.

The deeply blue eyes clouded for a moment, then were once more serene. "That is true. A sad and wasteful thing. But perhaps it will pass as all things pass with the healing of years. I too have lost those dear to me."

Tracy stirred her glass of tea with a tiny silver spoon and said nothing. Mrs. Erim had partaken of none of the sweet cakes, but she sipped the lemon-flavored brew and allowed silence to envelop the room. Only the spattering of rain against glass broke the quiet. Sylvana Erim, while she gave the impression of potential vitality held in check, did not waste her energies. Because of her ability to be still without being placid, she cast an atmosphere of tranquillity about her. Yet Tracy found herself increasingly on guard. She wondered what would happen if this well-controlled woman were angered, or severely crossed. She would not, Tracy thought, like to be the one to oppose her.

Mrs. Erim replaced her glass and saucer on the tray and moved slightly against her cushions. "Tell me—you are comfortable in the room you have been given in the yali?"

"It's a lovely room," Tracy said, her eyes lowered. "Thank you for inviting me to stay here."

"The water sounds will not disturb you or keep you awake?"

"I'm sure they won't," Tracy said.

"Good! Myself—I cannot endure the mooing of horns, the whistling of passing boats, the voices that carry across water. That is why I persuaded my husband to build me this house in the woods, where I can be quiet, undisturbed. Let us hope you will sleep well tonight. And do not worry about tomorrow. I myself will have a small talk with Mr. Radburn."

"You're very kind," Tracy said.

The interview had come to an end. She murmured that she would go to her room to unpack a few things, and took leave of her hostess. Mrs. Erim did not accompany her to the door, but somehow the houseman, Ahmet, was there, ready to open it as she went out. Silently he led the way back through the covered passage to the yali and saw her to her room. When she thanked him, he bowed his head and went away, moving rather like a shadow in his dark, ill-fitting suit, quickly lost in the gloom of the big salon. It was rather a shame, Tracy thought, as she went

into her room, that Ahmet was too late for the days of the Ottoman Turks. He would have looked well in a turban and flowing
robes.

After her visit with Mrs. Erim, she felt slightly more encouraged about remaining at least for a week. She could not fathom
the woman, or understand why she had aligned herself on the
side of a stranger who had little that was practical to offer. But
the fact that she appeared to have done so was a step in the right
direction. Granted one week, it would be necessary to find a way
to stretch it to two.

Tracy opened her suitcase and began to hang up a few things
in the cavernous wardrobe of dark walnut that was the single
out-of-harmony note in the modern bedroom. The white cat had
not stirred from its chair. As she moved about, it opened sleepy
eyes to stare at her briefly, then seemed to dismiss her as a person
of no consequence, and went back to sleep.

Before Tracy had finished unpacking, Halide came, lending a
bright splash of color in her red clothes.

"Hanimefendi," she said, and added one of her few English
words, "please?" as she indicated that she would take Tracy's
things away to be pressed. She admired each article of clothing
before she flung it over her arm and was interested in everything.

When the girl had gone with the few things Tracy had to give
her, she opened veranda doors and went outside. The rain had
lessened to a drizzle and in the dusk lights were coming on,
climbing the hills of the European shore across the Bosporus,
and marking the outline of a passing freighter. The strait was
narrow and winding in this section, more like a river than an arm
of the sea. Now that the last traces of daylight were vanishing
over Thrace on the European side, the Bosporus looked like black
marble, with light breaking its surface in oily swirls.

Without warning, as she stared at the water, pain swept through
her—the aching of a wound too new to heal, and the hurt as well
of an old, disquieting memory. Below the balcony dark water
swept softly past, treacherously deep and strong in its currents.
All through Turkish history these very waters had reflected the
wickedness of Constantinople—a city that raised spires to God
and cast loathsome secrets into the water that flowed at its feet.

She withdrew her eyes from the hypnotic play of the moving
surface and turned her attention to a lighted area below the jut-

ting balcony. It was stone-flagged, with stone steps running down to the water. Beside these steps stood Ahmet, with a boat hook in his hands. As she watched, Tracy heard the sound of a motor-driven craft turning from the main channel to come toward the yali. She could see the boat clearly as it neared the lighted landing. It was a caique with a high curved prow, decorated in a design of bright colors. Above the center portion of the boat an oblong of white canopy with gaily scalloped edges sheltered seats from the rain. A boatman stood in the stern, steering his craft toward the landing. Beneath the canopy sat a passenger, only his legs visible.

With well-practiced skill, Ahmet reached out with his hook, the caique was made secure with a tossed rope, and the passenger beneath the canopy stepped lightly from boat to landing. For an instant Tracy's fingers tightened on the damp railing of the balcony. Then she stepped back into shadow where she could stand unseen. As he crossed the paved area he glanced up at the house and light fell upon his face. It was a somber, rather craggy face with a dark, well-shaped head, the sides touched with early gray. Tracy had seen his photograph more than once and she had looked it up again before she left New York. The man was Miles Radburn. Did this unexpected return mean that she must face him tonight? At dinner, perhaps? Earlier she had been keyed to this confrontation, but now she shrank from the finality it might bring. Tonight she wasn't ready. Mrs. Erim had dissipated the need for immediate courage, and she was no longer braced for the ordeal of meeting him. Had that perhaps been the woman's intent, with her tranquil manner that seemed to dismiss the very thought of struggle as needless waste?

When Radburn had disappeared into the house below, Tracy returned to her room and closed the doors upon chilly dampness and the dark smell of the water. She could not settle down now, but paced the great expanse of gold rug, while the white cat opened its eyes and stared at her without expression. The room was growing colder in spite of the glow of coals in the mangal, and she turned on the electric heater and sat within the range of its radiance.

A knock on the door sent her flying to answer, anxious to know how soon the meeting would be upon her.

Nursel Erim came into the room, moving gracefully on her high heels, a touch of exotic perfume floating about her.

"I am sorry to disturb you," she said. "Mrs. Erim sends me to ask if you will mind having dinner in your room tonight. Then it will not be necessary to tell Mr. Radburn of your presence at once. A quiet talk this evening will prepare him for your appearance tomorrow morning. You do not mind?"

Tracy did not mind, and said so in relief.

The Turkish girl lingered, apparently unwilling to leave at once.

"You have all you wish?" she asked. Though she glanced about the room, her words had an absent sound as though they were an excuse for her lingering, rather than the reason for it. When she spoke it was almost as if to herself, as if Tracy's presence here were incidental and of no consequence.

"I have not entered this room for several weeks. Always the room saddens me. It is as if something of Mrs. Radburn remains. I feel angry when I come here. Angry because this very carpet, which my friend chose herself from a shop in Istanbul, should remain while she is gone."

Tracy heard her in silence. The girl stepped to shuttered doors and peered out into the rain. "Always she loved the water. Sometimes we ran off together and made boat trips so we might laugh and be foolish, with no stern looks to tell us we were not children. But there is no laughter left in this room. It is too close to the water she loved, water that betrayed her."

"She drowned, didn't she?" Tracy asked in a low, tight voice.

"Yes." Nursel nodded. "Out there within full view of the yali. Had anyone known, had anyone been at the windows to see, perhaps it might not have happened. It was on a gray evening such as this. Perhaps that is why it seems that this room is haunted by her presence whenever it rains."

Tracy must have made some small sound, for Nursel returned from her dreaming to look at her curiously.

"This disturbs you? I am sorry. These matters are of no concern to you. There is no presence of Anabel Radburn in this room for someone who never knew her. You must rest now. Later Ahmet will bring you a tray. This is convenient for you? You do not mind?"

"I don't mind," Tracy said. "Thank you."

"Then I will leave you here." Nursel cast a last glance around the room and her eyes lighted upon the cat. "You do not mind if the cat remains? If you prefer, I will take it away."

"Let her stay," Tracy said.

She waited until Nursel had gone. Then she went to the balcony doors and pulled cords that swung thick draperies of gold damask across them. She did not want to look out at the water now. Not when the night was so cold, so depressingly gray. The cat sat up and watched her with a certain wariness in its eyes and she went to stand before the cushioned chair.

"First of all," said Tracy softly, "we will have to change your name. I should probably cry every time I spoke it. You would do much better with something that sounds more Turkish. Of course no Turk would give an animal the name of a friend. But since I don't know anyone named Yasemin, perhaps that will do. How would you like to be called Yasemin?"

The white cat mewed delicately, though whether in acceptance or repudiation Tracy could not tell. She moved toward it without suddenness and picked it up firmly in both hands. Then she sat down in the chair within the beam of the electric heater and placed it in her lap. Yasemin neither spat nor scratched, but neither did she settle down to purr. She merely tolerated, without acceptance. Tracy stroked the soft fur and found comfort in the warmth of the small living creature in her lap.

Perhaps she and the cat both dozed a little, for when Ahmet knocked on her door, Tracy started up and found that an hour had passed. At her sudden movement, Yasemin leaped away and went to hide beneath the bed, as if she knew Ahmet Effendi of old and had no liking for him.

The man set the tray upon a table, removed silver warming covers, and prepared her food with the expert movements of one long experienced. Apparently Ahmet could do everything. She tried to speak to him as she watched, but he merely shook his head at her words, indicating that he did not understand English. When he had gone, showing her first the bell she might ring when she was finished, she called Yasemin from beneath the bed, prepared a few tidbits for the cat, and then sat down before the tray.

It was good food, attractively arranged. A small steak, whipped potatoes, buttered beans of a variety she did not recognize. Apparently Mrs. Erim's household ate well, as the French knew how to eat. The short nap had refreshed her, Tracy found, and both she and Yasemin finished their dinner with good appetite.

When Halide had taken the tray away and brought more coals for the mangal, Tracy let Yasemin out into the house, where she vanished at once in the direction of the stairs. In the bathroom hot water had been prepared and Tracy took a steaming bath in the big European tub.

Returning to her room, hurrying, lest by some misfortune she meet Miles Radburn in the hall, Tracy meant to go at once to bed. But again the water drew her irresistibly. She slipped a coat over her nightgown, turned off the lights in the room, and parted the heavy draperies to step out upon the veranda. The landing area stood empty and quiet, water lapping gently against the steps. The rain had stopped, and in the stillness she could hear distant voices from a village on the nearby shore. A well-lighted ship went past, its engines throbbing as it made its way north from Istanbul toward the Black Sea and the ports of Russia. Overhead ragged clouds raced, a touch of faint moonlight breaking through patches of torn gray. The water drew her eyes—black and seemingly still on the surface, yet with those deep and treacherous currents stirring beneath.

Somewhere in the village a man began to sing, and she heard for the first time the minor-keyed lament of Turkish music, repetitive and strange to Western ears, yet somehow haunting.

Again a sense of isolation swept over her. She was out of touch with all she knew and was sure of, abroad upon currents that might take her almost anywhere. Mrs. Erim, for all her calmly authoritative ways, was a woman with depths not easily read. The younger Nursel was also a puzzle, with her devotion to Anabel and her slight air of reserve that overlay all small courteous efforts toward a guest. She had yet to meet Dr. Erim, the brother. And tomorrow there would be the man she had come here to see— Miles Radburn. Loneliness and confusion engulfed her. Had she been right in this quest? Was there an answer to be found? She left the veranda door slightly ajar, turned off the heater, and got into the big comfortable bed, glad enough to be weary.

She slept heavily, wakening only now and then to strange sounds from the watercourse that flowed beyond her doors. Then waking not at all until the vociferous crowing of what seemed a thousand roosters began at the break of day.

3

For a little while Tracy lay beneath blankets and stared at a liquid shifting of patterns upon the diamond design of the ceiling. Through the opened slit of veranda door a flickering snake of watery light made its way into the room and told her the rain was over, the sun up and shining upon the Bosporus. She lay still a few moments longer, listening to crowing cocks and bleating goats. Then she slipped out of bed and went to look outside.

The hills of the opposite shore were newly green after the rain, and the Bosporus was a dark deep blue beneath a lighter sky. In coves across the water streamers of mist drifted, thinning as sunlight reached them. She could see the weathered wooden houses of a small village opposite climbing steeply upward. Across the strait in the direction of Istanbul, a great triangle of stone walls with a huge round tower at each apex mounted the steep pitch of hillside—apparently a medieval fortress.

But the morning air was cold and she soon closed her doors upon the brightening scene. The sun would help. Already its light restored her lagging courage, steeled her in a sense of purpose. Soon now she must face Miles Radburn and this morning she would be ready for him. She must be ready for him.

Halide brought her breakfast tray, with rolls and syrupy black Turkish coffee. Tracy sat in bed against plumped pillows with the table over her knees and breakfasted in unfamiliar luxury, regretting only the continental meagerness of the meal. This morning she could have managed the pancakes and bacon and eggs of a good American breakfast.

The room no longer seemed haunted and the white cat was not there to lend a slightly melancholy presence. She had difficulty accustoming herself to the room's vast expanses, however. The modern furnishings did not really suit the room, and she wondered if Anabel had chosen them, along with the gold carpet, in order to brighten its shadowy gloom. She and Miles Radburn seemed to have lived here for some time as permanent and privileged guests. Quite evidently Sylvana Erim regarded herself as a patron of the arts and she apparently had the wealth, thanks to her Turkish husband, to indulge her whims on this score.

By the time Nursel Erim came to fetch her, Tracy had put on a gray-blue frock, simply cut to her small waist and slim figure. Her one ornament was again the gold pin that was something of a talisman. She had brushed her brown hair to the shining perfection that was her one pride, and swirled it into a high coil on the back of her head. She looked neat, if not gaudy, she decided —and promptly felt like nothing at all the moment she beheld the vision of Nursel.

This morning's version of the Turkish girl was simpler as to coiffure and her heels were not so high, but she was no less smartly dramatic in tight black Capri pants and a blue Angora sweater that set her off to good effect. The sultans, Tracy recalled, had liked their ladies generous of curve, and while the dress might have changed from pantaloons to pants, the ample flesh was there and roundly enticing.

"Mrs. Erim wishes to speak with you," Nursel said. "She awaits you in Mr. Radburn's study."

"Is—is he there?" Tracy asked.

The other girl shook her head. "Always he goes for a long, very fast walk after breakfast. It is a British custom, I think? Soon he will return, but Mrs. Erim will see you first."

Miles Radburn's rooms were also on the third floor, overlooking the land side of the house across the drafty gloom of the big salon. Nursel escorted her to the door of the study and opened it for her. Beyond the expanse of a walnut desk piled high with books and papers Sylvana Erim sat in a leather chair. She said, "Good morning," pleasantly and indicated a chair. Then she moved a commanding finger that caused Nursel to close the door and obediently vanish. Mrs. Erim was accustomed, quite evidently, to a well-trained household. Tracy found herself wondering if tradition had trained Nursel to meek acceptance of this dowager rule. Away from Sylvana, the girl appeared to have more spark of her own.

"You slept well?" Sylvana asked of Tracy, and went on without waiting for an answer, gesturing widely with her hands. "You see? This, my young friend, is what you have come to contend with."

Tracy saw. She did not sit down at once, thus opposing herself in a small way to Mrs. Erim. It was better for her own courage if she did not give in too easily to this autocratic woman.

The huge room was no more tidy than the desk. Wall shelves were packed with books that lay in disorder, sometimes propped one against the next, sometimes in leaning stacks. In one corner stood a refectory table piled high with a conglomeration of papers and books, folders and portfolios. A large armchair of red damask held more of this hodgepodge in its stolid arms. The only oasis in the sea of disorder was a drawing table with slanted board that stood near veranda doors, a piece of work in progress upon it. At least the room boasted a tall, elaborate white porcelain stove that gave off a more comfortable warmth than that provided by an electric heater.

"I can see what Mr. Hornwright meant when he spoke of a housekeeper being needed," Tracy said wryly.

Mrs. Erim stiffened as if the words were a reflection upon her establishment. "He will allow the servants to touch nothing, you understand. He does not mind dust if it is not upon his drawing board. We manage to come and go behind his back, but you can see the difficulty."

Tracy could indeed. The task looked monumental in its most elementary steps, and, with the master of this confusion set in opposition to order, she had no idea of how she might proceed. Moving about the room, she paused before the drawing board where a long strip of cream-colored paper bore decorative Turkish script done in India ink.

Mrs. Erim noted her interest. "That is ancient Turkish calligraphy. Mr. Radburn has taken great interest in mastering the art of copying such script. Though, of course, he does not read it. But come—sit here, if you please. He will return soon and we must discuss this matter a little. I do not have good news for you."

Tracy sat down and looked at her hostess. Mrs. Erim had discarded her flowing robe and wore a gray suit that bore, like

272

Nursel's clothes, the stamp of Paris. Her long golden hair was caught into a coil on the nape of her neck and held by a silken snood. In the morning light her complexion seemed more glowing than ever. Again an air of calm assurance lay upon her. Clearly she expected those about her to fall in with her ways and Tracy braced herself a little. She must not let this woman intimidate her, or defeat her purpose in coming here.

"Last night I talked to Mr. Radburn after dinner," Mrs. Erim said. "He does not wish you to remain. He will not allow you to touch one paper of his material. But he agrees to speak with you. This, at least, I have arranged. When I asked that you be permitted to stay a week, he would not listen. The mood of the bear is upon him—and what can one do?"

Had Mrs. Erim worked for her or against her in this paving of the way? Tracy wondered. She did not trust the woman at all.

"Then I'll have to talk to him myself," she said, attempting a confidence she did not feel.

Mrs. Erim regarded her in silence for a moment. Then she rose in her graceful, unhurried manner and crossed the big room to the closed door of an adjoining room.

"Come," she said. "I have something to show you."

She opened the door upon what was obviously Miles Radburn's bedroom and stepped aside for Tracy to see. Here there was no confusion. The room appeared lived in, but crisply in order. The veranda shutters had been set ajar and morning sunshine poured in from a woodsy hillside beyond, warming the air a little and stage-lighting the room with a bright shaft that fell upon the bed.

Tracy spent no more than a glance upon the room itself, for her eyes were caught at once by a picture that hung above the carved headboard of the wide bed. It was the portrait of a young woman painted in a high, soft, silvery key—a little misty in its execution, except for the face which had been presented in slightly exaggerated focus. Tracy's fingers curled about the lower rail of the bed and she stood braced against the flood of emotion that washed over her. Somewhere, sometime, in one way or another, she had known the moment would come. Now it was here. From the wall her sister's face looked down at her, as elusive, as secretive, yet as strangely appealing as Tracy remembered, and almost as real as a living presence.

The picture showed a slender girl in a lacy white gown, her fair hair drawn loosely from her forehead and tied at the back of the neck with a silver ribbon. The curved cheek and jaw line of the partly turned head revealed a breathtaking beauty. The mouth had been touched with pale color, unsmiling and wide, but not too full of lip. Only the eyes had been emphasized to the point of distortion. They seemed closed, and dark lashes lay smudged against pale cheeks. One saw at second glance that they were not wholly closed. The girl in the picture gazed from beneath lowered lids, a faint, green-eyed gleam just showing. It was a face that hinted of tragedy, yet all in the same instant perversely promised joy. It was a young face, yet never carelessly young, the whole done with misty fragility—from which the dark smudging of the eyes stood out in vivid, unsettling contrast.

"That is Anabel," Mrs. Erim said. "His wife."

Tracy stared at the picture and waited for the room to settle. She had known this intensity of feeling must come, but she had not expected the portrait, had not been braced for it.

"She is the reason why this book will never be finished," Mrs. Erim said calmly. "Only three months ago she died tragically, as you may know, and the shadow of her suicide lies heavily upon all of us. Your Mr. Hornwright thinks only in practical terms of how many pages of script, how many prints must be made from Miles Radburn's drawings. To persuade Mr. Radburn he speaks of the healing value of work, but he does not understand the evil truth about this shadow."

Tracy drew her gaze from the portrait abruptly. The room had steadied, her vision cleared. "What do you mean by the truth?" she asked.

"This is not your affair." Mrs. Erim spoke with calm assurance, as though she reproved a child. "Your duty is to return home and make Mr. Hornwright understand that there will be no book. Nothing else concerns you here."

So this was why she had been invited to the yali. If permitted to remain, this was to be her accomplishment.

"You are against this book, Mrs. Erim," Tracy countered. "Will you tell me why?"

The Frenchwoman shrugged. "As I say, I am a realist. I have a practical nature. To a man who was once a fine artist, this work is a method of burying himself alive. It is a ridiculous thing that a child like yourself has been sent to deal with such a problem."

Tracy looked again at the picture. "Do you mean that he loved her so much that he can't bear to live without her? That all work has become meaningless to him?"

The veneer of calm flickered for an instant and threatened to crack, while the bright color in Mrs. Erim's cheeks flamed more intensely.

"What absurdity! You do not understand. Certainly he had no love for her in the last years of their marriage. She was wicked, depraved, beyond hope. At the end he despised her. But it is difficult for him to face this thing in himself. This is why he prefers not to be alive. He buried himself in such meaningless work as he does now long before her death."

This was not the first time Tracy had heard her sister spoken of in scathing terms. Yet even after Tracy Hubbard had ceased to be an adoring small sister and was old enough to face the fact that Anabel was sometimes less than perfect, she had never wholly accepted this verdict. The enigma of her sister still troubled her, as well as the question of whether there was more she herself might have done; whether some action of hers might have averted the final tragedy.

"Why did she die?" Tracy ventured. "Why would a girl who had so much take her own life? A girl who was so beautiful!"

The moment the words were spoken she saw that she had gone too far in pressing for an answer. She had forgotten the need for caution. There was sudden wariness in Mrs. Erim's eyes.

"It is a childish thing to parallel worldly possessions and beauty with happiness," Sylvana Erim said virtuously, overlooking the fact that her own manner of living seemed to contradict this tenet. "You will do well to content yourself with the task for which you have come. I must remind you again that Mr. Radburn's private concerns are not your affair. This is true, is it not, Miss Hubbard?"

The time had come to step back from the line she had overreached. "Of course they're not my affair," Tracy said meekly. "It's just that you showed me the portrait and my interest was aroused."

"I show you the portrait only that you may understand the folly of your errand. You will be wise not to mention to Mr. Radburn that you have seen it."

Tracy could feel the warmth in her own cheeks. Once more she felt like a child who had been disciplined and did not dare to answer back. Before she could attempt a reply, there was a knock on the study door and Halide's voice called urgently in Turkish.

At once Mrs. Erim led the way back to the study, closing the bedroom door behind her. "He is coming now. I will wait to introduce you, then leave you in his hands. When you wish to arrange your plane reservation home, I will be glad to take care of it for you."

Tracy could have wished for more time to recover from the impact of the portrait and from this exchange with Sylvana Erim. She felt as though the label of her identity had been stamped upon her, and she wished for Anabel's well-remembered trick of gazing beneath lowered lids that never revealed all that she was thinking.

The study door opened abruptly and a man stood upon the threshold. He was tall and leanly built. That he had once been a soldier was evident in the straightness of his back, the carriage of his shoulders, yet there was nothing in his bearing to suggest that he welcomed with interest what any new day held for him. His rather craggy face achieved that curious effect of being handsome which strong though ill-assorted features may assume in certain men. He looked older than his thirty-eight years and his face evidenced a somber quality, suggesting a loss of the ability to laugh.

"You look well," Mrs. Erim said. "It is a good morning for your walk. Miles, this is Miss Hubbard, the young girl who has been sent from New York to see that you proceed in your work with great dispatch." Amusement lighted her eyes. "I will leave you to settle the matter between you," she added and went to the door.

Miles Radburn opened it in silence and closed it after her. Then he turned and looked at Tracy without expression.

"Why Hornwright sent you, I'll never understand," he said, and Tracy noted that his years in America had not banished the British inflection from his speech. "Nor do I understand why you came on after I wrote you at the hotel. Perhaps you had better sit down and tell me what this nonsense is all about."

Tracy seated herself beside his desk, mentally rejecting the label of "young girl" that Mrs. Erim had placed upon her. Even as a child, she had sometimes felt herself older than Anabel. Miles Radburn stayed where he was, his hands busy with a briar pipe and pouch of tobacco, his eyes indifferent, no longer upon her. He had added up her sum total, found it of no consequence, and was already dismissing her. The very fact served to stiffen her spine still more. She must think only of how she could persuade this man to let her stay.

When the pipe was lighted to his satisfaction, he shoved a heap of papers carelessly to one side and sat on a corner of the desk, swinging one long leg. The blue pipe smoke carried a not unpleasant tang.

"Begin," he said. "Recite your piece. I've promised Sylvana I would listen. Just that and nothing more."

She sat up resolutely and faced him. "Mr. Hornwright feels that you are doing an important and distinguished book. Turkish mosaics have a significant place in the history of the world's art and—"

"Spare me that sort of sales talk," Radburn interrupted. "I know why I'm doing what I am doing. I'm curious only to know why you are here. There was a Miss Baker whose name I suggested to Hornwright. Do you fancy that you can take her place?"

She'd had enough of being talked down to—first by Mrs. Erim and now by this cold, rather frightening man.

"You're not ready for Miss Baker," she told him heatedly. "She would take one look at this—this mess!—and go straight home. Do you think she'd be willing to sneeze her way through all that?" Tracy waved a scornful hand at the refectory table, where the pile had reached so dangerous a height that an avalanche to the floor was momentarily threatened.

Radburn glared at her out of gray eyes that were without warmth, though he was clearly capable of anger.

"I can find anything I want at a moment's notice," he said. "I want no one coming in and mixing things up."

"Mixing things up!" Tracy echoed, forgetting that she was here to placate, to coax and cajole, to somehow endear herself so he would allow her to stay. "I never heard anything so silly in my life. Look—look at this!"

She left her chair like a small and impetuous cyclone and dived into the pile on the table with both hands. The avalanche tottered for an instant and then a good part of it went sailing off into space to scatter itself about the floor at Tracy's feet. Her indignation left her as abruptly as it had risen and she found herself regarding in horror the destruction she had wrought. She did not dare to look at Miles Radburn.

There was a long and deadly silence, broken by an explosion of sound. It was a sneeze. And having started, Mr. Radburn could not stop. He sneezed twice, blew his nose violently, unable to speak, and then repeated the explosion four more times in rapid succession.

Out of the past a sudden memory of her father's outraged face flashed into Tracy's mind and she suppressed a desire toward incongruous laughter.

"You're behaving just like my father!" she cried. "He wouldn't let anybody touch a thing in his study. But he couldn't really find what he wanted, the way he claimed. I was the only one who could straighten out his papers and keep them in any sort of order. So maybe I do have some experience that would be useful to you."

His sneezing spell subsiding, Mr. Radburn flourished his hand-kerchief. "Perhaps you can begin," he said coldly, "by picking up everything you've sent off onto the floor."

Tracy looked down at scattered pages of manuscript and draw-ings. "Where would I put it if I picked it up?" she asked reason-ably. "Surely not back on the summit of the mountain?"

A dark flush had engulfed Mr. Radburn's somber features and there were beads of perspiration on his forehead. Unexpectedly, Tracy felt sorry for him. After all, she thought, with that perver-sity of humor that so often seized her at inopportune moments, how did one deal with an intruder who behaved as she had?

"I'm sorry," she said contritely. "But you were way off some-where with your made-up mind and I had to get you to listen to me, to pay attention. I think I can be of some help without dis-turbing you as much as you think. I enjoy setting things in order and I don't chatter or make loud noises. You can pretend I'm not here. Besides, I do have a stake in this, you know."

"Why should I interest myself in your stake?" he demanded. "I have not asked you to come here."

Tracy went on as though she had not heard him. "I've been working for a couple of years at *Views*. It's a wonderful, exciting place where things are happening. Someday, if I'm useful enough, and enough of a burr under someone's collar, they'll let me into editorial work. I begged Mr. Hornwright to send me on this as-signment. I thought I could do a sort of housekeeping job before

Miss Baker came. If I go home empty-handed, it's likely that I'll be fired. Especially if I go home within a day or so of when I got here."

Everything she was saying was true. If it was not the whole truth, it must nevertheless sound convincing.

"This is a responsibility I refuse to accept," Radburn said. "It's not my affair."

Tracy regarded him almost pityingly. He looked like a man in whom all light and warmth had been wiped out. She turned from him and knelt on the floor before the scattered papers. There was an empty space beneath the table and she began depositing the sheets one by one in orderly heaps in that single clear space. Typed pages in this pile, carbon sheets in that. Penciled notes over there and sketches here. A special place for what appeared to be finished drawings of tile and mosaic detail. When the man behind her left his desk and moved restlessly about the room, she did not look at him.

"I am a short-tempered man," he said at length, and she knew that his voice came from near the veranda doors, where he must have paused before his drawing table. "I lack patience and I have no particular fondness for catering to women. I do not swear at the servants, but I am likely to swear at you if you annoy me."

Tracy looked up from a lovely mosaic pattern done in varying shades of blue. "If you swear at me I'll talk back," she said. "I don't like being sworn at. It will be more peaceful if you just ignore me and let me work." She turned the drawing over and saw the lettering on the back: *Sultan Ahmed.*

"This is from Sultan Ahmed's Blue Mosque, isn't it?" she said eagerly. "I must see that before I leave Turkey. And I want to visit St. Sophia—Ayasofia." She looked up at him and intensity was once more in her voice. "Mr. Radburn, will you let me stay for a week at least?"

He did not swear, though for a moment he looked as though he might. Then, to her astonishment, since she had not thought it possible, a fleeting smile lifted the grim corners of his mouth.

"One week," he said. "I will bribe you with a week. Otherwise you are likely to tumble the books from my shelves and engulf me in wreckage. Didn't your father ever swear at you?"

"My father is a gentleman," she told him with dignity. "And I was very young in those days. He only spanked me."

"An excellent solution," said Miles Radburn, and went grimly back to his painstaking calligraphy work on the drawing board.

Silence fell upon the room. Somewhat shakily Tracy settled herself cross-legged on the carpet, careful not to let her weight creak the old, old boards of the floor. She lifted her papers without a rustle. The occupation of her hands gradually calmed her, and she thrust back the small surge of elation that sought to possess her. A week would never be enough. Not only for this task—but for the other more important one that had brought her here. The questions she must have an answer to, for her own peace of mind. At least she had made a beginning. Mr. Hornwright might be astonished if he saw her now, but he would not be wholly displeased.

The work was unexpectedly absorbing. At least Miles Radburn had identified each sketch on its back. Before long she had a pile of Blue Mosque drawings alone, and others were beginning to emerge. The Mosque of Suleiman the Magnificent, of course, as well as numerous unpronounceable mosque and palace names she had never heard of—each with a pattern of its own. The variety of tile designs was amazing and endless. She made no attempt to read manuscript pages, but simply piled them up. They would have to be arranged by subject matter later. More than once she pressed a finger hard beneath her nose to avoid a sneeze. A dust cloth would be needed before any of this material could be put into a file, but for now she would be still as a mouse and continue her sorting.

While she worked she tried not to think of that portrait on the wall of Miles Radburn's bedroom. The enigma loomed larger than ever, and there was pain as well in any thought of her sister. Now she must deal only with the task at hand.

The morning passed quietly. Radburn worked at his drawing board and paid her no attention. No one came to disturb them, and when Tracy finally stole a look at her watch she found that it was nearly twelve o'clock.

"I'm going out for a while," Radburn said abruptly. "I presume someone will tell you what to do about lunch when the time comes."

He did not glance at the neat piles emerging beneath the shelter of the table, but went out of the room and closed the door firmly behind him. Tracy seized the moment to jump up and stretch widely. She would have to find some more comfortable way to work. Another table certainly, and a chair would have to be provided. Perhaps Nursel would help her. She would ask nothing of Mrs. Erim, who thought Anabel wicked and depraved, and who wanted to see Tracy Hubbard go home as soon as possible.

It was Nursel who at length came tapping on the door to summon her to lunch. The Turkish girl had changed from Capri pants to a full print skirt that gave her a flower-patterned grace of movement. She stood for a moment looking in astonishment at the heaps of sketches and papers beneath the table.

"He allowed you to do this? But it is a miracle!"

"He didn't allow me," Tracy admitted sheepishly. "I just started doing it and he didn't know how to stop me."

"Then you are not to go straight home as Mrs. Erim expects?"

Tracy shook her head. "I have a week. Then we'll see."

"Mrs. Erim will be surprised," said Nursel guardedly.

"And not pleased, I think," Tracy said.

Nursel made no comment. "Luncheon is ready. My brother and I would like you to dine with us, please. You have yet to meet Murat. Mrs. Erim dines in her own rooms in the kiosk. Come downstairs when you are ready."

Back in her room—Anabel's room—Tracy peered into the dressing table mirrors and found cobwebs in her hair and smudges on her nose. Her hands were grimy, and she set Miles Radburn down another notch in her estimation for being a careless and untidy man. Yet the bedroom had been as neat as a military barracks. There had been no disorder to distract from the effect of that stunning portrait on the wall.

If he had despised Anabel, why had he hung her picture there? The question persisted in Tracy's mind—one of the questions to which she must find the answer. But there was no time to puzzle now, with Nursel waiting for her. There was still the fourth member of this household to meet, and she must be careful during this meal. Careful to make no slips, careful to appear nothing more than they believed her to be. At least she was relieved to know that she need not face Sylvana Erim again immediately. There was a shrewdness about the woman that would seize upon any slip Tracy might make.

When she had washed in cold water and rid herself of smudges, she went down to the second floor. Nursel took her into a room which was apparently used as both living and dining quarters and which, she explained, she shared with her brother. Again there was a large Turkish stove to help against the chill. While Sylvana, the foreigner, had turned to old-fashioned, becushioned Turkish luxury in her rooms, the younger two had furnished their salon as though they could not decide between European and Turkish furnishings, and thus did justice to neither. As Turks, they had excellent taste, while their adaptations of much that was European left something to be desired. There were Middle Eastern touches of tilework and mother-of-pearl, fine carpets on the floor, and, in contrast, rather heavy graceless furniture of walnut or mahogany set stiffly at attention. Along one wall shelves displayed a collection of small art objects behind closed glass doors.

"My brother is busy in his laboratory so we will not wait for him," Nursel said. "There are times when he does not come to meals at all. He has made a study of diseases of the Middle East and at present he is working on a new drug for the treatment of a certain virulent eye disease."

"Will Mr. Radburn join you at lunch?" Tracy asked.

"Who is to know?" Nursel spoke lightly. "Our guest does as he pleases."

They sat at a table set for four, and a servant brought hot clear soup with crescents of vegetables in the broth.

"I must warn you that there is a crisis," Nursel said as they began to eat. "My brother does not ordinarily lose his temper. Perhaps he is not always a reasonable man, but he has a good disposition and is very kind when he is not angry. Today he is very angry with Mr. Radburn."

She would have left the matter there, but Tracy, eager to learn whatever she could of Miles Radburn, questioned her openly.

"What has he done to make your brother angry?"

Again Nursel's dislike of the artist was evident. "Yesterday Murat wished to use our caique to cross the Bosporus for an important appointment, but Mr. Radburn had taken it himself. My brother was most inconvenienced. There is a small motorboat also, but Ahmet Effendi had gone on an errand across the Bosporus in that. Murat is still much disturbed." Nursel's dark eyes danced with sudden sly mischief. "I must warn you that it is better for a woman to cast down her eyes and take no sides when my brother is angry. While he is a modern Turk and a great admirer of Mustapha Kemal, I can tell you he is given to the old beliefs when it comes to women. I am supposed to be emancipated. But you will see."

Her words and manner suggested that Murat's sister had a mind of her own that was not altogether acquiescent, for all that she seemed to move in obedient meekness about this twin establishment.

As they were finishing their soup, Dr. Erim appeared. He was a man of medium height, darkly handsome. Though he was a number of years older, the stamp of family resemblance marked him as Nursel's brother and his eyes were as large and lustrous as hers—true Turkish eyes. Thick black hair was brushed back from a fine forehead and his nose had an aquiline look that gave his face a faintly sinister cast.

He bowed over Tracy's hand gallantly, clearly a man who appreciated the company of women. He was more friendly toward her than anyone else in this house had been, with none of Nursel's suggestion of holding herself off even as she went through the gestures of hospitality. He asked Tracy pertinent questions about herself and why she was here, yet with no suspicious probing. Though he did not seem to take her work with *Views* seriously, he at least treated her as a woman. A fact that was somewhat reassuring after Miles Radburn's cool dismissal of her. At the same time she found Dr. Erim's attentive manner a little disquieting. This was a game she'd had little practice in playing. For Anabel it had come naturally, but Tracy had always recognized that she could not be another Anabel.

"It is pleasant that you have come to visit us in Istanbul, Miss Hubbard," Dr. Erim said. "Even though I fear this trip will prove a waste of your time."

"I've already begun work for Mr. Radburn," Tracy told him. "Why is it a waste of time if I help in the preparation of material for his book?"

Murat Erim shrugged. "This is work which should be done by a Turk. Mr. Radburn is an outsider. It is not possible that he will understand our ancient mosaics as a Turk would understand them."

Tracy found herself speaking up in defense of Miles's project. "Mr. Radburn seems to have done a great deal of research. The editors of *Views* feel that the book will be an important one."

"No doubt, no doubt," said Dr. Erim blandly and let the matter go.

During the meal he did most of the talking. He explained how the *dolmas* were made with vine leaves stuffed with savory rice, nuts, and currants, and extolled the Turkish predilection for flavoring everything with lemon juice. Tracy helped herself from the plate of freshly cut lemons on the table and found that a few drops improved the flavor of lamb.

While they ate, Dr. Erim spoke of his sister too, mentioning her almost in the same breath with the food, and as though she could no more hear him than could one of the vegetables on his plate.

"Nursel is an example of what Turkey is doing for women," he said proudly. "Today is not like the old times. Everything is possible for women now. You know that my sister received training to be a physician?"

Tracy looked at the Turkish girl in surprise, but Nursel shook her head, deprecating her brother's words.

"Please—Murat knows I did not continue with my studies. My father and my two brothers overestimated my ability. They were too enthusiastic about arranging my life in the new pattern. I did not complete my training."

"Nevertheless, she is now most useful in my laboratory," Dr. Erim said. "That is, when I can persuade her to help me there. She is often busy with social events, or with doing her hair in the latest fashion, or in helping Mrs. Erim with her perfume-making." He sniffed the air and made a slight grimace. "Even my laboratory has taken to smelling of attar of roses!"

"Which may improve it," Nursel said, faintly mocking. "Guinea pigs and mice do not of themselves furnish a pleasant atmosphere. If you wish, I will help you this afternoon."

They were halfway through the meal when Miles Radburn appeared, and at once silence fell upon the table. The artist took his place without apology for being late, but he did launch at once into an explanation about the boat.

"Sylvana has told me you were inconvenienced," he said to Dr. Erim. "I'm sorry. I'd supposed the boat was free for the afternoon, and there was a matter I wanted to check as soon as possible."

There could be a burning quality concentrated in Murat Erim's dark eyes. He was restraining himself with difficulty, it appeared,

284

though the reason for his annoyance seemed out of proportion to the cause.

"It would be better, perhaps, if you asked permission to use the boat first," he said, breathing a bit heavily.

"Of course I asked permission." Miles gave his attention to the soup. "Sylvana said it would be quite all right to use it for my errand. As I've said, I'm sorry if I inconvenienced you."

Dr. Erim stared at him, and Tracy thought uncomfortably that this was how hatred would look. She did not believe she had ever seen it exhibited so strongly in a man's eyes.

"There are times," Dr. Erim said, "when I forget that I am not master in my father's house."

Nursel flashed a sidelong glance at her brother and then looked at the food on her plate. Miles said nothing. It was as though, having made his apology, he had shut himself away from them, and Tracy remembered what Mr. Hornwright had said about a wall. Miles Radburn had gone behind one now and was indifferent to the others at the table.

Dr. Erim too fell into a silence that was heavy with resentment. Sitting next to him, Tracy noticed that he drew from his pocket a short string of yellowed ivory beads and began to play them through his fingers. Bead by bead, each one slipped along a cord until he reached the large finial bead that joined two ends of the strand in a sort of tassel. He toyed with the large bead briefly and then went on around the string again until the absent movement of his fingers seemed to calm him.

Nursel saw Tracy's interest and spoke to her brother. "Perhaps Miss Hubbard has never seen a *tespih* before. You must show her this one."

Dr. Erim started as though he had not noted the occupation of his hands, and held up the ivory beads with a faint smile. "We find that busy fingers often calm the mind and quiet the nerves," he said and handed the beads to Tracy.

The ivory was warm from his fingers as she ran the beads through her own. "Are they prayer beads?" Tracy asked.

Dr. Erim shook his head. "Not these. A proper strand of prayer beads must have exactly thirty-three beads in its length. These are shorter. I've heard the English call them 'fidgit strings.' They are only for the therapeutic purpose of busying the hands. You will see them in the hands of men all through the Middle East."

"How strange that women do not need the same outlet." Nursel raised her own pretty, well-manicured hands, wriggling her fingers. "I suppose we are expected to be so thoroughly occupied with household tasks that our hands are busy enough. Murat has many *tespihler* in his collection. You must show Miss Hubbard sometime."

"Why not?" Dr. Erim said. "Let me show her some of them now, while we wait for dessert."

With a key from his pocket he unlocked a glass cabinet against the wall and reached toward a shelf, where more of the beads were spread out in display or piled in glowing heaps of mixed color. He chose several strands at random and brought them to the table.

They were lovely things. Some of the less expensive were endlessly varied in their coloring. There were others of greater value made of ivory and amber. Some of the amber beads were still in their reddish, unaged state, while others were a golden, honey brown. All were smoothly rounded, without carving, to give a proper texture for the fingers. In the little heap on the table was a single tespih of black jet, gleaming darkly among the rest.

Dr. Erim reached into the heap and picked it up. "This is typically Turkish," he said. "A strand of black amber."

Tracy's fingers, moving idly among the beads, stilled. Perhaps it was only her imagination, but it seemed to her that everyone in the room was staring at the black beads in Dr. Erim's hands. Even Miles Radburn was paying somber attention. Ahmet, who had just come into the room with a tray of stemmed glasses containing rose sherbet, allowed his attention to flicker briefly over the glittering heap and focus on the black.

For Tracy, it was as if the sound of Anabel's voice echoed through the room. The high hysterical note of her sister's telephone call from Istanbul was so sharply clear in Tracy's mind that she half expected others in the room to hear and respond to it. Anabel had wailed something about "black amber"—though her confused words had meant nothing to Tracy. Now, in this house, the phrase had been repeated and it rang so insistent a note in her mind that Tracy could not let the moment escape without catching up these key words.

"What is black amber?" she asked.

Murat Erim dropped the black beads at her place. "It is a form of jet which is mined near our eastern border in a town called

Erzerum. It is a popular stone often used for pins and other jewelry, as well as for making tespihler."

Tracy picked up the strand. The smooth jet shone intensely black in her hands, but, though she ran the beads through her fingers several times, they seemed in no way remarkable.

Dr. Erim returned the black tespih to the heap and started to gather up the strands to make room for Ahmet's dessert plates. Then he paused and gestured toward the tespihler.

"You must choose for yourself one of these, Miss Hubbard. As a souvenir of Turkey. Please—any that you like."

Tracy thanked him, hesitating. She touched the black amber, picked it up, and it seemed to her that the room hushed, waiting. Carelessly she let the strand ripple through her fingers, discarding it, and chose an inexpensive string of gray-blue beads.

"It is very kind of you," she said. "May I have this blue one? It matches my dress."

"But of course," he said. "Keep it for yourself."

The moment of stillness, of waiting, was past. The room seemed to move and breathe again. Dr. Erim swept up the rest of the beads and replaced them on the shelves, locking the cabinet. Tracy held up her choice, allowing the tespih to dangle from her fingers, suddenly aware that Murat was looking, not at the beads, but directly at her with an odd, questioning expression on his face. Ahmet was no longer paying attention and Miles had again retired behind his wall. Yet Tracy had received the momentary impression that the attention of the room had been upon the black beads, and that Murat was interested in her rejection of them more than he was interested in the choice she had made.

Nursel broke the brief silence, making conversation almost nervously. "You must tell us about yourself, Miss Hubbard. What part of the United States are you from?"

Tracy dropped the tespih into her lap. Off guard, she answered readily. "I was born in the Midwest—in Iowa," she said, and at once could have bitten her tongue. But if it meant anything to Miles or the other two that she came from the state where Anabel was born, no one showed it and Tracy hurried on.

"I've always wanted to live in New York. I love the smell of printer's ink and I wanted to be in the center of publishing."

She knew she was chattering and found it difficult to stop. It was a relief when Dr. Erim, having recovered from his tiff with Miles Radburn, joined in the talk again. There was no further clash between the two men, and Miles still seemed unaware of how greatly he had annoyed the other. Tracy ate the delicately flavored sherbet and enjoyed a piece of *locum*—the richly sweet Turkish delight.

When they left the table, she turned hesitantly to Miles Radburn, but before she could ask about the afternoon he spoke to her curtly.

"I prefer that you let your—ah—housekeeping go for the moment. I won't be around to answer questions and I'd rather you keep out of my papers when I'm not present."

He did not wait for agreement, but went off toward the stairs. Ahmet held the door for Tracy, bowing as she came through, and she had a feeling that he understood Miles's words, indeed had a greater understanding of English than he pretended.

She returned to her room, feeling more than a little annoyed with herself. She had not needed Miles Radburn's presence that morning. She had asked him no questions. Yet only when she was angry enough did she seem able to face him with sufficient determination to gain her own way.

The gray-blue tespih was still in her hand and she studied it absently, thinking of the black amber. Had the sense of arrested attention she felt been wholly imaginary, or had everyone in the room really watched her when she held up the black beads just before she discarded them? The strand had seemed innocent enough in itself. Yet Anabel's frightened voice persisted in her mind. This too was part of the ominous puzzle that would not let her be until she found the answer.

She put the beads aside, ready now to face the thing she had been holding off throughout the morning. She must confront the fact of her sister's portrait on the wall of Radburn's room, with all the ramifications of why it was there, if, as Anabel had implied, he had turned against her. The urge to see it again was so strong that Tracy's next step seemed inevitable. With Miles Radburn away, this was the time.

She opened the door of her room a crack and listened intently. The vast gloom of the salon had a thick feeling of unstirred emptiness. She could hear the voices of servants from the depths of the house, but there seemed to be no one up here. She opened her door wide and looked across the nearly empty expanse toward the door of Miles's study. It stood slightly ajar and she went toward it, moving quietly.

WHEN SHE REACHED the study she paused again to listen. The inner silence was complete. Cautiously she pushed the door to a wider angle so that she could look into the room. And paused in surprise, for it was not, after all, empty. The houseman, Ahmet, stood before Miles's drawing table, apparently studying the script upon it in utter concentration. When he finally sensed her presence and looked up, his dark face did not change. He stared at her with unblinking eyes, his expression telling her nothing. After a moment he stepped back from the board, made her his usual polite bow, and gestured toward the calligraphy with one long-fingered hand.

"Hanimefendi," he said, "—this word of Allah."

The explanation seemed clear. For an uneasy moment she had felt there was something wrong about the man's quiet, absorbed presence in this room, but there was no reason why he should not, as a good Moslem, study the word of the Koran that Miles Radburn had copied.

"Do you read the old Turkish script, Ahmet Effendi?" she asked.

He shook his head without indication that he understood and slipped past her from the room. So softly and smoothly did he move that she scarcely heard his tread upon the stairs, though she stood in the doorway looking after him. When she was certain he had gone, Tracy crossed the study to Miles's bedroom door and opened it. Her heart began to thud in her ears, but there was no one there, and she went to the foot of the bed where she could best see the portrait of her sister.

This picture, she felt sure, had never been exhibited. It must have been painted during the early time of Anabel's marriage to Miles Radburn. She knew enough about his work to recognize the excellence of the portrayal, though the picture was unlike anything else he had done. The misty-silver quality that lay over the whole, with the lovely, tragic face emerging from it, the eyes in dark, dramatic contrast, was totally different from the usual Radburn touch. Working in a manner that was wholly virile, he had nevertheless intensified the femininity of his subject. As always, he was a superb draughtsman, and the excellence of the painting gave its emotional effect upon the beholder all the more impact.

Out of childhood memory haunting lines of verse came to Anabel's sister, and she spoke them aloud whimsically.

> This maiden she lived with no other thought
> Than to love and be loved by me.

But that was Annabel Lee, and this Anabel had been mistaken in her loving. In his portrait the artist had caught the very essence of her being—a sort of gossamer tension that had always frightened Tracy. The same look had been upon her that day eight years ago when Anabel had come to Iowa to tell her fifteen-year-old sister that she was to be married.

Tracy had played hookey from school that day in order to meet Anabel's train. They had gone to lunch together in a drab little restaurant, where they could sit in a booth at the back and hope to pass unnoticed. Anabel had been gay and electric, yet as gossamer as mist—hard to pin down. Never had Tracy seen her look more beautiful, more magical, and her own heart had ached a little in the old way—not only with love, but with something of envy as well. To be like Anabel—the wish had been a part of her for as long as she could remember, though she knew its foolishness, knew it must be thrust back, contradicted. It had seemed to Tracy in those days that Anabel would always have what she wished, merely for the taking. While Tracy, following inescapably in her shimmering wake, must compete with a vision she could never live up to.

At lunch that day Anabel had eaten like a bird and talked in high excitement. "I posed for him, Bunny darling," she said, using a pet name for Tracy that went back to Easter rabbit days. "That's how I got to meet him. He thought I had interesting bones, or something. And some sort of quality he wanted to catch on canvas. Then he began to worry about me—the way people do."

The high, light laughter made heads turn, and Anabel stilled it at once.

Yes—people had always worried about Anabel. Her mother had worried. Tracy's father, Anabel's stepfather, was the only one who had refused to worry. When Anabel had run away from home shortly after Tracy's twelfth birthday, he had not concerned himself. Indeed, he had probably been relieved to see her go. Tracy had hated him a little, and worried as much as her mother had.

Nevertheless, though their mother had suffered deeply—Anabel had always been her favorite—she had lacked the strength to stand up to her husband in Anabel's defense. Knowing this, Anabel would never come home. She wrote to Tracy now and then—quick, brief notes that did not say very much, while Tracy wrote long, though sometimes laborious letters because of her instinct to preserve whatever tenuous thread still bound Anabel to a family, if only through her younger sister. It had seemed necessary for someone to care about holding onto Anabel, and Tracy had never stopped trying. On the occasions when Anabel had come west it was to see Tracy secretly, never her mother or stepfather.

At home, life had been difficult for Tracy. Her mother had always blamed her for the occurrence that had brought matters to a head and sent Anabel away from home. At the time, Tracy had accepted her mother's evaluation and blamed herself, indulging in an orgy of twelve-year-old suffering and self-reproach. She knew better now; knew that she had been no more than a chance instrument. The fact that she had behaved with childish jealousy was not something to brood over for the rest of her life. Eventually, Anabel would have taken the same step whether Tracy had played her role or not. This was the continuing puzzle of Anabel—that she must hurl herself headlong toward disaster, when to other eyes there seemed so little need.

After Anabel had left home there were new walls around Tracy, and watchful suspicion, as if they only waited for her to do something wrong. She, who was accustomed to being open about all she did, who expected to be trusted, found herself faced with doubt and distrust on every hand. All because Anabel had gone before. Her love for her sister had been increasingly mixed with resentment. She knew now that this had been a healthy, self-preserving emotion, and sufficiently justified. But at the time she had not understood and there had been a sense of guilt. Even now that old feeling of being somehow to blame because she had been jealous of her sister reached out of the past to give pause to the grownup Tracy and make her question her feelings toward Anabel.

That day in the restaurant Tracy had tried to take blame upon herself for what had occurred to drive Anabel from home. But, as always, Anabel would not listen.

"It would have happened anyway, darling," she had said with unusual frankness. "You mustn't reproach yourself. Not ever."

She had gone on to speak of her coming marriage to a man who knew "almost all" about her, and who loved her as she was. She had refused Tracy's plea to make things up with her mother.

"I don't want to," Anabel had said and the words were final. There could be stubbornness in Anabel too, though of the kind that sometimes slipped away and left you seemingly unopposed when you had really been defeated.

"I'm sorry, Bunny darling," she went on, "but I never want him to meet my mother or your father. He thinks I'm all alone with no one in the world to turn to—which is almost true. He likes it that way. That's why I can't even tell him about you."

Her decision had hurt Tracy, yet she had accepted it. Anabel had found someone new to worry about her, someone closer at hand who could really look after her. The relief to that very young Tracy had been considerable.

They were going to visit Miles's relatives in England, and then go out to Turkey for their honeymoon, Anabel told her. Istanbul had always fascinated Miles as a painter. He wanted to try something besides portraits.

"He's so—so accountable and wonderful," she told her sister in warm excitement. "I can depend on him. He won't let me hurt myself. For the first time in my whole foolish life I'm going to be happy. And safe. When we're on our way, I'll send you something, darling, so you'll know everything is fine. Something that will make you think of me whenever you wear it."

Anabel had kept her word. By airmail had come the little feather pin that Tracy had worn ever since. A pin that said to her: "Here's a feather for your cap, Bunny darling. Wear it and remember me. You haven't done such a bad job raising me!"

So Tracy had worn the pin and warmed to the thought of Anabel's happiness, reassured that everything would now be all right for the sister she adored. Even then she had begun to suspect the flaw in Anabel that was like a crack in fine glaze—something for which there was no cure. But she closed her eyes to the flaw and kept her love and loyalty intact.

Now as Tracy touched her fingers to the pin in the familiar way and looked up at her sister's face, tears burned her lids. Anabel had not been safe, after all. Toward the end she had apparently been far from happy, and according to her Miles had not proved as dependable as she had expected. The faint green gleam of Anabel's eyes peered beneath the smudge of dark lashes and there was no telling what they saw, or what the girl behind them was thinking.

A voice spoke abruptly behind her, a bleak chill in the sound. "May I ask what you are doing in this room?"

Tracy whirled in dismay to find Miles Radburn in the doorway. There was more than a winter chill in his face. Anger burned beneath ice, and Tracy felt alarmed. Anabel had warned her of danger, and, though Tracy had somewhat discounted her sister's hysteria, she was suddenly afraid. She snatched at the first straw that offered.

"I—I'm sorry. I know I shouldn't have come in here. But Mrs. Erim showed me the picture this morning, and—and I couldn't resist coming to look at it again. It must be—I mean I've seen some of your other portraits—and this must be one of your finest."

"The picture is not on display, Miss Hubbard," Miles Radburn said. "If you are to stay for the week I've promised, you will have to resist such impulses. I suggested, I believe, that you stay out of my study this afternoon."

Tracy nodded mutely, unable to force words past the tight feeling in her throat, hardly able to see him through the blur in her eyes. He stood aside to let her return to the study. Then he went to his drawing table and seated himself on the high stool before it. She had been dismissed.

At the door to the salon she paused with her hand upon the brass knob. There was something he ought to know, and she could at least tell him this.

"When—when I came in a little while ago," she faltered, "Ahmet was here, studying that calligraphy strip you're doing. When I surprised him, he said those were the words of Allah and went away."

Miles did not trouble to look at her, nor did he comment. He simply waited for her to go, and if he had any interest in Ahmet's actions, he did not reveal it.

Tracy managed the toe latch at the bottom of the door awkwardly, and as she did so the white cat slipped past her into the room. With an air of being entirely at home, the animal sprang upon Miles's desk, moving so gracefully, so lightly, that not a paper was disturbed. There she seated herself and stared at the artist out of wide green eyes. Anabel's cat. The cat to which her sister had given Tracy's nickname of "Bunny." Out of loneliness, perhaps? Out of an aching for someone from home to talk to?

Miles raised a hand as if to cuff the animal from the desk. Outraged, Tracy moved first. She caught the white cat up in her arms and faced him defiantly.

"Poor Yasemin!" she cried, her cheek against the cat's pricked ears.

"That's not its name," said Miles sharply. "It's called—"

"Bunny," Tracy provided. "I know. That's a silly name for a cat. So I've renamed her. She's my cat now. While I'm here, that is. And any man who would strike a cat—"

He swore then. Quite loudly and firmly. Good British oaths that had the sound of a seafaring nation behind them. Tracy fled with the cat in her arms and heard the loud slamming of the door behind her.

She carried Yasemin back to her room and sat down with the small warm thing in her arms. She was in real trouble now. If ever Miles Radburn guessed who she was, he would send her straight home. She was sure of it.

"If only you could tell me about Anabel," she murmured to the cat. "Yasemin, what am I to do?"

Yasemin, however, had received enough of cuddling and human emotions. She scratched Tracy on the wrist, squirmed out of her arms, and leaped to the middle of the bed. There she washed herself neatly, sponging away the human touch with rasping tongue and firm pink paws.

Tracy stared at the scratch absently. What had happened might have been funny, she supposed—his getting furious and swearing at her over a cat. But it was not funny because of Anabel. Not only because of the phone call, but because of the letter she had received from Anabel more than six months ago.

Her sister had written that she and Miles had returned to Istanbul at the invitation of a good friend who had entertained them in her home during their honeymoon in Turkey. Miles was not painting just now, but he had developed an interest in Turkish mosaics. Mrs. Erim had offered him a base from which to operate in his research, and certain living arrangements had been made with her. All this by way of explanation. What Anabel wanted was to have Tracy drop everything and come out to Istanbul at once for a visit.

"If you'll come, I'll own up to having a sister," she had written. "I need you, darling. Things are going terribly wrong and I know it would help to talk to you."

It was not the first time Tracy had received such a summons. A few years after her marriage, Anabel had paid Tracy's expenses to New York one summer and Tracy had gone for a few weeks' visit against her parents' wishes. The way her sister looked had alarmed her. She had been thin and highly nervous. Flashes of the old gay Anabel had alternated infrequently with an Anabel who had only complaints about the dull life she led and resentment of what she regarded as her husband's neglect. Miles was away in England at the time. Had he been in New York, Tracy would have tried to see him, in spite of Anabel's wishes. As it was, she had discounted her sister's lamentations to some degree and tried to calm her and talk a little sense into her. For the most part the visit had been ineffectual.

Yet, strangely enough, Tracy had never lost her belief in some deep-rooted worth in Anabel. The good qualities were there, if only one could get at them. She was talented in so many ways. She could sing and dance, and if she had possessed a drive toward achievement she might have succeeded in the theater. Perhaps her most remarkable gift was the one of making life seem gay and carefree to those around her. She possessed a talent for laughter and for the generating of laughter. Even Nursel had felt this and had spoken of their running off to be free of sober faces and a restriction upon laughter. Yet the Anabel who had this gift for life was being destroyed by another Anabel. For some of the world's gifted there seemed to be this strange pull toward self-destruction that those who loved them could only watch in bewilderment and try, however hopelessly, to oppose.

Tracy knew only that she must hold to that slender tie by which Anabel allowed herself to be bound. After the visit to New York, she had continued to write the letters her sister seemed to want. It was all she could do.

Eventually she had been old enough to escape the impossible atmosphere that had been built up around her at home. By the time she moved to New York, however, Anabel and Miles were living out of the country and there were no meetings with them in the two years she had been in the east.

When Anabel's letter of summons had come six months ago, Tracy had felt both sympathetic and annoyed. She knew very well that Anabel loved to exaggerate and dramatize, and she suspected that nothing practical could be accomplished by flying to Istanbul with such dispatch as Anabel requested. Tracy might hold her hand and listen to her grievances and perhaps help her temporarily to a better balance. She wrote firmly to Anabel and she did not go to Turkey. She would come later, she promised. If she left now, while she was still a trainee in a new department, the company might not want her back. Anabel must understand how important this job was to her.

Anabel had not answered her letter, though Tracy had written again, promising to manage a trip during the summer. There had been a silence of months—which was not unusual. Tracy, absorbed and happy, free for the first time in her life, had put worry about her sister aside. Anabel would forgive her eventually, and Tracy had let the thread between them slacken.

Then, only three months ago, had come that wild and confused telephone call. Tracy had hardly recognized her voice, so upset had Anabel sounded.

"I never knew it would come to this!" she wailed over the wire. "I never knew Miles could be so wickedly cruel!"

This sounded like more of the usual thing and Tracy broke in, trying to quiet her, to make sense of what she was saying, but the girl at the other end of the wire ran on incoherently, and there had been a true note of terror in her voice.

"I need you desperately, Bunny. I shouldn't ask you to come —perhaps it would be dangerous for you to come. But there's no one else I can turn to. I must talk to someone. Someone who can get me away from here!"

Tracy spoke to her sternly then. "Anabel, listen to me! Get hold of yourself and tell me quietly what's the matter."

Anabel took a breath of air in a big gulp and went right on.

"It's the black amber again! It turned up yesterday and I know it's the end of everything. The secret is hidden with the Sultan Valide—remember that, if you come. And don't let anyone know you're my sister. If they don't know, they won't touch you. Bunny, I'm afraid—I don't want to die! Bunny—"

She broke off and there was a moment's silence in which Tracy pleaded with her to speak quietly, to explain. Then Anabel said in a whisper, "Someone's coming up the stairs." There was a long silence. Tracy held her breath, trying desperately to hear what was happening all those thousands of miles away in Istanbul. Then had come the most terrifying thing of all. Anabel had not spoken again, but she had whistled softly, incongruously into the telephone—the mere snatch of an old nursery rhyme: *London Bridge is falling down, falling down, falling down* . . . She whistled that much of it before the phone went dead.

The snatch of tune had taken Tracy back to her childhood in an agonizing wave of memory. When she and Anabel had lived at home, there had been many a secret signal between them in the form of nursery tunes they both knew well. *Here we go round the mulberry bush* . . . meant, "All's well. The storm is over." But *London Bridge* was the panic call. It meant, "Here comes ultimate disaster. Get ready for the roof to fall in." And it was never used except for desperate emergency.

That day, over the wire from Istanbul, Anabel had given her the disaster signal, their own secret "Mayday" call—and hung up the receiver.

Tracy tried at once to call Istanbul back. It had taken forever, and when someone speaking English had come on at last it was to say that Anabel was unable to come to the phone. Tracy asked for Miles, only to be told that he was out of town. In the end she had given up without identifying herself. She had tried to stem her own terror by telling herself that this was just the sort of wildly dramatic trick Anabel loved to play. But the conviction had persisted that this time the game was real.

The next day the news of Anabel's death had been in the papers, of front-page importance because of Miles's name.

Tracy had broken a long silence and telephoned her father in Iowa, only to be told that this was exactly what he had expected. This was the road down which Anabel herself had chosen to travel. It was the end she had deserved.

She cabled anonymous flowers for Anabel's grave and she began planning at once to get to Istanbul. She could not let her sister's sudden death, on the heels of that confused phone call, go unchallenged, unquestioned. Yet for once Anabel's words had bred a certain caution in her. She knew instinctively that if she went out at once, announcing herself as Anabel's sister, the questions would go unanswered. And she had a responsibility now. She had not gone to Anabel's help. She had regarded the earlier letter as the usual cry of "wolf!" But this time something had been dreadfully wrong and she could not rest until she knew what it was. She had never accepted whole-cloth the things Anabel had said about Miles. But now she must get to Istanbul and learn about him for herself.

She had lacked money for an immediate trip, or even credit to borrow for so wild a venture when she could not admit to being Anabel's sister. Then Mr. Hornwright had opened a door and she had dashed through without looking back.

As Anabel's half sister, she had been able to come here under her own name and identity, since even Anabel's maiden name was different from her own. As long as this incognito held, she would be safe from whatever threat Anabel had hinted at. The leads she had to follow were few: Anabel's outburst against Miles, which though not especially new, was more extreme. A reference to "black amber" and to someone referred to as a Sultan Valide who was in possession of a "secret." On the surface all wildly improbable. Yet Anabel had been frightened. Anabel had died. Driven to suicide by what degree of desperation? And by whom?

From what she had seen of Miles Radburn, he seemed the most likely instrument. She could imagine him driving a woman almost crazy. Particularly if she were so foolish as to love him. Yet there was the paradox of Anabel's picture on his wall. And there was Tracy's own voice of reason which told her that not everything Anabel said and did could be taken at face value.

If only there was someone to whom she could turn with trust and confidence. Now, sitting in the room that had been Anabel's she thought again of Nursel. The girl had seemingly been Anabel's friend and she was certainly no friend of Miles Radburn. But to what extent she might be trusted Tracy did not know. It was possible that Nursel might become an ally in her search for the truth.

She needed an ally badly in this maze of hidden motives and secretive behavior, yet she did not dare to trust anyone yet.

There were as many undercurrents in the murk of these problems as there were out there in the stream of the Bosporus, where Anabel had ended her life. Tension and dislike were evident between Dr. Erim and Miles Radburn. There was tension as well between Murat Erim and his sister-in-law, Sylvana, who held more power in this household than the brother and sister felt she should.

As Tracy sat there, turning futilely within the perimeter of her own thoughts, Halide tapped at her door. The maid carried a small pile of books in her hands and, when Tracy called to her to enter, she trotted into the room and deposited them on the table with a smile. Yasemin seized the opportunity and moved like lightning, flying through the open door as though she had waited here a prisoner.

When Halide had gone, Tracy looked wonderingly at the four titles. The books were all about Turkey. One was a modern guidebook which she had hurried through at home. Another was an account of Atatürk's campaign and reforms, and there was a book about the ancient peoples of Turkey. The fourth volume was an account of Ottoman Empire days, detailing the stories of fantastic wealth and power, with its deterioration into corruption and greed and shocking cruelty.

Mrs. Erim might have sent her the first two, and possibly the fourth, but surely only Miles Radburn would have in his possession the third volume. She opened to a flyleaf and saw that his name was written there and in the others as well.

Was this an apology for his loss of temper? she wondered. For the space of a moment she softened toward him and then smiled wryly at herself. She must never forget how attractive this man had seemed to Anabel in the beginning, and how wrong Anabel had, admittedly, been about him. It would be safer to dislike him intensely, to remember him as coldly frightening, as a man who could strike out violently at a cat. Somehow, she must dig in her toes and stay, but she must not be drawn into friendliness toward Miles Radburn.

Thus bolstered in her own determination, she sat down and opened a volume at random. She forced herself to read and tried to think about what she was reading. This was an account of Turkey's earliest inhabitants, the Hittites—a people of some consequence in the ancient world. They had been mentioned in the Bible. The lady named Bathsheba, who had led David astray, was a Hittite. Indeed, the Hittites had in their day rivaled the Egyptians and the Babylonians in importance. Behind them in Turkey they had left friezes and statues of remarkable beauty. After the Hittites had come the Semitic invaders and the conquerors from the West—from Greece and Rome. There had been a great intermingling of races so that Turks were Indo-European, with a dash of Mongolian thrown in.

All of which was undoubtedly fascinating to know. But the persistent echo of a nursery rhyme kept time with the words as she read, and Tracy could not care less about Turkish history at the moment. Indeed, she could not sit still in this room for a moment longer. She flung down the book and jumped up to get her coat. The afternoon was growing late and she must get outdoors and release this restless anxiety that would not let her be still. Only physical effort would serve. She'd had enough of the four walls of Anabel's room.

There was no one in the upper salon. The door of Miles's study remained closed. The white cat was nowhere to be seen. Tracy ran lightly downstairs to the marble corridor that bisected the ground floor and found her way to the door on the land side. Turning from the paved driveway that ran between yali and kiosk, she followed the path along the hillside above the Bosporus until it ended at a small gate set in the stone wall that surrounded the property. Beyond, the main road, having curved around Erim grounds, resumed its direction, running north, paralleling the water, though not close to it.

She expected the gate to be locked, but it was only latched, and she opened it and went through. The sun had dipped partially behind the hills of Thrace across the water, but there was still time for a stroll before it grew completely dark. She followed the scrubby grass along the road's edge so that she need not worry about passing traffic. The nearest village, apparently, was on the other side of the Erim property. Here were pleasant woods, still winter sere, though green shoots were beginning to push through the brown grass underfoot.

Curving, the road dipped toward the water and brought her at length to a large and ornate wrought-iron gate hung askew on dilapidated hinges, permanently ajar. To Tracy's mind there was always something both intriguing and touching about a ruin. She could not resist this one and stepped through the gap in the broken gate.

What had once been a fine garden spread before her in wild disarray. Vines and creepers and weedy shrubs had made a tangle of the place. All about were great plane trees and horse chestnuts with their candled blooms ready to bud anew with the coming of spring. A monstrous rhododendron hedge that would later be bright with blossoms had grown unrestrained, forming a wall that darkened the far side of the garden on the right. Straight ahead shallow steps led down to the water, their marble shimmering rosy-white in the lengthening rays of the sun. Beyond, dark water swept softly past.

The house rose on her left and, for all that it stood in ruin, the stamp of former wealth and eminence lay upon it. It was no ordinary house—there was too much marble showing through the curtain of shabby vines that overhung it. Once it had risen two stories above the basement floor, but she could see that toward the water the roof had fallen in upon the upper story and most of the wall on the water side had crumbled into the Bosporus. Yet a good part of the house stood intact, and she ventured toward the flight of marble steps that led to the marble framework of an empty door.

At the foot of the steps the pattern of a great circular mosaic lay partially revealed. It would be beautiful, she thought, if it were uncovered, but now it was earth-encrusted and weed-grown with the tangle that reached to the very steps. So romantic an invitation as the doorway offered was not to be resisted.

Tracy climbed the marble steps. The wooden door had rotted upon its hinges and fallen inward. She stepped over broken timbers and found herself inside the ruin. What remained of graceful arches that had framed windows on either side of the door revealed a fretwork of fine carving. Part of the ceiling was gone and the roof above as well, so that the house stood open to the water. What had once been a palace on the Bosporus had become a haven for lizards and mice, a nesting place for birds.

Worms and termites and general rot had broken the floor of the great central room in a number of places, and she stepped with care. One wall had bloomed with painted flowers that were now faded to a pale, dreamlike beauty. There was tarnished tilework over a doorway, and she studied it in the graying light from the water. Her sorting of Miles Radburn's drawings had given her a new interest in such things.

The rear of the house seemed fairly sound and further rooms stretched away in sheltered darkness. The sun had set by now and dusk was coming more quickly than she had expected. The chill in the air had intensified and a curious uneasiness possessed her in this haunted place.

Tracy hesitated on the threshold of a farther room, seized by a desire to flee from this crumbling, eerie place. Stepping cautiously, she went through the doorway into the next shadowed room beyond.

5

As SHE MOVED on, filled with uneasiness, yet held by a strange desire to persist, she felt something soft beneath her foot. When she bent to pick it up, she saw that it was a silk scarf. Its colors were washed out in the dim light, but it seemed to be a woman's scarf and she wondered at its presence here. She put it into the pocket of her coat and went on.

Around the turn of a dim hallway where a staircase led upward, she came to a sudden halt. Had she heard something? Was there someone else wandering about this ghostly place? The woman who had dropped the scarf, perhaps?

As she hesitated, a sound of whispering came suddenly clear, and then ceased to be whispering as someone spoke angrily aloud. Tracy drew back beneath the shadow of an arch, dismayed. The presence of others here seemed somehow less innocent than her own. The words were in Turkish. She could make out only that there seemed to be a man and a woman, and that they were arguing heatedly, their voices distorted and strained. The arguers must have been two or more rooms away, and Tracy started warily back along the course by which she had come, seeking the opening to the big main salon. Upon its threshold she paused, hesitating to step into the open where light from empty windows on the water would touch her clearly. As she paused, the man's voice rose above the other, speaking a name sharply. "Hubbard," he said and rushed on in Turkish, enclosing her name in words that had a menacing ring.

Her own name spoken in this atmosphere of angry conspiracy was terrifying. All the warnings of Anabel's letter swept back. Wanting only to escape unseen, Tracy started heedlessly across the floor, forgetting the rotting wood underfoot. As she stepped down hard, a board cracked, throwing her sharply to her knees. She could feel the scrape of splintered wood across one shin, the smarting of pain.

The noise of her fall betrayed her. Immediately the voices stilled. There was a breathless pause, followed by the sound of running feet, the hurried sounds of flight. She could not see them go, but they must have fled through another door and into the garden, rushing away in the gathering darkness. A guilty flight, it seemed, and she was glad they had gone without approaching her.

She gave her attention to her own predicament and pulled herself out of the hole into which she had fallen. She was examining her torn stocking, feeling gingerly of her skinned leg when a sound nearby made her look up sharply.

There was a fourth person there in the ruins. A man stood silhouetted against water and fading sky. There was something ominous about the motionless way in which he stood looking at her, faceless with his back to the light. He had made no sound when the others had fled, and she wondered if he had been there all along, spying upon them. She could only stand where she was, waiting for him to move, to speak. He broke the silence by addressing her in Turkish and coming toward her. She saw then that it was Ahmet. She did not trust or like this soft-spoken, silent man, but at least he was not a stranger. The hand she had touched to her leg was sticky with blood, and she held it out for him to see.

"I've hurt myself," she said. "Can you help me?"

He understood the gesture at least and came at once to assist her, moving with quiet assurance. "Come, please, *hanimefendi*," he said, and she limped out of the house and toward the gate, leaning upon his arm. As they walked slowly along the road, he muttered to himself in his own language. Since all Turkish sounded explosive to Tracy's unaccustomed ears, she could not tell whether he was commiserating over her injury, or complaining because she had interrupted the meeting of two he seemed to have been watching.

They had gone only a little way when a man appeared walking toward them. He moved at the pace of an evening stroller and, as she drew near, Tracy saw that it was Murat Erim. Ahmet greeted him, gesturing toward Tracy's bleeding leg.

"You have hurt yourself?" Dr. Erim said, hurrying to her in quick concern.

She explained that she had come for a walk and had been unable to resist exploring the ruined palace. It had been foolish of her to trust the floors, and of course she had fallen. As they walked back, he questioned Ahmet in Turkish and the man answered at considerable length. Before he had finished, Dr. Erim broke in upon his words, directing him to hurry on to the house.

"We will have warm water and bandages waiting," he said when Ahmet had gone off at a trot. "My sister is well versed in dealing with such injuries. Do not concern yourself. It is fortunate that Ahmet followed you, feeling that you might lose your way in a strange place. I had wondered at finding our side gate unlocked. It is where you came through, is it not?"

She had a sudden feeling that he might be dissembling, that he was abroad for some private reason of his own and was testing her in some way.

"It is where I came through," she admitted, and did not explain that the gate had been opened by someone ahead of her.

The houseman had apparently said nothing of the two who had taken flight, and Tracy did not contradict his account.

At the house Dr. Erim took her to Sylvana's rooms. Mrs. Erim had been working in the laboratory, but she left her perfume distilling to come upstairs. When she saw Tracy's scraped and bleeding leg, she sent Ahmet at once to find Nursel. Evidently Dr. Erim did not use his medical training in such matters and, when he saw that she was in good hands, he went away.

When Nursel came, bringing her first-aid kit, the wound was duly bathed and bandaged. Sylvana asked questions of her, but again Tracy kept her own counsel. She had happened upon some sort of hornets' nest and it seemed wiser to say nothing until she was sure of her ground. The fright she had felt over hearing the angry mention of her own name lingered. Her knowledge that two people whose identity she did not know had been discussing her heatedly under strange circumstances was no more reassuring than was the fact that Ahmet had been surreptitiously observing them.

When the bandaging was done, Sylvana Erim herself accompanied her to her room, gave her tablets for the pain, and suggested that she go to bed at once. It would not be necessary to get up for dinner—the meal would be brought to her. From now on, said Sylvana, Miss Hubbard must remember not to run about in unknown places after dark.

When Mrs. Erim had gone, Tracy got ready for bed. Now that

she was alone, anxiety swept back again. The fact that she had blundered unheedingly upon that clandestine meeting seemed to remove a little of the safety of her incognito. They could not know who she was, but if she stumbled upon some secret and gave cause for concern, her way might be all the more difficult in this house. Besides, what was their interest in her that her name should have been mentioned? Had it something to do with her working for Miles Radburn?

Just before she got into bed, she remembered the scarf in her coat pocket and brought it out. It was of finely woven silk, with stripes of dark plum color that alternated with cream and ran its entire length. The pattern had a faintly familiar look, but she could not remember where she might have seen it. She could not recall that Nursel or Sylvana had worn such a scarf since she had been here.

Sylvana's medication began to relax her, making her drowsy. She lay down on the bed without turning off the light and thrust the scarf beneath her pillow, too groggy now to puzzle about it. The tablets took quick effect and she fell soundly asleep.

She must have slept for two or three hours before Nursel tapped on her door and came in, followed by Halide with a tray. Tracy wanted only to wave the food away and go back to sleep, but Nursel insisted that she have something to eat. She supervised the matter of getting Tracy up against her pillows as if she were a helpless invalid, and set the bed table across her knees. Then she dismissed Halide and drew up a chair beside the bed.

"Now," she said pleasantly, "while you refresh yourself, you must tell me all that happened when you were injured. There is something strange here. I have said nothing to Sylvana or to my brother, but I do not think you have told them all the truth."

Tracy drank hot broth and found that the fog was clearing a little. With Nursel she felt less cautious and tongue-tied, and since the girl saw through her evasion, as the others had not seemed to, she gave her an account of exactly what had happened. There had been a man and a woman in the ruined palace, both engaged in angry discussion. And Ahmet had been there too, apparently watching them unseen.

Nursel listened intently, her slender hands clasped about her knees, a look of concern in her huge dark eyes.

"I do not know what Ahmet Effendi could be doing—watching

306

someone away from the house. This does not seem like him. He is not a good-tempered man, but he is very loyal."

"Why don't you ask him and find out?" Tracy said.

Nursel shrugged. "One might as well ask the Egyptian obelisk in Istanbul. Ahmet Effendi does not talk if he does not wish to talk. But I suppose it is his own affair if he wishes to spy on persons outside of this house."

"What if those two were someone from this house?" Tracy asked.

"Why do you think that?"

"I have no way of knowing," Tracy admitted. "But I heard someone mention my name. It was as though they were arguing about me in some way."

"About *you?*" Nursel echoed. "But this is very strange. You are sure it was your name you heard spoken?"

"I'm sure," said Tracy. She reached beneath her pillow and pulled out the scarf. "This is something I found when I went into the ruin."

The Turkish girl looked at the scarf as though it were alive and dangerous. "Please," she said in some agitation, "it is better if you do not tell this story to anyone. Not even to my brother. It will be better if you forget all this, if you know nothing about it."

"Then you know whose scarf this is? You know what this might mean?" Tracy asked bluntly.

Nursel's agitation seemed to increase. Her eyes were luminous with something like fear. "No, no, no—I know nothing! It is only that these matters are of no concern to you. Soon you will go home to New York, Miss Hubbard, and that will be for the best. This is not your affair."

Tracy wanted to say, "It is my affair. Whatever is going on here is my affair—because I am Anabel's sister." But she could not risk going that far with this girl whom she knew so slightly, for all that she had been Anabel's friend.

As if to conceal her agitation, Nursel rose and went to the balcony doors, opened them slightly, and stood looking out across the water. When she spoke again the course of her words took a surprising turn.

"Why did you go to this place—the palace ruins? What drew you there?"

"Why—nothing special," Tracy said. "I went for a walk and I

stumbled on the gate by chance. I was curious and went inside—
that's all."

Nursel nodded thoughtfully. "It is strange, but Mrs. Radburn,
who was also an American, loved this place. Often when she was
unhappy she went there alone. Sometimes I accompanied her,
when I thought she should not be by herself."

Tracy lay back against her pillow, her eyes closed. She had no
taste for the food on the tray. Was Nursel making some deliberate
connection between her and Anabel? But that wasn't possible.
No one had known of Anabel's sister. Nursel turned back to the
room with a slight gesture, as if dismissing the whole affair. Tracy
opened her eyes and spoke cautiously, watching the other girl,
trusting her not at all.

"This morning," she said, "Mrs. Erim showed me the portrait
of Anabel in Mr. Radburn's bedroom. The face in the picture
seemed so lovely. Was she like that—Mrs. Radburn?"

Nursel returned to her chair beside the bed. "She was like that
—and not like. Often she had the charming quality of a child. She
wanted always to be gay and lighthearted. She wanted to be the
heroine of her own little plays. Yet she was married to him—so
dark and heavy and serious. Oh, I could tell you stories about the
year they lived here! Have you seen the fortress on the other side
of the water in the direction of Istanbul?"

"I noticed the towers this morning," Tracy said.

"That is Rumeli Hisar. A very famous place in Turkish history. It was built to guard the Bosporus from the invaders,
though its purpose failed. There is a similar fortress on this side,
but smaller and not so interesting. One time we took Anabel to
Rumeli Hisar for a picnic—all of us. My brother and Sylvana,
even Miles. That was one of her wild, gay days. Something reckless
would get into her when she would be like—like a knife."

"What do you mean—like a knife?"

Nursel turned back to the room. "Very sharp and cutting in
her ways. She could hurt without thinking. Perhaps more like a
sword than a knife, with the ring of steel about her. Yes—that is
it! Like a blade hidden by folds of silk, ready to cut when one least
expected it. That day at the fortress she wanted to go to the very
heights. Miles forbade her. He said she had no head for high
places. But Anabel told him she could fly to the top if she chose,
and she proved it by running up those long flights of steps that

lead through the garden inside. We sat watching her and I was frightened. I cried out that someone should go after her, and Murat started the climb, but Miles stopped him. He said to let her go or she'd never get it out of her system. Perhaps he wanted her dead even then. It was a day in the springtime and the pink Judas trees were in bloom along the Bosporus. There is one that grows on a hillside outside the enclosure of the fortress walls. Anabel said she must see it from the very highest place. So she went up there, running like a gazelle, never looking back, never looking down. From the notch in the wall she could see the tree and she called to us that it was beautiful, enchanting, we must all come up there to see it."

The story thread broke off, and Tracy heard the emotion in Nursel's voice as she lowered her dark head.

"Never have I had an American friend, except when I was young and went to the American girls' school at Arnavütkoy across the Bosporus. That was where I learned to speak English. My friend was a girl of my own age whose father was an American Naval officer. But she was not like Anabel. No one else could be like Anabel."

No one else could be like Anabel, Tracy thought, and closed her eyes briefly. No one else had the wonder and excitement that had been Anabel's, or her extreme attraction for danger.

"How did she get down from the wall that day?" she asked.

"It was a dreadful time. I will never forget. She turned to call us to come and see the view from the opening in the wall. And when she turned she was forced to look down. The wall is high and narrow at that place, and there was a moment that caught at my heart. I thought she would fall before our very eyes.

"Miles saw what had happened and he shouted to her to lean back against the wall and wait there for him. He started up at once, but she did not wait. She wavered toward the steps and stumbled part way down the first level before she fainted there on a narrow ledge. It was only by good fortune that she did not roll over the edge. He reached her and brought her down from the heights. I could almost admire him then. He was strong and sure and he carried her all the way to safety before she wakened and began to struggle. Then I did not like him for long!"

Her words had a sudden ring of spite in them as she continued.

"When Anabel recovered she was hysterical—weeping, terrified.

Miles slapped her across one cheek. Brutally, cruelly. Never, never will I forgive him for that blow. Or for his actions—not only that day, but later."

One of Tracy's unpredictable and independent voices suddenly sounded in her mind. She had listened in dismay and she could have wept for Anabel, who was frail and fragile and never one to pit her strength against heights. Yet perhaps her sister had asked for stern treatment. What else could Miles have done, once he got her down, but shock her out of her hysterical state with a good slap?

"Did she quiet after he slapped her?" she asked Nursel.

The dark eyes widened in surprise, as if the other girl had expected indignation. "But of course. She wept afterwards—more softly. She was terrified of him, as she had every right to be—though I did not know this at the time. I did not know how much he wanted her dead."

The voice of justice was insistent, even though Tracy would have liked to shut it out. She was, after all, on Anabel's side. But the voice would not be still.

"It doesn't seem as though a man who wanted his wife dead would hang her portrait on the wall of his bedroom where he must look at it every day."

"Ah, but that is most easy to understand," Nursel objected. "What do you call it—the bed of thorns, the hair shirt of your Christian martyrs? He has a need to punish himself for what he has done. He is not without conscience, for all his wickedness. Part of the penalty he pays is to be unable to paint again. He will pay forever—but never enough. Never enough to bring Anabel back to life."

Nursel covered her face with her hands and was still. On one finger a star sapphire winked in the lamplight.

Again Tracy longed to say, "Anabel was my sister. If you were her friend, be my friend too. Help me to find the truth." But she did not dare. Though Nursel seemed increasingly frank, the time had not yet come. It was better to wait and be wise.

Nursel took her hands from before her face abruptly. Her eyes were sorrowful and there was a lingering tinge of fear, but there was no wetness on her cheeks.

"Give me the scarf," she said, suddenly urgent.

Tracy had thrust it beneath her pillow and she did not reach for it. "You do know who it belongs to. Why do you want it?"

"It is not wise for you to keep it," Nursel said obliquely. "It is possible that you might do great injury to the innocent if you tell others all that happened today. If you give me the scarf, it will be replaced where it belongs and no one will be the wiser."

Tracy hesitated, then made up her mind. "I'll give it to you. But not now. I'll give it to you before I leave for home."

Nursel was not satisfied, but she made a small despairing gesture. "You do not understand. Never mind. You are not finishing your dinner. I have disturbed you with my talk. Sylvana will be displeased if you do not eat everything. Come—the lamb is delicious."

Tracy wrinkled her nose. "I'm not hungry. Please take it away."

As Nursel rose to lift the tray from the bed table, someone knocked on the door and Miles's voice said, "May I come in?"

For an instant Nursel looked startled. Then she smiled at Tracy. "It is a new day in Turkey. Sometimes I hear my grandmother's voice and I forget. Will you speak to Mr. Radburn?"

She did not want to, but she could hardly refuse. "All right," she said grudgingly.

Nursel opened the door and the white cat flicked around Miles's legs and leaped into its corner chair. He ignored the animal and came to stand at the foot of Tracy's bed.

"I've just heard about your fall," he said. "I hope the damage isn't serious."

Was he too going to question her? Tracy noted again what a chill gray color his eyes were, how there was in him a lack of any light or human warmth except when he was angry.

"Only a scraped shin," she said. "I'll be all right tomorrow. I really don't know why I've been sent to bed."

"I suggest that you forget about work and rest tomorrow," he told her. "I'm going to the city in the morning and I don't expect to be at home at all. Take the day off and do as you like."

"What I'd like," said Tracy, raising her chin obstinately, "is to get to work and finish the job I've come here to do."

"I prefer not to lock my study against you," Radburn said. "Have I your promise that you will stay out of my rooms until I return?"

Remembering the way he had caught her—an intruder staring at Anabel's picture that afternoon—a flush swept into Tracy's cheeks and her determination crumbled. She could see his plan clearly enough. He would keep her away from his work and he would find new excuses every day until her week was up. Then he would send her home. At the moment she did not in the least know how to oppose the pressure that was being put upon her on all sides.

He seemed to gather agreement from her silence and gave her a stiff-necked nod. "Good night," he said abruptly and went out of the room.

Nursel made a rude face at the closing door. At least she had recovered from her upset emotions over the story she had told.

"I know what we shall do," she announced. "Since you are free tomorrow, you must come to Istanbul with me. I have an errand to perform for Sylvana, and there is a small jewelry shop I must visit for Murat. If your leg is well enough, perhaps you will wish to come with me to these places. There will be time to visit a mosque, perhaps. You must not leave Istanbul without seeing something of its wonders."

Since nothing could be accomplished here, Tracy accepted the invitation, but her sense of frustration increased. She was being forced to mark time on every hand. No door opened to answer the questions about Anabel which so troubled her. The few days granted for her stay already seemed to be slipping away with nothing achieved. At least time spent with Nursel need not be wholly wasted.

"I will leave you now." Nursel broke in upon her thoughts. "Sleep well, I am sorry that I burdened you with my unhappy memories. You must not give them a thought. It is all over now. Except for him."

This seemed an odd way to put it.

"What do you mean—except for him?" Tracy asked cautiously.

For a moment Nursel looked as though she would not answer. Her lips tightened and in her eyes Tracy had a disturbing glimpse of an anger that seemed brightly corrosive.

"I have not forgotten," Nursel said. "I do not mean to forget. One day he will make a mistake—and I will be waiting."

She picked up the dinner tray with its half-eaten meal and bore it away. When the door closed after her, Tracy sank limply back against the hard pillows. She was fully awake now, her thoughts ready to skitter back and forth and around in circles. Nothing that she had seen since she arrived in this household formed a logical, discernible pattern. On every hand there were contradictions.

Ahmet had been one of the three in the ruins of the old palace, but who were the others? Could the woman have been Nursel? Was that the reason for her interest in the scarf Tracy had found? As far as the two voices were concerned, there was no identifying them. They had been distorted in angry disagreement, and she could not guess whether the woman was someone she had met or a total stranger. It was the same with the second man. It might even have been Murat himself, pretending afterward to approach along the road, pretending to be surprised by the open gate. Since the language had been Turkish no accent had been identifiable.

The scarf was perhaps the main clue. Tracy drew it from beneath her pillow and once more studied the plum-colored stripes. Without warning a memory of where she had seen such material returned to mind. There had been a cushion or two in Sylvana Erim's salon made of this very stuff. But where that fact led, she had no sure idea.

Wasn't it probable that the roots of whatever was happening here now went back a few months ago to the time when Anabel had been alive? There was the dark hint of some desperate act behind her sister's death. "I don't want to die!" Anabel had cried—and gone almost directly to her death. If someone in this house was responsible, then reverberations of whatever had happened might continue for a long time after. Particularly if opposing forces of suspicion and concealment were still fighting some underground battle. If only she could know who concealed, and who suspected, so that she could safely choose sides. But friend, or foe, all wore masks, and with a wrong move on her part the ground could open under her feet with greater disaster promised than the physical fall she had taken through a rotted wooden floor that afternoon.

Since the answers were not easily to be found, she must stay out the week and longer. She must find the courage not to be bullied by either Miles or the dominating Sylvana. Nor must she be lulled into too-ready confidences with Nursel. Or flattered by the attractive Dr. Erim's suave, sympathetic attention. She must remain aloof from them all and in possession of her own will until she knew enough to take necessary action—if action of any sort was still possible.

Across the room the forgotten Yasemin settled more deeply into her chair, purring contentedly. The white cat had once more made Anabel's room her own.

6

In the morning when Tracy wakened she found her leg somewhat sore and stiff. But Nursel's bandage was still neatly in place and the discomfort would be minor. She was already looking forward to a trip to Istanbul and a space of time away from this house with its uneasy secrets.

When she was dressed and ready for breakfast, she started toward the stairs, noting on the way that the door of Miles Radburn's study was ajar. She thought of speaking to him before he left and went to the door. But the study was empty. Balcony doors stood open and a cool morning breeze played through the unheated room. As she looked about, the wind caught a sheet of paper and drifted it across the floor.

Tracy went to pick it up and then stood still in shocked surprise, staring at the space beneath the long table where she had left her stacks of sorted papers. The area was in complete confusion. Not a pile remained intact. Papers and drawings had been whirled helter-skelter, some thrown face down, some face up—all mixed together hopelessly.

The wind had done this, she thought, and went to close the doors. But when they were shut and the room empty of sound, she stood beside the tumbled papers and drawings and knew that no breeze could have created such disorder as this, and in only one part of the room. It was not the normal, heaped-high disorder of the table top. None of those papers had been touched, nor had those on Miles's desk.

Could he have done this in a moment of angry impatience? she wondered—to discourage her, to make her want to leave? But the act did not seem in character with what little she knew of Miles

Radburn. He would surely be open in his opposition. He would not resort to anonymous trickery like this. There was something spiteful about the act. But who was she to suspect? Not the shy and timid Halide. Not Nursel, who was beginning to seem a friend. Though at times the girl appeared capable of spite. And surely this was not the sort of thing Sylvana Erim would stoop to. Who then?

Ahmet, perhaps? Moving softly, secretly, aware that she knew of his secret watching in the palace ruins, taking this small revenge? But the act seemed less like an intent to her back than like a deliberate threat, a warning. It was as if someone said to her quite clearly, "Stop this pretense of work and go home. We do not want you here."

Tracy hooked her thumbs into the waistband of her skirt, turned her back on the scene, and went downstairs. In bright morning sunlight she felt more angry than fearful. She had been pleased with her small sorting task, and it was thoroughly aggravating to have hours of careful work go for nothing. She would not be stopped as easily as this. When she came home from the trip with Nursel, she would go straight to work and sort everything all over again. What had been done was not serious—just annoying.

As she reached the second floor she heard the sound of voices from the dining area and she went abruptly into the room, driven by the strength of her own indignation. She hoped to find Miles Radburn at breakfast, but he was not at the table. Only Nursel and her brother were there, discussing some matter earnestly in Turkish. When she walked in they both looked up with a surprise that told her the expression she wore might be on the combative side.

"I've just been in Mr. Radburn's study," she told them. "I found all the sorting work I did yesterday thrown into disorder. Have you seen Mr. Radburn? I'd like to hear whether he knows about this. Who would do such a thing?"

Nursel and her brother exchanged a quick look in which there was some meaning Tracy could not catch.

"Mr. Radburn left early for Istanbul," Nursel said. "We know nothing of this."

Dr. Erim rose to seat Tracy at the table, but he did not speak. In spite of his formal courtesy there was a change in him and he did not seem at all like the sympathetic man who had brought her home last evening after her fall. There was a smoldering in his dark eyes and he looked at her with an uncomfortable intensity. Something was very wrong. Tracy sat down feeling suddenly shaken.

"What is it?" she said. "What's the matter?"

Nursel recovered herself first. "You have taken us by surprise, Miss Hubbard. You are angry. It is distressing that your work has been disturbed. We are shocked, of course."

Murat Erim took no placating cue from his sister. Though he had not finished breakfast, he did not seat himself again.

"Perhaps it is better if you go home at once, Miss Hubbard," he told her shortly. "It seems that only trouble awaits you here in Turkey."

"But why should I go home?" Tracy asked, dismayed by this unexpected attack. "It's true that what I found just now upset me and made me angry. But I can straighten out the mess with a little more work. It doesn't make me want to give up and go home—if that's what was intended."

Dr. Erim put his napkin down with careful restraint, bowed to her without replying, and went out of the room.

Tracy turned blankly to Nursel. "What have I done? Why is he so upset? I should think he would want to know who has played this mischievous trick."

The Turkish girl did not answer at once. She gave her attention to breaking a roll, to buttering it delicately. Halide came with Tracy's breakfast and she waited until the girl had gone away. A notion was beginning to turn itself over in her mind.

"Did you tell your brother what really happened in that ruined place last evening?" she asked Nursel. "Did you tell him that I heard voices there? That I heard someone speak my name?"

Nursel seemed alarmed. "No—no, I have said nothing. It is another thing than this that disturbs him. Please—you must pay no attention. My brother has moods. Sometimes he is angry with me, sometimes with Sylvana, or with the servants. It means nothing. As you can see, he is not a happy man. Unfortunate circumstances have come upon us since the death of our older brother."

She paused as if uncertain of how much she might say, then came to a decision and threw reticence aside.

"According to our Turkish law what a man leaves when he

316

dies must be divided equally between members of his immediate family. Thus Sylvana, Murat, and I share equally in ownership of the yali. However, Sylvana prevailed upon our brother to circumvent the law during his lifetime by building the kiosk in her name, by turning much of his personal fortune which he amassed, not by inheritance but in his own exporting business, into outright gifts of money and jewelry to her. There was little left for Murat and me besides this house. We are dependent on Sylvana for most of what we have. And she holds the purse strings tightly. My brother is not one to live happily accepting what should rightfully be his from the hands of this Frenchwoman. Thus you will see that he may be easily upset."

"I can understand how he must feel," Tracy said. "But I still don't see why he should be angry with me."

Nursel sighed. "He does not mean to be inhospitable, Miss Hubbard. Please forgive us and enjoy your breakfast."

Tracy ate her rolls and coffee in silence and Nursel sat with her, making no further attempt at talk. She seemed pensive and subdued this morning. Perhaps she was already regretting her outspoken confidences to Tracy last night.

"Will you tell your brother," Tracy said, "that I have no interest in anything except the purpose for which I have come here." That was true enough. She needn't elaborate.

"And what purpose is that?" Nursel asked gently.

"Why—my work for Mr. Radburn, of course," said Tracy, but a faint prickling ran along the skin of her arms as if something had brushed her lightly in warning.

Nursel nodded. "Of course. I am sorry there has been this little upset. I will of course speak to the servants and see if I can find out who has played this unkind trick. The young girls who work for us are sometimes like merry children."

Tracy said nothing. She did not think this was the prank of a merry child.

"In any case," Nursel went on, almost in pleading, "let us forget the matter now and use our day pleasantly. Let us enjoy ourselves on our trip to Istanbul. Let us be happy this morning. This morning I wish to be like—like Anabel, with only the desire to be gay."

The coaxing words were hard to resist and Tracy's annoyance began to fade. "I agree," she said. "Let's not spoil the day."

Nursel cheered up with startling suddenness. Perhaps her air of meekness was something she used to keep out of trouble and to hide her own feelings. A girl who could be devoured by bitter anger at one moment, and in the next be close to sentimental tears, offered a riddle that was not to be easily solved.

The two set off soon after breakfast. Though it was late March, the day was a gift from spring—brightly warm and sunny. Budding promise showed along every tree branch, and overnight the grass had gained a fresh patina of green. Nursel drove as though she liked the feeling of the wheel in her hands and there was a new eagerness about her once they were away from the house, as if she too delighted in flinging off the shackles of its secretive atmosphere.

As Tracy stole a look at her, it was hard to believe that this poised and fashionable young woman was the same emotion-driven girl who had told her so much last night. She looked very beautiful today. Not a wisp of her smoothly lacquered hair stirred in the breeze from open windows, though Tracy's brown bangs were ruffled beneath the curve of her blue suede beret. The dangling earrings Nursel wore caught glints of sunlight and danced with every movement of her head, giving her an air of careless lightheartedness. The clips at her earlobes were circled by tiny blue stones, and the lower teardrops of silver framed larger stones of the same flawless blue.

"How pretty your earrings are," Tracy said.

Nursel smiled at the compliment and, when she slowed the car for the next turn, she reached up to pull the trinkets off and held them out to Tracy.

"Please—they are yours. Wear them in happiness."

"Oh, but I couldn't take them!" Tracy said in dismay. "I didn't mean—"

Nursel dropped them into her lap. "It is a Turkish custom. You cannot refuse or you will offend me. If I did not like you, I would not give them. May I call you by your first name, please? As you will call me Nursel."

"Of course," Tracy said, touched by the friendly gesture.

"You know, do you not, that we Turks have possessed last names for only a handful of years? Before that there was great confusion. Now we are westernized and we have chosen last names for ourselves. But we still cling to the use of first names. It is more comfortable."

"Thank you, Nursel," Tracy said and clipped the pretty things to her own ears. She loved the dancing feel of the earrings against her cheeks. Anabel had worn earrings like this, and never the dull button variety Tracy permitted herself. For a moment Tracy felt almost as elegant as Nursel, as glamourous as Anabel.

With a graceful gesture, the Turkish girl had endeared herself. Nevertheless, Tracy wished that a faint reservation did not mar her feeling toward the other girl. Earrings or no, Tracy could not be wholly comfortable with Nursel Erim. She had the feeling quite often that the Turkish girl was hiding something.

Nursel gave her an approving look as she clipped on the earrings. "They become you," she said. "And of course the blue color will keep you from harm. Or so the ancient Turkish belief tells us."

In Turkey, Tracy recalled, blue was the color used to ward off the effects of the evil eye. She had already seen babies and small children with blue beads woven into their hair or worn as necklaces. Car radiators sometimes wore a string of such beads, and donkeys often wore them around their necks.

The car had left the ferry and was following a main thoroughfare of modern Istanbul. A long strip of plane trees, still bare of leaves, divided the two lanes of traffic, and great concrete government buildings flying the Turkish Crescent and Star rimmed one side of the avenue. As the road dipped toward old Istanbul across the Golden Horn, Tracy sat up eagerly to watch for the famous skyline.

The Golden Horn was that curving, narrow strip of waterway that opened from the Bosporus and bisected Istanbul, separating the old from the new. There were two bridges across it—one the newer Atatürk Bridge, the other the ancient Galata, which they were now approaching. Across Galata Bridge had traveled the caravans of the ancient world. Today the horses and camels had given way to motor vehicles of every description, packed in close formation as they streamed back and forth across the water.

As they drove toward the beginning of the bridge, the skyline came into sight and Tracy drew in her breath. With rain and fog banished, it was a magical thing—a great pyramidal mound of solidly packed buildings from which rose the domes and minarets of a myriad of mosques. There was little color, Tracy saw. Istanbul was a gray city, even in the sunlight. But the grace of its minarets, the perfected architecture of dome rising upon dome, gave the whole an almost ethereal grace.

They slowed for the bridge traffic, and Nursel identified a structure here and there. To the left, near Topkapi Palace, which the French had called the Seraglio, rose that marvelous structure built by the Emperor Justinian in the year A.D. 537—the divine St. Sophia, once a church, then a mosque, and now a museum to house the relics of its own great history. Somewhat higher was the Blue Mosque, while nearer the center was a far vaster building—the mosque of Suleiman the Magnificent.

They were on the bridge now and traffic ran bumper to bumper, with a stream of pedestrians crossing by means of the walks on either side. The waters of the Golden Horn were filled with boats of every description. Below the bridge on the right ran what seemed to be a street paralleling the bridge at water level. Here fishing boats were drawn up and men peddled their fresh wares to purchasers on the bridge.

"A portion of the Galata floats on pontoons," Nursel explained. "It is opened only once each day. At four o'clock every morning it swings open to let boats in and out of the Golden Horn. Two hours later it is closed again and traffic is once more allowed to cross. To see the bridge at dawn when it is open, to see it close and the traffic flow across again is a wonderful thing. Once my brother brought me here for the sight."

On the far side as they left the bridge, the narrow cobbled streets of Stamboul, as the British had called the old quarter, swallowed them and it was necessary to drive slowly, for now there were donkeys and peddlers and pedestrians crowding every thoroughfare. Yogurt sellers, candy peddlers, purveyors of drinking water vied with each other for the right of way. Boys, with brass trays hanging from chains and laden with tiny coffee cups, ran about skillfully without spilling a drop. Nursel drove into the maze of streets and up the hill to find a place to park.

"We are near the Covered Bazaar," she said. "We will go there first and I will complete my errands."

Once they were on foot in the steep, cobbled streets, Tracy caught the smell of dust that was the smell of Istanbul. The slightest stirring of air sent the dust that lay between cobblestones and along every ledge and gutter edge into a swirling dervish dance.

They crossed the courtyard of a lesser mosque where pigeons thronged, being fed by passers-by. Beyond rose the arched entryway to the Covered Bazaar. Set in stone above the pointed arch that gave final entrance to the bazaar was the insignia of the Ottoman Empire, with its emblem of crossed flags. The stream of men and women that went in and out of the entrance wore European dress for the most part, and the faces were those of any cosmopolitan city where races mingled. Here and there Tracy saw men carrying tespihler in their hands, or with strands of beads hanging partially out of pockets.

Once through the arch, they were in the maze of the bazaar itself. It was, Tracy found, a city of tiny shops gathered beneath arching stone roofs that had been stained and weatherbeaten by the years. At intervals high windows let in a watery semblance of daylight. For the most part, however, the lighting was by electricity, and the small glass window of each shop glowed with warm light. Off the first stone corridor other corridors opened, and still others upon those, until Tracy was soon lost in the web.

The shops were apparently gathered into communities, each group selling one type of goods. They passed window after window heaped high with gleaming golden bracelets—vastly popular with girls from the villages, Nursel said, since they still counted their worth as brides by the number of gold bracelets they might string upon their arms. There were shops where nothing but slippers and shoes were sold, and where the smell of leather was strong. There was a street of copper shops, another that sold only brass, and there were endless rows of small jewelry stores.

It was into one of these that Nursel went on her first errand. So small was the shop that its exterior consisted of no more than a narrow show window and a door. Inside was a small counter behind which there was room for a single shopkeeper. The space before the counter could hold no more than two customers comfortably at one time. The young man behind the counter greeted Nursel by name and at once brought stools for his guests. He was tall and well built, with bright, intent dark eyes and a smile that showed the flash of fine teeth.

"This is Hasan Effendi," Nursel said.

The young man bowed gravely and murmured in English that the *hanimefendi* did his shop honor.

Tracy sat upon her stool and studied the fascinating array

within. Every inch of the tiny space held shelves on which were displayed beads and brooches, rings and amulets and tiny ornaments.

"You have the tespih for my brother, Hasan Effendi?" Nursel asked.

The young man reached into a drawer behind him and laid upon the glass counter a tespih strung with beads of fine green jade. Nursel studied them with interest.

"Murat will be pleased," she said and gave them to Tracy to see. "These will be a valuable addition to my brother's collection."

The string was like others Tracy had handled yesterday—a short string with finial beads and no clasp. In her fingers the jade felt exquisitely smooth and was cool to her touch. When Nursel took them back and asked the price, a gentle, almost teasing bargaining began between buyer and seller. The good-natured banter quickly concluded, Nursel paid the sum agreed upon and put the small package in her handbag. Then she spoke to Tracy.

"You will excuse us, please, if we speak in Turkish? Hasan Effendi is the son of Ahmet Effendi and I have a message for him from his father."

While they spoke together, Tracy studied the young man with new interest. His good looks and well-built frame held little resemblance to the wiry Ahmet. Until he began to frown. Then they seemed kin at once. She did not like the way he scowled, or the somewhat harsh note that came into his voice. Once more Nursel cast down her eyes in the old meek way, though this seemed a little strange when the man on the other side of the counter was a shopkeeper and the son of a servant in the Erim household.

It was possible that he sensed Tracy's surprised interest upon him, for he suddenly broke off, smiling, and reached into a box beneath the counter.

"Perhaps you would like to see the tespihler I will soon send to Mrs. Erim, *hanimefendi*," he said, and cast a handful of bead strands upon the counter before her.

Tracy leaned closer to see the colorful array. Automatically she looked for black amber, but there was none in this collection. Nursel, after a glance, seemed to dismiss the display with indifference.

"I am sure Mrs. Erim will be pleased to have them, Hasan

Effendi," she said politely. "She is eager to assist you in the success of this shop, just as she is eager to help her villagers."

The look of Ahmet was in the son's eyes again—a little sullen, darkly resentful. But he did not answer. As they left the shop, he came with them to the door and stood looking after them as they walked away.

Once they had turned a corner and were out of sight of the shop, Nursel flung off her air of meekness and became herself again.

"It is very difficult for Hasan Effendi," she said. "Our elder brother sent him to school for a time, but after he died Murat did not wish to continue Hasan's education, for there was so little money. Nor is Sylvana interested in spending the money—though she could afford to. So this young man is forced to work in a small shop. He is ambitious, however, and perhaps he will one day finish his education and become an attorney."

"He seemed angry with you when we left," Tracy said, probing.

Nursel seemed undisturbed. "It does not matter. It is nothing. The behavior of Mrs. Erim infuriates him. Perhaps this is a good thing. Come—we will go this way. I have now an important purchase to make for Sylvana."

As they walked down still another corridor, Tracy saw that along the edge of the walk marble heads and busts, a broken pedestal or two, portions of a marble pillar had been piled carelessly —all fragments with the stamp of age upon them.

"Shouldn't some of these things be in a museum?" she asked in wonder.

Nursel's shrug was expressive. "Who is to know how such things find their way into the bazaars of Istanbul? All through Turkey there are ancient ruins still to be excavated. Undoubtedly pilfering goes on. Ah—here is the place I am looking for."

She had stopped before a shop that was larger than the others, perhaps a combination of three or four thrown together. The show windows were dusty and far less cluttered, displaying only a few fine articles of silver, copper, and brass. It was as if this shop knew its own worth and was above tawdry commercial display.

As Nursel entered, the shopkeeper came respectfully to greet her. He signaled to a boy to bring wooden chairs for the guests, and they were seated in the bare main aisle. The shop was rather dark and the smell of dust lay heavily upon it, yet Tracy sensed that all about were objects old and rich in value.

The boy who had brought the chairs disappeared, to return shortly with a copper tray on which were set small cups of Turkish coffee. Tracy sipped the thick, bittersweet brew determinedly.

When they had been refreshed and Nursel and the shopkeeper had exchanged courtesies, he brought out the treasure for which she had come. The object was large and fairly heavy and he bore it before him with a ceremonial air. A sharp word to the young boy sent him scurrying to fetch a table upon which it could be placed and a cloth with which to dust it.

Tracy saw that it was a very grand and dignified samovar. Its copper luster was tarnished and dull, but beauty of form remained. Above the large water compartment rose tiers or racks and lids and a tall copper chimney. Below was the curving base on which the whole thing rested. A handle over the spout was fanned and ornamentally embossed, fancy as a peacock's tail. On either side of the tank were strong handles by which the heavy piece could be lifted.

The boy handed the dustcloth to his master, backed fearfully away from the copper beauty, and bolted to the rear of the shop.

Nursel smiled. "He is afraid. He knows the story of this samovar. It is perhaps more than two hundred years old. In the old times the finest samovars came from Russia, but this was made in a village in Anatolia. You can see how beautiful the workmanship is. Always we Turks have valued artists and, when the Sultan of that day found so fine an artisan in a small village, he brought him and the samovar he had made to Istanbul. There the man was given an important place at court and encouraged in his work. Unfortunately, he was one who enjoyed intrigue. Perhaps he was not as clever at court affairs as he was clever with his hands. It seems that he came to a sad end and his head floated down the Bosporus in a basket."

Nursel walked around the samovar, touching it respectfully now and then.

"The most romantic part of the story comes later," she went on. "The samovar was given at last to the Sultan's mother, the most powerful woman in the Empire. For many years it graced her summer palace on the Bosporus. Unfortunately, she was stabbed to death and the samovar outlasted her. Later the samovar was placed in the Topkapi Palace museum. Many years ago it was stolen from the museum and disappeared, only to come to light recently in Istanbul's bazaars. What a marvelous treasure for Sylvana to own, though I wish that Murat had found it first."

Tracy regarded the samovar with interest. "Won't it be returned to the museum?"

Again Nursel made her graceful little shrug. "Perhaps it will be. But for now Sylvana may enjoy it and she will also enjoy making Murat envious." She sighed as though she foresaw further tensions at the yali with the coming of the samovar.

There was no bargaining here. Apparently the price had been arrived at between Sylvana and the shopkeeper, and Nursel had only to pay him the not inconsiderable sum.

When they returned to the car, the shopkeeper accompanied them, bearing the treasure wrapped carefully in Turkish newspapers and tied with string. The boy, it seemed, would not carry it. He had run away to hide until the samovar was gone from the shop.

When the large package had been placed in the back of the car, Nursel suggested that there was time for Tracy to see the Blue Mosque before lunch. They drove a short distance and then parked again.

"I am sorry I cannot go in with you," Nursel said. "I must not leave Sylvana's treasure alone in the car. But you may enter and look around as long as you wish. I am content. There is no hurry."

The great mosque was a pyramid of domes rising upon domes, with the largest one crowning the top. At each of the mosque's four corners rose a slender minaret, encircled by small bands of balcony, as rings might encircle a finger. The two extra minarets —six was a greater number than any except those possessed by the great mosque in Mecca—stood somewhat to the side.

Tracy's eyes were filled with the soaring grace of the architecture and she stood looking up at the domes for a long while before she walked across the wide courtyard to the entrance. She had read that Sultan Ahmed had so admired Justinian's St. Sophia that he had copied the outer form of it in this mosque.

Near the entrance an aged Turk pointed to large soft slippers she could put on over her shoes, and held out his palm for her tip. Shuffling in the ungainly coverings, she stepped into a world of flying arches and vast domes, all floating in a shimmer of blue light. Far above, high windows circled each dome and graced each arch, flinging sunlight into the heart of the mosque, only to have its gold transfused by the expanse of mosaic until the air seemed blue as an undersea cavern. Tracy stepped onto soft layers of carpet, dozens of which were arranged in orderly rows, covering every inch of the floor. A sense of spreading, soaring space was all about her, not only overhead, but all around at floor level. There were no pews to break up space as was the case in a Christian church. The carpets were there to be knelt upon, and only four enormous fluted columns interrupted the open vista.

So varied was the decoration of tilework, with its flaunting of blue peacock tails, its stylized reproduction of blue roses and tulips and lilies, its giant inscriptions from the Koran that adorned pillar and dome and arch, that the eye soon wearied and Tracy ceased to see detail, but was absorbed into the vast blue atmosphere.

The hour was nearing for prayer, and the Faithful, having performed their ablutions in running water outside the mosque, were coming in to kneel upon the carpets, gathering in a mass toward the front of the edifice. There were no women among the worshipers who faced Mecca. The men who passed Tracy paid no attention, undoubtedly accustomed to tourists and intent upon their own purpose. A low, carved stand in the form of a giant X held a huge Koran, its worn pages open to be read by whomever pleased.

Overhead wires had been strung across the space, and from these hung glass lamps which had once contained oil and wicks for the lighting of the interior, but now boasted unromantic glass bulbs for electricity. In her huge slippers Tracy shuffled beneath them toward one of the outer galleries, her senses dulled by the very blueness and the vast assortment of detail. The wall pulled in her perspective a little and she rounded a turn of the corridor to come to a surprised halt. A few feet away a man stood before an easel, intent upon his painting. She saw that it was Miles Radburn.

She stood where she was, watching him, uncertain whether to advance or go quickly away before he saw her.

7

AN UNEASY PRICKLING stirred at the back of Tracy's neck and she smiled ruefully. Her hackles were rising, undoubtedly, at the very sight of this man. She moved nearer, trying to walk without scuffling, in order to see what he was doing before he discovered her there watching him.

His dark, rather saturnine head was bent toward the work in progress on his easel. He was, of course, painting in blue—an assortment of blues that made up one of the far-flung peacock panels over his head. Meticulously he was filling in tiny wedges and feathery curves, and she marveled that he could do such work. Once he had been a painter of men and women, known for the swiftness with which he could cut through exteriors to the essence of his subject in quick strong strokes. He had done just that in his painting of Anabel. How could he turn now to this painstaking detail, so lacking in any human quality?

He must have sensed her presence, for he looked around and recognized her without welcome. Tracy braced herself. She did not like the uneasiness she felt with this man, the inclination to flee from something half feared and not understood. For this very reason she stood her ground.

"Touristing?" he asked. "What do you think of all this?"

She did not believe he really cared what she thought, but she tried to give him a true answer. "It overwhelms me. I get tired of trying to look at it all at once. I suppose I keep wanting to see a human face somewhere in all that sea of abstract design."

"The Moslem religion forbade the depicting of humans or animals," he reminded her. "Mustapha Kemal changed all this, but it's why artists used to turn to architecture and mosaics to express themselves. They produced some of the finest work of this sort that's ever been done, as a result." He waved a hand toward the interior of the mosque. "Of course a lot of what you see there now is stenciling. Unless you look closely, you can't always tell it from the real tile. Many of the less famous mosques have finer work preserved in them."

He turned back to his painting and she watched him for a few moments longer. When it appeared that he had nothing more to say to her, she intruded upon his silence.

"Did you happen to go into your study before you left this morning?"

He answered carelessly. "Only when I first got up. I had no time after breakfast. My stuff was in my car and I wanted to get an early start."

"I went in," she said quietly. "Someone had gone through the sorting I did yesterday and whipped everything into complete disorder."

She had his attention now. He stared at her, his face expressionless.

"That means it has begun again," he said.

His words had no meaning for her, yet they had an ominous ring.

"What do you mean? What has begun again?"

"The work of our evil genius. Our poltergeist, or what have you. Was any damage done to my papers and drawings?"

"Not as far as I could see," Tracy admitted. "It was as though a child had mixed everything up."

"It was not a child." He continued to regard her with an odd concentration. When he spoke again his words took her by surprise. "Those earbobs you're wearing—I suppose you found them in the bazaar?"

Startled, her hands flew to the earrings she had almost forgotten. "Nursel gave them to me. I admired them and she took them right off and handed them to me. She wouldn't let me refuse."

He nodded. "You have to be careful what you admire. The Turks are a wildly generous and hospitable lot. But you shouldn't wear the things. They don't suit you."

"But I like them," she said, beginning to breathe hard.

He set down his palette and brush on the folding stand beside his easel and came over to her. Before she knew what he meant to do, he pulled off the clipped earrings and held them out to her. "That's better. Now you're all of one piece."

She was both outraged and disconcerted as the earrings dropped into her hand. Suddenly old memory was strong. It was as if she were a young girl again and her father had just thrown her first lipstick into a wastebasket. The words he'd spoken so long ago rang in her ears as if she heard them now, "Don't try to look like your sister Anabel. Just be yourself."

But she was not a child now, she thought indignantly, and Miles Radburn had no authority to tell her what she might wear. Nevertheless, the old feeling of having made herself ridiculous— because she could never be like Anabel—possessed her as it used to do, shattering all self-confidence.

"What do you mean—all of one piece?" she faltered, hating the very uncertainty of her words.

He went calmly back to his easel and began to put his painting things away. "Don't blame me for seeing as a painter sees. How is your barked shin?"

"It's all right, thank you," she managed in a choked voice.

He continued without looking around. "You ought not wander around old ruins in the dark. If you get into trouble so easily, perhaps you'd better not stay in Turkey until your week is up."

This was exactly what Dr. Erim had said at breakfast, and she found she was tired of being told to go home. She walked away without another word, her chin stiffly atilt. She would not be scolded and frightened, and she would not go home.

Halfway across the courtyard she clipped on the earrings again. They set up a small defiant dance against her cheeks, and she told herself that it made no difference if Miles Radburn was right. Even if she wasn't the type for dangling earrings, even if she was no match for Anabel's memory, he had behaved in an outrageous manner. She would wear what she liked and do as she pleased. But he had spoiled her delight in the baubles and she would not readily forgive him.

He must have put his painting things away rather quickly, for he caught up with her before she left the courtyard.

"There's something you ought to see," he said. "Hold on a minute."

She reminded him coolly that Nursel had been waiting for her quite a while, but he brushed her words aside.

"You wanted to see something of Istanbul. Look up there."

They were close to one of the minarets, and she looked straight upward at a tiny balcony that circled one needlelike finger near the top. The tower seemed unbelievably tall and thin, and the man who had climbed the stairs within it and stood upon the balcony seemed small as a puppet figure. The muezzin wore no robes and carried no trumpet. In his black business suit he stood within the high circle and cupped his hands about his mouth. His long, wailing cry was almost lost to them on the wind, so they heard only a faint warbling. Then he turned and cried out again, and this time the call to prayer came toward them and they could hear the liquid sound of the words:

"Allahu akbar! La ilaha illa' llah!"

"'God is most great . . . there is no God but God . . .'" Miles Radburn repeated softly.

Tracy found that she was unexpectedly stirred by the sound. Her indignation was fading in spite of herself.

"Even this is passing," Miles said, as the man completed his calls and disappeared into the darkness of the minaret. "There are a good many mosques these days where you'll find the muezzin sitting comfortably on the ground, warbling into a microphone. Can't say I blame them. I climbed a flight of stairs inside a minaret once. Those fellows have to keep in trim, even if their flocks are falling off."

"There seemed to be a great number of men coming into the mosque," Tracy said.

"Mostly of the older generations, I suspect. It's too bad some of the younger Turks are turning away from religion—with nothing to put in the place of what they're chucking out."

"There were no women," Tracy mused. "I saw only men kneeling on the carpets inside."

"The women are in separate niches at the back," Miles said. "You'll always see a few sitting cross-legged, keeping out of the way of the men but no less devout. Shall we go along now and find Nursel? Perhaps you'll both have lunch with me."

The earrings bobbed against her cheeks, but she no longer felt defiant. She did not particularly want to lunch with Miles Radburn, but something in her had quieted, temporarily at least. An unspoken truce had been declared. An uneasy truce, perhaps, because his strange words about a poltergeist lingered at the back of her mind, as well as his quick changing of the subject after he had spoken.

Nursel was waiting patiently in the car. She accepted Miles Radburn's invitation to lunch with the guarded courtesy she adopted toward him. Tracy had a feeling that Miles himself did not suspect how thoroughly he was disliked by Nursel Erim. Further evidence, perhaps, of the blank side he turned toward the feelings of others. Further evidence of the barrier he placed between himself and the world.

Again they drove a short distance and left the car in an open place not far from the Spice Bazaar. When they got out, Nursel explained to Miles about the samovar—that she dared not leave it behind.

He lifted the ungainly package out in its newspaper and string wrapping. "I don't suppose this is the same one . . ." he began.

Nursel broke in quickly. "Yes—it is the same. Sylvana purchased it long ago. She waited to bring it home because it might remind you of unhappy things. But now a little time has passed."

"Yes," Miles said, "time has passed. We'll take it with us and see that no harm befalls it. Though I gather that it has weathered history better than those who have owned it."

Together they walked through crowded streets. Near the Spice Bazaar the roadway was filled with cars and taxis, with carts and horses and donkeys, with teeming humanity. Awnings overhung open stalls where spices were sold and flapped in the wind above fruit stands. The Istanbul smell of dust was pleasantly cut by the scent of Eastern spices and the odor of ripe fruit.

The restaurant in the Spice Bazaar to which Miles took them was very old. They climbed narrow stairs to a room at the top and were shown to a table near a deep window that overlooked Galata Bridge and the Golden Horn. A glass chandelier hung from the dome of the ceiling and there was blue and black tilework around the walls.

The menu was in English as well as Turkish, and Miles ordered for them—swordfish on skewers, alternating with bits of bay leaf, tomato, and lemon slices. Tracy looked out the window toward buildings across the Golden Horn in newer Istanbul, where an ancient fire tower topped a mound of less picturesque buildings than graced the old quarter.

"We build only in stone now," Nursel said. "No longer are wooden houses permitted. Istanbul has burned down too many times."

On a nearby wall hung the familiar picture of Mustapha Kemal —Atatürk—that Tracy had begun to see everywhere.

Nursel saw her eyes on the picture. "My father fought with the Ghazi, as they called him—the Victor—in the campaign that saved Turkey. Ahmet Effendi was with him in those days also. My older brother and Murat and I grew up on stories of those times. Ahmet Effendi would have given his life for my brother, as he would for Murat also."

"But not for you?" Tracy asked.

Nursel smiled. "I am a woman. It is not the same. Still he is loyal to any of our family. Even to Sylvana."

She began to discuss the current political situation with Miles, and Tracy found herself watching him as she listened. Even now, when he had invited them to lunch, he remained somewhat absent, lapsing into an occasional moody silence almost in the middle of a sentence. She had again the feeling that she was looking at someone who had ceased to be alive. Ceased deliberately.

The swordfish, when it came, was delicious. Mediterranean waters and those of the Marmara and the Bosporus all offered their wares to Istanbul, and fish was a favorite food with the Turks.

Not until the meal was half over did Miles put a sudden question to Nursel, giving her his full attention for the first time.

"You know about what happened this morning?" he asked.

Nursel stared at her plate. "Yes, Tracy has told me."

"It sounds like the old game starting up again."

"Perhaps it is a warning." Nursel smiled, attempting to treat the subject lightly.

"It won't be easy for anyone to frighten Miss Hubbard away," Miles said. "I suspect she'll make a stand."

"Of course I will!" Tracy felt the earrings dance vehemently against her cheeks. His unexpected support braced her to further resist leaving.

He did not let the matter drop. "From what quarter do you think such a warning might come?" he asked Nursel.

"I make only a small joke," the Turkish girl said. "I do not know who does this thing." But she sounded uneasy.

"Last time there were hints dropped that it might be Anabel

playing these tricks," Miles pointed out. "What happened this morning seems to indicate that it couldn't have been."

Nursel spoke quickly. "I have never believed this of Anabel! But, please—it is better not to talk of such things. This—poltergeist, as you say, is only mischievous. He does no harm."

"He frightened Anabel half out of her wits," Miles said. "Tracy is made of sterner stuff. Perhaps she'll frighten him." He flashed his unexpected smile upon Tracy. "After all, she has managed to intimidate me. Perhaps your Turkish spirits had better look out for themselves."

This was no longer a joke to Nursel. "One must not speak aloud the name of evil," she protested.

A spark seemed to have been lighted in the bleak inner landscape of Miles's being and now it burned more intensely.

"I don't agree. I'm inclined to think that evil has a name—a human name. Perhaps there are times when it's better to cry it as loudly as possible—even from the rooftops. Once the name is known, of course."

Nursel said nothing more, withdrawing herself pointedly from so distasteful a subject. Apathy fell upon Miles again. They finished the meal with little conversation, but Tracy could not forget the glimpse she'd had of unexpected fire in the man who had been Anabel's husband.

It had been surprising to see his indifference kindle into something verging on excitement. True, it was a dark excitement and Tracy had the uncomfortable feeling that a hint of violence might lie beneath the surface. Yet it showed him alive and not wholly indifferent to what happened around him.

When the meal was over and they left the restaurant, Miles carried the samovar to Nursel's car, packing it away again in the rear seat.

"I believe I'll start home myself," he said. "I need to get on with that strip of calligraphy I'm doing for Sylvana. And I want to have a look at our mischief-maker's new trick."

Tracy caught him up at once. "In that case, I'll start cleaning up the muddle as soon as you've looked it over. Then I can get on with my work."

For an instant he seemed disconcerted. As they drove off, Tracy glanced back and saw him staring after the car with an expression that seemed part annoyance, part dismay.

On the trip home, crossing on the ferry, and driving along the road on the Anatolian side, she and Nursel talked idly and at random, not touching again on the subject of Miles Radburn or the disturbance in his study. Questions teemed in Tracy's mind, but she dared push them no further at the moment.

When they reached the yali Halide came to carry the samovar upstairs.

"Come with me while I take it to Sylvana," Nursel suggested. "It will be amusing to see her open it. She has coveted this for very long."

As the three climbed to the second floor of the kiosk the door of Sylvana's salon was flung suddenly open and a sound of angry voices reached them. Dr. Erim appeared abruptly at the head of the stairs and it was clear that he was enraged. Though the argument was in Turkish, there was no mistaking Murat's anger or Sylvana's indignation.

As he started down the stairs, Halide squealed and ducked out of his way with the samovar and Tracy drew back against the rail to let him pass. Nursel reached a hand toward her brother, but he brushed it aside and rushed downstairs. Whatever had occurred, the quarrel had been thorough.

"I am sorry," Nursel said. "I must go to him. I must learn what has happened. This time she has pushed him too far. Please—you will take the samovar upstairs to Mrs. Erim."

Thus directed, Tracy and Halide climbed the remaining steps. Tracy had no desire for an encounter while Sylvana was in a temper. Her own presence in this household was too uncertain, too tenuous. There was, however, no avoiding what was to come. Sylvana stood in the open door of her salon, clearly struggling to regain control of herself. Her air of calm was gone and she seemed at the point of angry tears.

She glanced impatiently at Tracy, then saw the package in Halide's arms. She seized upon it as a distraction.

"Good—you have brought home the samovar!"

There was no opportunity for Tracy to slip away. She was waved into the room in Halide's wake and could only watch uncomfortably as the maid placed her burden upon a table and Sylvana began to rip away its covering. The great, handsome thing emerged into view, and at once assumed an aristocratic air, as if its presence made any place a palace.

As Sylvana walked about the samovar, exclaiming raptly in French, her hands clasped in admiration, the fury of her quarrel with her brother-in-law died out a little. Her color remained higher than usual and she was far from tranquil, but the samovar was indeed serving as a distraction.

"It has been neglected," she said, touching the plump sides with admiring hands. "Of course I shall not use it, but the exterior must be polished to a fine gloss. This I will do myself."

She spoke to Halide in Turkish, apparently explaining to the village girl where the samovar had come from, perhaps something of its story, for Halide's eyes began to widen. Suddenly she backed away as the boy in the shop had done, and ran out of the room.

Sylvana laughed, something of her surface tranquillity restored. "Our girls from the villages are still fearful and superstitious," she told Tracy. "They cling to the old ways in their customs. You notice that Halide keeps her head covered. That is because it is still regarded as unseemly to let a man see one's hair."

She circled the small table upon which the samovar stood, admiring it anew, pointing out to Tracy the art that had gone into its creation.

"The Anatolian Samovar!" she said softly. "That is the name by which it is called. Of course such a thing is not in itself evil, as Halide imagines. It has merely been witness to much wickedness. Legend has it that the Sultan's mother was drinking tea made from this very samovar on the afternoon when she was stabbed to death. The ruins of her summer palace where she died are only a short distance from this house."

"The ruins I explored yesterday?" Tracy asked.

"Yes—the very same. How is your injury?"

"It doesn't bother me," Tracy said.

Sylvana's attention could not be drawn for long from her new treasure, and she continued with her story.

"The accounts of tragedy that surround the samovar go on and on. The strangling of a young prince occurred in its presence. With all the princelings there were in the harem, there was much jealousy and those who stood close to the Sultan were always in danger of their lives. Both because of ladies who wanted their own sons to succeed to the throne, and court officials who feared their power might be usurped. All the Bosporus area has a history of wickedness to curdle the blood. It is said that a man died much later when the samovar was stolen from the museum. How fortunate that I am a Frenchwoman and am able to savor such stories without being frightened by them!"

Tracy's attention had begun to wander. Now that she was here, she remembered the scarf she had found in the ruins last night. Her glance moved about the room, seeking. This was surely the place—yes, there was the pattern among cushions on a divan below the windows. A pattern of plum-colored stripes.

She picked up the cushion. "What very pretty silk this is."

Sylvana nodded absently. "Yes—it is from Damascus. I bought a length of it last year."

"It would make a lovely scarf," Tracy mused.

Sylvana patted the samovar and circled it possessively, her interest upon her treasure.

"I don't suppose you have any of this material left?" Tracy persisted.

Sylvana glanced indifferently at the cushion. "No, it has all been used. The last of it went into a scarf. A gift I made for Nursel." Then her attention seemed at last to focus upon Tracy. "I understand that Mr. Radburn will permit you a week here after all. You are working? How does the task progress?"

"Not very fast," Tracy said. "There are too many interruptions." She watched Sylvana's face, wondering how much she knew of what had happened in Miles's study.

"It surprises me that he has consented to have you remain. Perhaps, Miss Hubbard, there is something about this work of yours you have not wished to tell us?"

Tracy had no idea what she meant, but she was on guard at once. "I don't understand," she said.

"No matter." Sylvana's smile was enigmatic. "I must not keep you when you are so busy. Thank you for bringing me the samovar."

Thus dismissed, Tracy left her presence, newly concerned. She followed the covered passage back to the third floor of the yali. On the way she pulled off her coat and when she reached the upper salon she dropped it on a chair, drew off her beret to run her fingers hurriedly through her hair. The earrings tapped her cheeks lightly and she pulled them off, tucked them into the beret. It wasn't necessary to prove her independence by wearing them now.

8

As Tracy walked toward the door of Miles's study she saw that he had left it open to the warmth of the springlike day, and through it she could see him working at his tilted drawing table. Again he seemed completely absorbed. He was working in black ink, as he converted the intricate details of a photograph into the large, decorative calligraphy.

He glanced up and saw her in the doorway, caught the expression on her face.

"You're watching me the way you did in the mosque this morning. What does that look on your face imply?"

"I'm sorry if I stared," she said as she went into the room. "You were concentrating so hard that I didn't want to interrupt you."

He made a sound of exasperation. "There's more to it than that. What were you thinking just now?"

His mood had changed completely from that of lunchtime. He was neither smiling nor darkly excited. Once more she felt uncertain, but at least she would not dissemble.

"I was wondering how you can work at that sort of thing. It's as though someone who has created cathedrals turned to copying a hedge maze."

For a moment she wasn't sure whether he would fling his brush at her angrily and dismiss her from the room, or simply retire behind his granite barrier. He did neither. To her considerable astonishment he laughed out loud. The sound was not altogether cheerful, but it was better than his scowl.

"Hornwright should know just how you've tackled this job. I'm not sure he understood what he was inflicting upon me, or the risk he was taking in sending you out here. At least you speak up,

337

however foolish your conclusions may be. But I must ask you to remember that I am your problem only as far as this book is concerned."

Her own sense of humor revived with disconcerting unexpectedness and she found herself smiling at the picture he had evoked.

"I'll try to remember," she told him cheerfully.

"Good!" he said, sounding stiffer than before in the face of her good humor. "Now perhaps you can get on with your housekeeping. I can't endure that disturbance under the table much longer. I prefer my own forms of disorder."

She knew he meant his words to sting and was all the more determined to remain unruffled. She went to the table where the morning's mischief still awaited her, pulled up her skirt, and sat down cross-legged like the women in the mosques. She would not think of the spite behind this havoc for the moment. She would simply sort things back into their respective heaps and leave all other problems for later. The problem of Nursel, for instance, and the scarf that belonged to her.

The room was quiet except for the faint rustle of papers. As she worked, Tracy found herself once more interested in the project itself. She dipped into manuscript pages concerning the work of the Seljuk Turks, and read a little here and there. Apparently the Seljuks had left behind tiles and mosaics of surprising beauty in their mosques and mausoleums. Coming before Islam, there were even occasional human representations and animal pictures in some of their work. In their pigments they had used a great deal of turquoise and white, dark blue and indigo and gilt. A pink shading seen in some of the mosaic panels, as Miles pointed out in his text, was due to an ingredient used to hold the tiles together. Several reproductions in color revealed the imaginative beauty of Seljuk work.

So complete was her absorption in seeking out drawings which matched the text that she was startled when Miles spoke to her.

"When I came into the house a while ago, I heard what sounded like a bang-up fight going on between Sylvana and Murat. Do you happen to know what was wrong?"

She was surprised that he would question her on affairs of the household. "I've no idea what it was about," she said. "Just as Nursel and I came upstairs, Dr. Erim burst out of Mrs. Erim's salon and rushed off. Nursel went after him and I haven't seen her

338

since. Halide and I took the samovar to Mrs. Erim, and she seemed terribly upset over what had happened. Though of course she made no explanation to me."

Miles returned to his calligraphy and again there was quiet in the room. Tracy's work went faster now as she reached material she had sorted before. When Miles spoke again it was in a milder, more reasonable tone, as if he wanted to persuade her of something.

"I suppose that the recording of details about mosaics and their history may seem like mere copy work and note-taking, yet it's a task that needs to be done. So much is falling to ruin and accounts ought to be preserved. Until a comparatively few years ago there was no written history in Turkey, you know, and there hasn't been enough consultating of what archives exist. Few translations have been made. I'm not doing this alone. A number of people are helping me get this record together. When it's finally in a book, the result will be worth accomplishing."

Tracy looked up. From her place on the floor she could see across the top of the intervening desk to where he sat on a stool, bent above his drawing board. Shadows emphasized the craggy features of his face and marked the unhappy slant of mouth corners, hiding the coldness that so often repelled her. An odd warming toward him stirred in her and she saw him as a man more dedicated than she had guessed. A man who worked with integrity at the assignment he had given himself.

Hesitantly she ventured a question. "But couldn't almost anyone do the actual copy work and free you to get on with the writing of the book?"

"This particular work happens to interest me," he said, his tone dry.

She considered him more sympathetically than she had ever expected to, wondering how to probe and explore, how to discover the true identity of the man who had been Anabel's husband. Perhaps a bold frankness was the only way to smoke him out from behind his wall.

"Mrs. Erim thinks there will never be a completed book," she said, "and that you don't really want to write it. She wants me to go home and tell Mr. Hornwright that it will never be done—so that he will call the whole thing off."

"What do you think?" he asked.

339

"How can I tell? You sounded just now as though you believe in this work. But you don't seem to move it ahead very quickly."

She wondered what he would say if she told him that Nursel believed the work was a hair-shirt process—a sort of punishing of himself for his treatment of Anabel in the past. But she had gone far enough for the moment and she did not dare put the thought into words. In an odd way she found that she was more reluctant than before to goad or bait him. She had begun to consider him not only as Anabel's husband, but as a man in his own right.

"Mrs. Erim may have her reasons for not wanting to see this book finished," he remarked. "The same reasons, perhaps, that led to this quarrel with her brother-in-law. It's possible that she's right and you are wasting your time here, Tracy Hubbard."

She no longer believed that Mrs. Erim was right, but before she could say so, he glanced toward the door.

"Listen!" he said.

From the direction of the stairs came the sound of high heels clicking briskly along. Miles bent above his board again. Tracy caught the scent of Sylvana's rose-drenched perfume as she came to the door of the room.

"I may speak with you, Miles?" Mrs. Erim asked.

Tracy had never listened to her voice before as an entity in itself. She noted its faintly querulous note, and a slight stridency in the higher pitches. It did not seem as tranquil as her manner.

"Of course—please come in," Miles said.

"There is a little trouble," Sylvana murmured as she entered the room. Clearly she had not seen Tracy sitting on the floor watching her over the top of the desk. Her air of composure had returned. From her blond hair drawn into its neat, heavy coil on the nape of her neck, to the tips of her smart black pumps, she looked undisturbed. If one did not listen to the faintly importunate note in her voice, one would think her wholly poised.

"First," she went on as Miles waited, "I think this American young girl must go home at once. It surprises me that you have permitted her to remain, when—"

"The American young girl is right over there," Miles said, cocking an eyebrow at Tracy. "Perhaps you would like to tell her why you think she should go home?"

Sylvana Erim was not in the least disconcerted. She glanced

calmly across the desk at the top of Tracy's head and gestured her toward the door.

"If you please? I wish to speak to Mr. Radburn alone."

Tracy looked at Miles as she stood up. "I'd really like to know why Mrs. Erim doesn't wish me to stay."

"I am sure you know my reason very well," Sylvana said.

Miles nodded toward the door. "Suppose I call you when we're through."

Mrs. Erim came at once to stand beside the drawing board, paying no further attention to Tracy. As she went out of the room, Tracy heard her exclamation of pleasure.

"This is beautiful work! The best you have done, my friend. The buyer in New York will be enormously pleased. There seems to be a sudden demand for Turkish calligraphy to use as decoration."

Tracy closed the door softly and sped across the salon to her own room. She had endured enough for one day. Somehow she must draw into the open at least one of these currents that flowed beneath the surface of life in this house. Sylvana, she knew, would tell her nothing. Dr. Erim appeared to be angry with her for some reason. But there was still Nursel, and it was time for the Turkish girl to be brought into the open.

In her room Tracy unlocked the drawer and took out the scarf she had found last evening in the palace ruins. With it folded into her purse, she went in search of the girl who had been Anabel's friend.

Nursel was not in her own room, but when Tracy questioned Halide on the lower stairs the maid gestured in the direction of the laboratory in the kiosk.

Tracy had not been in this lower section of the hillside house before, except to climb the stairs. The area seemed to be made up of a large main room, brightly lighted, with two or three smaller rooms opening along one side. The big room was rimmed with cabinets, and there were tables of equipment and shelves on which labeled cages of mice and guinea pigs were kept, lending a slightly zooey smell that was lessened by the hovering aura of perfume. At the far end Dr. Erim worked with two young assistants and he did not look up as she came in.

A light burned in one of the small cubicles and Tracy heard

someone humming a plaintive Turkish tune. Tracy looked in and found Nursel, dressed in a white lab jacket, working intently with a glass measuring phial. She glanced up and smiled at Tracy.

"You have come to visit me? Good. Please come in."

Tracy stepped into the small room, where a strong odor of sandalwood for the moment dominated weaker scents. On wall shelves were innumerable glass bottles, labeled and grouped in perfume families—the animal, the flower scents, the plant perfumes.

"Do you distill the oils yourselves?" she asked.

"Sometimes in spring and summer Mrs. Erim does this," Nursel said. "But it is a difficult process and it is simpler to work with essential oils and extracts already prepared. For me, it is the blending, the combining of scents that is interesting. Tell me what you think of this."

She unstoppered a small flask and put a dab of scent on the pulse place on Tracy's wrist. It was necessary to leave the atmosphere of sandalwood and step outside in order to catch the delicacy of lilac, very light and fresh.

"Lovely," Tracy said as she returned to Nursel. But she had not come here to talk about perfume. "Are you very busy? I'd like to have a talk with you, if it's possible."

"I thought you had returned to your sorting," Nursel said. "Has Mr. Radburn grown restless again?"

"Mrs. Erim wanted to see him alone. I think she wants to convince him that I should be sent home at once. Do you know why she feels this way about my being here? After all, it was she who invited me out in the first place."

Nursel bent above a glass tube, pouring carefully. "Perhaps I can guess. But I do not think she will give Mr. Radburn her true reason for wishing you to go home."

Over her shoulder Tracy glanced toward the end of the long room. Dr. Erim seemed wholly concentrated on his work and betrayed no evidence of noticing her at all.

"Could we go somewhere else to talk?" she asked Nursel.

"But of course." The other girl finished her immediate measuring and put a stopper in the glass tube. "This will wait." She sniffed at her fingers and wrinkled her nose. "These essences which Sylvana prefers are too heavy for me. Wait—I will cleanse my hands and we will go where no one will be near."

342

She washed her hands in a basin and then reached for a sweater from a rack, handing it to Tracy.

"Put this on—it is a little cool outside. I have my coat near the door. Come—I will show you something."

She did not speak to her brother as they left the building, and he paid no attention to their going. Outside they followed an up-hill path through the woods until they reached the summit of a small hillock, still on Erim property. Here a little summerhouse had been built, with arched doorways and open latticework walls. During warm weather it would make a charming haven of cool shade. Nursel stood outside its door and directed Tracy's attention to the view.

From this height a great stretch of the Bosporus could be seen in the sunny afternoon—a winding strip of navy-blue ribbon separating Europe from Asia. In the direction of Istanbul a filmy haze hung low like the concealing veil of a harem beauty. Nearer at hand across the strait the stones of Rumeli Hisar shone golden in the light, unlike the black aspect the fortress took on after the sun had set.

"It is beautiful—our Bosporus, is it not?" Nursel said. "But how strange the currents are down there. The Black Sea is not very salty and it causes a cold surface current to flow down the strait toward the Sea of Marmara. From the Marmara a warmer, more salty undercurrent flows in the opposite direction toward Russia. Different kinds of fish are caught in these two bands. If you look from your window at night, you will see boats with bright gasoline lamps being held over the sides to attract fish into the nets. But enough of such matters—you have not asked to speak with me because you wish to know about fish. Come, here is a rock where we may sit in the sun and talk."

The rough stone surface had been warmed and dried during the bright afternoon. The two girls sat upon the boulder and were quiet for a little while. There seemed no way to go about this delicately, Tracy thought. She drew the silk scarf from her handbag and held it out.

"I'll return your scarf to you now. I know from Mrs. Erim that it is yours."

The other girl hesitated for just an instant. Then she took the scarf and opened the striped length. The plum- and cream-colored folds ran like liquid through her fingers, dropped into a pool of warm color in her lap.

"You were the woman in the ruined palace yesterday, weren't you?" Tracy said.

The girl's dark head bent over the scarf and she did not look up. At last, when Tracy thought she might not answer, she said softly, "Yes, it was I."

"Ahmet was there," Tracy said. "He was watching you. And there was a second man. All rather secret."

Nursel's head came up and she looked at Tracy with her bright, dark gaze. A gaze less gentle now, a look in which there was no meekness.

"Secret—yes. But not the affair of anyone else."

"Except that you were talking about me," Tracy said. "I've been wondering why ever since. Whoever spoke my name was angry at the time."

"And you do not know why?" Nursel asked.

"How could I know why? Was it perhaps Mr. Radburn who was with you? Or your brother?"

Nursel sighed and began to ripple the scarf through her fingers as though she needed to keep her hands busy, as men did with their tespihler.

"If I tell you something, will you keep my secret? Though because of Ahmet Effendi, perhaps it is a secret no longer. He does not approve. If I tell you this, I put myself in your hands. Give me your promise that you will say nothing."

"I'm not likely to run to Mrs. Erim, or to your brother, or Mr. Radburn with confidences," Tracy said.

For a moment longer Nursel studied her, as if probing for an answer as to whether or not Tracy could be trusted. Then she nodded.

"An American promise is better sometimes than a European promise. Perhaps you will be my friend, as Anabel was my friend. The man who came to meet me in that place last evening was Hasan."

Tracy repeated the name blankly. "Hasan?"

"You do not remember? In the Covered Bazaar today—the small shop where I bought the jade tespih for Murat. Hasan is Ahmet Effendi's son."

Tracy recalled the young man at once, remembering the dis-

344

trust she had felt as she had listened to the harsh note in his voice as he spoke to Nursel. She remembered too that there had been what she recognized now as a certain familiarity between him and Nursel.

"I wish to marry Hasan," Nursel confessed. "But his father is old-fashioned and does not think such a thing suitable. My brother would be furious. He does not know. He has a great sense of position and he would oppose my marriage and I could do nothing unless I ran away. But Hasan is in no position now to afford a wife. Later, perhaps. Waiting is hard, but I must wait and let no one know until the proper time comes. Then I will laugh at anyone who tries to interfere. I do not like this—that Ahmet Effendi was watching. Soon I must speak to him. I must persuade him that we will wait."

"Would Mrs. Erim be against this too?" Tracy asked.

Nursel made a small sound of scorn. "Sylvana would be happy to see me leave the yali. She would like to turn us all out and fill the house with her friends and her entertainments. There is no loyalty in her toward the family of my father or older brother. Murat opposes her, while Ahmet Effendi remembers that our brother cherished this woman and brought her into our home. That he gave her everything it was possible to give. Ahmet Effendi's first loyalty was to our brother, after our father."

Nursel's bitterness was intense, and it seemed a release for her to put it into words. As she listened, Tracy glimpsed the anger and pain that underlay Nursel's attitude of meek obedience toward Sylvana, and toward her brother as well.

She touched the other girl's arm in sympathy. "I'm very sorry. You have my promise that I won't tell anyone. But I still don't understand why you were speaking about me in that place."

"It is because you have brought a new unrest into the house. Because where you are trouble will follow. Like the thing that was done to your work this morning. I do not like such a happening. It is like a beginning of what happened before, and it is very disturbing."

"Do you think it could have been Sylvana who played that trick?" Tracy asked. She had not thought this likely before, but after witnessing the end of Sylvana's quarrel with Dr. Erim, and after the brief scene in the study just now, she was less than sure that tranquillity was the true keystone to Sylvana Erim's character.

345

Nursel drew up her knees and clasped her hands tightly about them. "Sometimes it is better not to think. Not to see."

"I don't like to play ostrich," Tracy said. "What did Mr. Radburn mean this morning when he spoke of a poltergeist? What do you mean when you say the tricks have begun again?"

"This I do not wish to speak about," Nursel said. "When such tricks were played before they were a prelude to trouble. Perhaps to death."

"The death of—of Mr. Radburn's wife?" Tracy asked.

"The death of your sister," said Nursel softly.

For a moment the quiet in that high, sunny place was intense. For a moment it seemed to Tracy that she could not have heard the word Nursel had spoken—"sister." But there was no mistaking the way the other girl was watching her, her eyes darkly intent and questioning.

"How long have you known?" Tracy asked.

Nursel sighed softly, as though it might be a relief for her to let this secret be known.

"I knew from the moment when Sylvana phoned me in town and told me to go to the hotel to pick up an American whose name was Tracy Hubbard."

"You knew—and you said nothing?"

"It seemed that you wished to keep this a secret," Nursel said. "I gave you many opportunities to tell me and you said nothing. I feared you would suspect from my manner toward you. I could not be easy."

"But how could you have known? Anabel told me often that she let no one know she had any family."

"Yes—she explained this to me." Nursel plucked at the folds of silk in her lap. "She said nothing until the last time I saw her. The very morning of the day she died. She was wildly unhappy, distraught, not herself. Miles had been wickedly cruel to her. He had gone away from her in her time of great need. She sent me after him. She sent me to the airport to bring him back before he could leave for Ankara. But I was too late. Before I agreed to go, she was nearly hysterical. In that time she told me of her little sister in America. The sister she had sent for—who would not come to help her. The sister who had failed her."

"I suppose that's true," Tracy said and did not explain about the crying of "wolf."

346

"Then why do you come here now? Why do you come under this pretense of working for Miles Radburn? Why do you come here to fool us all and pretend that you know nothing of Anabel?"

It was difficult to face Nursel's accusing look. Difficult under the circumstances to know what course to take. The ground had jarred open beneath her feet.

"There are reasons," Tracy said. "It's a long story."

Nursel waited, but Tracy did not go on. She could not bring herself to speak of Anabel's hysterical phone call.

"You've kept my identity to yourself?" she asked Nursel. "Even though you knew who I was at our first meeting, you didn't tell the others?"

"Not at once," Nursel said.

Tracy sat up straight, bracing herself. "Who else knows of this now?"

"I am sorry." Nursel sounded acutely apologetic. "It did not seem proper to me that Murat should not know. Last night I told him the truth. He is indignant that you should play such a trick upon us. That is why he was not very polite to you at breakfast."

"Now I can understand. You've told no one else?"

"Murat thought Sylvana should know also, since, in a sense, this is now her house. So he tells her today while we are in Istanbul."

Tracy remembered the veiled allusions in Sylvana's speech and understood them now. Probably at this very moment Sylvana herself was telling Miles Radburn, and Tracy could not believe that he would keep her here one moment after he knew the trick she had played upon him.

Nursel spoke gently, as though she guessed Tracy's thought. "I do not think Sylvana will tell Miles the truth about you. She would be afraid he might want you to stay, that you might ally yourself with him as Anabel's sister—against her."

"But why? I don't understand—"

"Because she does not want him to finish this book. In the beginning it was an excellent excuse to offer him her home, her hospitality—because he was doing this worthy record of Turkish history. But now it takes all his time, all his attention. He cares for nothing else. And this she does not like. It is because of Miles that she quarreled with my brother today. Murat wishes him to leave this house. But Sylvana waits for him to forget Anabel and

347

accept the tranquillity and peace with which she wishes to surround him—at her own price."

Tracy stared at her, waiting.

"She is infatuated with him—that is what I mean."

This revelation was somehow the most disturbing of all.

"She's older than he is," Tracy objected. "And how could he—
after Anabel—?"

"How upset you are, little one," Nursel said, sudden amusement
brimming her eyes. "You are not, like Sylvana, a realist. You have
indeed been an ostrich since coming to Istanbul. Sylvana claims
her age is forty-one. She is only three years older than Miles. As
my brother's widow, she is a wealthy woman. She can offer this
man the safety of a cocoon in which to dull his sense of guilt. In
the end she will have her way. Unless Murat can stop her. About
Sylvana we can do nothing, but the prospect of having Mr. Radburn in our house forever is not a pleasant one. If I marry Hasan,
I will escape. For Murat—what is there? He cannot bring himself
to take a wife under circumstances as they exist. Of course he
could go to Ankara, as the Turkish government wishes him to do.
He would be given a fine modern laboratory connected with our
best hospital. But he will not go. This is our father's home—it
should belong to Murat. He is determined to stay and drive Miles
away. Perhaps even Sylvana."

This was all readily understandable. There was only one part of
it that Tracy could not accept.

"I think you underestimate Mr. Radburn," she said firmly. "I
can't believe that he would take Sylvana seriously."

"So—you too are falling under his spell? This I do not understand. I do not like this man myself. And I have seen what he has
done to Anabel—to your sister. It is a sad thing if you follow in
her steps."

Tracy dismissed Nursel's words with an indignant exclamation
and went at once to the question of Anabel.

"That's ridiculous. But tell me what it is he did to her. You've
mentioned his cruelty and said several times that he is wicked—but
you haven't explained."

Nursel flung the bright scarf about her shoulders and stood up.
"We have talked enough of such things. I have no proof. If proof
could be found I would tell you. Otherwise it is only the making
of empty words. The air is cool up here. Let us return."

Tracy rose quickly and put out her hand. "Wait! There may not be another chance soon for us to be alone. Tell me how she died that day—I've never known any more than what was in the newspapers. Why was she out on the Bosporus alone in a boat?"

"This we have never understood," Nursel said. "Except that she meant to die. He had left her in anger and she did not wish to live. This is the only explanation possible. She took a boat from our landing—not the big caique with the engine, but a small motorboat, a boat for short travel, or for fishing. It was misty, dark and cold and rainy. She did not use the motor, we think, but rowed out into those swift currents, where she lacked strength to handle the boat. It had capsized long before they found it. Her body was recovered the next morning, below Rumeli Hisar. All that night we waited anxiously—with Miles gone to Ankara, and no help from him."

Tracy stared at the blue strip of water, winding so peacefully toward Istanbul, with its treacherous, reverse current underneath, flowing back to the north. Tears were wet upon her cheeks. Anabel had always lacked physical strength. She had been delicately made, finely boned—the fragile gossamer girl of Miles's portrait. She would have known that she'd be helpless out on that stream. What extreme desperation had driven her to choose that way to die?

Standing here on this hilltop, with the very waters in which her sister had drowned flowing at her feet, the intensity of feeling in Tracy made her faint and a little ill.

Nursel was watching in some concern. On impulse the other girl leaned to kiss her lightly on either cheek in the Turkish fashion.

"Please—you must not grieve," she said. "I do not know why you have come here secretly, but perhaps in time you will tell me this."

Tracy braced herself determinedly, blinking away both tears and faintness. She owed it to Anabel to find courage in herself and to go on.

"For one thing I'm here because I have a job to do," she said. "I'm sure Mr. Hornwright would never have sent me here if he'd known I was Anabel's sister. And I don't think Mr. Radburn would like it if he knew. Is it necessary to tell him?"

"I will not tell," Nursel promised. "I also believe Sylvana will

349

not tell. But Murat will consider it his duty to inform Miles of this. He does not like the man, but he will do what he believes to be correct. Not at once, perhaps. He will examine the matter carefully with his scientist's mind before he acts. So perhaps there is a little time."

"If Mr. Radburn has to know, I'd rather tell him myself," Tracy said. "But not right away. I need a few days' grace first." Time, she thought—time to fight her way through the mists that still engulfed Anabel.

"Then you must speak with Murat yourself," Nursel said. "If you like, I will arrange this for tonight. Sylvana is having a small dinner party in her house and Miles will be there. I, also. But Murat will not attend her parties. There will be time for you to speak with him alone after dinner this evening."

As they started down the hill together, Nursel slipped a hand through the crook of Tracy's arm in a gesture almost affectionate. It was as if she wished to transfer something of her feeling for Anabel to Anabel's sister.

On the way back to the house Tracy asked one of the questions that remained unanswered. "I still don't know why you were talking about me with Hasan in that place yesterday, or why you both sounded so angry."

"You must understand," Nursel said. "It is necessary for me to discuss with Hasan all that is of importance to me. So of course I have told him this thing about you. He argued with me that I must tell the others. He was angry with me that I did not at first wish to do this. Today at the bazaar he reproached me again. A man does not always understand that a woman's small fibs may be necessary."

"But why should he feel that way about me?" Tracy found it disturbing to realize that this young man should harbor strong convictions about her when he did not know her at all.

"Hasan never liked my friendship with Anabel," Nursel admitted. "He wishes me to have no friendship for her sister."

Another thought occurred to Tracy. "Then Ahmet must know about me too—since he was listening to you yesterday."

"It is possible this is true," Nursel said absently, more concerned with the fact that Ahmet must have overheard her personal words with Hasan.

Somehow Tracy felt more uncomfortable about Ahmet's knowledge of her identity than about having Sylvana and Murat know who she was. From the first Ahmet had seemed the traditional plotter of Turkish legend, and she could not free herself of this impression.

As they walked down the hill, Nursel, at least, flung off her pensive mood and became once more lighthearted. As light-hearted as she had seemed this morning, Tracy recalled, when she was going into Istanbul to see Hasan.

"You must not disturb yourself," Nursel told her comfortingly. "I do not always do what men may tell me to do. I have the new independence."

Tracy wondered about that. Perhaps Nursel's independence was mostly wishful thinking. When Murat ordered, she seemed always ready to perform, used by him perhaps more than she herself realized.

"But what about Ahmet?" Tracy persisted. "Now that he knows about me, do you think—"

"Do not worry," Nursel broke in with reassurance. "Since Ahmet Effendi detests Miles also, you need not fear that he will tell him anything. Everyone will now wait in silence—to see what you will do. Except perhaps Murat."

The picture of that silent waiting carried no reassurance for Tracy. As they reached the kiosk and she left Nursel to her per-fume blending and returned to Miles's study, Tracy found herself thoroughly dismayed by the fact that for a good part of the time that she had been in Istanbul the people whom she trusted least had been fully aware of her identity. After all her reluctance, Anabel must indeed have been distraught to give away her secret at the last moment.

That Miles did not yet know offered little comfort. This meant that the moment of telling him could not be postponed too long, or someone else would speak to him first. Yet it must be post-poned for a little while, lest he send her home just when she was beginning to get a clearer picture of the relationships within this house.

Her immediate hope for concealment now lay in Murat Erim's hands. But it would be hard to face a man who was already indignant about her deception and ask a favor of him. The im-mediate prospect was thoroughly unsettling.

9

MILES HAD GIVEN up work on the strip of calligraphy and was sitting at his desk, reading and jotting notes with a pencil. He barely looked up when she entered and he did not question her long absence.

She was glad enough to slip in unnoticed and return to her work. The interview with Nursel and its resulting revelations had left her shaken. One of the things she liked least, though she had flinched from considering it at the time, was Nursel's implication that Tracy herself might be falling under the spell of Miles Radburn.

This, of course, was ridiculous. Because she could not always trust Anabel's claims, Tracy had tried in the beginning to be open-minded about him. Once she had met him, antagonism had flared between them and she had been at a loss to know what his true feeling toward her sister might have been. Today he had surprised her several times, leaving her further confused by the riddle he posed. But that did not mean she could be charmed by him, as Anabel had been charmed in the days before her disillusionment. This was not the problem.

The problem that confronted Tracy was how to explain why she had come here without letting anyone know that she was Anabel's sister. In her confidence that no one could know of her existence, she had painted herself very neatly into a corner from which there now seemed no easy escape.

"If you're going to sit under a table in that ridiculous fashion," Miles said abruptly, "you might at least stop sighing. I can hardly think for your breathing. Come along and we'll find you a chair. Maybe that will help."

It was uncomfortable to meet his eyes, she discovered. The role she had been playing in this house was no longer a safe disguise. She felt thoroughly self-conscious and all too easy to read.

Miles went into the central salon, picked up the round table, and bore it back to his study, velvet covering and all. Tracy chose the most solid of the four straight chairs and followed him. He planted the table in an empty space with an air of furious impatience, and she put the chair beside it. When she had gathered up some of the papers and drawings under the long table, she sat with her back to Miles and went to work. She was careful not to sigh, and she tried not to think about anything but Turkish mosaics.

They worked the afternoon out in silence. After a time Miles put aside his book and began to write busily with a pen. Not until it was past five o'clock did he stack several sheets together and bring them to Tracy.

"I presume you can type?" he said. "Perhaps you can prove your usefulness and copy these pages for me when you have time. There's a typewriter in the corner over there—one that speaks English. You've made me feel guilty about the manuscript part of this book. If you're to stay on for a time and protect that job of yours at *Views*, we'd better prove that there's something here for you to do."

She heard his sudden kindness in surprise. "I'll type it right away," she said and glanced at the handwriting to make sure she could read it. The strong script was legible and familiar. She remembered it well from the curt note he had sent to her at the hotel.

"I'm going to stop for now," he said. "I want to get out for a good walk before I have to dress for Sylvana's dinner tonight."

He stood for a moment beside her chair, as though waiting for her to look up at him. She recalled that he did not like to leave her in this room when he was out.

"Would you like me to stop now?" she asked.

"That's not necessary if you want to work a while longer." He drew a key from his pocket and laid it on the table beside her. "I've found an extra key for this room. You can keep it, if you like. Bolt the balcony doors when you leave, and lock the study door after you. Then there'll be no more interference with your work."

She looked at him, puzzled over his changed attitude, feeling in-

353

creasingly guilty. "What did you mean about a poltergeist? Who do you think did this?"

"Poltergeist is as good a word as any for a mischief-maker. Perhaps it will stop now. I see no reason why anyone should try to frighten you into leaving. Let's forget about it unless something else happens. There seems to be no real harm behind it."

Tracy wondered, remembering that both Miles and Nursel had spoken of Anabel being frightened into desperation. Besides, there was a reason why someone might want to drive her away. A reason Miles knew nothing about—the fact that she was Anabel's sister.

He left her to her work, and the sense of his unexpected kindness stayed with her. He had, after all, considered her future at Views and was trying to safeguard it for her—while she was tricking and deceiving him in a way that could only bring his anger and contempt upon her when he discovered the truth. Nursel's hinting had been ridiculous, but nevertheless Tracy found that while she might not mind Miles Radburn's anger—that was something she had already dealt with—his contempt would be something else. She turned from the thought of it with a distaste that surprised her.

After he had gone she had bolted the veranda doors. Now and then as she typed, she glanced uneasily at the open door to the study. Once when the clatter of typewriter keys was still, she thought she heard footsteps in the salon. But, though she went to the door and looked out, no one was there.

At length she finished her copy work and returned to her room. She was glad to have Yasemin slip in with her for company. The fact that everyone in this household except Miles knew she was Anabel's sister made her seem far more alone than before, and doubly vulnerable. What else could anyone think except that she was here because Anabel had told her something, because she was following some definite lead? They could not know how very little had been given to guide her. Only that mention of black amber, of some secret and Anabel's desperate cry. "I don't want to die!" she had wailed—and gone out on the Bosporus in a boat she could not handle.

By now Yasemin had accepted Tracy. She permitted herself to be stroked and petted and finally settled down to dreaming in Tracy's lap, offering an illusion of companionship. The two of them stayed quietly where they were until Halide brought a tray to the room, with a note from Nursel.

Murat was working late in the laboratory tonight, Nursel had written, and would eat over there. So perhaps Tracy would prefer to have this early tray in her room. The servants would be very busy later with Sylvana's nine o'clock dinner party. Nursel had talked to her brother and he would see Tracy at eight-thirty. She was to go to the living quarters Nursel shared with her brother. He would await her there.

Tracy was grateful for this smoothing of her way and glad that she need not face Dr. Erim at dinner. For the moment she must put aside her fearfulness about the encounter and find a way to pass the time.

Again she and Yasemin shared a meal, and afterward Tracy picked up one of the Turkish books Miles had loaned her and began to read of Ottoman times, of the legends and scandals that clung to those days. She found a rather gruesome elaboration of the story Nursel had told her on her first trip across the Bosporus in the car ferry—about the harem ladies who were dropped into the shallows off Seraglio Point when they displeased or bored a reigning sultan. There had been one such sultan who had made a thoroughly fresh start by ordering a hundred concubines tied up in sacks that were well weighted with stones at the feet, and gathered and tied tightly below the chin so that no struggling would be possible when they were dropped into the Bosporus. Sometime later a diver had gone down into these waters and found the hundred ladies all standing up on the bottom, their long hair streaming in the current, swaying as if they performed some macabre dance.

The story was too vividly told for comfort and it added much to Tracy's uneasiness in a room that overlooked the Bosporus. When it grew dark, she went out upon the balcony and stood watching the night scene once more, reminding herself that the Ottoman Empire was long gone and Istanbul today was probably no more wicked than any other modern city.

Out on the dark waters she saw fishing boats moving, and the lights Nursel had described that would attract fish. Voices came clearly across the water, and now and then the whistling of a passing steamer added utterance to other night sounds. On the far side Rumeli Hisar stood dark and lonely, its towers black against the sky.

The thought of Anabel was strong and constant. It would not let her be.

She was glad when it was time to face Dr. Erim. Any sort of action was welcome by now. She brushed her hair until it shone and renewed her lipstick. As a last touch she clipped on the blue earrings that had been Nursel's gift. To charm Murat? she wondered wryly. Or merely to keep away the evil eye?

Nursel's brother waited for her in their sitting room. When he opened the door at her knock, she saw that he had spread a number of objects from his collection over the surface of a carved ebony table. He held a small satsuma bowl, turning it in his fingers, playing with it as he had with his tespih. She sensed in him something of an Oriental love for objects that could be savored by touch as well as by eye.

As he invited her into the room, she saw that he was no longer the angry man she had seen today at breakfast. There was a gentle, almost poetic sadness about his dark features. She noted again how arrestingly handsome he was, how naturally graceful in his movements—and how aware of feminine company.

"First—I must apologize," he said. "This morning I was extremely disturbed. I fear I was rude to a guest."

"You had every right to be annoyed," Tracy said frankly. "I suppose I've done a very foolish thing."

He drew her to a chair and piled cushions behind her when she sat down. "It is your right to do as you wish. I was disturbed because I thought at first that Radburn had brought you here, knowing very well that you were Anabel's sister, and that he was keeping this fact from us."

"Oh, no," Tracy said quickly. "Mr. Radburn doesn't know. That's why I've come to talk to you—to ask you not to tell him."

He stared intently at the small bowl in his hands, then set it on the table next to a small brass Buddha. "This we must discuss a little," he said. "There are certain aspects of this affair I would like to understand."

"I'm not sure I can explain," Tracy admitted. "I've acted mainly on impulse, I'm afraid. When this opportunity to come to Turkey arose so suddenly, I was afraid to tell Mr. Hornwright that I was the sister of Miles Radburn's wife. He might have thought I'd be an unsettling influence and no help in moving this book ahead."

Murat nodded gravely, watching her with an uncomfortable intentness. Suddenly he moved to bring a standing lamp closer so that its light would fall upon her, reveal her every expression. The inquisitor testing a prisoner? she thought wryly. His words surprised her.

"No—I can see nothing of Anabel in your face. Not the slightest look of her. Your expression is different, your way of speaking. There is no resemblance that I can find."

"That's true," she agreed. "People have always pointed it out. And I've always wished I were more like her. I've never seen anyone as beautiful as Anabel."

He did not disagree, or deny, but his sudden smile was for her and not for Anabel. "I can see that it would be difficult for any girl to have a sister, even a half sister, like Anabel. But I think you can make yourself very interesting and pretty. I am glad to see you wearing such feminine earrings this evening."

"Nursel gave them to me," she said shortly.

"They become you. It is possible that in your growing-up years you have tried not to be prettily feminine because you believed you could not compete with Anabel. Is this not so?"

The conversation was taking so unexpected a turn that Tracy could only stare at him in astonishment.

Again his smile lifted for a moment the sadness that seemed to touch him tonight. "You are surprised that I compliment you? But why? You are a most feminine person. But you must be a little more frivolous, a little more fashionable, perhaps, in your dress."

"I can't ever be like Anabel," she said.

"No, you cannot be like Anabel. Your long hair, with the coil at the back becomes you, and such touches as the earrings you are wearing. Perhaps a dress less severe? You will forgive me for speaking frankly? Nursel can teach you much."

Tracy thought of Miles snatching off the earrings because they did not suit her, and the memory made her laugh. She was no longer angry because of what he had done. It seemed amusing that in this one day two men had reacted in so opposite a fashion to a pair of dangling blue earrings.

Her sudden smile must have touched a near-the-surface sensitivity in the man, for he winced. But at almost the same instant a much louder burst of laughter came from beyond the glass doors that bordered the veranda on the uphill side. Tracy glanced toward them and saw that lights glowed brightly all through the second floor of the kiosk and the chatter of voices and laughter was reaching them with the arrival of each new guest.

Murat frowned and went at once to close the draperies, jerking them in annoyance across the glass.

"She is forever entertaining," he said. "She knows everyone in Istanbul. The French ambassador is here tonight, and several government officials. Tonight she will be showing them the samovar, boasting of her find, proving once more how clever she is. When it should not belong to her at all."

Tracy pondered that. "You mean because it should be returned to the museum?"

"That, of course. Though, since she has considerable influence in high places, she will be permitted to keep it for a time. No, there is another reason."

He hesitated as though he could not decide whether to continue. Then he fixed Tracy once more with his keen, dark gaze that was so different from Miles Radburn's. Miles's cold look seemed to glance off without penetration. It was as though he seldom saw the one he looked at. This man's eyes hunted for the meaning that was essentially a part of the person who held his attention. Tracy felt uncomfortably that it would be difficult to keep a secret from him.

He pulled a carved chair away from the table and turned it so that he could sit astride it, facing her, his arms folded upon its back.

"I will tell you," he said. "I will tell you why that woman has no right to the samovar. She stole it from Anabel Radburn."

Tracy waited, suddenly alert and wary.

Murat studied her reaction as intently as though, without speaking, she might tell him something. "Perhaps I have said this too strongly. It was your sister who first found the samovar, dusty and unnoticed in a shop in the bazaar. From the first it seemed to speak to her. There were times when one suspected that she had some sixth sense few others possess. She managed to unearth the samovar's story and it enchanted her. At once she wanted Miles to buy it for her. The shopkeeper recognized tardily that he had a treasure in his hands and asked a fantastic price. Radburn did not care for the thing or its history, and he would not pay the price or bargain with the man. He did not want to encourage such whimsies in his wife. He said she could not have it—though she nearly broke her heart over the denial. Some months later it disappeared from view in the shop, and Anabel was forced to stop going to Istanbul to visit it. She had made a habit of this. We knew of it, though she did not tell her husband."

Murat's hands sought for a cigarette and lighted it. "You do not smoke? Good. Turkish women, like Turkish men, smoke too much today. Nursel—and Sylvana as well. I prefer a woman who does not smoke. But to return to the samovar. Anabel stopped begging for it, and there was peace again during the few days before her death. Only recently I learned that Sylvana had gone to Istanbul and made a payment on the samovar, knowing well that Anabel had set her heart upon it. She left it hidden at the back of the shop until she could bring it home without offending Mrs. Radburn.

"After your sister's death, she hesitated to produce it immediately and remind Miles of the unhappy quarreling over it. But now she has come into the open and has it for herself. Not that she truly appreciates it as a work of art. She is simply one to covet what others value."

So Nursel had not understood her brother's attitude about the samovar, Tracy thought. She had believed he would envy Sylvana for possessing it.

"I do not like to see that evil object come to my father's house," Murat went on darkly. "Though perhaps it was ordained from the first to be brought here."

"Do you believe that?" Tracy asked.

He smiled a little tightly. "I am a Turk as well as a scientist. We are an emotional people, Miss Hubbard. Outwardly we may at times seem stolid and reserved. We are not explosive and given to expressing our slightest feelings without inhibition, as are the Greeks who live among us. But we have existed with the idea of Kismet too long not to have a certain fatalistic cast to our thinking. It is perhaps a thing that holds some of our people back from making faster progress. Though I believe we learn to do for ourselves today and do not always wait for God to act. Perhaps there is something I can do about this samovar."

"So it won't cast its evil eye upon this house?" Tracy asked dryly.

He shook his head. "You are making fun. It is clear that you are not at all like Anabel. She had great belief in evil as an entity in itself."

"I think she believed in goodness too," Tracy said quickly. "She loved to give happiness to those around her. When she was young there was always gaiety and happiness wherever Anabel was. She believed that happiness was something she could hold in her hand, and she was always reaching for it."

"Yet in the end she opened her fingers and let it slip away," Murat said.

Tracy wanted the discussion to go no further. It was time to push her reason for this interview, to extract from him the promise she needed.

"As I've said, I'm here tonight to ask you not to tell Mr. Radburn who I am. At least not right away."

"I have no liking for Radburn," Murat said. "I do not care whether he knows about this or not. Except that he is still a guest in this house and that even an unwilling host has certain obligations. Perhaps you will tell me now why you have come to Istanbul under a pretense and still do not wish this man to know your identity."

She tried very hard to sound convincing. "It's just that I'd rather tell him myself. But not right away. If I can get into this work a little more deeply first, then perhaps he will let me stay."

"Why are you so determined to stay?"

"Because I have a job to do," Tracy told him, aware that she had begun to sound a little dogged.

"I see. We travel in circles and again you do not wish to tell me the truth. Perhaps it is none of my affair. No matter—I have something for you." He went to the cabinet where the remainder of his collection was displayed and took something from it, brought it to Tracy. The object was a small, tightly corked glass vial filled with a pale liquid.

"It is perfume," Murat said. "You may open it if you like."

She twisted the cork from the neck of the bottle and sniffed the light fragrance. It had a touch of sweetness without being cloying, and there was a woodsy scent to it that reminded one of some cool, mossy place where ferns might grow, warmed indirectly by the sun.

"This was Anabel's formula," Murat said. "She told me the recipe. There is oak moss in the base, a touch of ylang-ylang, and other ingredients as well. Your sister was fascinated by Sylvana's work with perfumes, but my sister-in-law would not trouble to teach her anything after a first attempt. Anabel's hands moved too swiftly, with too great carelessness, so that she broke some of Sylvana's equipment. After that, only Nursel would trouble to teach her. In a sense it was a game Anabel played, though she had some talent for it, I think. To encourage her I ordered from her an essence—for a lady whom I described to her. That small bottle of scent was the result. You may keep it, if you like. The lady was imaginary, based perhaps on Anabel herself."

Though Tracy had refixed the cork, a hint of delicate fragrance lingered on the air. It was as light and gay as Anabel herself had once been and she found it hard to swallow past the lump in her throat. The man was watching her with his air of gentle sadness, and she was suddenly aware of a possible significance behind everything he had said and done in this room tonight.

"You were fond of my sister, weren't you?" she said in wonderment.

At once the gentleness was gone and the sadness with it. He was on guard against her, alert and ready to deny.

She spoke again, quickly, as she stood up. "I'm glad to have this. Thank you for it. Will you at least let me tell Mr. Radburn who I am in my own way? If you will, I'll waste no more of your time."

"Very well," he agreed, still watchful. "It shall be as you wish."

He came with her to the door, but when they reached it, he did not open it for her, but paused with his hand on the knob.

"Before you leave," he said, "perhaps you will tell me why you were eager to choose the black amber tespih yesterday, and then deliberately discarded it."

He saw too much. He sensed too much. Now she could see what had been done to her. Murat had calmed her, appeared to sympathize, complimented and advised her—and then he had struck home to the heart of the thing he wanted to know.

"I don't know what you mean," she managed. "I don't especially care for black jet—why would I choose it?"

"Yet you wanted *that* tespih. I saw the wish in your eyes and it made me curious."

The very flush in her cheeks was giving her away, but she could not reach for the doorknob with his hand still upon it and she had no answer for him.

"It is a very strange thing," he mused. "This affinity for black amber. Anabel chose the jet at once when I offered her a tespih from my collection. I wonder why? Did you perhaps receive a letter from your sister before her death? Did she tell you anything that might be useful to you here in this house?"

She was warned now. The smell of danger was in the air and she knew how careful she must be.

"Yes—Anabel wrote me a letter. She wrote that she wanted me to come to Istanbul for a visit. I couldn't make the trip at that time. Perhaps I failed her by not coming. So it was necessary for me to come now, even though too late."

"What you might call a sentimental pilgrimage?" He opened the door for her, bowing slightly. "I have enjoyed your visit," he said, and there was a note of mockery in his voice.

She thanked him again for the perfume and for his promise. The door did not close at once behind her, and she knew he must be watching as she climbed the stairs.

The third floor seemed bleak and cold and empty when she reached it. The dim chandelier scarcely dispersed the shadows. But she had left a light burning in her own room, and there light and warmth welcomed her. Yasemin had waited. The mangal was freshly stoked with hot coals.

Anabel's eyes had been faintly green, Tracy thought. Was that one reason Miles so violently disliked this cat with green eyes?

She sat down and uncorked the perfume vial again. Woods and moss and sweetness—gay as a light summer breeze. She had not thought enough of Dr. Murat Erim's role in this picture. Samovar and sweet perfume and black amber—a pungent mixture of Turkish intrigue.

At least she knew something about Dr. Erim that she had not known before. His very resistance to her question had given her the truth. Murat Erim had been in love with Anabel. Where that fact led she could not tell, except that it might account for Murat's antagonism toward Miles Radburn. Miles's own indifference toward the other man seemed to indicate either that Murat's interest in his wife had remained ineffectual, or Miles did not care one way or the other. Somehow she found the latter hard to believe.

In any event, each of those who knew that Tracy Hubbard was Anabel's sister was intent in his own way upon seeing her go home as quickly as possible. This fact left her all the more certain that she was on the verge of some discovery. A discovery that would surely have to do with the ominous leitmotiv of black amber.

Yet Miles, who still did not know her identity, was the one she feared most, and she could not yet bring herself to tell him the secret the others knew. She would do it. But not yet.

The next few days passed quietly enough. Since she had a key to the study and Miles no longer minded if she worked in the room alone, she could go and come as she liked and was thus able to keep busy. None of her neat piles of paper had been disturbed again. No further untoward tricks had been played upon her. When it came to Turkish history, her education was growing apace. Miles had put a great deal of work into this book, she was discovering. At least into the first half of it. In recent months, it seemed, he had slowed down, perhaps losing the impetus of his first interest.

Once or twice she managed to coax him into telling her something of the places he had visited around Turkey, about the discoveries that were still being made. Then his interest would seem to kindle. But it did not last and he would quickly fall back into listless plodding. Sometimes he would sit at his desk staring at nothing, or he would fling himself impatiently from the room and go for long walks along the Bosporus.

For several afternoons in succession he gathered up his painting equipment and simply disappeared. Yet at these times he went on no distant trips, for his car remained in the garage and he would return too quickly to have been far away. After such disappearances restlessness and impatience would lie more heavily than ever upon him. He offered no explanation and it was not for Tracy to question him, however much she might wonder.

Except for mealtime, and not always then, she saw little of Murat and Nursel. And she saw nothing at all of Sylvana.

The day of her twenty-third birthday came, but she mentioned the fact to no one. Anabel had made much of every birthday of Tracy's. Even after Tracy was grown, Anabel would remember and some surprise always arrived on time, revealing that affection and imagination had gone into the choosing of a present. Once or twice Anabel had been ill, but even then some token gift had come, to make Tracy laugh and think warmly of her sister.

This would be the first birthday with no Anabel to remember it. The knowledge that all the good and lovely things Anabel had once been in the young Tracy's affection were gone forever came sharply home, bringing with it a further realization of loss.

Tracy was glad to spend the day working quietly and to avoid the rest of the household except for Miles. He was deep in one of his long silences and seemed not to know that she was about. During the afternoon he went out, as usual not mentioning where he was going. Tracy worked alone until Halide came with a not un-expected summons to Sylvana Erim's quarters in the kiosk. Ever since her talk with Nursel several days before, Tracy had known this moment must come. Sylvana, being in possession of the truth, would not be content to let matters go indefinitely.

As she followed Halide, Tracy touched the feather pin that was one of Anabel's imaginative gifts. She felt closer to her sister today than she had felt for a long while.

10

SYLVANA'S SALON, THOUGH perfumed as always, was not aglow with lamplight this afternoon. Instead, all draperies had been drawn aside from the windows to allow full daylight to possess the room. Sylvana sat against piled cushions on her divan, not reclining as a Turkish lady of the past might have done, but with her straight French spine upright, and one arm resting upon an inlaid table beside her. The scene was arresting, not only because of the golden-haired woman in a saffron yellow gown, but because the Anatolian Samovar occupied the table beside her in all its copper splendor. The exterior had been burnished to a rich gleam, and highlights reflected the saffron of her dress.

"Please come in, Miss Hubbard," Sylvana said without moving her head. "It will not disturb Mr. Radburn if we speak together a little."

Today the scent of Parma violet engulfed her as Tracy entered the room. She saw that Miles had set up his easel near a window where the light was good and he stood with a brush in one hand, and palette in the other, his attention wholly concentrated on the canvas before him.

So this was what his recent afternoon absences had meant. Apparently he was painting again—painting Sylvana Erim and her samovar. It did not help Tracy's equanimity to find him there. With so present an opportunity, who was to know what Sylvana might have told him? Or what she might now say in front of him?

Tracy took her place on the lower divan where she had sat before on the day when men from the villages had displayed their wares for Sylvana.

"Mr. Radburn tells me that you are proving yourself of more help to him than he expected, and that your work progresses well." Sylvana spoke without disturbing her pose.

"I'm glad," Tracy said, and ran the tip of her tongue along her lips.

Miles paid no attention to either of them. He wore a frown between dark brows, as though he did not care for what he saw evolving upon the canvas.

"Perhaps you know by now just how much longer this work will occupy you?" Sylvana questioned. "A week more, do you think? Two weeks?"

"I'm not sure," Tracy answered carefully. "Mr. Radburn has ordered a proper file for me from Istanbul. As soon as it comes I can arrange his material in folders with a cross index. In the meantime, I am retyping pages of manuscript that have been revised. There's still a great deal to be done. I understand that much more information must be collected, many more drawings made before it will be possible to select those that are most representative."

She was echoing Miles now, giving the very excuses he gave for continuing his work indefinitely.

Sylvana remained outwardly tranquil, but one hand moved in her lap, the gesture faintly impatient.

Miles spoke at once. "Keep your hand the way it was. I want that ring to show. It will be the only touch of green in the picture."

"He will not let me see," Sylvana murmured plaintively to Tracy, and turned her hand so that the great square-cut emerald flashed, its light caught and thrown back, coppery-green, in the plump, burnished sides of the samovar. "He says I must not see this portrait until it is completed. But to return to the matter of your work, Miss Hubbard. Once this file you speak of is arranged, perhaps Mr. Radburn will then be able to keep his own work in order. Or perhaps I may be able to help him achieve such order myself."

The woman's hands were quiet now, her blue eyes calm, but her lips had tightened just a little. It was not hard to imagine that Sylvana might harbor a special feeling for Miles Radburn. But if this was true, what was his response? Tracy found herself glancing at him quickly, almost anxiously.

He laid down his brush and stepped back from the canvas, regarding it with disapproval. "Get to the point, Sylvana. Tell Tracy what it is you want."

"The English are so blunt," Sylvana murmured, but there was a look about her that said a Frenchwoman might be blunt too if the purpose served her. "I will tell you then. Of course I do not wish to hurry you beyond reason, but I have invited several friends who are coming from Paris to visit me. As you can see, your room and the one next to it, both being on the Bosporus side of the yali, are considered most attractive to visitors. I am sorry, but—"

"You'll want me to move, of course," Tracy said.

Sylvana permitted herself a slight smile. "I am glad that you understand. Perhaps you will not be sorry to leave this particular room, Miss Hubbard?"

Tracy stiffened at this reminder that the room had been Anabel's.

"Why should she want to leave it?" Miles asked.

The answer came blandly. "The sounds of the Bosporus, the cold, the damp, of course. For myself—I do not care for those rooms."

"If you need the space," Tracy said, "I can return to Istanbul for the remainder of my stay. I believe there are buses that come out here. I can manage."

"That would be difficult and inconvenient," Miles said. "How soon are these guests of yours coming, Sylvana?"

Mrs. Erim raised an eyebrow in mild reproach, but she gave in with seeming grace. "It is possible that we can postpone this visit for a little while. I do not of course want to inconvenience you."

"That's fine," said Miles.

Tracy found that her fingers were tightly interlaced in her lap. The battle had been won, with Miles's help, but she did not feel particularly reassured. Sylvana Erim's full arsenal of weapons would not be wasted in vain display. Tracy did not think that this apparent surrender meant a great deal. She left her place, presuming that she had been dismissed, but Miles spoke to her again.

"Come here and take a look," he ordered. "While I never let the subject of a portrait breathe over my shoulder and start objections before I am finished, I sometimes welcome an outside eye."

Though she wanted only to escape, Tracy stepped behind the easel to look at the picture. The portrait had not progressed very far, but the tones in which he meant to paint were indicated.

There was to be no mistiness here. He was doing Sylvana Erim in shades of gold and copper that made the canvas gleam with light. Already the samovar's shape was evident, and a saffron flow of color that was the form of the woman on the divan. There was no detail as yet, and he had not touched her face. Tracy wondered if he were merely playing with color at this point in order to postpone the moment when he must come to grips with his subject and really paint.

"The thing doesn't come to life," Miles muttered. "The colors are good and so is the general composition—woman and samovar in that juxtaposition. But it doesn't live."

"Dear Miles—you must not be discouraged too quickly," Sylvana put in. "You have grown unused to the brush. This will come. You will recover your touch, and without doubt this portrait will bring you great fame."

"It's not fame I'm thinking about," Miles said. "It's the loss of interest in painting anything at all that troubles me. Theoretically, I want to paint. But, specifically, I don't find a subject that sets off the necessary spark of energy."

Miles's inference that he found her less than inspiring did not please Sylvana. She looked as though she might burst through her veneer of calm, thus further irritating Miles. Tracy spoke quickly to distract them both to a safer topic.

"How beautiful the samovar is now that it has been cleaned and polished. Are you planning to use it for serving coffee, Mrs. Erim?"

"Never! But certainly not!" Sylvana protested. "One does not give a museum piece common usage. Even the polishing I have done myself. There was a green film in some places—which has prevented corrosion of course. But the samovar has received rough treatment. There are scratches and dents. I have disturbed it as little as possible. It is enough to beautify the exterior."

Tracy was studying its detail for herself, and a small amusing circumstance caught her eye.

"Do you see?" she said to Miles. "There in the samovar?"

He stared at the great gleaming thing and a faint quirk lifted one corner of his mouth. "That's rather interesting," he said and picked up his brush.

Tracy stepped back, not daring to watch him. The reflection in the copper curves of the samovar was not flattering to Mrs. Erim. If he chose to develop it, she would be even less pleased.

Sylvana stirred against her cushions. "What is it? You must tell me what you see."

"Don't wriggle, please," Miles said. "I'll give you a chance to rest in a moment. Let me catch this first. And don't ask questions. If I pull it off, you'll see it in plenty of time."

Sylvana sighed and settled back. The emerald winked on her finger and repeated its green fire in the samovar's mocking reflection. Tracy noted for the first time that just below the tall chimney a circlet of blue beads had been hung.

"Why is it wearing a necklace?" she asked.

Sylvana smiled. "That is Halide's notion. It is the only way I can get the girl to come into the same room with the samovar. She thinks the blue will halt its evil emanations."

"I like the beads there," Miles said. "A good Turkish touch. I'm not sure Halide isn't right about the emanations. Nor am I sure the blue beads are strong enough magic to protect us."

He worked for a while longer and then stopped with an impatient gesture and began to put away his painting things.

"Nothing comes right today, and I've tired you enough for this sitting, Sylvana. Will you give me a hand with this stuff, Tracy?"

As Tracy moved to help him, Sylvana spoke with calm authority. "I wish to see Miss Hubbard for a few moments, please. I will send her to you later."

It was clear that the unpleasantness for which Tracy had braced herself earlier was coming, and she waited, standing once more with her thumbs hooked into the belt of her dress in her attitude of resistance. She caught Miles's amused glance upon her before he took his equipment away, but that merely strengthened her determination not to be put down, no matter what was coming.

As he left, Nursel slipped into the room in the manner of one who did not expect to be sent away, and Tracy wondered if she had come to watch the final performance, in which Anabel's sister was to be sent home.

Idly the girl paused beside a table where a box stood open. "I see you have received the new shipment of tespihler from Hasan Effendi," she said.

Sylvana nodded carelessly. "The demand for them in New York seems to be growing. I can help the young man a little by buying such things from him."

Nursel dipped her hand into the box and scooped up a bright handful of beads. Tracy watched as they slipped through her fingers. Among the blue and red and brown she caught a brief gleam of shiny black before the beads clattered into the box.

"Perhaps there are other ways in which Ahmet Effendi's son could be helped," Nursel said without looking at Sylvana.

Tracy paid little attention to the older woman's indifferent reply. The dark refrain had been sounded again. Meaningless, or otherwise? There had been no black amber among the beads Hasan had shown them in the shop. At what point, in what manner had these been added? Their presence would seem of no significance if it were not for Tracy's memory of a voice on the telephone and the desperate whistling of a nursery tune.

Sylvana's attention returned to Tracy. She did not ask her to sit down, but spoke out frankly. "Murat has told me that you are the sister of that unfortunate girl who caused us so much trouble, so much grief."

"That's true," said Tracy and felt again the dryness of her mouth. "I'm Anabel's sister."

"May I ask why you have come to Istanbul without giving us this information in which we would all naturally be interested?"

Stiffly Tracy repeated the reasons she had given to Murat and to Nursel, and nothing she said rang convincingly in her own ears. Sylvana listened with calm attention, and the samovar beside her gave back an oddly malevolent reflection.

"You expect us to believe this story?" she said when Tracy finished.

"It's all true," said Tracy, knowing very well that it was true, but that it was not enough of the truth.

"I have thought of this for several days," Sylvana said. "I have taken no action because I wished to consider the matter fully. Since the truth is now known to everyone in this house, it would seem natural to me that you must now inform Mr. Radburn. But you have not done so?"

Tracy shook her head and stood her ground. She could only hope that the churning of unreasonable fright that had risen in her so suddenly did not show. The sight of black amber beads had been unnerving.

"You have kept silent because you know he would send you home at once? Is this not so?" Sylvana prompted.

"I don't know what he would do," Tracy said. "I have a job to finish here. When it's done, I'll tell him. Just before I go home."

"Do you truly think I will permit such a thing?" Sylvana asked. "You are a foolish young girl. Mr. Radburn has begun to paint again. This portrait may be his salvation. I will not have him upset by such an occurrence. Tomorrow I will arrange for your passage home by plane. You will leave on the day after. I make myself clear?"

Tracy took a long slow breath. "I've offered to move into Istanbul. There's no reason why I need to stay in this house if you want my room."

Sylvana made an impatient movement with one hand, breaking her outward pose of calm. The samovar at her elbow reproduced the movement in miniature in its smooth copper surface, adding a baleful interpretation.

"As I say, you will be on the plane day after tomorrow," Sylvana told her. "If you are not, I will explain the truth to Mr. Radburn myself and see that he sends you home. I think he will not be pleased with what I tell him."

The trembling of inner anxiety was about to possess her utterly, Tracy knew. All the cards were in Sylvana's hands and her bluff was being called. She made one last effort.

"What if I tell him myself, Mrs. Erim?"

"That is as you please," Sylvana said. "In that case, I will of course add my own comments. Perhaps it will be pleasanter if you leave as you have come—saying nothing. The disturbance, the—the trouble to you will be less."

Tracy made up her mind and started toward the door. "Never mind. I'll ask Mr. Radburn myself. I'll tell him you want me to leave at once. Perhaps he won't need to remain in this house to finish the book. It's surely possible for him to move elsewhere and get the work done. Since this painting is not going well, he may prefer a change."

Nursel gasped softly. Sylvana did not speak until Tracy reached the door.

"For a few more days then," she said in a choked voice. "A few days only. After that you will leave. It is not necessary to speak to Mr. Radburn of this now."

Tracy went quietly from the room. She had won another reprieve, but at some cost to herself. Inwardly she was shaking. She did not welcome Nursel's company when the Turkish girl came after her in a rush.

"That woman!" Nursel cried softly. "It is she who should be sent from this house. No one else. But, please—it is better if you do as she wishes. It is better if you go away soon."

"Why should I?" Tracy demanded. "Why do you want me to go home? Why are you on Sylvana's side?"

Nursel's answer came indignantly. "I am not on that woman's side. Never! But I think it can be that you are walking into trouble. I think you are not enough afraid of how Mr. Radburn may—may change you. There are matters which I understand and you do not. If you go now, perhaps all may be well. If you stay—then one must rely on fate and hope for the best."

Now that she was away from Sylvana, Tracy's sense of rising panic had died a little. "I will not go," she said.

Nursel gave up with a shrug. "But now you will tell Mr. Radburn the truth?"

"I don't know," Tracy said. "I don't know when I'll tell him. From now on I'll just have to play it by ear."

The expression puzzled Nursel, but Tracy did not stay to explain. She could no longer hide her distress and confusion and she fled Nursel's company, hurrying downstairs and along the passage to the yali.

Miles was in his study cleaning brushes when she burst in upon him. He looked at her without pleasure.

"What now?"

"Mrs. Erim wants to send me home immediately," Tracy told him, sounding more than a little excited. "Everyone wants me to go home, including Nursel!"

Miles scowled at her. "Perhaps they're right. Certainly you're a disrupting influence for all of us. No—don't put your thumbs in your belt and turn in your toes like a pigeon. I like quiet, gentle women. And *you* are what Hornwright sends me!"

She could only regard him in outrage. On top of everything else, this was too much. She was on the verge of blurting out the whole truth when Miles tossed down his brushes impatiently.

"Stop looking as though you were about to explode. We've both had enough for today. Go put on your coat and tie something over your head. Hurry back and we'll go out to tea. You need a change and so do I."

"I don't want any tea!" Tracy cried indignantly. Tea—at a moment like this!

He pushed her toward the door without gentleness. "Well, I do. Now hurry up. And don't come back here looking like a bomb about to go off."

Again she fled, this time to her room. She was furiously angry with Miles Radburn. Which, at least, was strengthening. Indignation would help her to stand up to him. The time had come to tell him the truth and she must face the fact and go through with it. She repaired her lipstick and tied a scarf over her head with overly emphatic movements. Except for the flush in her cheeks and the brightness of her eyes, she was once more in control of her emotions. It had been ridiculous of course to let Sylvana upset her. Partly her reaction had been the fault of that samovar with its queerly malevolent reflection. Once she had seen the image, it haunted and disturbed her, though she did not know why.

Miles was waiting when she returned to the study. He had put on a jacket and a cap and he appeared eager to be outdoors and away from the yali.

Downstairs Ahmet hovered near the landing, watching as the boatman helped Tracy into a boat smaller than the caique. She was aware of the old man's watchfulness as Miles started the motor and they set off from shore. When she looked back she saw him standing there, as if observing their direction.

There were no larger craft going by at the moment, and their course was clear to the opposite shore toward which Miles turned the prow of the little boat. They moved at a slight diagonal, and Tracy sat on the wooden cross seat in the stern and lifted her face to the wind.

Beneath them the water flowed still and dark. At the moment the surface seemed deceptively unruffled, hardly appearing to move as the little boat slapped its way across the strait, leaving a churning white froth behind. The cool, clear air was reviving to breathe and carried with it none of the dust of Istanbul. Nor any hint of roses or Parma violet. Tracy felt calmer now and in better control of herself.

Their crossing attracted two young boys, who came down to the stone embankment on the opposite shore. The boat nosed in among fishing craft, and Miles accepted the help of the boys in landing. It was more difficult here to climb from small boat to embankment, but Tracy managed it with a minimum of scrambling and the help of Miles's strong grasp.

They stood on the edge of a road down which motor traffic traveled in a fairly steady stream. Across the road an open-air space filled with small tables and chairs climbed the hill beneath tall plane trees, newly in bud. Though the sun had sent a veneer of warmth across the area, most of the tables stood empty.

"It's mild enough for tea outdoors," Miles said. "Let's go up there away from the road."

He found a table toward the rear of the terraced hillside, and they sat in wooden chairs that teetered a little on uneven ground. A waiter came for their order and Miles gave it in Turkish.

At a table nearby a man sat lost in contemplation as he smoked his narghile, and Tracy watched him draw smoke through bubbling water and long coils.

"Like the Caterpillar," she said dreamily.

"That's better," Miles approved. "You're cheering up. What is worrying you? What does it matter if Sylvana scolds? You're involved in nothing but the job you're doing for me. And that's not a life or death matter. For you, at any rate. I'll give Hornwright a good report, if that's what concerns you. Even if Sylvana wants you gone, it's not terribly important."

This was the least of what was worrying her, but she could not say so. The time for decision was upon her, yet she could make no decision. She could only bask in the sun and watch the hypnotic bubbling of the narghile, and listen to Miles's voice.

In the summertime, he told her, particularly on weekends, this place would be filled most of the time. There were many of these tea spots along the Bosporus to which Istanbul people liked to drive. This was one of the most popular. But now they were here ahead of the season and could have it almost to themselves.

Before long the waiter brought a small samovar to their table and a plate of *simit*—round, braided rolls, sprinkled with sesame seed. Tracy filled the teapot from the spout and placed it on the rack to steep, as she had seen Sylvana do. She broke a piece of roll and the breeze blew sesame seed about. Out on the water a tug-drawn string of barges moved upstream in leisurely fashion, leaving a creamy wake behind. Across the strait, some distance below the yali, rose the towers and walls of Anadolu Hisar, the opposite fortress. The scene was disarmingly peaceful and without any sense of tension.

As she bit into her roll Tracy thought again of the fact that today was her birthday.

"My birthday cake," she said, holding up the bit of simit. "Today I'm twenty-three."

Miles bowed his head gravely. "Congratulations. I'm glad we came out to celebrate."

There might be a way to make him understand, she thought, crumbling the roll in her fingers. There might be a way to tell him. She began almost as if she were talking to herself.

"There's something I remember that occurred on my twelfth birthday. A new one always reminds me. I've never forgotten because it was an unhappy day, with the sort of things happening that can never be erased."

Miles had relaxed since coming across the water, as if he had left strain behind him at the yali.

"Tell me about it," he said.

She hesitated, seeking the right words. If she told her story well, this might be the way to reveal that she was Anabel's sister.

11

TRACY BEGAN IN a light, uncertain voice that grew stronger as she went on and was caught up by the thread of her own memories.

"My parents seldom let me have a party. My father was a doctor, and he did a lot of writing as well. Medical articles. He was a very serious, busy man. He had his office in our house and he didn't like noisy children around. But this time my older sister prevailed on my mother, so the occasion was special. It was to be my day, with everyone coming to see me, bringing me presents. I suppose it went to my head a little. I had a new dress. Mother said I looked very nice, and the other mothers who came said so too. The spotlight was all mine, and I felt practically giddy with conceit and excitement.

"Then my seventeen-year-old sister came home from her dancing school lesson—and everything changed. She didn't intend what happened. She was only being herself. But from the minute she came into the room the party started to be hers. She could charm people of any age and she loved to do it. She loved to be loved and to amuse and please. So she sang for us a bit and she danced. And in a little while no one remembered about me, because how could anyone remember with her in the same room?"

Miles was listening more attentively than she would have expected.

"So your nose was out of joint?" he said.

Tracy nodded. "I was terribly jealous. I loved my sister and admired her and looked up to her. But I couldn't be like her and sometimes I was green with envy. When I turned green enough that day, I slipped away from the party and went to my father's

376

office. I knew nobody would miss me, and that made everything worse."

As she told him what happened next, it was almost as if she lived the scene again. She forgot the Bosporus and the man with the narghile. She nearly forgot Miles himself. Only one part of her remained vigilant, watchful, lest she mention Anabel's name before it was time.

It had been after visiting hours when she left the party and went into her father's office. He was working in deep concentration over papers on his desk. In his preoccupation he hardly noticed as she came into the room. She curled up in a corner armchair where he sometimes let her sit and read, if she didn't disturb him by talking. She had done no reading that day. She began to cry very softly to herself, wallowing in self-pity and disappointment because she was of no consequence at her own birthday party, and people always forgot about her when her sister was there. Through the walls of the room and down the hall, party sounds filtered and the sound of her sister's singing.

Tracy had not thought consciously at the time of why she had come to her father's office, but the reason was there, as she understood later. Dad was her sister's stepfather. Her sister's real father was dead. Dad was the only person who never succumbed to her sister's charms and her coaxing ways. Perhaps there was envy in him too—envy of another man's child. Especially since Tracy's mother always melted with love for her first daughter and was reluctant to heed his criticism. As Tracy very well knew, she compared her younger daughter with the older a dozen times or more a day, and always to Tracy's disadvantage. Now, by coming into her father's presence, Tracy left the magic circle and reached a haven where her sister's charm exerted no effect.

Unfortunately, she had been a little whimpery in her weeping and after a while her father noticed. He glanced around at her impatiently and told her to blow her nose. If she was to stay, she'd have to stop sniveling. He did not ask why she was crying, or show any interest in the cause. He was busy and her presence annoyed him.

She had managed to be silent after that, not even blowing her nose very loudly. A strange thought had come into her mind. A mature and rather bitter thought for a girl of twelve. She had realized quite clearly in that moment that the only reason she liked her father at all was because he did not like her sister. It was a strange sort of thing to hold in common with him, and she did not feel very proud of herself because of it.

After a time even her silence irritated him, and he flung down his papers and turned around. "Out with it!" he said. "What's the matter that you aren't back at your own party where all that uproar is going on?"

She gulped once or twice before answering. Then she blurted out the truth. "My sister's there. It's turned into her party. They don't want me any more."

"I should think not," he said, "if you behave like this—creeping away like a little coward. Come along and I'll get rid of your sister for you. Then you can be belle of the ball again. And I can have peace in this room at least."

As he left his desk, Tracy scrambled to her feet in alarm. For some reason this was the last thing she wanted. She knew perfectly well that her father would not pat her cheek, or cuddle her, or tell her he liked her best. But he would prove again in another way that he did not approve of her sister. Though his intention was to reinstate Tracy, he would wreck the party completely. It would not be hers or anybody else's when he was through with what he might say to the older girl. So she told him hurriedly that she was fine now. That she had recovered and didn't mind any more. He did not push the matter, though he clearly thought her change of heart further evidence of weakness.

She flew out of the room and went back to where her sister was singing her own croony version of a popular tune. Anabel sat cross-legged on the floor with her cornflower-blue skirt fluffed over her knees, and the children crowding in about her. Always they wanted to touch Anabel, to cling to her when she was near, and always it overjoyed her to make them happy. Now they swayed to the beat of the tune she was singing—a song with non-sense words that was current for the season.

Tracy sought her mother and slipped into the warm curve of her arm. An arm that moved automatically, as a mother's arm does, to hold any child that comes within its circle. Yet Tracy knew that all her mother's loving pride was focused upon her older daughter. In that moment twelve-year-old Tracy had faced the truth once and for all. A truth she had been trying all her short life not to face. She had known consciously and without any doubt that she could never be loved by her mother as the older daughter was loved.

A certain pride had possessed her then and made her hold her head high. She watched her sister with that love she had always given her, however laced with envy and hurt it might be. It was at least to her credit that she had let no one know how she felt. And she had not cried again.

The narghile bubbled softly at the nearby table, and fragrant smoke drifted toward the grownup Tracy where she sat with the man who had been Anabel's husband. There was more to the story, but she sought a diversion to postpone the most painful part of this telling.

"Our tea will be dreadfully strong," she said. "I forgot about it."

"I like it that way," said Miles.

She put small spoons in the glasses so they would not break and poured the hot, strong tea. Hot water from the samovar spout diluted her own. When the brew was sweetened and lemon slices added, Tracy subsided into silence, still under the spell of the story she had not yet told fully.

Miles raised his tea glass. "Here's to Tracy when she was twelve! A young lady of honesty and courage. You learned rather young to accept an unpleasant truth and live with it bravely."

She sipped the tea. "No—I didn't. That's the trouble. The story isn't done. If it was only what I've told you, I don't think I'd have remembered every detail after all these years."

"Then you might as well tell me the rest," he said.

It was strange that she should find him so willing a listener. She sensed an understanding that she had not expected. He did not belittle, or discredit, or sympathize falsely, and she felt drawn to him and unexpectedly trusting.

What had happened later had left a wound that had not healed for a long time. She began to relate the rest, keeping her voice carefully even and bare of emotion. Birthday cake and ice cream, candy and self-realization had not mixed too well in Tracy's interior and she had gone to bed early that night, feeling queasy. Going to sleep early, she had awakened later in the night and begun to think despairingly of her disappointing day. Her sister was asleep in the next room and the house was quiet. The illuminated dial of the clock on the dresser told her that her parents must be in bed and asleep now too. In the lonely darkness in which only she was awake, she could hug to herself all the misery of her resentment against her sister and let it grow and swell almost to the bursting point, like a grotesque balloon.

In the next room she heard the older girl get up and move around softly. Tracy stayed very still listening. She heard her sister go to the window, heard the unlikely bird chirp from the driveway below. This was not the first time such a thing had happened, and she knew what Anabel would do. It was always frightening and inevitably it threw Tracy into an anguish of indecision. If she went to her parents in their room at the front of the house, she would get her sister into dreadful trouble. Yet if she did not it seemed that terrible trouble would come to the other girl.

She listened intently while her sister dressed. She heard her slip out of the room and down the stairs, heard the faint squeak that was the kitchen door opening. Followed by silence. She told herself virtuously that what her sister was doing was wrong, that her parents must be told. She got out of bed, shaking a little, and went into the room where they slept. She wakened them and made it clear what had happened. She could remember her father swearing as he dressed, her mother weeping. Dad had gone searching up and down the streets without success. Tracy, watching from an upstairs window, and no longer pleased with her betrayal, was the first to see her sister come home. She leaned out the window whistling a quavery and out-of-tune *London Bridge* to let her know that everything was indeed "falling down." Anabel, forewarned, was still undaunted. She looked up at Tracy with a smile and waved her hand in a thumb-up gesture that signified courage—or perhaps only recklessness.

When she came in there had been a dreadful scene downstairs, with the older daughter weeping at last, and Tracy's father shouting ugly accusations. It was all quite horrible and Tracy had been thoroughly sick at her stomach.

Her sister, for once shaken and frightened herself, came upstairs and found her in the bathroom. She bathed Tracy's green little face and soothed her and helped her back to bed. She put aside her own grave troubles for the sick younger one, giving her the love and care and consideration Tracy had longed for all day. How bittersweet that comfort had been.

"So that's the way it was," she finished. "That's why I've never forgotten."

"Because you betrayed her?" Miles said. "Yes, I can see that. Yet you were doing the right thing. Your parents had to be told about this."

Tracy shook her head. "The right thing, but for the wrong reason. I didn't do it to save my sister from harm. I did it because I wanted to punish her for being beautiful and popular. And most of all because my mother loved her best."

She picked up the tea glass with a hand that reached blindly because of the mist before her eyes.

"A few weeks later my sister ran away," she went on. "She couldn't endure the way my father treated her, and for a long time I blamed myself for driving her out."

"But you grew up," Miles said. "And probably she did too."

Tracy sipped her cooling tea. "Yes, I grew up and I learned enough to know that she would have run away anyhow, no matter what I did. It would be foolish of me to go on blaming myself for something that happened when I was twelve years old."

"But you do a little, don't you?" Miles took her glass and set it down and held her hand in his own. His fingers were firm about hers, and there was strength and reassurance in his grasp. She wanted to cling to the comfort his hand offered. At that moment she liked him enormously and did not question the warmth she felt toward him.

"It was all so long ago," she said. "I know it's foolish to remember. But I suppose I'll always wonder if I could have helped her more than I did. Perhaps I could have tried harder to understand whatever it was she wanted. Not just then, but later on when I was old enough. She was a wonderful person, really. There was so much about her that was good. I think she could have made something fine of her life."

"Was?" Miles asked.

"My sister is dead," said Tracy. She drew her hand from Miles's and touched the feather pin beneath her open coat. This was the moment. This was the time to tell Anabel's husband the truth. Yet she was helplessly mute.

Out on the strait a ship moved toward Istanbul. As it glided by, white and shining in the sunlight, Tracy could see beyond it the silver-gray shape of the yali showing among trees on the opposite shore. The whole reason for her being here swept back on a wave of pain.

"I'm sorry," Miles said, his tone surprisingly kind. "But of course it's futile to reproach yourself, or to ask questions that can't be answered. Perhaps there are those who can never be helped."

"We have to try," Tracy said fervently. "Someone has to try! There are too many who give up easily with the ones like my sister." She was aware of his long, perceptive look and knew that his thoughts had turned to Anabel. Had he done all he could for the woman who had been his wife? she wondered.

"I knew a girl very much like your sister," Miles said, startling Tracy by coming close to her thoughts. "My wife Anabel was charming and gay as your sister must have been. And as thoroughly bent on self-destruction."

Tracy waited, knowing that this might be the brink of the very answer she was seeking.

"Of course the story is that I drove her to her death. You've heard that, I expect. But she had only one interest in me by that time. The fact that I was angry and walked out on her wouldn't have meant a thing. Something happened while I was gone. Perhaps I can even guess what it was. But I'm not sure who was responsible. I don't know who could have wanted her dead as desperately as that."

"Nursel says you did," Tracy told him. "She says you wear a hair shirt by keeping your wife's portrait on the wall of your room. In order to punish yourself for her death."

The words did not seem to anger him. "A plausible enough explanation, I suppose. If I were that sort of man. I'm not. There was nothing I wouldn't have done for Anabel."

He had given her an answer. His answer, at least.

"Why do you stay here?" she asked him. "Why don't you work on your book somewhere else and get away from this place?"

It was almost a relief to have him regard her with more normal impatience. "Do you think it's this book that matters most to me now? I believe in its worth and I'll get it done sometime, of course. But for me it's painting that matters. How do you think it feels to be a sort of cripple—because I want to paint and can't?"

"But why here?" Tracy persisted. "Perhaps you'd paint again if you went away."

He was silent for a long moment. "I've tried it," he said at last. "I'm pulled back every time. It's here the thing left me and it's here I must recover it."

She had the curious feeling that he had turned some corner in his thoughts and had abruptly ceased to speak the truth. The feeling that this was a story he had told often—with the truth well hidden behind it.

"What of your portrait of Mrs. Erim?" she asked. "Isn't this a step toward painting again?"

"I'd like to keep Sylvana content for the moment," he admitted. "But I haven't the slightest desire to immortalize her on canvas. Nothing went right this afternoon until you called my attention to an odd trick of reflection in the samovar. I've decided to experiment with it and find out where it leads. It's a change in my approach, at least. Perhaps not a happy one."

She listened uneasily, still sensing concealment in his words. "It is only because of your painting that you want to stay on at the yali?"

He glanced at her and then quickly away. "Call it a matter of unfinished business, if you like. But don't poke about trying to satisfy your curiosity." His face had darkened and there was a sudden warning in his eyes. "Do your work. Get it done and go home. Play in the shallows, if you like, but stay out of the deeps."

She gave him look for angry look, yet in the very instant of her indignation she sensed it was a pretense. She must pretend anger so that he would not guess that she remembered his brief kindness and the touch of his hand holding hers in reassurance. There was a sense of loss in knowing that moment would not come again.

He pushed his chair from the table. "Shall we return?"

Tracy rose without a word and they went down to the landing. She got into the boat quickly, and when Miles had tipped the waiting boys he pushed away from shore.

On the return trip he paid no attention to her, but kept his eyes upon the far shore. Tracy faced him on the crossboard seat, intensely aware of him—of the rough-hewed look of his face, of dark hair growing thickly back from his forehead, of eyes that had no knowledge of her now, but which she had learned could be warm as well as chill. How far away he seemed there in the stern of the boat with his hand upon the rudder. Eons removed from Tracy Hubbard, who could never be as Anabel had been at her fascinating best. "I would have done anything for Anabel," he had said—and her portrait hung upon his wall, reminding him always of what he had lost.

As they neared the shore, she realized that in returning he had headed the boat farther up the Bosporus. They were approaching the broken palace with its overgrown gardens, where Tracy had wandered that day when she had come upon a tryst in the ruins. When they came opposite cracked marble steps, Miles cut the motor and let the boat drift idly.

"Do you know what this place is?" he asked.

"Only that it's where I fell and scraped my leg the first day I was here," Tracy told him.

"As a matter of fact it's a spot with considerable history behind it. It was a palace in the old days—belonging to the Sultan's mother. The Sultan Valide as she was called. Neither a sultan's wife nor mother was ever called a sultana—that's a word the English created."

Tracy's attention was fully arrested. "A Sultan Valide lived here?"

"This particular one died here—stabbed to death by an enemy among her own ladies."

"In the presence of the Anatolian Samovar," said Tracy softly. She was thinking in sudden excitement of Anabel's confused reference to the Sultan Valide who knew a secret. A secret hidden perhaps in the old palace ruins?

"The samovar again!" Miles said with some impatience. "Did you know that it's one my wife wanted to own—before Sylvana apparently purchased it behind her back?"

"Yes," Tracy said. "Nursel told me."

"Sylvana did me a favor, as a matter of fact. Anabel had a taste for tales of wickedness and evil. The opposite facet to the side of her that looked toward the light, I suppose. She made this old ruin and its gardens her own place. She was always running away to hide here and put on her little amusements."

Tracy watched him, not wanting to stop this reminiscing, or to miss a word, yet touched by an old pain. He did not notice, his attention wholly upon the crumbling building on the shore. Its arched windows and broken veranda were close to them now. The boat seemed to drift in a pocket of quiet made by a jutting point of land that held them away from the main current.

"Once when I looked for her here," Miles said, "I found her putting on one of her performances. For an audience of nightingales and lizards." There was momentary tenderness in his voice. "Like your sister, she could dance and sing a little. She was tripping around over broken floors, making up little steps and singing to herself as though she occupied a stage. She could be an entrancing person. When I applauded she came running to me like a child."

Listening, Tracy could see Anabel there among the ruins, moving as though she were the very spirit of this haunted place, delighting and entrancing in her own special way.

"I might have thought of Ophelia when I found her here," Miles said, "except that Anabel was not mad. Or if she was, it was a sort of madness that often made her more appealing than any woman I've ever known."

The old hurt that was now a new hurt deepened in Tracy. She studied the ruins above the boat, understanding better than he knew. This was what Anabel had been like, possessed of her own special magic, or madness, holding those who loved her with a bond that only strengthened with her perversity and need for protection from herself.

"Well, it's done now!" The change in Miles's tone made her look at him quickly, and she saw in his eyes an anger that startled her.

The quiet of the tiny cove was shattered by the sudden sound of the motor. Their little boat cut through the water as though the very speed of its movement gave vent to Miles's need for turbulent action.

Tracy clung to her seat, wondering that she had ever thought him a man in whom all emotion had died. She had glimpsed just now a degree of anger that she shrank from in alarm. Never would she understand the complexities of his nature. With such a man anything was possible—love and hate, perhaps vengeance. But vengeance against whom? Was his anger against someone who existed in the present, or was there some violence that Miles Radburn had brought down upon one who had incurred his anger in the past? Anabel, perhaps, with her ability to subjugate and repel almost in the same breath? His mood had changed so swiftly from tenderness to rage.

They reached the yali quickly and as quickly his emotion subsided, outwardly at least. He seemed cold again and far removed from all feeling.

Ahmet was waiting as they came ashore. The old man stood back until they were out of the boat, and then slipped silently away through the passage. Was he off to the kiosk to report to Sylvana, as he had perhaps been instructed to do? For the first time Tracy thought of the fact that Mrs. Erim would not approve of this excursion Miles had made across the Bosporus, taking Tracy with him.

But she could waste no concern upon Mrs. Erim. Or even upon Miles and his hidden angers. Not now. Since the moment when he had spoken of the Sultan Valide, she had known what she must do. This was the time, if she could slip away without being seen.

Unexpectedly, Miles was studying her as though she puzzled him for some reason.

"Thank you for tea," she said, stiffly polite, and glanced at her watch. It was nearly five.

He said nothing. It was as if he had become acutely aware of her, as if he searched for an answer to some troublesome problem that had its source in Tracy Hubbard. She had the feeling that he might be asking himself why he had spoken out so frankly to a stranger who meant nothing to him. Perhaps wondering why she had confided in him. She understood, but he could not. He had no idea of the invisible bond that drew them together.

The moment lasted briefly. "I believe I'll walk over to the village," he said, turning curtly from her. His gesture rejected whatever had held his attention, rejected perhaps, the possibility of friendship between them.

The boatman was busy getting the small craft into its place in the boathouse under the yali and Tracy stood watching for a moment until she was sure Miles was out of sight. Then she slipped through the marble corridor of the ground floor and went through the far door to the driveway. No one was there. There was no one at the windows of the kiosk on the hill above. She slipped quickly away up the same winding path she had followed on her first exploration. Winter shrubbery offered little shield for her going, but as far as she knew no one saw her.

She found her way to the side gate. Again it was unlocked. Probably because Miles had gone through. But the village lay in the other direction and she would not meet him now. She hurried along the road, knowing her way.

As she walked, she thought again of Anabel's words. Miles himself had given her a possible answer to them in the fact that Anabel had often gone to the old ruins where the Sultan Valide had once reigned. Perhaps she had hidden something there that she was trying to tell her sister of in that last hysterical effort.

Rounding the turn in the road, Tracy saw the iron gate askew upon its great hinges and she began to run, lest some car come suddenly along the road so that she would be seen entering the old garden.

She went through the gate quietly and trod softly across flagstones, where grass and weeds had sprung up in rebirth. Heavy brown brush cut off the view of the front door and she welcomed it, since it would hide her from the road. She hurried past spiderwebs spun across bushes and ran lightly over the pebbled mosaic below the marble steps.

Even as she moved there was a sound within the house, and before she could halt her headlong pace a man came through the door and stood awaiting her. It was Murat Erim.

12

~~~~~~~~~~~~~

TRACY STUMBLED TO a halt, staring at the man in the doorway. He did not seem nearly so surprised to see her as she was to see him. Indeed, he smiled at her easily and came down the few steps to her level. She did not like a smile which touched his lips but did not reach black, unfathomable eyes.

"I have startled you," he said. "I am sorry for that. I did not hear you until you were through the gate. You enjoyed your boat trip across the Bosporus?"

"Why—yes," Tracy said. "We—we had tea on the opposite shore."

He nodded. "I supposed as much. There is a fine view of the water from this place. I could see your boat drifting close to the walls on your way back. I was just in there, you see—at the embrasure of the windows." He gestured toward the house behind him. "You will forgive me—I could not help but hear you speaking together of Mrs. Radburn. It seems he still does not know that you are her sister?"

"No," Tracy said. "I haven't told him yet." She wanted only to get away, to keep to herself the secret of why she had come here.

"As Mr. Radburn mentioned, this was a place your sister loved," Dr. Erim went on. "A place she visited often. Sometimes I used to wonder why. But when I asked, she only laughed and would not tell me. It is possible that you know the reason?"

Tracy shook her head. It was ridiculous to be afraid. This man meant her no harm. Indeed, he had been kind to her in the beginning. But now he probed dangerously near the truth, and she tried to find an explanation that would put him off.

"It's because Mr. Radburn said my sister loved this place that

388

I've come here. It interested me the first time I saw it, and knowing she was fond of it made me want to see it again."

"And I have disturbed your solitude," Dr. Erim said regretfully. "But perhaps you will bear with my presence a little longer. Come —let me show you about. Having hurt yourself the other time, you had no opportunity to appreciate this place where a Sultan Valide once lived."

He held out his hand and she felt compelled to go up the steps and into the house with him. His manner remained formal and stiffly proper, but she knew he was watching her in an oddly intent way—as if he waited for some revelation on her part.

He showed her the safest passage as though he knew the ruins well, and led her from room to room. Here, where plaster crumbled from a wall, there were exquisite mosaics to be seen. Beyond was a door that had been ornately carved, and in another room portions of the elaborate ceiling with its diamond-shaped sections could still be seen. All the while Dr. Erim spoke in his low, cultured voice, as though he were a curator of art conducting a visitor upon the rounds of a museum. Tracy went with him, trying to respond with suitable sounds, but finding little to say.

When she had seen all of the musty, crumbling first floor of the place, they returned to the main salon and stood where the floor was least damaged, watching the Bosporus flow by outside arched windows.

"They say it was in this very room that the Sultan Valide was stabbed," Dr. Erim said gently.

There had been enough of this hinting, Tracy decided, this queer creeping about through an old ruin, as if something dramatic were about to happen at any moment. Or as if they waited for a ghost to appear. She did not like it. She'd had enough.

"I'm not a bit like Anabel," she told him, forcing a light tone. "I'm not romantically enchanted just because this was once a palace. Nor am I frightened because a murder was committed here."

"You do not believe that the past, when it has been bloody, may lay a hand upon the present?"

"Only so far as the present grows out of the past," said Tracy.

"Ah—but that is the important thing, of course. There is still a present in this place, even though it belongs to the past."

"I don't know what you mean," Tracy said.

He discarded his gentle manner and turned so that his back

was toward the light that fell through arched and empty windows. She could no longer see his dark, sensitive face, but there was something faintly menacing about the vigilance of his poised body, as though his very stillness was a threat.

"Where do you think she hid whatever it was she had to hide?" he demanded. "In this very place, perhaps? I have often thought so, but, though I have searched many times, the house does not give up its secret."

Tracy stared at him and the skin crept a little at the back of her neck. "I don't know what you're talking about," she repeated.

"I think you know," he said. "You know or you would not have been so interested in the black amber tespih. There is significance in your interest—of that I am sure. But the beads would do you no good—is that not so? Because they are not the same ones your sister Anabel took. A few things were recovered, but neither that nor any of the other things she stole were found among her possessions afterward. Although we searched for them carefully."

"Anabel—stole?" The words came out in a whisper.

"I am sorry to say this is true. We would have given her what she liked—but no, she must slip about the house at night and take first this small thing, then that. Several articles from among those Sylvana was shipping abroad were taken. Nothing of great value, but important to Sylvana since she meant to sell them abroad and get money for her villagers. It was a sad thing to behold, this sickness of your sister's—this taking of that which did not belong to her. I myself remonstrated with her, but to no effect. Indeed, she laughed at me, as she sometimes laughed at all of us." His face darkened at the memory. Murat Erim did not care to be laughed at.

Tracy wanted to say that she did not believe a word of this. That Anabel was no thief. That she would never have been guilty of pilfering. But the truth was that she did not know her sister well enough to champion her blindly. Behind heavy white lids that green gaze had peered out at the world, never telling all, preserving Anabel's secrets. It was even possible that Murat Erim was telling the truth.

"I don't know anything about this," Tracy managed. "It's hard to believe that Anabel—"

"She was very beautiful." Murat's tone was sorrowing. "But she was also, I think, dedicated to evil. Perhaps without being wholly aware of the fact. Perhaps that is why she had an affinity for this place, with its tragic, evil history. It is perhaps why she wanted to possess the samovar for herself."

This time Tracy responded with angry indignation. "I've never heard anything so silly in my life! I knew Anabel. She did foolish things sometimes, but she was a warm, loving, generous person. There was nothing evil about her."

Murat moved toward the window and light touched his face, glinted in his eyes.

"You do not believe then, that just as a person may be, without knowing it, a carrier of some certain disease, another may be a carrier of evil? Not being evil in themselves, perhaps, but bringing evil to others?"

His voice, so quietly persuasive, held her arrested, frozen, as though in this place, in the crumbling ruins of this palace on the Bosporus, such things might be true and believed in. But the good sense that was so strongly a part of her nature rejected the fancy.

"I don't believe anything of the sort," she said with conviction. "What did Miles do about—about what you claim was stealing? I suppose he knew?"

Murat Erim made a gesture that was wholly of the East, fatalistic—a movement of his head and hands and shoulders that said many things: *Who knows? What is one to believe? What can one do?*

"But didn't he do anything?" Tracy persisted. "Didn't he try to stop her?"

"She would deny everything," Murat said. "And Sylvana did not wish us to worry him. She felt she could handle this matter herself."

Tracy stood in stricken silence, staring out across the Bosporus, where the sun dipped toward the hills of Thrace. Along the broken floor at her feet the arched shadows were many and long. Because she was so still, the small sound came to her clearly—a skittering in the rubble of the next room.

Murat turned at once toward the sound—so faint, so slight. Perhaps only a mouse in rotting woodwork, or a small garden snake wriggling away. Then there was a faint mew and through a shadowy doorway stepped Anabel's white cat. Yasemin paused on the sill and regarded them without surprise, her green gaze unblinking. Murat Erim moved first. He picked up a bit of broken masonry from the floor and flung it with violence at the cat. So quickly did he move that Tracy could only watch in shocked silence. She fully expected the animal to be injured with the force of the blow, but the cat was quicker than the man. Yasemin sprang away and hid herself in a broken place in the floor, looking out at them with only her nose showing and her great green eyes, her ears laid back warily.

"Don't hurt her!" Tracy cried. "Why did you do that?"

She ran toward the cat to lift it from the cavity in the floor and keep it safe, as she had done the time Miles had tried to cuff it. But Yasemin spat at her and leaped away, this time vanishing through the door to lose herself in the weed-grown garden.

Tracy turned indignantly, to find that the man was smiling at her in his enigmatic way.

"Often Anabel used to bring the cat with her when she visited this place," he said. "Since she is gone, the animal has made the ruin its lair. There is good hunting here. But how strange, since you are Anabel's sister, that the cat does not like you, does not trust you."

"I don't suppose she knows who I am," said Tracy, tartly amused. "Sometimes she likes me. She's been frightened by too many people. She doesn't trust anyone now."

"Perhaps she thinks you will betray her." He spoke softly, almost as if he did not want the white cat to hear, yet as if he mocked at himself the while. "You know the legend of this cat, do you not?"

"I know Anabel made a pet of it," Tracy said. "And I don't understand how grown men like you and Miles can be so cruel."

"Then you do not know. Come—we will start home, and I will tell you on the way."

The place held nothing for her now. It would reveal nothing until she came here alone. She let him lead her from the house and out of the garden.

When they were on the road, he told her the story and she listened to him with an increasing disquiet that she could not stem.

"Anabel made much of this small cat. Again and again she told us mockingly that if anything ever happened to her she would return and inhabit that small white body. She would look at us out of those green cat's eyes. And then we would be sorry for whatever we had done to her. We would be afraid—and with justification. She could be extremely annoying with this game of hers, this foreboding of trouble to come."

"She didn't want to die," Tracy said out of the chill that held her.

"She did not need to die," said Murat, his tone suddenly harsh. "If she had listened to reason . . ." He broke off and when he spoke again there was sarcasm in his words. "You do not believe in this story of the cat?"

"Of course I don't believe it. And surely you don't either?"

"Sometimes I do not know exactly what I believe. But I think it is not this. I dislike the animal and I would like to see it gone."

"Why did my sister have this foreboding that something might happen to her?" Tracy asked.

The man beside her stiffened. "It is to be remembered that she died by her own will."

"So I understand," Tracy said. "But if that's true, what drove her to it? You've just said she did not need to die."

He walked beside her with his head averted. "Perhaps it is Mr. Radburn who can tell you why she died. Why do you not go to him with your questions?"

"I mean to," Tracy said. "That's why I've come to Istanbul—to find the truth behind my sister's death."

"So? It is as I thought. But let me tell you this one thing, Miss Hubbard. Whatever you find, there will be no scandal, no smirching of the good reputation of my family. If you understand this, there will be little trouble for the remainder of your stay. If you do not—" He flicked a finger in the air and left the words unspoken.

They had reached the gate and he opened it and allowed her to go through. "I will leave you now," he said, and went off through the grounds in an opposite direction from the house.

Tracy hurried to the yali and went inside. Downstairs there seemed no one about to notice her return. When she reached the third floor she saw that Miles was at his desk. He looked up and called to her without questioning her absence.

"Will you do an errand for me?" He held out the strip of paper on which he had done the decorative calligraphy. "I've finished this. Will you give it to Mrs. Erim, please?"

She took the paper and stood for a moment studying it, wondering if she should tell him about her encounter with Murat in the ruined palace. But to tell him would be to betray her own special interest in the place, and this she was not willing to do.

She left him and went by means of the second-floor passage to the kiosk. On the way she stopped again to admire the handsome piece Miles had done. Though the curves and arabesques had no meaning for her, the strip fascinated her and she could imagine how well it would look framed and hung upon a wall. No wonder the Turks had used their script as a form of art, since the painting of men and animals was forbidden them.

In the other house she found the same state of lively confusion she had encountered on her first meeting with Sylvana. Villagers were here again, presenting their craftwork to Mrs. Erim's critical eye. Apparently a different group came every week, bringing her their wares.

Once more Ahmet hovered in the background, quietly watchful and in control of the visitors. Nursel was there too, her eyes bright with interest, her hands respectful as she handled the lovely things. The great samovar had been removed from Sylvana's elbow and stood regally in its place of honor on a carved table, reflecting the whole colorful, excited scene in its coppery tones.

Nursel dangled a pair of silver filigree bracelets at Tracy. "Are they not lovely? This is some of the best work I have seen. Sylvana has done well to encourage these people, scold them a little, and insist upon the best. She will not allow them to fold their hands and wait for Kismet."

Mrs. Erim paid no attention to Nursel's words as she discussed business matters in Turkish with a headman from the village. When Tracy gave her the strip of calligraphy, she broke off to study it.

"Ah, but this is excellent! The finest work Mr. Radburn has done." She held it up for the men to see, and they exclaimed in admiration of an ancient art, though undoubtedly few could read the script.

She set it beside her on the divan and spoke to Tracy. "Perhaps tomorrow Mr. Radburn will lend you to us. We will need every hand possible to assist us in the packing and wrapping of these articles. Now I have enough for shipment to America. Everything will be carried over to the second-floor salon in the yali and if the day is not too cold we will work there. I do not like clutter about me here."

"I'll be glad to help, if it's all right with Mr. Radburn," Tracy promised.

She stayed long enough to look at a few of the articles and listen to the arguing and declaiming. All Turks loved to talk, it appeared, and part of their pleasure in this event lay in the discussions that went on between the men and Sylvana.

When Tracy left she returned to her room. The door stood ajar and when she went in she found Yasemin asleep on the bed. Lying beside the cat was one of the Turkish books Tracy had been reading.

The circumstance was mildly puzzling. She always closed her door when she went out, though she did not lock it. And she was sure she had left the book on the table with a marker in it. Since Yasemin, for all the whimsical faculties Murat Erim might attribute to her, could not open doors or read books, it was clear that someone had been in the room. Perhaps only Halide.

As she reached for the book, she saw that something bulky lay between the pages. When she flipped it open she found that a black amber tespih marked the place. The sight was utterly chilling, bringing with it the memory of Anabel's words on the telephone: "It's the black amber again! It turned up yesterday."

Tracy stared at the place the beads had marked and saw that someone had underlined a passage in ink. Since it was a passage she had read before, the marking was new. Meaning sprang out at her from the page and she began to read the flowery paragraph again, word by word.

The Bosporus has always been a receptacle for ugly secrets. A head floating downstream in a basket, or bodies of those whom a sultan might fear tumbling in its waters. Perhaps a harem beauty neatly tied in her sack and flung into the shallows off Seraglio Point, to stare with sightless eyes at the wickedness men have for so long hidden beneath the innocent blue surface. Beautiful and treacherous, this is a watercourse to give one pause. Is it to be trusted today any more than it was in the past? To which of us does it still promise an evil retribution?

That was all. The single gruesome paragraph had been marked and left for her to read. Marked by the string of black amber beads. She examined the strand briefly, but it told her no more than the black tespih in Murat's collection had done. She did not expect it to. An inkling of the use made of the beads with Anabel was dawning in her mind. This was the "poltergeist" again, intending to tease and torment and frighten. Black amber, it appeared, was being used as a warning.

She took the cat into her lap and sat in a chair. Yasemin yawned with wide pink mouth, rubbed her head against Tracy's arm, and went to sleep again, purring softly.

Who in this household would do such a thing as this? Was Anabel's sister indeed too close to the brink of discovery for comfort? Perhaps Tracy Hubbard was more feared than she had suspected.

She whispered into one white ear of the cat, "I won't go home!" If she was as close as this, she would stay and find out what it was that someone wanted so terribly to conceal.

But though her words sounded brave enough, the sense of an evil that was all too imminent had settled upon the room. This was more than mischief. She found herself recalling Murat Erim's words. Was it possible, as he claimed, that the past could lay a continuing hand upon one's physical surroundings? That past tragedy could mark the present with an extra dimension, sensed if not seen? There must have been times when Anabel sat in this very room, frightened and tormented by such tricks. So tormented, perhaps, that she was driven at last to her death in Bosporus waters.

"They won't do that to me!" Tracy whispered fiercely to Yasemin. She would stand up to them. She would beat them at their own game! Whatever had been done to Anabel would not succeed with Anabel's sister.

13

THAT NIGHT NURSEL and Tracy dined alone in the yali. Dr. Erim
had received a sudden call from Istanbul and had gone there to
spend the night. Miles was dining in the kiosk at Sylvana's
invitation.

Tracy considered bringing the Turkish book to the table to
show the underlined passage to Nursel, but it was better to trust
no one, to be suspicious of everyone. The trickster might be more
concerned if she carried this off by saying nothing. She would not
even tell Miles Radburn what had happened.

She did, however, tell Nursel about having tea with Miles
across the Bosporus—something Nursel already knew from the
well-informed Sylvana. And about what Miles had said concerning Anabel and the ruins of the old palace.

"Did she really like to go there?" Tracy asked.

"This is true," Nursel agreed. "It is of course a conveniently
lonely place. Always Anabel loved to be alone, except for the
white cat which was often in her company. In the last months
she did not enjoy being with her husband. This I understood
later when we learned the terrible thing he was doing to her."

"What terrible thing?" Tracy asked, once more baffled and annoyed by Nursel's hinting.

The other girl shook her head gently. "Please—it is better to
allow all this to be forgotten. I do not wish to speak of it. If you
wish to know, ask him."

Tracy let it go for the moment. "I went to that place this afternoon, after Miles told me about Anabel," she said. "Your brother
was there."

397

Nursel glanced at her quickly. "You did not tell him of the time when I met Hasan there—when Ahmet Effendi saw us?"

"No, of course not. I've never mentioned that to him."

"I am afraid he is suspicious." Nursel sighed. "If he wished, he could make much trouble for Hasan."

"I don't think he was there looking for you," Tracy said. "He told me he thought Anabel might have hidden something in those ruins. He said there was a time before her death when she began taking things that did not belong to her. Do you know if this is true?"

Nursel did not look at her. She toyed with the food on her plate, studying it with grave concentration before she answered.

"You must not concern yourself," she said finally. "Anabel was not well. There was much to disturb and frighten her. The small articles she took perhaps made her briefly happy. She could be like a child in her wish to possess what was pretty and shiny and bright."

"Like black amber beads," said Tracy, half to herself. "What is there to know about black amber?"

"It is only that such beads were a part of Anabel's derangement toward the end. She behaved as though she believed in magic and spells. Black was the color of magic, she said, and the black amber was a stone for the working of black magic. For a little while in this house it was the way it must have been in the old days in Turkey, when everyone was governed by superstitious beliefs."

"I suppose it was more of the same thing with the cat?" Tracy said. "Your brother told me Anabel said that if harm came to her she would return and watch this house through Yasemin's eyes."

Nursel's faint smile was rueful. "Yes—but she did not use the name you have given the cat. She said she would come back and watch us all through Bunny's eyes. That foolish name by which she called the animal. She would hold the small white thing up to her cheek and stroke it and threaten any who might injure her with this promise of what would happen after her death."

Through Bunny's eyes.

Tracy found herself no longer hungry. She could swallow nothing past the tightness in her throat. Now she understood the secret little game Anabel had been playing with the cat. Anabel had been saying in effect, "If anything happens to me, my sister will come and she will watch you. She will find out what drove me to my death and she will punish you for it." How like Anabel to comfort herself with such a fantasy.

Nursel saw her face and reached out to touch Tracy's hand across the table. "Please—you must not be frightened. There is no harm in this cat. *I* have no fear of it. The men drive it away to show they are brave and not superstitious, though you can see that they are remembering and are disturbed. Even my brother, who is an intelligent man, dedicated to his work and with nothing to fear, becomes uneasy when the white cat is present. Women are not so foolish."

Tracy was glad when she could leave the table and slip away to her room. She took with her scraps of uneaten food on a plate for Yasemin, and the cat awaited her with confidence as though she knew she would be fed.

In her room Tracy watched Yasemin eat with her delicate, tidy manners. She sat in the chair by the veranda doors and thought about Anabel, who had at the end trusted only one person in the world—her faraway younger sister. Yet even in her cry for help, she had thought of possible danger for Tracy. If her warning had only been more coherent, if only she had named a name. Now someone in this house recognized Tracy as an enemy and was embarked on an effort to frighten her away. With mischief and with the warning sign of black amber. Perhaps with nothing more if it stopped there. Yet Anabel had said, "It is the end of everything." Would it mean the end of everything, the tumbling of the last bridge for Anabel's sister as well?

No—that wouldn't work with Tracy Hubbard. It must not be allowed to work. The pattern of following Anabel must not continue.

During the evening she did not venture from her room. Yasemin at length tired of her company and went to the balcony doors. When Tracy let her out she ran along the veranda with a flick of her plumy tail, past the empty room next door that had once been Miles's, and on around the corner, on her own nocturnal pursuits. Tracy closed the door against the cold and got into bed. For a time she sat up, trying to absorb herself in Turkish history—though not from the book with the marked passage. It was impossible to concentrate, however. Her thoughts went round their endless circling, and somehow always returned to Miles.

How foolish if Sylvana Erim thought she could win this man for herself. Or for any other woman to think she might win him, for that matter. Foolish indeed the woman who came to love him.

Unbidden, the memory of Miles's hand, strong and firm about her own, returned, and with it a sense of painful loss. Again Anabel had gone ahead of her. The pattern still held.

She put out the lamp beside her bed and turned her head against the pillow. The patch beneath her cheek was quickly damp and she did not know why she cried, except that welling up in her were old defeats and old longings and old loneliness. Always where Anabel had been, nothing could ever be right for Tracy. Yet this had been neither Anabel's fault, nor Tracy's.

She slept fitfully for a time, and then could not sleep. After that she lay wakeful, listening to the creakings of the old wooden house, astir on a windy night. Massive doors and shutters rattled, and loose panes of window glass set up a clatter, until Tracy's every nerve was alert. It seemed that footsteps moved everywhere, that all the house was on the prowl. At last restlessness drove her from her bed. She flung her coat around her and opened the doors to the veranda.

It was the dark of the moon and scudding clouds hid the stars. Across the Bosporus most of the lights had gone out and there was little radiance anywhere, except for lamps on fishing boats out in the strait. She stood at the rail with a shoulder to the wind and watched the black water flowing below the jutting balcony. Its surface caught a wavering ladder of light cast from the dim lamp that burned all night at the house landing. There were no ships passing, and the lapping of water over stone steps seemed the only nearby sound in the night. It must be well past midnight, and yali and kiosk were soundly asleep. Everyone was asleep except Tracy, who had been drawn to this dark, pointless vigil.

She was about to return to her warm bed when she heard a slight sound behind her, and whirled. The veranda lay still and empty. No white cat emerged from the shadows. Her bedroom was dark, and she knew the door to the salon beyond was locked. Yet there had been a sound somewhere near. The closed shutters of the room next to hers were the old-fashioned shutters of a Turkish house, left perhaps from the days of the haremlik, with their latticework and lozenge-shaped openings—meant for someone to see through without being seen.

An eerie conviction was upon her that eyes indeed watched behind the shutters. That someone in the room beyond had moved, making the slight sound she had heard. She wondered what would happen if she pulled the doors suddenly open to reveal whoever stood hidden there. It took all the courage she possessed to make the quick move. But the shutters resisted her. They were latched from within the room.

Her very gesture terrified her. She stood in full view of a watcher who knew she suspected his presence. She began to edge toward her room, afraid to make another sudden move lest he unlatch his door and be upon her. But there was no further sound, no pursuit. She was opposite her door when a faint splash from the water reached her. She looked over the rail and saw one of the fishing boats gliding past not far from shore. She had a single glimpse of its light before something blocked it from view. There was no sound of a motor, no sound of oars, just that faint dip and splash that she had heard. Strange that such a boat seemed to be coming so silently in toward shore. She wondered if it was approaching this house, and looked down at the landing again. Something seemed to move in deepest shadow, as though another watcher observed the boat.

Again there was a sound from the room next to hers—like a door being opened and softly closed. The sense of watching eyes was gone. Tracy ran through her own room and unlocked the door. In the dim light from the chandelier above the stairs, she saw a man running lightly down. It was Miles Radburn, and she knew that he had gone to meet that boat coming so quietly in to shore over the dark Bosporus.

She did not hesitate. She dared not wait, lest timid fears hold her back. She dared not count the risk. This was an opportunity to find out what stirred in this house, what midnight excursions might have roots in a past that had once involved Anabel.

Her bedroom slippers were soft upon her feet and they made less noise upon the stairs than the old house voiced of its own accord. She stole to the second floor, where all was empty and quiet. Both Murat's bedroom door and Nursel's were closed. Murat, of course, was away in Istanbul. The door of their shared salon stood open, and she saw that it and the main hall were heaped with the merchandise Sylvana Erim must have sent over from her house. Evidently preparations had already begun for the work to be done tomorrow.

Tracy wasted no second glance on heaped tables and piled-up chairs. Moving more cautiously now as she rounded the lower bend of the stairs, she went toward the lower corridor that ran from front to back of the house. There were no lights on below. Only the faint light from high over the stairs kept the marble corridor from being utterly black. She could see no one, hear nothing. Step by step she ventured down the lower stairs and stood upon cold marble.

At first she thought the corridor empty. Then she realized that a darker massing at the end near the boat landing was the figure of a man. His back was toward her as he faced the water, and she did not think she had been seen or heard. She could not go that way. But there seemed to be no one near the door at the other end that opened on the driveway, and she ran toward it soundlessly, thankful that marble did not creak. The door was locked with a huge, old-fashioned key and there was a more modern lock as well. She hoped the turning of the key, the click of the lock would not be heard. In a moment she had the massive wooden door partly open. It would creak if she opened it wide, so she slipped through the crack and was outside where the wind was rising, hiding all other sounds.

The area between the two houses lay quiet. In the garage the car Murat Erim should have taken to Istanbul stood in its place, but she did not pause then to question its presence. Wind swept between the two houses and whipped at her coat, stung her bare ankles, tossed her hair. She fled from the lighted area around the corner and found herself in the dark garden. Here grass deadened the sound of her steps, and there were the black forms of bushes and trees guarding her all about. She picked her way carefully, able to see but little, moving in the direction of the water. At the corner of the house she blended into the thick darkness of a hydrangea bush and started toward the landing.

There was nothing there and no one. No small fishing boat with oars muffled had come in to shore. All stood empty and without life. Only wind ruffled the dark waters of the Bosporus. Yet she had been sure the boat was approaching the shore. There would have been no time for it to dock and get away again. She had been sure, too, that a figure had stood not far from where she stood now, watching. And she had seen Miles come downstairs.

The very emptiness of the place was somehow alarming. She had gone far enough. She turned and hurried back through the garden by the path along which she had come, knowing her way now and able to distinguish objects in her path. She reached the front door and found that the wind had blown it shut. It had latched itself behind her, and she could not get in. Whether she liked it or not, there was nothing for it but to return through the garden and go around to the water side.

She approached the landing warily, but it stood empty as before. There was no tide in these waters that opened eventually to the Mediterranean, but the wind was pushing the Bosporus into a squally pattern, sending dashes of spray against the landing, so that she felt the wetness upon her bare ankles as she ran toward the corridor.

Here she did not hesitate, lest she be silhouetted to watching eyes against water and sky as Miles had been. She darted into the gloom, relieved to find the corridor empty. There was something almost eerie about the way everyone had vanished, and she wanted only to regain the safety of her own room and lock the door behind her. There had been no time to be frightened, but now cold tremors seized her and she found that she was terrified without knowing what there was to be terrified about.

She ran upstairs as quietly as she could, and shut herself into her room. But she did not go to bed. She did not take off her coat. She stood for a time on the balcony again, watching the water and the landing below. Nothing stirred. There was clearly no one there. Once it seemed that she heard not too distant sounds from the water, but nothing was visible close in, and such noises were usual all night long. Out on the water the lights of fishing boats moved like fireflies.

When she tired of watching the landing, she closed the balcony doors and set the inner door ajar, listening now for Miles's return upstairs. Again there was only the usual creaking of stairs and house. More than a half hour had passed since her excursion and it began to seem probable that he had returned to his room earlier. There was no purpose to be gained by listening all night for footsteps that never came any closer. Then, just as she was about to close her door and go back to bed, a sudden clamor arose from the floor below. She heard Miles shouting, "No, you don't! Drop that stuff! Drop it!"

Tracy ran toward the stairs and down them. In the big second-floor salon two figures struggled together. Something crashed with the sound of breaking glass and a strong scent of heliotrope flooded the air. The larger figure that was Miles won its struggle with the smaller more wiry one—Ahmet. Miles held the captive by the loose cloth at the back of his jacket, shaking him roughly. The odor of heliotrope bathed them both, bathed the very air about them.

As he shook the fellow, Miles ran his hands over Ahmet's pockets, divesting them of assorted contents. He flung objects away from him across the floor. A comb and coins and other small articles skittered toward Tracy. She bent to pick up two strings of beads. One was the somewhat greasy brown tespih she had seen often in Ahmet's fingers. The other was of black jet.

"Were you stealing for yourself?" Miles demanded. "Or is this something you do for your master?"

It was a strange question, and by way of reply Ahmet turned upon Miles a look which indicated that he understood the words and was angered by them.

Miles went on and Tracy wondered if he deliberately baited the man. "Perhaps this is a matter for the police. Perhaps it is now time to show everyone the source of our thefts."

Before Ahmet could manage an answer, Nursel's door opened and she came from her room wearing a flowing green gown, her black hair long upon her shoulders, her dark eyes wide with alarm.

"What is it?" she cried. "What has happened? Miles, what has Ahmet Effendi done?"

The houseman ceased to struggle and turned limp. Cautiously Miles released his hold. "I'm not sure. He seems to have been taking stuff from this merchandise of Sylvana's." He gestured to the floor about him, where Ahmet had dropped an armload of goods. "A queer assortment. Pillows and embroidered bags and table linens. Suppose you ask him to explain."

Nursel questioned the man in Turkish while Miles listened. Ahmet shook his head in sullen refusal and would not answer. Abruptly a new voice spoke from the head of the stairs, and Tracy turned to see Dr. Erim standing there. He regarded the tableau for only a moment and then strode to Ahmet, addressing him without excitement, coolly, quietly. Ahmet hung his head as if in shame, as if admitting his iniquity. When Murat had listened for a moment or two to what appeared to be mumbled confession, he turned to the three who waited.

"If you please—the occurrence is over. I will deal with Ahmet Effendi myself. I see that a perfume bottle has been broken—let us open windows to air the room."

He followed his own suggestion with the veranda doors, and Ahmet, after another dark look at Miles, began to gather his scattered possessions from the floor. Tracy held out the two strands of beads and he took them from her sullenly.

Nursel came to Tracy. "Can you tell me, please, what has happened? Why does Ahmet Effendi touch such things for which he has no use? I have asked him, but he does not tell me the answer. Nor does he tell my brother."

"Perhaps he meant to sell them," Tracy suggested.

Nursel looked indignant. "He has been trusted for many years in this house—almost like one of our family. I cannot believe he would do such a thing." She lowered her voice for Tracy's ears only. "Hasan, his son, will be most upset. I do not know—perhaps it is better if we do not tell Hasan."

She threw a concerned look at Ahmet, still pocketing his belongings, and saw the broken scent bottle on the floor.

"But what a sad thing! It is Sylvana's perfume bottle that has been shattered, the perfume wasted. Sylvana will be annoyed. She ordered this container herself from a village glass blower. I cannot understand what Ahmet Effendi can be doing with that or with any of these things."

Neither could Tracy. And there were other things she did not understand. Miles had said nothing of the boat, if he had seen it, or of being in the corridor below—if this had been the figure she had seen. But he was not through with his notion about summoning the police, and he said as much to Murat.

The other man answered coldly. "We do not take such action with one who has served us as long and faithfully as Ahmet Effendi has done. There will be no reporting of this to the police. You understand? If you are so foolish as to take some action, my sister and I will protect Ahmet Effendi. We will deny that anything has happened."

Tracy glanced at Nursel and saw that her eyes were downcast. It was clear that she would do exactly as her brother wished.

Miles turned his back on Murat and spoke to Tracy. "I don't know how you got into this, but it seems to be over. You'd better go back to bed."

Tracy started up the stairs. As she looked down over the rail she saw Murat gesture Nursel away and take Ahmet into his bedroom. Tracy continued upstairs and Miles followed.

As they reached the upper floor Miles sniffed at himself ruefully. "I need an airing too. He spilled most of that stuff over the two of us. Deliberately, I think. If the bottle had merely slipped out of his hands, it would have broken on the floor. But he got the stopper out first, so it went all over him and over me."

"But why?" Tracy asked. "Why would he do that?"

"Who knows? Perhaps to cover up some other smell? Don't ask foolish questions. It's too late at night."

His tone was snappish and she snapped back. "I have plenty of questions to ask, and I don't believe they are foolish!"

He took her firmly by the arm and marched her to her door. "There's just one question I'm interested in now. How did you get down there so fast?"

"I was out on the veranda," she said. "I think you know that. I saw a boat coming in toward the landing. The same one you were watching."

"By the dark of the moon," he said. "This was a good night for it. Go on. What else did you see?"

"Nothing," she admitted. "I ran downstairs after you to find out what was going on. But by the time I got to the landing there was no one there."

"Exactly my deduction," Miles said. "The boat comes in elsewhere, I suppose. Have you ever considered that it might be wiser for you to stay out of an affair like this?"

"As you are staying out of it?" Tracy asked.

"It's my business, not yours. I'll thank you to keep still about having seen me go down there."

Her feeling toward him was one of greater irritation than ever before. "Why should I keep still? What are you trying to hide?"

He looked at her with such exasperation that she feared he might shake her, as he had shaken Ahmet. She backed away from him hurriedly.

"You do smell quite dreadful," she said.

He neither shook her nor swore at her, though he might well have done both. "From the moment you arrived in this house I haven't known what to do about you. That sister you told me of would have had her hands full trying to keep up with you. Now —will you go to bed and stay out of this from now on?"

His look told her that she was pushing him too far, but she had to stand her ground. "No," she said, "I won't keep out of it."

He put his hands on her shoulders, but he did not shake her. Quite astonishingly he pulled her to him and kissed her on the mouth—with great impatience and a sort of rough tenderness. Then he shoved her away.

"Now will you go home? Slap my face, if you like, and go home. Get out of this! You're way beyond your depth in dangerous waters and you don't belong here. You can't remain any longer."

She felt a little sick with shock because two totally opposing currents were charging through her in almost the same instant. To her distress, she liked being kissed by Miles Radburn. She liked it that he had wanted to kiss her. And then he had told her why he'd kissed her and the current had flashed distressingly the other way. Her eyes were bright with outrage and her cheeks flaming, but again she stood her ground.

"I *do* belong here. I *am* involved. Nothing you can do will change that. Anabel was my sister and I belong here as much as you do."

He stared at her while color drained slowly from his face, leaving it pale and cold. Abruptly he turned on his heel and walked away from her across the salon. She watched him go. Watched him disappear into his own room, where the portrait of Anabel would look down upon him with its secret green gaze.

Feeling thoroughly shaken, she went into her room. She had left the veranda doors open and the air was cold. She closed them with hands that shook and caught the sweetish odor of heliotrope upon her own person. It was a dreadful, sickly smell. She knew she would detest it for the rest of her life. It was on her coat and she flung it off to escape the scent and shivered in her thin nightgown. Quickly she got into bed and lay beneath cold sheets thinking. But not of Ahmet, or of the larger events of the night. She could remember only that Miles had kissed her in order to anger her and be rid of her. He would never forgive her for being

Anabel's sister, or for the hoax she had played on him. While she, after all her resolution, her determination never to follow in Anabel's footsteps again, was moving helplessly down a road that could lead only to pain and frustration she had brought upon herself. No matter how hard she tried, she could not put out of her mind and her heart the man Anabel had loved. The man others claimed was responsible for Anabel's death.

14

IN THE MORNING Miles was up and out early and Tracy did not see him at the breakfast table. She went downstairs, to find Murat and Nursel breakfasting alone. Ahmet was nowhere in evidence.

Dr. Erim greeted her cheerfully enough and rose to pull out her chair. "Good morning, Miss Hubbard. We are sorry you had to lose your sleep because of the disturbance last night."

She undoubtedly looked as though she had lost sleep, Tracy thought. She murmured a "good morning," and waited for Halide to bring her coffee. She needed it strong and thick today.

Nursel smiled at her sadly. "Murat and I have been discussing this foolish act of Ahmet Effendi's. He has been all his life with us. For servants to take small items of food—this is not unknown in Turkey, as in other countries, but to do such a thing as this! How will you deal with him, Murat?"

"Unfortunately, it is not in my hands," Murat said stiffly.

Tracy knew he was thinking of Sylvana.

"Does Mrs. Erim know what has happened?" she asked.

Nursel rolled her eyes heavenward. "She does not know. I am afraid of what will result when she learns. But my brother and I are also discussing another matter. I have suggested to him that if Ahmet Effendi has done such a thing before, it is possible that your sister was judged falsely and blamed for taking what she did not take."

Murat shook his head in disagreement. "This I do not believe. Certain articles were found in Mrs. Radburn's possession. There is no question about what she was doing."

Tracy looked at her plate and did not speak. Her head ached

409

and her eyes felt heavy. At the moment it was impossible to concern herself with Anabel's behavior or Ahmet's guilt.

"Last night I told Mr. Radburn that I am his wife's sister," she said. "Have you seen him this morning? Has he mentioned the fact?"

"We have not seen him," said Nursel. "But do not be concerned—we will protect you, even if he is angry. When you wish to go home we will arrange it—at any time you wish!"

She wasn't concerned, Tracy thought. She was simply numb and shocked and sickened. Because of the discovery she had made about herself last night and which she could not manage to live with this morning.

As they were about to leave the table, Sylvana appeared. For all her bright, calm air of efficiency, Tracy sensed again her single-minded determination to bend persons and events to her own use and eventual profit. Yet it was not entirely clear what lay behind this desire to rule, to manage, to manipulate. Tracy remembered the odd distortion that had appeared in the samovar reflection and the interest Miles had shown in it. Had that accidental glimpse revealed a disturbing truth about Sylvana that Miles had recognized?

Glancing at Murat, however, she knew that he was not fooled by the woman. Dr. Erim, at least, saw her with a contemptuous clarity he scarcely tried to conceal as he told her curtly what had happened last night.

Sylvana took the account with a tranquil acceptance that seemed faintly exaggerated.

"We cannot do without Ahmet Effendi," she decided at once. "I cannot imagine how this household could be run without him. Every servant has faults and makes mistakes at times. If nothing has been taken, and if you have reprimanded him, I think we must give him another chance."

"I have spoken to him," said Murat. "I believe there will be no more trouble."

"Good. I shall add a few words of my own and then we shall go on as before—yes?"

Murat shrugged and left them, to retire to his laboratory in the other house. Within Tracy's hearing no one had asked why he had come home unexpectedly last night, and he had offered no explanation.

"Where is Ahmet Effendi now?" Sylvana inquired briskly.

"He has remained in his room downstairs, waiting to be kept or dismissed," Nursel said. "He is very gloomy. Would you like me to bring him here?"

"Not now. Let him commune with Allah for a time. Perhaps he will chasten himself sufficiently. Undoubtedly he took these things to give to his son Hasan to sell in that poor little store. Come, let us begin sorting the articles which must be shipped. Then we will start the packing. Is everything ready?"

As Sylvana spoke she had moved into the main salon where the disturbance had occurred last night. Behind her back Nursel looked at Tracy and shook her head vehemently, denying the implication that would have involved Hasan. She did not argue openly with Sylvana, however. Tracy might have admired her more if she had. Always Nursel gave before the slightest pressure, no matter what her inner feelings might be.

The tall green porcelain stove in the salon had been lighted earlier, and the room, for all its vast reaches, was not uncomfortable in the springlike weather. Halide came to help and later one of the girls from the kitchen joined them. Wrapping paper and twine had been set out and there were shears and cardboard and large boxes. Sylvana gave crisp instructions and insisted upon wrapping each breakable object herself. When she discovered that the bottle of heliotrope scent had been smashed, she seemed more annoyed than she had been over the actual thieving.

"Such carelessness! It is difficult to forgive Ahmet Effendi for this. But of course one of my special scents would have been a fine thing for his son to sell in the bazaar and he would try to take this."

Nursel went so far as to make a clicking sound of disagreement with her tongue, but Sylvana seemed not to hear, or ignored it if she did.

Tracy sat at a table, wrapping various articles—a shepherd's bag, handwoven and embroidered in brightly colored wool, a shallow bowl of beaten copper, silver jewelry, and innumerable tespihler.

After a time Tracy's hands moved automatically and she paid little attention to the talk around her. The problem of Miles must be faced. She must see him and talk to him, perhaps tell him of Anabel's phone call, show him the strand of black amber left between the pages of the book with a passage marked. She must

411

tell him why she had come here, try to make him understand her need for secrecy. He had sounded last night as though he knew something of what went on in this house. He had accused Ahmet of working for a master—meaning Murat? How much of a thorn of trouble between Miles and Murat had Anabel herself been? It was possible that Tracy and Miles might help each other if they pooled their mutual knowledge.

Yet even as her thoughts turned along a practical course, there was an aching in her that would not be quiet. Ever since she had come here, she had been moving surely and inevitably toward Miles Radburn. Even in moments of antagonism the chemistry of attraction had been drawing her to him. When Nursel had warned, she would not listen. Had she been more honest with herself, she might have felt the strength of the current before she was helplessly caught up in it.

But no—she would not accept that! She was not helpless even now. Anabel had drifted with whatever current had caught her up. But this was not for Tracy Hubbard. It was nonsense to believe that she could fall in love so suddenly that she was unaware of what was happening until it was too late. Or—the pendulum swung again—was this the fundamental and irreversible truth that she must now face—that in spite of herself she was in love? Because of Anabel this would be a particularly difficult thing to accept, and she winced away from it in her own thoughts.

Sylvana's voice broke in upon this unhappy circling. "Are you dreaming, Miss Hubbard? If you please—we cannot waste good twine like that."

Tracy apologized and unwound a few wasted lengths of twine. She was well aware that Sylvana regarded her with cold distaste today. Beneath all that mock calm, the woman was still angry because Tracy had defied her and remained at the yali. But at least it would not be for long. Now that Miles too wanted her to go, Tracy's days in this house were numbered. With that thought came further realization of the cause behind her hurt and confusion and self-blame. Miles had loved Anabel first. He still kept her picture on his wall. Last night he had rejected Tracy Hubbard unequivocably. It was this that hurt so much and would not release her from pain.

Again Sylvana's voice cut into her thoughts, drawing her back to petty reality, whether she liked it or not.

"Where is the strip of calligraphy Miles has made for me?" Sylvana was asking. "I have a cardboard roll in which to place it so that it will not be damaged in mailing. I thought it was here among these things, but I do not find it."

At once a search began for the Turkish script. It was not among the articles in the big room where they worked. Nor could Nursel or Sylvana find it in the living quarters Nursel shared with Murat, where other articles had been piled. Halide was sent to the kiosk to search for it there, but returned empty-handed.

Sylvana shed her air of tranquillity and began to look seriously disturbed. "I have several regular buyers for these pieces in New York. Miles has contributed his time for this work and the money goes with the rest to the villagers' fund. This must be found."

Tracy remembered Ahmet's odd interest in the piece when she had surprised him in Miles's study.

"There's still Ahmet," she suggested.

"He would not take such a thing," Sylvana said. "Still—we must be sure."

"Let me speak to him," Nursel offered. Her concern about Hasan's father was evident to Tracy, but Sylvana lacked the key to an understanding of Nursel's feelings.

"Yes—it is time," Sylvana said. "Bring him here, whether he has the script or not."

Nursel hurried away. During her absence Miles came indoors from his walk. He would not have stopped on his way upstairs if Sylvana had not spoken to him.

"I am sorry that I will not have time to give you a sitting for a day or so," she said. "As you can see, we are well occupied. This will take up all of today and perhaps some of tomorrow. After that, we will continue with the portrait."

"The painting can wait," Miles said.

He did not look at Tracy and she could sense his displeasure with her, his continued rejection. She gave her attention to tying a secure knot in carefully apportioned twine and pretended not to know that he was there.

When he had gone upstairs, Sylvana spoke again to Tracy. "I think we shall not tell Mr. Radburn about this small matter of the calligraphy. Assuredly it will be found. He would be disturbed if he thought his contribution had been carelessly treated."

Tracy said nothing. Perhaps she would tell Miles, perhaps not, but she wondered at this small effort at deception on Sylvana's part.

A few moments later Nursel returned with Ahmet. Last night the man had seemed murderously angry with Miles, then apologetic with Murat. Now he had returned to his usual sullen, uncommunicative self.

Nursel produced the rolled-up script and placed it before Sylvana. "What has happened is nothing for us to be excited about, I think. Ahmet Effendi tells me he has only borrowed this. He took it to his room yesterday, thinking you would not mail it at once. Then, after what happened last night, he was upset and forgot to return it."

Sylvana unrolled the strip of paper and spread it out upon a table. Then she spoke to Ahmet in Turkish.

He answered her readily enough, repeating the names of Allah and the Koran several times. As they talked, Tracy stepped close to the table to study Miles's careful, precise work, once more fascinated by it. The ancient calligraphy had been truly beautiful with its vertical lines, its dashes and loops and convolutions. There were bows like small crescent moons, and lines that wriggled up and down like the moving body of a snake. All meaningless to eyes that could not read, but endlessly intriguing as a pattern. Miles must have reproduced the script meticulously.

In one corner was a sort of hatchwork design with small ripples around it like falling leaves. This Tracy had not noticed before and she studied it, puzzled. Before she had come to a conclusion, Sylvana picked up the script, rolled it into a cylinder, and slipped it inside the mailing tube. She spoke a few more words from the table to Ahmet and he bowed to her and went away, looking not at all repentant.

"I suppose it is reasonable that this piece should interest him," Sylvana said. "Ahmet Effendi can read the old characters as young Turks cannot, thanks to Mustapha Kemal. I do not believe Atatürk did only good for Turkey. So much of the old and picturesque is gone."

"This is true," said Nursel dryly. "Before I was born my mother wore a veil and my father a fez. Murat and I are no longer able to be so picturesque."

Sylvana sat down at a table to address the tube, paying no attention.

Nursel whispered to Tracy, "We will not tell Hasan. I do not know why Ahmet Effendi is so foolish, but he will continue to work here and I do not think this will happen again. Hasan would be worried about his father."

Tracy scarcely listened. A clear picture of the calligraphy as she remembered it lingered in her mind. A picture that was without the crosshatching and falling-leaf design in one corner. Had Miles added some further touch after the script had been delivered to Sylvana? Or might Ahmet have been so whimsical as to have put in something of his own—perhaps out of his knowledge of what was correct in Turkish writing? Both seemed unlikely. Apparently Sylvana had noticed nothing. Or wished to notice nothing.

Uneasiness began to grow in Tracy's mind. This was something Miles should know about. And he must be told before Sylvana sent the tube off in the mail and it could not be examined.

She worked for a little while longer and then told Sylvana she would go upstairs to see if there was anything Miles wanted of her.

Sylvana objected as though she could not bear to agree with any suggestion Tracy might make. "He has promised me we could have your help today. We have only today and tomorrow to finish this work. The shipment must be ready to be sent at the proper time. I myself will deliver it to the airport—where it will go by air freight."

"Perhaps I'll come back," Tracy said.

She went upstairs to Miles's study. The door was closed and she stood before it a moment, waiting for the thumping of her heart to quiet. She detested this excitement in herself at the mere prospect of seeing him. She would have none of it. Where Anabel had gone, she would not follow. But when she rapped on the door the sound had a hollow and hesitant ring to her ears.

Miles called, "Come in."

She stepped into the room and closed the door behind her.

"There's something I want to tell you," she said.

He sat at his desk with a sheaf of manuscript fanned out before him. There was no welcome in his eyes as he looked up. Not even in the beginning had she seen his expression so remote, so coldly forbidding.

"I have nothing to say to you," he told her. "I have only one

415

thing to ask—that you go home at once. There's nothing else I want of you."

It was difficult to stand her ground, when he looked like that, but she fought back an inclination to retreat.

"I won't leave until I have a chance to talk to you. I want to tell you why I came. About what brought me here."

"Why you came or what brought you here has no interest for me. I've no taste for hoax players. You had only to say who you were the moment you arrived."

"And what would you have done if I had?" Tracy demanded.

"I'd have refused to let you stay, naturally. If you came as far as this house, I would have sent you home before you took off your hat."

"That's exactly what I thought!" Indignation restored her courage. "That's why I didn't tell you. I intended to stay."

He returned his attention to the papers before him, waiting for her to go. But there was still something she must report, whether he liked it or not.

She spoke quickly. "Ahmet took your strip of calligraphy to his room yesterday without telling anyone. I think it's possible that he added some characters of his own to the script. Sylvana is going to mail it and I thought you ought to know."

He left his desk before she had stopped speaking and went past her on his way downstairs. She followed him to the stair bend to watch the scene below.

Sylvana and Nursel turned from their work in surprise as he broke in upon them.

"I'd like to have another look at that calligraphy piece before you send it off," he told Sylvana.

She waved the cardboard tube at him. "But I have already packed it to mail. I am about to seal it."

"Let me see it before you do." He held out his hand.

For a moment it seemed that Sylvana might not oblige. Then she gave Miles a brittle smile and handed him the tube.

He drew out the rolled sheet of heavy paper, uncurling it so that he could study it carefully. Tracy leaned upon the rail and watched.

After a moment he nodded. "Something has been added. Something I didn't put there. Halide"—he turned to the little maid —"find Ahmet Effendi. Bring him here."

416

Sylvana objected quickly. "I have already spoken with the man. He has been reprimanded for what happened last night. I do not wish to disturb him further."

Miles repeated his words in Turkish and Halide flew toward the stairs, with only a backward glance of apology for Sylvana.

"I'm sorry to interfere," Miles said quietly, "but when I turn out a piece of work I don't want it tampered with by amateurs. Did neither you nor Nursel notice anything different about it?"

Sylvana's usual manner of calm affection toward Miles had begun to show signs of cracking. "It looks exactly as before to me," she insisted. "As for Nursel—she would not know. She is not familiar with this work as I am."

At that moment Sylvana glanced toward the stairs and saw Tracy leaning on the rail. The flat blue surface of her eyes took on a baleful expression. She had an outlet now for mounting tension.

"You are a maker of trouble!" she accused. "Whatever this is, it is a small matter and we do not need such a disturbance about it."

"Miss Hubbard is going home," Miles said. "She's going back to New York as soon as I can send her there. She will cause no further disturbance of any kind."

Nursel stared at the star sapphire on her finger, aloof from the discussion, while Sylvana looked pleased. "It is time you agreed," she said.

When Ahmet appeared, Miles showed him the script, pointing to the hatchwork in the corner, to the curving lines that had been added. "What is this? What do you mean by tampering with my work?"

Ahmet understood English well enough when he pleased, but he answered with the Turkish gesture of the negative, throwing his head back abruptly. He had seen nothing, done nothing, added nothing. *Allah ashkina*—for the sake of God, would they not believe in his innocence?

Miles shrugged and let him go. "He doesn't mean to talk. Nevertheless, someone has put in several additional characters and I'm not at all pleased."

As Ahmet turned away, Tracy saw again the look of dark resentment he gave Miles. A look to which Miles seemed indifferent.

Sylvana was increasingly displeased. "Is this of consequence? I am sure my purchaser in New York will not know the difference. I cannot believe these small scratches have so much significance."

Miles studied the script for a moment longer. "Perhaps you're right. If it's important for you to mail this at once, then I won't object."

Sylvana's smile rewarded him, though it seemed a bit frayed around the edges and the flat blue gaze was without warmth. "Thank you, my good friend. It is important to me only because I do not like to disappoint the buyer who has ordered this calligraphy and has someone waiting to purchase it from his store."

"Very well," said Miles. "But after this, let's have no fancy additions to what I've done."

Sylvana seemed about to answer sharply, but when he had rolled the script and put it carefully into the tube, taking his time, she accepted it without a word. Miles went upstairs past Tracy. She had to hurry to catch him before he shut himself into his study again. She reached the door just in time.

"You'd better watch Ahmet," she said breathlessly. "He dislikes you intensely. I wouldn't feel comfortable if someone looked at me like that."

"Thank you, Miss Hubbard." Miles was elaborately polite. "I must take lessons from Ahmet Effendi. I'd like to learn his method of frightening at a glance. Then perhaps I could persuade you to go home without further delay."

He went into his study and she found the door closed in her face. She stood looking at it stupidly for a moment. Then she went back to her room and lay down on the bed, feeling more frightened than she had at any other time in this house. Her fear was not for herself, but for this man who openly detested her and would not recognize his own possible danger.

15

FOR THE REST of that day Tracy was of little help to Sylvana. She did not need to placate the woman now, or to keep to any commitment Miles might have made in offering her services. Nor did she mean to accept the order from him to go home at once. She would stay until they sent her home forcibly. Now there was something she must still do this very day.

In the afternoon she picked up Yasemin for company, and she and the white cat went again to the ruins of the Sultan Valide's palace. Today it seemed a melancholy place, for all that the sun was shining. At least it was empty. There seemed to be no one here ahead of her and she had no sense of a hidden watcher. She set Yasemin down and the cat ran off on a hunting expedition, while Tracy began her own search. There were only two places she did not attempt to investigate. She avoided the veranda with its rotting wooden arches and broken roof, since it looked to be an exposed and unlikely hiding place. Its floor overhung the water, and she had no wish to trust its boards beneath her feet. The stairs and second story looked even more treacherous, and she doubted that even Anabel would go up there. Room by room, however, she went through the lower floor of the house.

She suspected that her search would be useless since Murat had apparently done a good deal of looking himself, without result. Still, there was the chance that some inspiration would come to her, that she might find some answer, simply because she had once known Anabel.

The main difficulty, of course, was that she did not know what she searched for. Had Anabel hidden something in this place, or perhaps discovered something hidden here? What other "secret" was possible?

If it was a hiding place she looked for, a thousand crannies offered concealment. Rotted floors presented pockets by the score. Stone crumbled and could be moved to form apertures. Plaster had fallen away, leaving bare lath exposed, offering possible compartments in the very walls. Only marble stood solid, and even that was cracked in places.

When she had wandered outdoors in the garden, she found that vines and weeds and newly budding shrubbery grew in a vast tangle, with secret concealment likely almost anywhere. What particular place among all these would have suggested itself to Anabel—if, indeed, this was the answer?

Tracy poked here and there in a desultory fashion, with no inspiration coming to her. Her efforts were as useless as Murat's had apparently been. She wondered again what his interest in such a search could be. What did he know? How deeply had he been involved with Anabel?

Once more she stepped through the marble doorway and was in time to see Yasemin vanish into the same large hole in the floor of the main room that she had hidden in when Murat had threatened her. A place, perhaps, with which she was familiar. With quickening interest, Tracy called to her and Yasemin mewed in plaintive alarm from within the hole. Today going in had apparently been easier than coming out.

Tracy knelt on a board she thought least likely to crack beneath her weight, and reached gingerly into the splintery hollow beneath. Something blocked the way. It seemed to be something loose that must have moved when Yasemin crept in, wedging itself against her exit as she turned around inside.

Tracy scolded gently as she worked the object free. "You could get caught in there and starve to death, you foolish little cat. No one would ever know where you were. You must be more careful in your hunting."

The object felt like an oblong box with a slippery plastic wrapping around it. Excitement grew in her and she worked earnestly until it came free in her hands. She lifted out the closed wooden box and laid it upon the floor beside her. At once Yasemin sprang free, her white fur streaked with grime and splinters of wood. She went off a little way and set herself busily to work, washing and tidying.

How fitting that Anabel's cat should be the one to lead her sister to whatever had been hidden in this place. Tracy stared at her find. The package was the size of several cartons of cigarettes. She pulled off the plastic wrapping and found that the wooden lid had already been pried loose and came off easily. Inside were a number of lumps of some substance she could not identify. The stuff looked rather like thick pats of porous, yellow-brown dough. Or even like dried manure. When she crumbled a bit of the substance it came away in her fingers. She pressed together a small wad the size of her thumb and wrapped it in a handkerchief. Then she sniffed her fingers and turned her head away. The odor was sickeningly sweet.

What this box and its contents meant, Tracy could not be sure. Someone had hidden it here. Ahmet, perhaps? Had the fishing boat that had veered in toward shore last night come, not to land at the yali, but farther upstream at the marble steps of a ruined palace?

It was time to go—and quickly. She had discovered something she had not been meant to find. Perhaps not Anabel's secret, but someone else's. Perhaps something far more dangerous and illicit than anything Anabel could have been involved in. A faint illumination, a suspicion was beginning to form at the back of her mind. She shivered as she replaced the wooden lid and plastic covering, slid the parcel into its hollow in the floor. She hoped she could approximate its original position so that no one would guess it had been moved. The small lump of yellowish-brown stuff was in her pocket, and she wondered if her whole person was permeated with the smell. She had better go home at once and get rid of it.

She was suddenly aware of her exposed position and she glanced around hastily. Overhead the sun shone through a break where roof and upper floor had crumbled into ruin. The empty palace rustled faintly with its own sounds of deterioration. Birds sang undisturbed and the Bosporus lapped gently nearby. Otherwise stillness lay upon the ruins and their surrounding vegetation. Yasemin sat unconcernedly washing her fur with an energetic pink tongue. The cat, being a nervous creature, would have told her if any watcher was about.

Nevertheless, she felt increasingly uneasy. All too well she remembered other encounters in this place. The very first time she had come here, Ahmet had appeared suddenly from the veranda. That was one place she had not looked into. She glanced toward it hastily now, but all seemed quiet and at peace. The wide arch of a doorway opened upon the overhanging gallery above the water. Through splintered wooden balustrades the Bosporus was visible. Examining the expanse for the first time at floor level, Tracy saw something that brought a catch to her breath.

The toe portion of a man's shoe, sole upward, protruded its tip past the place where the arch met the floor. It lay motionless as though the shoe had been tossed there carelessly. Moving as quietly as she could, Tracy went toward it.

As she peered around the arch she saw the man who lay there face down upon the broken floor. One leg was fully extended, the other drawn up to his body. His head lay cradled in the crook of an arm and he was fast asleep.

Tracy fled the house, picking Yasemin up on her way. Out upon the road she met no one, but she hurried as though pursued. She had recognized the man who lay sleeping on the veranda. He was Hasan, the son of Ahmet.

The side gate to the Erim grounds stood open when she reached it, and Miles Radburn leaned against a gatepost, smoking his pipe and staring expressionlessly at the sky.

She went toward him and at once the white cat sprang out of her arms, streaking through the trees toward home. Tracy came to a quick decision. From her pocket she took the wadded handkerchief and held it out to him.

"Will you tell me what this is, please?" she asked, sounding stiff and unfriendly as she remembered their last encounter.

He caught the odor at once. "Good Lord! What have you been into?"

"I don't know," Tracy said. "It smells rather sickening, doesn't it?"

He opened the handkerchief and looked at the contents with an expression that told her nothing. "You'd better tell me where you found this."

She told him exactly and he listened without comment. From his pocket he drew a tobacco pouch and put the lump, handkerchief and all, into it. Then he rubbed his fingers with tobacco until he had satisfied himself that the odor was sufficiently disguised.

"You probably smell of it thoroughly," he said. "You'd better go back to the house and take a bath."

"Or douse myself with perfume the way Ahmet did last night?" Tracy said.

Miles made no reply. He was staring at the sky again as though he had not heard her.

She spoke impatiently. "Just tell me what this stuff is. You owe me that, at least."

He grimaced. "You don't know how to stay out of trouble, do you? All right—it's opium. Crude opium, my innocent. Now that you know, what use do you mean to make of the information?"

This was the inkling that had stirred at the back of her mind. Turkey, she knew, grew a good portion of the opium poppies of the world as a legitimate business intended for medical use only.

"Then this means that Ahmet is mixed up in a smuggling operation?" she asked.

"I have no idea," said Miles remotely.

"His son Hasan is there now. I found him sleeping on the veranda."

"And I suppose you wakened him to announce your find?" Miles asked.

"Of course not! I got out of there as fast as I could."

"May I congratulate you on such excellent judgment," said Miles.

She had no time to be angry with him now. She went on, half to herself. "I've read about Turkey's exporting of opium. But the poppies are grown under government control, aren't they?"

"At a place called Afyon Karahisar," Miles informed her. "Afyon means poppy. It's a long way from here. Three hundred miles, at least."

"And this isn't the season for poppies," Tracy mused.

"All the better time for moving the stuff after it's been secretly stored for a few months. Farmers have been known to withhold a portion of their production for greater profit. Inspectors have been known to take bribes. The stuff is easily hidden and could be moved gradually toward Istanbul and the outer world. The undercover drug traffic is always a worry to Turkey. In the last few years everything has tightened up and all precautions increased. But still a quantity slips through."

"What are you going to do?" Tracy asked. "Will you call the police and turn this information over to them?"

"I shall do nothing," Miles said, his tone coolly remote. "I advise you to do the same."

She could only gape at him in dismay. "But I should think—"

"Don't think about things you're ignorant of," he said, suddenly angry. "Go wash off that smell and forget what you've stumbled on. Can you understand that much in simple language and get out of here? Go home, American. Go home to the Hilton at least!"

Again he had made her furious, but she could think of nothing to say in the face of his determination to be rid of her. She wheeled abruptly and walked through the gate, following the path that led to the house. She walked with angry resolution. Not until she reached the point where the path turned, and the gate would be lost to sight, did she stop and look back. Miles had closed the gate and was strolling leisurely off in the direction of the ruined palace. To inspect the cache? To retrieve it? Uneasily she hoped that he would not linger there and be caught by Hasan, alone and away from the house. What that young man's part in this affair might be was as much a question as everything else. She had half a mind to turn back, but she knew very well what he would say to her if she did.

When she reached the yali, she obeyed one set of instructions at least. She drenched a handkerchief in Anabel's perfume that Murat had given her, and thrust it into the pocket of her coat where the opium smell was strong. Then she went into the bathroom and by luck found water still hot in the tank so that she was able to have a thorough scrubbing at once.

She got into the huge tub and worked with a brush upon her skin until she glowed and the sickly sweet odor was gone from her person. While she was scrubbing she remembered Yasemin. She had handled the cat and she wondered if the odor might have rubbed off on white fur. Perhaps she had better go in search of the animal when she was bathed and dressed.

In the meantime she lay back in the tub and tried to think about her discovery and its significance. Into her wondering slipped the persistent ghost of Anabel. Was this matter, after all, apart from Anabel? Her sister must have been involved in some desperate and dangerous affair to sound as frightened as she had on the telephone. Was it this? Had she learned something of a boat that came along the Bosporus by the dark of the moon?

A second question came to mind as well. Was Ahmet working with Hasan, if it was he who had hidden the box? Were they working together for someone else in this matter—someone in this house? Which of the three—Nursel, Murat, Sylvana? Or perhaps for two of them, or all working together?

She did not want to think of Nursel, but she must. It was difficult to know whether the girl was for or against Ahmet. Nursel worried about him because of Hasan. Yet Ahmet apparently opposed her marriage to his son as strongly as Murat would have done. Why had Hasan been idly asleep there in the ruins?

Or was Sylvana back of this? She would have no moral scruples, Tracy felt sure, and she had deliberately protected Ahmet. She would not have him discharged and she had dismissed as unimportant his tampering with Miles's calligraphy piece. Perhaps this was because she valued Ahmet as a servant, as she claimed, or perhaps it was because she already knew very well what had happened during the night and was concerned lest he be unmasked. Of what significance was the change Ahmet might have made in Miles's script? This question seemed especially baffling.

The third person who might be involved was Dr. Erim, and here Tracy drew a blank. The man was an enigma. There were contradictions in him that left her always undecided. He might well be involved in some sort of intrigue, and he too had been tolerant with Ahmet. Murat had claimed an overnight trip to Istanbul last night. But if he had gone at all, he had returned early; when Tracy had gone outside she had seen his car in its place in the garage. And later he had come in from outdoors.

Anything was possible—anything.

When she left the tub and toweled herself dry, she felt no wiser than before. She wrapped herself in a woolly bathrobe and went into the hall just as Miles came up the stairs. They met at Tracy's door and he regarded her grimly.

"You smell a bit more wholesome, at least," he said. When she would have opened her door, he put a hand on her arm, his voice low. "I had a look for myself and found the stuff. But this is only a fraction of the picture. The rest may be a good deal more frightful. And more dangerous. I meant it when I asked you to go home

425

at once. Your work for me is over. There's no point in your staying."

Stubbornly, she would not answer. She drew her arm from his touch and went into her room. There was nothing more she could say to Miles Radburn.

When she was dressed she searched for Yasemin. The white cat was in none of her usual haunts, and Tracy could find her nowhere.

The remainder of that day and all of the next passed slowly. The work on the shipment was completed, and with Ahmet's help Sylvana took it to the airport. Afterward there was little for Tracy to do. Miles would not let her work on his files, or remain in his study. No further mention was made of her going home, but she was left so completely to her own devices that she began to wonder if staying could serve any useful purpose. If she were away from Miles, perhaps she could begin to forget him. Futile and foolish though her feeling for him might be, she could no longer hide it from herself. She had indeed followed Anabel. Yet she was no mooning schoolgirl to enjoy the pangs of unrequited love. It would be wiser to take a decisive step that would remove her from his too immediate presence.

But even as she thought about this in sensible terms she knew with another part of her mind that leaving Turkey at this time was impossible. Her discovery of the hidden cache of opium had pointed to an involvement with far larger elements of danger than any she had hitherto suspected. Those who trafficked in drugs did not play nursery games. Miles was in possession of knowledge that made him vulnerable, and she knew that he waited only for the right moment to use it. *If* they gave him time. Feeling as she did, she could not turn her back and go home knowing the danger of his position. As long as she stayed she might be useful in some unexpected way. At least she would be one other person on his side, whether he welcomed the fact or not.

On the third day after her discovery in the ruined palace, Tracy sat alone in her room. It was late afternoon and the day had been a lonely one. She wished for the white cat's presence, but she was beginning to fear that it had run away.

The wind had begun to rise, whining through window cracks and about the eaves, while gray clouds scudded overhead. A storm seemed to be blowing up.

As she sat there idly, Nursel came tapping upon her door and looked in with an apologetic smile.

"I may enter, please? We have neglected you. You are unhappy, that is clear. And Miles does not permit you to work for him. We have all seen this. But now I bring you something to make everything better for you."

Tracy put no trust in the girl's apparent friendliness. Nursel bent with whatever wind was blowing and she was thoroughly under her brother's thumb. Now she came into the room and laid something upon the table beside Tracy. The airline insignia on the folder was plainly in sight. Tracy stiffened in resistance.

"Sylvana sends this," Nursel said before she could speak. "Everything is arranged. Your flight to New York leaves tomorrow morning. If you like, I myself will drive you to the airport."

"I'm not going until Mr. Radburn sends me away," Tracy said.

Nursel moved graceful shoulders in one of her delicate shrugs. "Then let us not speak of it. I have done as Sylvana wishes. There is another matter that brings me to speak with you. I have kept silent because you have great love for your sister and I have respected this. But now you must know the truth—not only of Anabel, but also of her husband."

Tracy watched the other girl warily. She would listen, but she would not necessarily believe.

Nursel seated herself on the edge of a chair and went on, speaking softly, as the story she told took shape. There had been a party in the kiosk on the day before Anabel died. One of Sylvana's famous parties, with many important personages from government and diplomatic circles present. Always Sylvana cultivated friends in important positions. Miles had come alone to the affair. His wife was ill, he said, and was not able to appear.

"Nevertheless, Anabel came," Nursel said. "We were standing about talking before dinner. I was not far from the stairs and I saw her first. But I could not reach her, I could not stop her. No one could have stopped her, I think."

In her telling Nursel omitted no detail. Anabel had worn a misty, gray-green gown that night, softly draped. Her arms were bare, her golden head rising on its slender, fragile neck, her green eyes huge and intense. Across the room Miles saw her and started toward her. Before anyone could reach her, she deliberately called the attention of the guests to herself. She flung out both slender arms in a gesture of entreaty, the soft inner flesh exposed.

"Look!" she cried. "Look at what my husband has done to me!"

A dreadful silence had fallen upon the room. Laughter and talk died, heads turned and eyes stared. Sylvana herself stood frozen and helpless, and for an instant not even Miles could move. The accusation was tragically clear. Where veins neared the surface of the skin were the betraying bruises left by a needle.

Anabel had laughed then, mockingly, laughed in Miles's face as he came toward her.

"You know I will die of this!" she cried. "In the end I will die of it. Then you will be rid of me and free to do as you please."

There had been hysteria in her voice and she would have said more, but Miles reached her and picked her up bodily. She did not fight him, but lay limply in his arms, as if the effort she had made had exhausted her. He carried her down the stairs and back to their rooms in the yali.

Nursel broke off and covered her face with her hands. Tracy could only stare at her in horror.

"The next morning Miles went away," Nursel said. "He abandoned his wife in her time of greatest need and disappeared. She could not face what had happened, what she herself had done to condemn him in public. Yet she was the victim, not the one who had committed this wickedness. Afterward she must have known there was no hope for her anywhere and she dissembled that day. She fooled us all. We knew she was ill, suffering from a withholding of the heroin he had been giving her, but we did not think she would take such action. She slipped away in the early evening and managed to get the small boat out on the water with no one knowing. She did not want to live."

"But why?" Tracy said. "Why would he do a thing like that? I don't understand—"

"Nor I," said Nursel bitterly. "He is a man I have never understood. I have not wanted to tell you this thing which can bring you only grief. But he has drawn you also under his spell. You must know the truth and escape him."

"What if you aren't telling me the truth?" Tracy asked bitterly. "What if I say I don't believe you? You aren't your own woman, you know."

Nursel regarded her curiously. "What is this—I am not my own woman? What do you mean?"

Tracy found herself speaking out of her own pain and despair, seeking to discount anything Nursel might say.

"You talk about independence for Turkish women!" she cried. "But you act like those women who hid behind veils and scampered for the haremlik at the sight of a man. You never stand up for yourself. You never stiffen your spine and go your own way. Because you don't know how to be yourself, I can't believe anything you say."

Nursel rose and went quietly to the door. "I am sorry for you," she said. "If he blinds you in this way, the end is foreseen. But you may ask him, if you like. Tell him what I have told you and ask him for the true answer."

She slipped out of the room and went softly away. Her steps were light upon the stairs and left behind a ringing silence.

16

TRACY DID NOT know how long she stayed where she was, unable to think clearly. She felt ill to the point of nausea. The room about her seemed tight and close, the air stifling.

Hardly knowing what she did, she put on her coat and went into the hall. Miles's doors stood closed across the salon. She could not bear to face him now. What had Nursel told her—the truth or a fabrication of lies?

There was no one in sight as she went downstairs and through the lower corridor to the garden. She wanted to be outside in fresh air where she could walk vigorously and be alone. Physical action might stop the whirling confusion of her thoughts. Wind from the Black Sea blew sharply cold as she followed the path through graying light. The treetops were whipping now with the threat of coming storm. She did not care. She would welcome a storm. She would stand in it and let it quiet her, let it quench the rising of an anguish she could not bear to face.

The side gate was unlocked and she went through. It was not likely that she would meet anyone in the ruins today. Not with a storm coming up. She could not walk slowly and she began to run along the road. Once a car went past and she glimpsed astonished faces staring. She ran headlong, stumbling more than once, nearly falling, picking herself up to run on. The first drops of rain struck across her face with stinging force and she put her head down as she ran.

It was because she scarcely looked where she was going that she ran full tilt into him there on the road. He had heard her coming and turned so that she ran straight into his arms. He held her, steadied her for a moment, then set her on her feet and she raised startled eyes to the face of the man she wanted least of all to see —Miles Radburn.

She wrenched herself away from him. "Let me go! I don't want to talk to you. Leave me alone!"

He took his hands from her arms. "Where are you going? There's a storm coming up."

"I don't care!" she cried and ran from him down the road.

She did not look back or stop running until she reached the gate of what had once been the palace of the Sultan Valide—that place of ill-omen to which Anabel had come so often. Perhaps she could find something of her sister here that would help her. Something that would restore her to belief in both Anabel and Miles, help her to refute Nursel's terrible words.

She scarcely heard the rumble of thunder and did not mind wet slashes of rain as she stumbled through the garden and up marble steps. Within the house faded flowers bloomed dimly, tranquilly, barely discernible upon the wall in the stormy light. Toward the rear of the big salon a portion of the upstairs floor and the roof above were intact. There the rain could not reach her. She took care at least to walk carefully across the broken floor. As she passed the hiding place near the door, she bent to look in, but there was no obstruction visible. The parcel of opium was gone. When she reached the sheltered corner of the room, she stood against the wall and listened to the storm crash about her. The wind made a dreadful sound, howling through the broken house. Its intent was surely to flatten the whole structure into final kindling wood and tumble the very blocks of marble. A corner of the remaining roof, two stories above, lifted and flapped as though it would ride off upon the wind at any moment. Perhaps this was the time when the whole haunted building would topple and crash into the waiting black waters of the Bosporus.

Yet so great was Tracy's inner anguish that she could not be physically afraid. Even when lightning flashed and she saw its forked tongue strike downward toward the water, she was not afraid of the storm.

At least its fury prevented her own feelings from rising and engulfing her. The very uproar numbed her, kept her from thinking. With all the trembling and creaking, the thrashing of tree branches against paneless windows, she could only endure mindlessly, without ability to reason and think.

Then, through the storm clamor, a sound close by reached her —a faint creaking nearer at hand. It was like the squeaking of a rope that held a boat to dock or shore. The sound focused her attention, and she began to search idly for its source. It came from inside the house apparently, and across the vast room. Her eyes searched the far side where rain pelted in and found the cause of the faint, rhythmic squeaking. Something lay upon the floor, just inside what had once been a balcony door. Something she had never seen there before. It was a large rock, and about it had been tied a length of rope that stretched tautly from rock to balcony, disappearing over the rail. It was this rope, moving slightly against the rail, that caused the sound. As though a small boat might lie in the water beyond, tossed by the waves, its swaying weight bringing about a slight movement of the rope that held it.

She left her dry corner and stepped into the roaring wetness. Lightning flashed brilliantly and the thunder that followed marked it as very near. She reached the rope and felt the wet tautness of it in her hands, felt the weight beyond. Something fairly heavy had been tied here in this curious place. Rain drenched her hair and ran in rivulets down her face and into her collar. Her hands were slippery wet. She followed the rope to the rail and looked over. In the dim light she could see no small boat in the roiling water below. A wave splashed her as she leaned upon the rail, and she saw that something hung there over the balcony, something heavy that did not pull up easily when she began to haul on the rope.

She leaned closer, bending toward the water, trying to make out the thing that moved toward her up the side of the balcony. Suddenly she saw the wet white head, the ears that were no longer pricked in wary listening, the drowned eyes with the green no longer showing. A cry of horror choked in her throat and she pulled fiercely on the rope until the bundle came over the rail and fell onto the floor with a heavy clatter.

In that instant lightning brought everything vividly sharp for a fraction of time and the terror that lay at her feet was fully revealed. It was not only that poor Yasemin was dead—it was the terrifying, heart-shaking way in which the little cat had died. What had been done was more cruel, more horrible than anything Tracy could have imagined.

432

In the full revelation of the lightning flash she had seen the face of ultimate evil. Vicious evil that could place a small white cat in a sack weighted with rock, a sack tied beneath the chin in the old, dreadful way, leaving it to hang over a balcony rail till Yasemin had drowned in surging black Bosporus waters.

Tracy put both hands to her mouth to keep from screaming. Terror engulfed her—as it was meant to do—and she fought against the sickening waves of it.

Then Miles's arm was about her shoulders, drawing her back from what lay upon the floor, forcing her gently toward shelter at the rear of the room. When rain no longer washed over them in a torrent, he held her quietly and she dissolved into tears and trembling in his arms.

She did not scream now. She clung to him and wept. He held her close and let her cry.

Against his shoulder she wept out her terror and anguish. He soothed her and dried her wet face with his handkerchief. When at length he kissed her, she clung to him, returning the touch of his lips with something like fury. Around them the tumult died a little. The voice of the wind dropped a decibel and the house ceased its wild complaining. Lightning flashed more dimly and thunder rumbled farther away.

"It's stopping," Miles said against her cheek. "We'd better go back to where it's dry and warm. Then you can tell me all about this."

She flung out a hand in the direction of the water. "Yasemin!" she choked. "Anabel's little cat."

"I know," Miles said. "I saw."

Reason was returning a bit at a time. "I was meant to find it. Someone knew that I come here—as Anabel used to. It's another warning. The first one was the disturbance of my work. Then a paragraph was marked in a book." She blurted out the story of the underlining she had found in one of the volumes he had loaned her. That marking of a story about drowned harem ladies. If someone had wanted to frighten her, this was a way to manage it. If he had not been here—she broke off, and Miles held her tightly to still a new onslaught of shivering.

Outdoors a trace of late sunshine touched the water to blue and brightened the wet garden.

"We can go now," he said.

433

"Let's bury her first," Tracy pleaded.

The earth of the garden was soft. Miles found a stick and a broken piece of tile and dug a grave beneath the rhododendron bushes. With gentle hands he freed the white cat from the ignoble sack and laid it into the hollow. Tracy helped him scrape earth over the small sodden body. She had recovered herself now, recovered the power to be angry.

"They can't frighten me like this!" she cried. "Such wickedness has to be exposed. Not just for Anabel's sake. It's a bigger thing than that."

She remembered then. Nursel's words, the story of Sylvana's party. As they stood there in the dripping garden beside the white cat's grave, she told him all that Nursel had said. His mouth was tight as he listened, his eyes cold again and on guard. The look of his face began to frighten her and she ended piteously.

"It's not true, is it? It can't be true? Nursel didn't understand. Or else she was making it all up."

He shook his head. "She wasn't making it up. It happened just as she says. It's true. All of it."

"But—heroin? Then it must have been Anabel who was lying. You couldn't have—" she choked again. "I don't believe it!"

For a moment he stood looking at her, his face haunted by memory. Then he spoke in the old, curt way.

"It's true. All of it. Come, we'll go back now."

She went with him in silence while a new fear possessed her. The face of evil was one thing. It could even be accepted and confronted—if only there was someone nearby to be trusted. Someone who was good and sound and not given to the wicked harming of others. If there was not . . .

He did not speak until they reached the gate to Erim property. "Now will you go home to New York?" he said. "Use the plane ticket. Sylvana consulted me, and I told her to go ahead with the arrangements."

She shook her head numbly. She could not answer him with words. There was no one to whom she could turn. Yet she must stay and see it through. She owed this to Anabel, to herself. And even to a small white cat. She was no longer certain of what she owed to Miles.

Inside the gate he paused. "You'll get back to the house all right by yourself? I'm not going in yet."

434

She nodded and went away from him, following the path to the yali. As she passed the kiosk she saw lighted windows on the laboratory floor. Above there were no lights in Sylvana's windows. Tracy stole past silently and slipped into the house. Not even Ahmet watched her from the shadows. She reached her room without meeting anyone.

The room awaited her undisturbed. There was no black amber warning, no marked pages in a book, no white cat lying asleep on the bed. Her throat tightened, but she would not give in again to useless tears. The terror was there and it must be dealt with. First, however, she must find the way to unmask its face.

The room was a haunted place. There were two ghosts to inhabit it now. One a girl and one a little white cat. Tracy could see them both at every turn. She could see Anabel sitting before the dressing table with the mirrors that had once returned her image. Anabel sleeping in the huge bed where Tracy had slept. And Yasemin everywhere. They had not known what the Bosporus held for them—those two. Was a third ghost now intended to join their company? Another for whom Bosporus waters could mean cold, smothering death? This was the threat promised to Anabel's sister if she did not leave Istanbul.

She paced the big room from wall to wall and tried to shut such thoughts from her mind. She must think only of finding the answer. An answer that lay in what had happened to Anabel. Perhaps in the very marking of her arms with a needle that had brought her narcotic oblivion. By his own admission administered by Miles.

But she could not accept this as a fact. Even though Miles himself had admitted the truth of Nursel's words, she could not believe it to be the whole truth. There was more here—something that went deeper than seeming evidence indicated.

She could endure the room no longer. She knew, as she had known before, that she must somehow recapture Anabel—find again the very essence of her sister's spirit. Not the sad spirit that haunted this room, but the joy-giving girl she had once been. Perhaps the portrait would bring her back. If Miles had not yet returned to the house, this was her chance.

She crossed the salon to the door of his study and knocked lightly. There was no answer and she went in, closing it softly behind her. The last light was fading beyond the hills of Thrace, and here on the land side of the house the room was dim with shadows. She fled them and slipped through the door to the bedroom. In the moment before she flicked on the light to face her sister, she tried to erase from her mind the picture Nursel had put there, the image of a desperate, hysterical girl displaying ugly marks on her arms, denouncing Miles. It was the Anabel of Tracy's childhood who must help her now. The Anabel Miles had painted in the early years of their marriage.

She touched her finger to the switch and faced the wall where the picture hung. The shock of surprise made her stand blinking for a moment. The portrait of Anabel was gone. In its place above his bed Miles had hung the unfinished, unframed portrait he was painting of Sylvana Erim. The substitution was in itself a disturbing thing, but Tracy had no interest in Sylvana's picture and she would have turned from it if the samovar had not gleamed so brightly in the painting that it drew her attention.

Instead of turning away, she went close to the canvas to study it in some astonishment. The portrait of Sylvana had progressed little since she had last seen it. Perhaps a bit more work had been done upon the dress, but the face was still an empty blur. Miles had given his time to the reflection in the samovar and he had portrayed it in full. The bulging copper sides had distorted Sylvana's image and made a mocking caricature of it—this Tracy remembered. But a mocking caricature was not what Miles had painted. With deliberate intent he had created a miniature of something far worse. Line by line Sylvana's face had been cunningly altered to reveal avarice, cruelty, deceit.

The thing had been subtly accomplished—there was no flagrant distortion. At first glance the intent might have been missed. But it was there—an implication of all the evil of which the human soul might be capable, all reflected in a face that was still Sylvana's.

Once she had looked, Tracy could not withdraw her fascinated gaze. She stood shocked and wondering, not a little frightened. The miniature was a revelation, not only of Sylvana, but also of Miles Radburn himself.

When she heard the outer door of the study open, she did not move from her place before the picture. She was beyond caring if he found her here. There was nothing she could say to him at this moment, but perhaps it was best that he know what she had discovered.

She heard steps approach the bedroom door she had left ajar. There was a light tap upon it, and Sylvana's voice called out sharply, "Miles? I may see you, please? There is an urgent matter—"

She did not finish, because Tracy went swiftly to face her in the doorway. Sylvana was the one person who must not be put on guard by seeing the picture before Miles intended her to see it. Tracy tried to block the opening, but Sylvana pushed past her into the room. At once she saw the portrait on the wall. Its presence did not seem to delight her, as might have been expected.

"But this is amusing!" she exclaimed tartly. "He has taken down the picture of his wife and set mine in its place."

"You're not supposed to see it until it's finished," Tracy warned. She could only hope that Sylvana would miss the reflection in the samovar.

"Then we will not tell him I have seen it," said Sylvana. "You do not expect me to turn away when I have this opportunity to discover exactly what your sister's husband has painted."

There was left only the possibility of distraction. "I found the cat," said Tracy abruptly, her gaze fixed upon Sylvana's face.

The woman gave no sign that she understood. Much of the time she had absolute control over her own reactions. Now, if she knew about the cat, she was well prepared to conceal the fact.

"The animal was missing?" she asked carelessly, and stepped closer to the wall, the better to examine the portrait.

"Someone put Anabel's cat into a sack weighted with stones and hung it by a rope over the balcony of the Sultan Valide's palace. Yasemin was drowned. And her body was left there for me to find. Do you know why?"

Sylvana had stiffened, and there was a glitter to the blue surface of her eyes. But it was the portrait upon which her attention was fixed. She had seen what Miles had painted there and now she saw nothing else.

Watching her, Tracy half expected the woman's face to change before her eyes, to take on the ugly revelation of Miles's portrait. Sylvana stared coldly at the picture, her eyes hard and bright, yet still without emotion. If she had ever known an infatuation for

437

Miles Radburn, it was over. Perhaps it had ended long before, when she had found him a dangerous enemy within her household.

Sylvana stared for a long moment without speaking. Then she turned and went out of the room. The sound of her high heels upon the floor of the salon had a sharply purposeful ring. There was no telling what the woman now intended. Tracy knew she must find Miles at once, warn him, let him know all that had happened.

But when she ran downstairs she found that the garage where he kept his car stood empty. Both car and man were gone, and she had no idea where. The thought that he might have left the yali for good came uneasily to her mind. But surely he would not go away and leave her here alone. Not after the way he had held and soothed her after Yasemin's death. Not after the gentle way he had kissed her. As Anabel had said, he was *accountable*. Yet later Anabel believed she had been wrong, and he was a man whom Tracy, after all, did not really know. It would be better for him if he forgot everything except his own safety and left Istanbul for good. In which case she ought to do the same.

Her heart had no interest in listening to reason. It told her that he would return, and she knew that she could not leave the yali herself and have him walk unwarned into some trap of Sylvana's making.

Since the only safe haven seemed to be that of her room, Tracy went back to it. There she locked herself in, drawing the draperies across the balcony doors, shutting out the last daylight. When she had packed her suitcase and was ready to leave, she sat down to wait. If Miles returned to this floor, she would hear him.

Time had never passed more slowly.

During the evening a tap on her door startled her. She called through the panel before she drew the bolt. Nursel answered, and after a moment's hesitation Tracy let her in.

"I have brought you something to eat," the girl said, setting down the tray. "My brother is most disturbed. It is best if you avoid him. Please—I may stay a little?"

Tracy wanted no company, least of all Nursel's, but to reveal the fact might make her seem afraid.

"Of course," she said. "Thank you for remembering me."

438

She sat down to onion soup and forced herself to eat, deliberately silent, while Nursel watched in concern.

"It is a terrible thing about the small cat," the other girl said at last. "Sylvana has told us."

So—in spite of the portrait—Sylvana had heard Tracy's words very well.

Nursel stirred uneasily in her chair in the face of Tracy's silence. "What does this terrible happening with the small cat mean to you?"

From beneath the table, Tracy drew the book Miles had loaned her and opened it to the passage where a black amber tespih still marked the place.

"This was left in my room," said Tracy, holding up the beads. "And a passage in this book has been underlined."

Nursel shivered at sight of the tespih and would not touch it. The beads seemed to mean more to her than the words in the book.

"It is as before," she murmured. "This is what your sister called the 'black warning.' It has come again. Someone wishes you ill. Someone wishes you to go away."

"I've begun to suspect as much," said Tracy. "In fact, I can even guess the connection between the marking in the book and what was done to Yasemin. I suppose the next logical step will be me."

Nursel stared at her. "You do not mean—"

"Of course I mean. Me—in a sack weighted with rocks and tied about the throat. Isn't that what is being threatened? Only it would be harder to manage in my case. Because I would fight."

Nursel bent her head and covered her face with her hands. "You must leave this place at once. You must leave Istanbul."

"Who do you think is behind this?" Tracy persisted. "Is it your brother who has behaved in such a monstrous fashion? Or perhaps Ahmet? Or Sylvana perhaps? Or was it you?"

Nursel did not raise her head. "It is better if you do not risk any more anger against you in this house."

"Don't worry," Tracy said. "I've already packed my suitcase. I'm ready to leave. I'll lock myself in tonight, and tomorrow Miles will come to take me to the airport."

"This is the best way," Nursel murmured faintly. She sat up, drawing her hands from before her face.

439

Tracy studied her curiously. "Don't you ever blame yourself, Nursel?" she asked. "Don't you ever suffer qualms because of what happened to Anabel, or what might happen to me?"

"I—I do not understand," Nursel faltered.

Tracy went on without pity. "I've said it before. I'll make it stronger now. You let your brother dominate you. You lower your eyes if Sylvana scolds. You run their errands. You probably do exactly as Hasan tells you to do, except when you're sure he won't find you out. You don't like Miles, yet you never stand up to him. You don't even stand up to me!"

There was shock in Nursel's face.

"You do not appreciate!" she cried. "I have been your friend —as I was Anabel's friend, and you do not—"

"But never a good enough friend. Never a good enough friend to either of us. Perhaps if you'd been a little braver, Anabel would not have died. Perhaps if you were just a little braver now, nothing dreadful would happen to me."

Nursel left her chair in agitation and ran to the door. "You do not understand! I cannot speak—I cannot! All would be destroyed. But soon, *soon* the matter will be ended. This I know. Perhaps by tomorrow. But it is best if you do not stay for the ending. You are not involved. It is not your affair."

"You forget," said Tracy. "Because of Anabel, it has always been my affair."

Nursel pulled open the door with a despairing gesture and rushed through it. Tracy locked it after her and sat again in her chair.

The encounter left her drained and limp, as reaction set in. She was a fine one to taunt Nursel, to criticize her for not acting, when blame lay so heavily on Tracy Hubbard for that very fault.

Oh, *where* was Miles? Why didn't he come?

Once she tried to read to pass the time, but found it impossible. Always the underlining of words about drowning and weighted sacks interposed themselves upon the page, and she saw again the stiff, sodden body of a white cat. Now and then she paced the floor of Anabel's room and looked into Anabel's mirror at her own pale face. And she waited for Miles.

She did not undress to go to bed, but at one o'clock she lay down and, at some time or other, with her clothes on and covered by a quilt, she fell asleep. She heard nothing until the soft tapping on her door began. Her light was still on and her watch said three-thirty. She flew up from the bed and ran to the door.

"It's Miles," his voice said softly.

As she opened the door a wave of relief that had nothing to do with reason flooded through her. It did not matter that he had marked Anabel's arms with a needle, or painted that hideous picture of Sylvana. Nothing mattered except that he was here and she loved and trusted him with all her heart. But when she would have clung to him, he smiled wearily and held her away.

"I waited till now so they'd give up expecting me. If anyone is watching, it will be for me to come by car on the land side. But I've left the car on the opposite shore. I've hired a small boat. Come quickly—I'm taking you across."

"I'm ready," she said. "I've been waiting for you."

He picked up her suitcase. The house was still except for its usual creakings. They stepped lightly on the stairs and there was no Ahmet waiting for them in the marble corridor below. Miles hurried her toward the boat landing, where a man sat waiting in a hired boat. Miles helped Tracy into it and followed her. Their boatman used the oars at first, rowing strongly out upon the black current. It was not wholly dark. Above the fortress of Rumeli Hisar hung a widening crescent of moon, brightening the towers and spreading a ladder of light across the water. They headed toward the fortress and did not start the motor until they were well out upon the strait. Among fishing boats and other night traffic, the sound of the motor was lost in the voices of the Bosporus.

They ran in a diagonal toward the opposite shore.

17

ON THE FAR side Miles's car awaited them near the wide stone landing. While he paid the boatman, Tracy stood looking across the water toward the yali. There were lights on that had not burned when they left. Near the house landing a light bobbed as if from a boat pushing out upon the water. She touched Miles's arm.

He stared across the water. "Someone's up after all. Let's move along. At least we've got a head start."

They got into the car and he backed onto the road and turned in the direction of the inland highway. The road was almost free of traffic and Miles knew it well. They picked up speed, leaving the Bosporus behind as they reached the crosscut into the city.

"Where are we going?" Tracy asked.

Miles was curt. "To the airport."

"But what about your book? All your papers?"

"I'm not leaving," he said. "I'm going to put you aboard the first plane possible—a plane to almost anywhere. Then I'm coming back."

"I won't go," Tracy said. "I won't get aboard a plane alone."

His face was grim as he watched the car's headlights pick out the road ahead. "You'll go. You have no choice. Do you think I want you to wind up in a sack the way Yasemin did? You know too much for your own safety."

"But not enough!" she wailed. "I won't go away and leave you. Do you think you're not vulnerable too?"

He reached out his hand and covered her own. "Hush. Be quiet. Listen to me. I want to tell you about your sister."

She slid down in the seat and closed her eyes. She did not know

442

what was coming, or whether she wanted to hear it or not. But the time for the truth had come. She could turn from facing it no longer. He began without emotion, and as he spoke she could conjure up her sister's secretive green eyes watching the world with their sidelong glance.

"I first knew Anabel when she began to work for me as a model," Miles said. "Her contrasts, the elusive quality of her fascinated me and I kept trying to capture it on paper. While I painted, she used to talk to me about her friends and about her life in New York."

"Did she tell you about her family?" Tracy asked.

"Never about her family. Never about anything that had happened to her at home in Iowa. I found that she was running with a worthless crowd in New York and I tried to get her away from them. I didn't know for a while that she had been taking narcotics. When I found out—I married her."

Tracy sat up and stared at him in the dim light from the dashboard.

He nodded. "Fairly insane, I'll agree. Against the best of advice, I had to play the rescuer of a lady so obviously in distress. I was in love with her then—though in my own way, not in hers. Partly, I suppose, I was in love with the way I had painted her on canvas. After we were married, I took her out of New York to be cured. She was loving and grateful and, for a time, devoted to me. I suppose we were happy in an uneasy sort of way. I painted her as I saw her that first year and put more into the portrait than I knew."

"She came to see me before you were married," Tracy mused. "She believed that everything was going to be wonderful from then on. She thought she was going to be happy—and safe."

"I remember too." His tone was dry. "I believed in all this and I thought I could keep her safe."

"Yet she went back to drugs. Why?"

"Who knows? Who can say whether it is childhood environment, or the accident of circumstance, or something in the genes that drives a person like Anabel? In spite of all I tried to do, she took up the habit again whenever she found an opportunity. I saw her through two more so-called cures. That's when I came to abhor the creatures who are behind this vicious traffic."

443

Sylvana, Tracy thought—that miniature of evil he had painted. "When Sylvana's invitation came to visit her here in Turkey, I seized on it," he went on. "Anabel was pulling out of her last bout, and I thought we'd be safe for a time in that quiet place on the Bosporus. For more than a year I hadn't been able to give myself to painting. I'd been going downhill for a long while anyway. I didn't care enough any more. I had always been interested in Turkish mosaics, and I decided to do a study of them for my own satisfaction. Sylvana was generous and made us welcome. Or so I thought. And I believed the trip would offer a haven for Anabel. But at the yali someone began giving her heroin again. Someone who wanted to destroy her."

There was silence in the car. Tracy hugged her arms tightly about herself, waiting.

Miles's eyes were on the rear-view mirror. "There's been a car on the road behind us for some time. Up in this rolling country, I can see for a couple of hills back. It means nothing, perhaps. But that was a boat leaving the yali."

Tracy turned and saw the distant headlights. Miles stepped up the car's speed and the other lights fell away.

"Was it Sylvana who gave her the heroin, do you think?" Tracy asked. "Because she wanted you herself? Because it was an easy way to be rid of Anabel? I saw that picture you painted—the reflection in the samovar."

"I'm not sure about Sylvana's infatuation. Sometimes I think she has used me mainly to torment Murat and let him know he lacks the money to be master in his own house. Once you'd called that reflection to my attention, I could see the portrait in no other way. I found something I wanted to paint—my hatred for the predators.

"But there was more than possible infatuation to furnish a motive. I believe that Anabel stumbled on some dangerous knowledge. It's even possible that she was actively involved. By playing on her need for the drug, she could have been made a useful tool in this beastly undercover affair that was going on. In any case, she must have known where the heroin was coming from. The source, that is, behind those needle marks on her arms. Once she brought me some beads. A black amber tespih. Nothing unusual. But she sounded strange when she asked me to consider it. I didn't pay much attention at the time, and she changed her mind and took them away. When I asked her about the tespih later, she wouldn't explain."

"The beads were a warning," Tracy said.

"Perhaps. But I think they were more than that. I think they must have been used as a signal. Though I'm not sure exactly how."

By now they had reached the sleeping suburbs of Istanbul, though Miles hardly lessened his speed. The tiered white balconies of new apartment buildings came into view, and the road dipped at length toward the water. They passed the great white cake ornament that was Dolmabache Palace and followed a narrowing road.

Tracy, lost in her own thoughts, hardly noticed the increasing traffic that was slowing them down at last. There was still so much that she wanted to know.

"Why have you kept Anabel's picture on your wall ever since her death?" she asked.

His voice was cool again. There seemed no emotion left in him but fury, and he kept that hidden from view a good part of the time.

"Because I wanted to stay angry," he told her. "I didn't want to lower my guard, or to forget what had been done to her. But when I started that portrait of Sylvana, I had a far stronger reminder and I could let Anabel rest."

It was hard to imagine Anabel resting, or at peace. In life she had always been moving, seeking. Even her joyous moments were never quiet.

"Tell me what really happened that night when Anabel came to Sylvana's party," she begged him. "You've told me you were giving her drugs, but you haven't told me why."

He hesitated so long that she began to think he would not reply. Then he lifted a hand from the wheel as if in relinquishment.

"It's not something I like to talk about to Anabel's sister, but perhaps you had better know. I don't suppose you've ever seen a heroin addict in the throes of what they call the withdrawal syndrome? It's pretty ghastly. Sweats and chills. Running nose, running eyes. Pains in the back and the abdomen. Twitching and shaking and repeated vomiting. In England addicts are treated a bit differently than they are in America, you know. They are permitted doses of drugs to keep them going as they taper off.

Sometimes they're able to lead almost normal lives. I'd got myself a hypodermic syringe and a medicinal supply in case I had to deal with an emergency. With a serious addict the drug must go directly into the bloodstream. I tried to relieve her suffering until I could put her in professional hands. I went to Ankara that last day to consult a man I knew there about her."

So he hadn't simply abandoned her, after all. "But if someone in the house was giving her heroin—"

"The supply was suddenly stopped. To make her suffer, I suppose. Perhaps to keep her under control. She came to me in desperation. But she wouldn't tell me her source. My endurance was nearly at an end. I said I would help her this time, and then there would have to be an end to it. I'd see her through once more—but after that I wouldn't try again. Or at least I told her that. I thought I might shock her into taking hold of herself. So I gave her one more shot. I hadn't marked the veins in her arms as she tried to make everyone believe that night. That had taken years to accomplish, and I'd given her only occasional shots. She took care to wear long sleeves most of the time. When the drug began to wear off, she remembered what I said and she chose that way to punish me, to put me in the wrong with all those who were present. Indeed, if it hadn't been for Sylvana's discreet intervention, I might have found myself criminally liable, while the real culprit went free."

"How could Anabel do such a thing if she loved you?" Tracy felt sickened, revolted.

"Love is not an emotion the narcotics addict is capable of. Except love for the drug he's taking. Nothing else matters. Eventually he becomes incapable of loving or responding to love. Everything of that sort had been dead between us for years. I owed her the best I could give her because she was desperately in need, and she was my responsibility. But I couldn't love her as a man loves a woman. When a heroin addict is sober, he's full of terrible guilt and rage and self-pity. After a shot he becomes lethargic and sleepy. All he wants is to indulge his dreaming. In either state she had no feeling left for me, unless it was occasional anger."

A bitterness she had never felt before surged up in Tracy. An unfamiliar bitterness against her sister. "My father was right about her! When I remember how I envied Anabel and how I believed in her and tried to help her in all the small ways I could—"

446

"You did help," Miles said.

"I shouldn't have! It would have been better for me if I'd let her go. Better for you if you'd never tried to save her!"

He was silent for a little while. When he spoke again his tone had changed, as though all anger, all the old bitterness had drained from him. "Have you forgotten what you said to me a few days ago when we went across the Bosporus for tea? You were the one who said somebody had to try. You said most people were too ready to give up with the ones like your sister."

"But I didn't know the truth then," Tracy said miserably. "If I'd known, I couldn't have—"

He touched her hand lightly, quieting her. "If you'd known, you'd have tried even harder. You aren't the giving-up sort. Anabel was worth trying to help, you know. In spite of everything."

Tears were wet upon her cheeks. What he said was true. Even though the goodness and worth had been somehow lost and all effort hopeless in the end, it had been necessary to keep on trying, to keep on loving. Miles had given her sister back to her.

"I think she tried to free herself at the end," she told him. "She telephoned me in desperation the very day she died. She tried to tell me about some dangerous secret." She did not add that Anabel had spoken out against her husband as well. Now Tracy understood why that had been. "I think she wanted to break away and save herself. That's why she wanted me to come. Because I'd always given her support, even though I didn't know how much was going wrong. I want to believe that she tried at the end. What do you think happened that day when she went out in the boat?"

"I don't know," Miles said. "That's one of the reasons why I've stayed in Istanbul."

"Just as it's the reason that brought me here," Tracy said. "I don't want to go home yet. I can't go home without knowing."

"What good will it do you to know? This part is my job, not yours."

There was no use in arguing with him. Time enough for that when they reached the airport. She couldn't change his mind while they were in the car. Her eyes were dry now, her determination strong.

The traffic on the streets had increased as the sky brightened with early light. They were hardly moving now. Behind them cars were crowding in, slowing everything to a crawl.

447

Suddenly aware of what was happening, Miles looked about in dismay. "Good Lord! I'd forgotten the bridges. They were opened at 4:00 A.M. to let boats get in and out of the Golden Horn. Now they won't close to permit traffic across until six o'clock. We've got to get out of this."

He searched for a turnoff into a side street, but it was already too late. Gradually all movement had come to a halt. The traffic leading to Galata Bridge penned them in. Unless they got out of the car and walked away, they would be here until the bridge swung shut again. Down near the water men with small boats were offering to ferry pedestrians across, but that would do them no good.

Miles glanced at his watch. "Another half hour at least. What a stupid thing to do. I've been concerned with other matters."

Tracy turned anxiously to see what lay behind in the brightening light of dawn.

"At least, if there's someone following us, he'll be caught too," she said.

Miles nodded grimly. "We'll make up time on the road to the airport."

Over the Bosporus behind them the sun was rising out of Asia, and a soft rosy light touched the city that lay ahead across the Golden Horn. Rounded domes and the spires of minarets were turning to glinting rose and gold. The towers of the Seraglio glowed in the rising sun. All about, napping car drivers stirred, restless now and eager for traffic to move again. But still the bridge had not closed the gap.

"At least this gives me a chance to show you something," Miles said.

He opened a compartment in the dashboard and took out a brown paper parcel.

"Look inside," he said and handed it to her.

She unwrapped the paper and saw that it held one of the large shepherd bags, wool-embroidered and fringed, that Sylvana liked to ship abroad. She looked at it, puzzled.

"I got curious the other night as to what Ahmet was up to," Miles continued, "and I began to put two and two together. Before Anabel's death there was an accusation made that she had been stealing articles from Sylvana's shipments, though she denied everything when anyone asked her. After her death nothing was found among her possessions to indicate that the claim was true.

448

Perhaps because someone else got there first and cleared everything out. I can guess now what she was about. She must have been collecting evidence. Like this bag."

Again Tracy looked at the bag in her lap, but it told her nothing.

"When things quieted the other night I went back and stirred around in the stuff Sylvana was planning to wrap for mailing the following day. I was curious enough to look pretty carefully, but perhaps, because of my earlier interruption, the job wasn't finished. This was all I found. Look inside."

Tracy opened the bag and saw that instead of the rough self-material that usually made up the interior of such bags, this one had been given a plain cotton lining. When she reached into the bag she found that a bit of the lining had been ripped up to reveal a sheet of plastic underneath. She looked at Miles.

"That inner plastic bag is filled with white powder spread out carefully over the whole," he said. "It's a hundred per cent pure heroin. I checked with a laboratory friend, who tested it for me. These shipments are not likely to be too carefully examined by Turkish customs, since they go out under Sylvana Erim's philanthropic protection. Nor have the U.S. customs caught on as yet. The concealment has been clever, and the shipments always seem above reproach. Probably most of the things shipped are innocent. Whoever manages this at the yali must take the stuff to his room, where he can work on it at night before a shipment is made."

"So that's what Ahmet meant to do?" Tracy folded the package, feeling a certain repugnance about handling it. "For Sylvana, or for Murat?"

"I can guess, but I'm not positive. You already know what I think."

Tracy remembered the portrait and nodded. "Then there must be an accomplice in New York?"

"Undoubtedly several. This is no small operation. It could be that the buyers who accept these things to sell in their stores aren't necessarily involved in what is happening. Seemingly casual purchasers in the stores could have the stuff spotted and pick it up."

"But—how would they know what to choose if most of the shipment is untouched?"

"I think we'll have evidence of that shortly," Miles said. "I've made a phone call to New York. There will be someone on watch

449

for whoever buys that strip of calligraphy Sylvana sent by airmail to a Third Avenue dealer. I noticed the address on the mailing tube. Remember those marks you spotted on the script? I think there's a code involved. Whoever receives that strip will know exactly which goods to buy to get the smuggled heroin."

"And Anabel knew," Tracy said.

"Maybe she even helped for a time," said Miles. "She couldn't bring herself to blow up the whole thing and cut off her own supply of heroin."

"She must have known that opium was brought by water and hidden in the ruined palace, since she spoke of the Sultan Valide when she telephoned me."

"Exactly. The way she haunted the place, she could easily have happened on the truth."

"Even Yasemin knew about that hole in the floor," Tracy said. "She led me to it. But there's still a long step from the raw opium we saw in that box to pure heroin."

"Not so long as you might imagine. There's no need for fancy stills and elaborate equipment, you know. The process can be managed with ordinary kitchen utensils and a few chemicals bought from a drugstore. Ethyl alcohol, ammonium chloride, sulphuric acid, and a few other cozy little items. From the crude opium you get morphine, and from morphine comes diamorphine. Heroin is the trade name for diamorphine, the final step. The whole operation takes only a little knowledge and some hours of time. It could be done anywhere."

"Perhaps in one of the laboratories in the kiosk?" Tracy said softly.

"Of course. I've often wondered how much of Sylvana's perfume operations were a blind. And if Anabel's interest in perfume-making grew out of something she happened on down there. Now I have the proof, and all I need is to know which of them stands behind the operation. I have to be sure, no matter what I suspect."

Tracy was thinking of something else. "If Anabel was involved in all this, how could anyone withhold heroin from her as seems to have happened at the end? Wouldn't she have made sure of a supply from the articles she took—like this bag?"

"She was no beginner to get relief through sniffing heroin. And she had no needle. I kept watch for that. Besides, this is the pure stuff and as much as a tenth of a gram will kill. It would need to be cut back."

On ahead the windows and towers of old Istanbul were beginning to catch the full rays of the rising sun. The rounded mound of buildings shimmered in golden haze, like a splendid Arabian Nights vision floating above the Golden Horn. But Tracy could see only the evil at its heart. An evil that had threatened Anabel's very life. And now would threaten Miles if he returned to the yali. "It's all so dreadful, so horrible," she murmured. "I never imagined!"

"Now you're imagining too much," he said. "It's time to think of something else." He reached into his pocket and drew out a small packet and handed it to her. "I picked these up for you in a shop off Taksim Square. See what you think of them."

He was trying to distract her and she did not want him to succeed. Without interest she removed the cover of the small box. On a bed of cotton lay a pair of earrings delicately carved in ivory. They were neat button clips, etched in minute fretwork. Modest earrings that would not dangle. Quite suitable for a girl who could never be like the Anabel of Miles's portrait.

He was watching her. "I can see that you don't like them. What's wrong?"

The last twenty-four hours had been too much. She was beyond being rational and sensible. These earrings were a verdict that she would not accept.

"Murat said I ought to dress in a more fashionable and frilly way," she told him. "He thought dangling earrings suited me and made me more feminine."

Miles's snort disposed of Murat Erim. "You're quite feminine enough as you are. Besides, he's not the one to listen to. The man was half in love with Anabel himself. He probably thinks you ought to pattern yourself in your sister's image. Even though he turned against her at the end."

So Miles had known about Murat. Of course there would have been no need for jealousy under the circumstances that had existed.

"Forget about Murat," Miles went on. "And forget Anabel for the moment. While you're often a thoroughly exasperating young woman, you are at least, as I've told you before, all of one piece. You fit yourself. You wear yourself well. Simplicity is your style.

And so is your long shining hair that you wear so neatly. Earrings that dangle are not for you."

"You've never approved of me!" Tracy cried, still lost to reason. "All you want is to send me home and—"

"Stop being an idiot!" he said roughly. "That doesn't suit you either. What I shall do without you once you've gone back to New York, I can't think. The prospect looks fairly dull and bleak."

"But you said—"

Cold fury was upon him again. It was in his eyes, in the set of his mouth, and she shrank from the sight of it.

"I said I wanted you out of this. I've been trying to keep you out of it all along. There's a demon to be unmasked and I don't want you around when it happens. I've been using delaying tactics on my book for months while I tried to get to the bottom of what's going on. And then you come out and disrupt everything. Cause for Anabel's actions can be traced clear back to her childhood. But the immediate and terrible blame isn't yours, my prickly darling, or mine either. It belongs to the creature who drove Anabel to her death. Even if I'd stayed at the yali the day she died, a way would have been found. If only she had come to me—but she didn't."

Tracy stared at the city across the Golden Horn. She found to her surprise that her spirits had lifted enormously, in spite of everything. The spires and domes looked unbelievably beautiful in the morning light and she wasn't angry any more. Miles had called her his darling. He was concerned about her. He didn't want her to be like Anabel. Surreptitiously she clipped on the button earrings.

"Traffic's beginning to move," Miles said, and started the car.

Tugboats in the water had pushed the floating section of the bridge into place. All about them cars, motorbikes, bicycles, handcarts—with pedestrians on the far edges—were coming to life, beginning to move.

Neither Miles nor Tracy saw the man who slipped through the traffic behind them until he suddenly opened the back door of their car and got in. There was nothing of friendliness in the look Murat Erim turned upon Miles as he spoke.

"When you cross the bridge," he said, "you will take the turn I indicate."

Miles glanced at him in the rear-view mirror. "I will if it's the way to the airport," he said, inching the car into the narrowing stream that approached the bridge.

Murat Erim lifted his right hand briefly and Tracy saw the automatic in his fingers. "It is better if you do as I say. Since we have come this far, there is something I wish to attend to."

Tracy sank down in the front seat. Miles gave no sign except for the tightening of his hands on the wheel. It was easy to guess what had happened. Murat had been in the boat that set out in pursuit across the Bosporus. It was the car he drove whose headlights they had seen behind them on the hills. He could not catch them on the road to Istanbul, but he had counted on the bridge to hold them for him. Somewhere back on the road he must have left the car and come forward on foot, searching through waiting traffic. By their bad luck he had reached them in time.

"How did you happen to spot us when we left the yali?" Miles asked casually.

"Unfortunately, we expected you on the land side," said Murat. "Ahmet Effendi did not realize a boat had come and gone until you were out on the water. Then he came to summon me. Our start was late. After we crossed the Bosporus I borrowed a car from a friend. Ahmet Effendi is now at the wheel. For the time being, your car will be more convenient for me and he will return the borrowed one."

"Would you mind telling me what you're up to?" Miles asked.

"Did you think I would let you leave the country if it was possible for me to stop you?"

"I meant to return, never fear," Miles said. "It's Miss Hubbard who will get aboard a plane."

"She will not," said Murat flatly. "If she had gone home to New York in the beginning, she might have remained uninvolved. But now you have committed her by your own actions. As you committed Anabel. We will end this thing today. And we will end it in my way."

Tracy remembered Nursel's words, ". . . soon, *soon* the matter will be ended." Nursel must have known very well what was in the air.

Miles said nothing more, but gave his attention to driving. Solidly packed cars were moving slowly over ancient Galata Bridge. On the sidewalks masses of people streamed across the Golden Horn, coming from and going toward old Istanbul. In the water on either side of the bridge, a curious pattern was evident. A good many ships and boats anchored in the Horn had drawn aside to

453

let other craft flow through the opening. Now, on their right, a mass of seacraft of every size flowed out toward the Bosporus, while on the left all that were willing to be shut in for another twenty-four hours had entered the upper reaches of the Golden Horn.

At the far end of the bridge a traffic policeman directed the cars, and Tracy saw Miles glance at him speculatively. But the man was interested only in keeping the way open, the cars moving. In the back seat Murat was alert, his hand hidden, but ready.

On the far side he indicated the course and the car followed a cobblestoned street up the hill. Tracy lost count of the turns they took, the labyrinth of narrow streets they followed, until Murat at length gestured Miles to the curb.

"This is good," he said. "You will get out, please, both of you, and go upstairs ahead of me."

Miles hesitated for a moment before he left the car, and Tracy knew he considered opposition. But there was little chance of summoning help in this remote Turkish street. When Murat jerked open the car door and gestured, Miles got out, turning back to extend a hand to Tracy. She felt the warm, reassuring pressure of his fingers, and tried to take heart.

18

THE HOUSE WAS very old—one of the now forbidden wooden houses of an older Istanbul. Weathered to a smoky brown, it rose flush with a sidewalk too narrow for more than one person to pass at a time. There were three tall, narrow stories above a basement, and from the second floor two old-fashioned Turkish balconies overhung the sidewalk, rather like suspended sentry boxes.

When Miles hesitated at the doorway, Murat prodded him and motioned Tracy to go ahead. The entryway was darksome, unlit, and there was a smell of long-stale cooking. The wooden stairs turned crazily upward, and sagging treads moved and creaked beneath their feet as they climbed to the third floor. Here Murat called out and a door opened upon the darkness, blinding them with morning light.

Ahmet's son, Hasan, stood silhouetted in the doorway. He was already up at this early hour and indeed looked as if he had slept little during the night. He greeted Murat respectfully and, if he felt surprise at this early visit, he did not show it, but stepped back to allow his visitors to enter the single room he occupied. After the dark stairway, Tracy stood blinking and uncertain in the small bright room.

A rumpled bed occupied the greater part of the space. There was a table with books upon it near a window where sun poured through. A porcelain stove stood against one wall, cold and unlighted.

Murat spoke to the young man, regarding him with a disapproving eye. He spoke in English, as though he wished to make sure the foreigners understood.

"You have served me badly, Hasan Effendi. You were set to watch at a time when watching was important, and you failed by falling asleep. It has been necessary to repair your mistake."

Hasan ceased to smile. "I do not fall asleep, *efendim*," he denied. "I stay in the house of the Sultan Valide and I remain awake and watchful."

There was nothing like setting one thief against another, Tracy thought, and interrupted abruptly.

"I saw you there asleep on the veranda of the ruined house, Hasan Effendi," she said. "You were very sound asleep. You did not hear me at all."

"Thank you, Miss Hubbard." Murat bent a mocking look upon her and went on sternly to Hasan. "It is better if you do not lie to me. We will now return to the yali and you will accompany us there. Your father wishes this. It is possible that we may give you an opportunity to make up for your negligence."

Hasan bowed his head submissively, offering no objection, and when Murat turned to Miles, Ahmet's son flung Tracy an oddly enigmatic look. Where she might have expected resentment, he seemed almost pleased.

"It is necessary for you to understand, Mr. Radburn," Murat continued, "that the end has come for you. This matter will now move as I wish. Any resistance on your part may result in an unfortunate accident. You understand what I say to you?"

"I think I'm beginning to," Miles said.

Murat gestured to Hasan to go downstairs first, and then to Miles and Tracy to follow. When they reached the car, Miles was put in the driver's seat, with Murat beside him, while Tracy got into the back with Hasan.

Though the blockage around the bridge had been broken, morning traffic was still heavy and moved at a crawl in this congested area.

Under cover of noisy city sounds, Hasan spoke softly to Tracy. "Thank you, *efendim*, for informing the Doktor of my negligence in falling asleep."

Tracy stared at him, trying to read the brown eyes and the face she had seen wear dark scowls directed at Nursel. Former anger seemed to have given way to a surprising mood of cheer.

"But you told Murat you were not sleeping," she said. "So why are you pleased when I told him you were?"

456

"I knew he would not believe me," Hasan said. "You confirmed what I wished him to know."

This oblique approach was too much for Tracy, and she attempted no comment. When they were across the bridge and moving toward the car ferry, Hasan spoke to her again.

"I wish to thank you for befriending Nursel. It is well. I, personally, will see that no harm befalls you in whatever may come."

Such an offer of friendship from this young man, who had not in the beginning approved of her, was astonishing, but Tracy did not stop to question it now.

"It's not myself I'm afraid for," she said quickly. "What does Murat intend to do about Miles?"

Hasan's face darkened. "It will be as this man deserves."

"But why—why?" Tracy pressed. "Why does Murat—"

"You speak my name?" asked Murat from the front seat.

"Why shouldn't I?" Tracy asked. "I want to know what is happening. Why are we being taken back to the yali as if we were prisoners?"

"This you will know soon," Murat said. "Let there be no talking now. If you must choose your friends unwisely, then there are consequences you must suffer. As it was necessary for your sister to suffer the consequences of her acts."

From then on there was silence. During the brief crossing of the Bosporus no one left the car. There were people all around going to work, but there seemed no one to whom an appeal by foreigners in trouble could be made. Miles remained alert and watchful, but he took no step toward freedom. On the Anatolian side early morning traffic had quickened and he drove with concentrated assurance. Whatever faced them at the yali, Miles's courage had not been shaken and Tracy tried to take comfort from the knowledge.

When they reached the house Nursel was waiting for them. She smiled briefly at Hasan, but scarcely glanced at Miles or Tracy.

"Ahmet Effendi has returned," she said. "All is ready."

"Where is Sylvana?" Murat asked.

Nursel moved her eyes in the direction of the kiosk across the drive. "She has breakfast in her rooms. We will find her there."

"Good," said Murat. "We will go there now. The moment is here. It is time for the truth to be known."

On their way upstairs in the kiosk Ahmet slipped out of the

shadows of the upper salon, where he had apparently been watching, and joined them.

In Sylvana's room, Nursel drew uneasily apart, as though she wished to leave all that might happen here to others. Not once had she met Tracy's eyes. Ahmet had a quick, almost scornful look for his son, and Tracy saw the young man lower his eyes.

Mrs. Erim seemed surprised and not a little annoyed with this invasion of visitors before she had finished her coffee and rolls. When she saw Miles, her eyes sparked with anger and she would have spoken to him indignantly if Murat had not stopped her.

"Let us waste no time. I have brought your accomplice back when he would have escaped from the country and left you to suffer all consequences alone."

Sylvana made an effort to recover an illusion of serenity. "What nonsense are you speaking? What do you mean—accomplice? Accomplice for what?"

"It is not necessary to dissemble," Murat told her. "We know all that you have done. Where is the samovar?"

For the first time Tracy glanced about the room, missing the now familiar gleam of burnished copper.

"Why do you wish the samovar?" Sylvana asked. "This morning I shall dispose of it. I shall have it thrown into the Bosporus from the boat landing. It is an evil thing which has brought great trouble upon me. All—all the misfortune that has come upon this house is the fault of that evil object." She looked at Miles. "That one could see me as you have painted me is the blame of the samovar!"

Murat ignored this outburst. "What have you done with it? Tell me at once where it is!"

"I do not like this tone in which you speak," Sylvana said. "But it is there—in the corner, hidden from view so that I will not see the wicked pictures it makes."

Ahmet went to the indicated corner, where scarves and cushions from the divans had been flung to hide the samovar. He pushed them aside and pulled the samovar into view.

"Open it," Murat ordered. "Remove the lids, Ahmet Effendi."

The old man worked quickly, taking off the copper chimney, removing the other parts until the charcoal tube and hot water chamber stood open. Murat himself went to the samovar and reached through the narrow neck into bulging depths. A moment

458

later he drew out a plump plastic bag, packed like a sack of salt. But the white powder it held was not salt. Balancing it on his palm, Murat extended it toward Sylvana.

"This contains perhaps a kilo. A little over two pounds of pure heroin. You see—we know all. We have the final evidence. We know the crime you have been committing under cover of the Turkish goods you send abroad. We know how you have operated with this Englishman's help. You managed to use his wife Anabel also, until she became difficult to control because of her own addiction. Now you have brought in the young sister as well. This is a terrible thing."

Sylvana gaped at him in horror. She seemed to have lost the power to speak, even the power to stand, and she might have fallen if there had not been a divan for her to sink upon.

"We know all that is to be known," Murat continued ruthlessly. "We know that you have ceased to trust your accomplice and that he has tried to escape today, lest you betray him entirely."

Miles broke in. "This is a pack of lies!" he cried, and took a step toward Murat. At once Hasan stood warningly at his elbow.

Tracy glanced at Nursel and saw that the girl had shrunk back in her chair as though she wanted to take no part in what was happening.

Murat ignored Miles's outburst. "You can see that we have enough evidence to put you in prison for many years," he told Sylvana.

"Perhaps I shall go for the police now, Doktor?" Hasan inquired, his tone false. In spite of Murat's threats about prison, Tracy suspected that the police would not be informed. This was a further ruse to control Sylvana.

Dr. Erim shook his head. "Not yet. Perhaps I will offer this woman an alternative. I do not wish to have the reputation of my house disgraced, or my work discredited with the government. I wish only to have Sylvana abdicate her claim to my brother's property and wealth. If she will sign over all that belongs rightfully to me and my sister, I am willing to let her go free."

Miles's outrage was evident. "You mean that even if she were guilty of narcotics smuggling, you'd release her, allow her to leave the country without punishment so she could commence her operations elsewhere?"

"A strange question," Murat said, "coming from you. I do not care what she does, so long as it is stopped in this house. The punishment will, I think, be enough. I have been waiting for this moment for a long time. The signal of the black amber has appeared recently. On the dark of the moon a boat comes down the Bosporus to the ruins. You think I do not know this, Sylvana? Many times when the moon is right I have watched, but nothing happens. This time I go to the palace ruins and find Ahmet Effendi there also. My good and faithful Ahmet. He too has been watching. He tells me that strange men have brought the box ashore to hide it in the broken floor of the house. When they leave, he opens it and finds crude opium from which Sylvana makes the heroin she sends abroad."

Sylvana cried out, and he silenced her with a gesture.

"On this night when I come upon Ahmet Effendi, there is the open box at his feet. I send him back to the house while I examine everything for myself. At the yali Ahmet Effendi has attempted to pick up some of the articles Sylvana meant to send from the country. He wishes to see if heroin has been hidden in them. He has taken the strip of calligraphy as well, to study it for the code we know is being so cleverly used. Of course Mr. Radburn is angry when he finds what Ahmet Effendi is trying to do. Perhaps it is you, Miss Hubbard, who are helping these two—you who are being used, as your sister was used?"

"That's ridiculous!" Tracy cried.

Murat went smoothly on. "You can see that I know everything. Ahmet, Hasan, Nursel—all have worked together with me to expose this woman and her accomplices. Now there will be an end to such things in this house."

Sylvana started to rise from the divan, and Hasan stepped forward to thrust her back with a none-too-gentle hand, apparently eager to reinstate himself in Murat's favor. At once Ahmet spoke to his son in Turkish, clearly reproving him. Then, paying no attention to Murat, the old man went to Sylvana and addressed her gently in his own language, as if he were reassuring her, as if he still remembered that she was the cherished wife of a master to whom he had been devoted.

Murat watched in displeasure, but he did not reproach the old man.

"There's a point you seem to have missed, Dr. Erim," Miles

said, speaking more quietly than before. "You and I appear to be working on the same side without recognizing the fact. Why else do you suppose I've remained here since my wife's death, except to learn the truth?"

Murat threw him a look in which there was a certain triumph. He was paying Miles off, Tracy thought. Paying him off with malice because of Anabel, with whom Murat had for a time been in love. She realized with growing dismay that Murat might not even care whether the words he spoke about Miles's complicity were true or not, providing he could injure the other man.

"Be quiet!" he told Miles. "I do not care for more of your lying words. When I am done with Sylvana, your turn will come, my friend. For the moment you will go to one of the empty rooms on this floor and remain there. Hasan Effendi—you will guard him well?"

To Tracy's dismay, Murat took the revolver from the pocket of his jacket and handed it to Hasan. That young man looked enormously pleased as he gestured Miles from the room.

Murat did not wait to see them go, but turned at once to his sister. "You have the documents ready for Sylvana?"

Nursel brought forward a folder of papers she had held in her lap. Sylvana's eyes had a blank, glazed look as if she did not wholly comprehend what was happening. Her fingers would not grasp the pen Murat tried to thrust into her hand. Ahmet and Nursel stood watching. For the moment, no one was thinking about Tracy Hubbard.

She had remained near the door, and she slipped through it unnoticed in the wake of Miles and Hasan. Across the salon Miles had been ushered into a room and Hasan stood in the doorway, the revolver held confidently in one hand, his back to Tracy.

She ran downstairs, pushing past a startled Halide and out into the garden. She had no plan, no purpose—she wanted only to get away before someone remembered her and she too was imprisoned in that house.

The familiar path beckoned and she ran through newly leafing woods toward the side gate. Out on the road, she turned from the direction of the palace ruins and hurried toward the village. Perhaps there would be someone there to whom she could turn for help. Perhaps she could find a telephone and call Istanbul. Or go to the police.

But as she walked, turning these plans over in her mind, their futility grew increasingly clear. The barrier of language was too great for her to hurdle. The red tape of going to any authority would be immense, or of putting a call through from a place where no one spoke English. The time which any sort of action would take defeated her.

She did not know how much Murat might be concealing in his accusation of Sylvana. She did not know how far he might go in order to silence Miles. Certainly there had been a threat in his words. The stake was high for all of these people. Once rid of Sylvana and her hold upon the Erim wealth, they all stood to gain. Even Hasan, whose help with his education had been cut off when the older brother died and there was little money left for Murat and Nursel. Under other circumstances Nursel might have been an ally to whom Tracy could turn for help. As things stood, she would certainly do as her brother and Ahmet and Hasan ordered her to do. Aside from her Turkish heritage of obedience to the male, she too stood to gain. Once Tracy had hoped to sting her into action, but that hope had dimmed completely.

Only Tracy Hubbard was still free to stop what was happening. Yet she could think of no possible way in which she might take action swiftly.

More and more she distrusted the scene she had witnessed in Sylvana's room. As she followed the road, her mind turned it over again and again, allowing it to spin through her thoughts like a reel of film that could be replayed while she watched and listened to it all over again. The conviction was growing in her that something was vitally wrong with both picture and sound. Sharply, acutely wrong. Not just because of Murat's false accusation that Miles was as guilty as he claimed Sylvana to be. Something was missing. Something that Tracy could not find in Sylvana's shocked and helpless state, in Nursel's downcast eyes and uneasy manner, or even in Murat's triumphant anger. The thing that had not appeared was the face of evil. The face that Miles had painted in the samovar reflection.

She had reached the streets of the little village that ran uphill from the water. This was apparently the day for an open market, and she saw that stalls had been set up, displaying fruits and vegetables, articles of clothing, all sorts of oddments. Her attention was solicited by eager sellers as she went by, and on any other day she would have stopped to look. Today she passed the stalls without pause. Once she nearly stepped on one of the numerous cats that abound in every Turkish city and village. The animal spat at her and leaped away.

When she had escaped the bustle of the market, she found a stone wall where she could sit undisturbed in the sun. She knew that she could not linger idly. Somehow she must act. After what she had just witnessed, she could not believe in Sylvana's guilt. And from the gentle way Ahmet had treated her, she did not think he believed in it either. Miles had painted the evil he saw in the crime, but he had not painted Sylvana.

Whose, then, was the face she must identify? Whose was the wickedness that had returned Anabel to the taking of drugs, played tricks to frighten and threaten and eventually destroy by driving her to her death? Tracy had not seen that face as yet. The mask was still in place, the identity hidden. Yet there must be some way in which to snatch the mask away and expose the truth. But how—how?

A small, plaintive mewing sounded nearby. Tracy turned, startled, as a white cat sprang onto the wall to sit inquiringly behind her. A cat not unlike poor Yasemin, though perhaps a little larger and not as well groomed. It was the same breed, however, and its eyes were as green as the eyes of Anabel's cat.

Tracy put out a coaxing hand and the cat did not leap away. It seemed more friendly than Yasemin and was willing to come close and rub its head against her hand. She stroked it gently and talked to it for a moment or two. Once it looked up at her as though the sounds she made were puzzling and unfamiliar. Still, it was a friendly cat and after a moment it stepped into her lap and settled down to a pleasant purring.

The beginning of a plan stirred in Tracy's mind. What if there was a way, after all, to get behind the mask? Here was a chance— wild and fantastic, perhaps, but still a chance. And nothing else had offered itself. She bent above the purring white creature in her lap.

The cat offered no resistance, but hung limply willing when she picked it up. It cradled itself against her shoulder with none of Yasemin's suspicion and allowed itself to be carried as Tracy started back toward the yali.

She had no knowledge of custom when it came to Turkish cats.

463

They swarmed everywhere and were always being chased from restaurants. But if she seemed to be kidnaping somebody's pet, there might be an outcry that she would have no way of answering. However, she met no one as she followed back ways to avoid the busy area of the market. The cat, undoubtedly, would find its own way home from the yali, once she set it free.

When she reached the road, she hurried so fast that once or twice the cat set its claws uncertainly into her shoulder. Tracy soothed it and went on without slackening her pace. When she neared the gate, she put the cat under her coat, where it made no objection to the warm shelter that hid it from view.

She avoided Sylvana's kiosk and went directly to the yali, passing no one on the way. She climbed the stairs to the second-floor salon where, clearly, she had the upper house to herself. Everyone must still be across the way in the hillside house. The test she considered must be made as unobtrusively as possible and with only one person at a time. Perhaps that very fact made the whole idea impossible. How, for instance, was she to see Sylvana alone?

For the moment she could only wait and do nothing. Sooner or later she would be missed, and the likely place to look for her was here. She held the white cat in her lap, shielded by a fold of her coat, whispering to it soothingly, petting it into a continuous purr of contentment.

The big, empty salon stretched in echoing shadows about her, replete with the usual creakings that haunted the old wooden house. The big green porcelain stove stood cheerless and unlighted, and the room seemed damper and colder than the outdoors.

When steps sounded on the marble corridor below and someone started up the stairs, Tracy sat up expectantly, breathing more quickly, her hand tightening without intention upon the warm fluff of the cat. But it was only Nursel coming up the stairs. Of course she was the messenger they would send, once they remembered Tracy Hubbard. She drew the coat more closely about the cat and waited.

As Nursel came around the bend of the stairs, she saw Tracy sitting there, and paused. Her eyes moved evasively from Tracy's own, and it was easy to guess that the girl was torn by feelings that warred within her and left her not without a sense of guilt. If only it was possible to play upon this guilt.

"My brother wishes to see you," Nursel said in a low voice.

"Then let him come here," Tracy said. "I'm tired of being ordered around. I'm not guilty of any wrongdoing and I'm not a prisoner in this house. Or am I?"

Nursel sighed. "It is better if you do as Murat wishes. He will not like it if I return without you."

"That's your problem," said Tracy boldly. "Are you planning to take me to him by force, perhaps?" She braced herself mockingly in her chair. She did not believe Nursel would attempt any such thing. With all the stubbornness in her Tracy meant to stay where she was and force them to come to her—one at a time, if that was possible. Nursel moved somewhat uncertainly toward her, and at that moment the cat mewed in protest against a hand that had forgotten to be gentle. The Turkish girl stopped in her tracks.

"What was that?" she asked in surprise.

The moment for the first test had come. "Why, it's Yasemin, of course," said Tracy and drew back her coat.

The white cat sat up and stared at Nursel out of sea-green eyes. Then it struggled free of Tracy's restraint and sprang through the air. Nursel froze where she stood, and Tracy saw her face, saw the reaction of shock, the rousing of superstitious terror. Nursel started backward out of the cat's path, crying out in fear. Without warning, the mask was down and the face behind it revealed. The thing that Miles had painted in the samovar reflection was exhibited in all its frightening reality for anyone to read.

Tracy touched her tongue to dry lips. "Did you think you could send Anabel twice to her death? Did you think she would not return to accuse you? You'll never be free in all your life of what you've done!"

Nursel recovered herself and clapped her hands furiously at the cat. There was a wild brightness in her eyes. "This is not Yasemin!" she cried.

"Of course it isn't," said Tracy softly. "How could it be? You drowned Anabel's cat in that dreadful way and left her for me to find. You thought you could frighten me into running away, didn't you? It was you all along who played tricks on Anabel, and then on me. On Anabel because she had discovered what you were doing. She knew it wasn't Sylvana. Or your brother Murat, whom you've duped so wickedly. It was you who gave Anabel drugs to keep her quiet. You could control her for a while that way, couldn't you? And you managed to poison her mind against Miles. But what did you do in the end to send her to her death? You might as well tell me, Nursel, since I know everything else."

The wildness had not died from Nursel's eyes, but she veiled them now with lowered lids and made an effort to control herself. "We cannot speak together here. If you wish to know the answer to such questions, then come to my room."

She circled the cat warily and walked toward her bedroom door. For a moment Tracy hesitated. It would be better to remain here in the open, but she was not particularly afraid of the other girl now that she knew where true danger lay. There was much more she needed to know. As yet she had no proof of Nursel's guilt that anyone else would accept. She bent to pick up the cat and followed Nursel into her bedroom.

She had never been in this room before, and she found it crowded with huge black walnut furniture and heavy draperies that shut out the sun. She blinked for a moment in this murky twilight, trying to orient herself. Nursel went to a cabinet across the room and took from it some object wrapped in a handkerchief. When she turned she made no effort to veil what Tracy had seen in her eyes.

"You are as foolish as your sister!" Nursel said. "How I have despised you! Telling me always that I am meek and too easily managed—that I can be used by anyone. When it is *I* who have used these others. They are not so clever as they think. Murat believes what I wish him to believe. Sylvana walks stupidly into every trap I have set. Hasan kneels at my feet and will do all that I ask for love of me—though I let him have the illusion that he rules. Of course it was I who devised the calligraphy code and made the changes. And now I must deal with you—another silly Anabel!"

She whisked away the handkerchief and Tracy saw the thing in her hands. It was an object that had not only the look of evil, but the look of death. Yet, strangely, she was not afraid. With sudden clarity she knew her own identity. She was Tracy Hubbard and she would not flee across the Bosporus in a boat she could not handle, as Anabel had done in her terror. *This* was why Anabel had gone, of course—the death Nursel held in her hands. Miles's words flashed through Tracy's mind: "A tenth of a gram will kill." Anabel must have known it would come to this. And she had lacked the strength and courage to stand and fight.

Tracy found that she was keyed to a pitch of excitement so heady that it filled her with a queer confidence. Knowing that death was inches away, she did not move. She had only herself to depend on. Herself—all of one piece, as Miles had told her she must be.

The door behind her stood open, but if she tried to escape, the other girl would be upon her at once. If she so much as opened her mouth to scream for help, the plunge of the needle would come. She had only words to fight with. Perhaps with words there was still a chance.

"Anabel told me about the black amber, you know," she said almost conversationally. "That was the signal, wasn't it? Of opium coming down the Bosporus?"

Nursel watched her warily, not altogether certain, in spite of the weapon in her hands.

"I suppose it was Hasan who set the black amber among the other tespihler so you would know the load was expected," Tracy went on. "And it must have been you who retrieved the box from the ruins."

For an instant amusement flashed in Nursel's eyes. "My foolish brother sets Hasan to guard the opium, to watch who comes to take it away. How we have laughed over that! Hasan had only to spend the hours sleeping, so that it would seem to Murat that Sylvana had taken the box while Hasan slept. When of course it was both Hasan and I who took it away when we were ready. Sylvana has made an excellent dupe for fooling Murat. It was a simple thing to make him believe that it was she who hid the heroin in the samovar."

"You've used them all cleverly," Tracy said. "But not cleverly enough, Nursel."

The other girl took a step forward, and Tracy cried out in warning.

"Don't come near me or it will be the worse for you. Don't make the mistake of thinking I'm like Anabel. You haven't the nerve to use that thing on me. You've always had someone to do your work for you—someone you could hide behind. Now you have only yourself. You're the one who must do this, Nursel. Only you. And I don't think you can."

467

As her eyes grew accustomed to the dim light, Tracy could make out Nursel's face more clearly now. She saw the wide, dilated eyes, the lips that trembled—the uncertainty.

"You're a disgrace to all Turkish women!" Tracy taunted. "It's a good thing others aren't like you. Trafficking in drugs, tricking and cheating and ready to murder!"

The cat in her arms squirmed, but Tracy held the writhing body, heedless of claws.

"Anabel never meant to kill herself!" she cried. "She was foolish enough to run away from you, instead of standing to fight. Anyone who turned on you could beat you down. It's you, Nursel, who are foolish and weak."

Nursel screamed in a queer, hoarse way and lunged toward her. Tracy had been waiting for the moment. She flung the cat directly into Nursel's face and dashed out of the room. Behind her she heard the frenzied squalling of cat and woman.

Miles was coming up the stairs. He rushed past her toward the outcry, and Tracy turned back in time to see him set his foot upon the syringe where it lay on the floor. The white cat sprang frantically away and fled through the salon. Nursel had gone thoroughly to pieces. She sagged against a chair, screaming imprecations that gave her away with every word.

There was a sound of running on the stairs, and Tracy whirled to see Ahmet brandishing a revolver and apparently in pursuit. She cried out a warning to Miles, but he did not move as the old man reached the doorway.

"There is the woman who has betrayed your son," Miles told him. "She will tell you all you want to know."

Ahmet made no gesture toward Miles. He stood in the doorway, listening, comprehending. He looked older than before, more shriveled and wrinkled in his shabby suit.

"You'd best take her to Dr. Erim," Miles said. "He will have to face the truth now and see where the real guilt lies."

Ahmet had pocketed the gun. He went directly to Nursel, and she did not resist as he took her arm.

When they had gone away, Miles drew Tracy out of the dark, crowded room and up the stairs to the empty third floor. She found that she was trembling as reaction set in.

"You're all right?" Miles said. "She didn't touch you?"

"I'm all right," said Tracy. "The cat—if it hadn't been for the cat—!"

He held her tightly. "Don't talk about it. It's over now."

"But Hasan had the gun. How did you get away?"

"Ahmet is no fool. Apparently he's had some doubts about what Murat was cooking up. He knows Sylvana well, and he began to think as I did, that her collapse was due to fright, not guilt. Murat was obviously convinced of Sylvana's guilt, and thus could not be the one himself. That left only Nursel. When Murat sent her to look for you, Ahmet took things into his own hands. He demanded the gun of Hasan, who handed it over, not knowing what his father intended, and he told me to go after Nursel. I had a tussle with Hasan, but he'll be quiet for a while. I came over here as fast as I could."

"I needed you and you came!" said Tracy, weeping against his shoulder, not caring how ridiculous she sounded.

Miles chuckled. "Obviously you didn't need me at all. You had everything very well in hand, my determined young American."

He held her away from him so that he could look at her, held her not very gently, and shook her a little. She stopped shivering and weeping and recovered herself with a single deep, indrawn breath.

"Are you sure who you are now?" he asked.

She nodded. "I'm not Anabel. Not in any way at all. And I don't have any more secret wishes to be like her. You've taught me a better way."

"You've taught yourself," he said. "And now, shall we get that book done between us?"

"Here?" she asked, astonished.

"Certainly not. You're going to help me pack my books and manuscript and then we're going back to New York. You'll not be out of my sight again. I can't get on with my painting until after we're married."

She gulped and did not argue. The matter was clearly settled. She didn't quite believe it yet. She would have to get used to the idea, but she knew she would do so blissfully.

"What will you paint? Is there something you want to paint now?" she asked him.

"A leading question," he said. "You, of course," and he bent to kiss her. "You'll sit for me without benefit of reflections in a sam-

469

ovar—I don't want to be misled again. You'll wear the sun in your hair, that feather pin in your lapel, and ivory earrings for your ears. You'll put up your chin and thrust your thumbs in your belt —and I'll paint you with love and tenderness."

She smiled at him joyfully. Two things, she knew, would never appear in his picture. There would be no hint of Anabel, except for happy memories evoked by a pin. And there would be no tespih of black amber. The warnings were over and done with, the Bosporus ghosts were stilled forever as far as she and Miles were concerned.

She kissed him back without restraint, and with his arm about her they hurried toward his study where the last of their work in Turkey awaited them.